SPECIAL MESSAGE TO READERS

This book is published under the auspices of

THE ULVERSCROFT FOUNDATION
(registered charity No. 264873 UK)

Established in 1972 to provide funds for
research, diagnosis and treatment of eye diseases.
Examples of contributions made are:—

A Children's Assessment Unit at
Moorfield's Hospital, London.

Funding research into eye diseases at the
Great Ormond Street Hospital for Sick Children.

The Chair of Ophthalmology at the
University of Leicester.

The Ulverscroft Children's Eye Unit at the
Great Ormond Street Hospital for Sick Children,
London.

You can help further the work of the Foundation
by making a donation or leaving a legacy. Every
contribution, no matter how small, is received with
gratitude. Please write for details to:

THE ULVERSCROFT FOUNDATION,
The Green, Bradgate Road, Anstey,
Leicester LE7 7FU, England.
Telephone: (0116) 236 4325

In Australia write to:
THE ULVERSCROFT FOUNDATION,
c/o The Royal Australian College of
Ophthalmologists,
27, Commonwealth Street, Sydney,
N.S.W. 2010.

A TOUCH OF TERROR

The year is 1860, and although Laura
Lambourne has been married to Sir Matthew
Merrick for several months, she has never
actually seen her husband's face. Forced into
a marriage ceremony in which the groom
remains hidden behind the curtains of his
canopied bed, Laura nevertheless begins to
love the gentle voice that tells her exotic
stories of adventures on the family sugar
plantations in the South Pacific. Finally,
Laura learns the horrific truth about her
husband's malady.

SARAH FARRANT

A TOUCH OF TERROR

Complete and Unabridged

ULVERSCROFT
Leicester

First published in Great Britain in 1980 by
Robert Hale Limited
London

First Large Print Edition
published 1999
by arrangement with
Robert Hale Limited
London

British Library CIP Data

Farrant, Sarah
    A touch of terror.—Large print ed.—
Ulverscroft large print series: romance
1. Love stories
2. Large type books
I. Title
823.9′14 [F]

ISBN 0–7089–4099–4

Published by
F. A. Thorpe (Publishing) Ltd.
Anstey, Leicestershire
Set by Words & Graphics Ltd.
Anstey, Leicestershire
Printed and bound in Great Britain by
T. J. International Ltd., Padstow, Cornwall

This book is printed on acid-free paper

1

'. . . . earth to earth, ashes to ashes, dust to dust, in the sure and certain hope of the Resurrection . . .' A sharp nudge from Mama's elbow was intended to remind me of the solemnity of the occasion but, instead of hearing the voice from heaven, I heard her hardly audible hiss of, 'Laura, remember where you are and take that smirk off your face!' It gave me cause to wonder if I had indeed been guilty of such a heinous offence? No, Mama must have been mistaken, for, though I had heartily disliked in life he whose remains were now being interred, my upbringing would never permit that I should show aught but a straight face at a funeral.

And what a funeral! Nothing had been overlooked that could proclaim to the world the esteem in which the late Mr Wilfred Cheadle had been held by his family and all who had been fortunate enough to have dealings with him or his many business interests. The church had been filled with mostly male mourners who now surrounded the grave, standing bareheaded in the pouring rain and ankle-deep in sticky wet clay, for even the heavens wept to see the burial of such a person as Uncle Wilfred. Yes, he would have liked that! He had ever liked to see other folk made uncomfortable. In any event, he had never let an opportunity pass by in which he could make me feel ill at ease, and now here he was, snug and dry in the coffin he had designed and had made long before he fell ill and died, whilst everyone else was exposed to the keen east wind and the icy rain falling with such persistence on this day of mid-November. And, although I had not been aware that I smiled, the whimsical notion had passed through my mind that, if we were constrained to linger here for much longer, some folk might develop chills leading to pneumonia, expire in due course and follow he whom we now mourned into the hereafter; and thus, just like some potentate of long ago, whose slaves were slain upon his death, Uncle Wilfred would continue to have an entourage to do his bidding in the afterlife as assiduously as they had done in this one.

And now the ornate casket, made to his own specifications whilst he lived lest any should dare to skimp the ostentation and dignity he considered due to him when he was no longer in a position to raise his hectoring voice in protest, was lowered to rest upon the clammy bosom of Mother Earth, and at last we were quit of him and would shortly be able to go home!

That must surely have been the uppermost thought in the minds of most people present, or at least to get back to warmth, shelter, and dry clothes. The glutinous mud in which we had been standing clung to the hems of my gown and petticoats, my boots and woolen stockings were sodden and within them my feet felt like blocks of ice; and though my bonnet and upper part of my cloak were comparatively dry owing to Mama sharing the protection of her umbrella with me, I was chilled to the bone. Yes, condolences were brief. Aunt Isobel Cheadle, Cousin Albert, and his wife Ondine were the recipients of hurried words of comfort uttered in the same breath as refusals to return to the former residence of the deceased and partake of the cold luncheon awaiting the delectation of the mourners, and so it was that only the immediate family and Mama and I were transported back to No. 19 Grosvenor Crescent in the foremost crepe-hung carriage, followed by Mr Peppercorn, the Cheadles' solicitor, and his clerk in the second, and the senior household servants in a third.

The house was cast in an identical mold to its neighbors: double-fronted, with sash windows on either side of a pillared portico that sheltered five steps, with spear-topped railings guarding the area steps that led down to the basement. Within, it was always cool even on the hottest summer day, and during the winter months, it was like living in a barn! Although it was of fairly recent construction, there were draughts amany, the main rooms were spacious and the ceilings lofty; and though Uncle Wilfred had been quite a rich man, he had never been one to squander his money on such things as roaring fires. The small ones he judged to be sufficient for health and comfort were indeed so from his point of view, for he had always sat squarely in front of them; and, as women carried more flesh about them than did men, his wife and sister-in-law, who was my mother, had no need of artificial warmth; and young people, which referred

3

to my little sister Theophania, known to the family as Tiffany, and myself never felt the cold anyway! Did we not, indeed?

Really I should not refer to her as little, for on the day of Uncle Wilfred's funeral she was fourteen, almost a woman, with the promise of becoming a beauty that even her ill-fitting, makedo clothes could not hide. I am five years her senior, but as I am not over-tall she already nearly matched me in height, and I foresaw that in years to come it would be as though we had been made as a pair, but that he who had fashioned us had run short of materials and that Tiffany had received her full share of everything but I had to be content with just a little less, or just a little more when it would have been better to be endowed with the former. My hair is flaxen, long and thick; hers is of golden hue and thicker, longer, silky and softly curling. My eyes are blue, hers are bluer with darker, lengthier lashes. Her nose is a nicer shape than the one that adorns my face, her lips more full, her teeth a shade more even; and though I am slender, her waist is the trimmer but at bosom and hip she was even then a little more voluptuous, though her hands and feet were smaller than mine and destined to remain so. Also, alas I must confess it, she had a happier, more forgiving nature than I did, for despite being excused from attending the interment of Uncle Wilfred on account of her youth and the added fact that she was but newly recovered from a severe head cold, she had actually wanted to go, whereas I had submitted to the mummery with ill grace and only because I knew I must.

The horses' smart clip-clop slowed, then stopped. The carriage steps were let down, and once the bereaved family had descended from the vehicle, Mama and I were able to alight and scuttle with more haste than dignity to the only shelter we could hope to obtain, and that solely bestowed on us for the sake of charity, for we were poor relations. No, that is untrue for we were no blood-kin of the Cheadles, my mother being the widowed elder sister of Aunt Isobel Cheadle, the deceased's second wife. But the walls and roof of the unwelcoming house were sufficiently stout to combat the elements, and after groping our way across the hall and up the first pair of stairs (for the blinds were drawn close at every window), by common consent we went our separate ways to try and restore some degree of comfort to our shivering bodies. Aunt Isobel bore Ondine away to her own bedchamber, for Cousin Albert and his wife had their own residence a short distance away, but that gentleman obviously considered that he and Mr Peppercorn would best be employed by discussing a glass of brandy apiece, and they disappeared in the direction of the morning room where it was probable that a small fire would be smouldering; Mama entered her chamber, leaving me to climb another flight of stairs, which would enable me to reach the floor where was the small room allocated to the use of my sister and myself.

Tiffany was sitting on the brass-beknobbed bed she and I shared, but at the sight of my bedraggled appearance, she instantly rose, exclaiming, 'Laura, you poor dear! Here, let me help you,' as with

5

numbed fingers I tried to untie my sodden bonnet strings. 'I knew you would be wet, but I did not imagine you would return in this state. Never mind, I have made all ready. I have been down to the kitchens for hot water for you, and I begged Alice to fill a stone comforter, and I have wrapped fresh stockings, petticoats and even drawers around it so you should be dry and warm in no time at all. Oh, Laura, just look at your boots!'

'I know, but everyone else's are in the same condition. The churchyard was a quagmire.'

'Give them to me, and I will put them in the corner until later. They can be dried out in the kitchens after luncheon.' Gingerly, she took them from me and placed them on the bare scrubbed boards that with the concession of two small rugs, floored our bedchamber. 'How is Aunt Isobel? Is she greatly upset?'

'No more than she was when we set out. I think she is mastering her grief quite well,' I answered, for even to Tiffany I hesitated to voice the unworthy suspicion that our so-recently-widowed aunt was more relieved than grieved at the death of her spouse. But then, how could anyone truly mourn the passing of a person so singularly unlovable as the late Wilfred Cheadle? He had been a large, well-fleshed man, with thinning hair through which a shiny pate had gleamed, and he affected muttonchop whiskers to adorn a countenance which in health was ruddy. He had been a man who held strong opinions on every subject, opinions that none would venture to contradict, for he was also a bully with a chancy temper that grew ever more uncertain as his last illness progressed. Aunt Isobel had been his second wife, he being a widower many years her senior when she went to him as a young bride. Cousin Albert, the child of his first marriage, was twelve at that time, and he remained the sole heir, for my aunt failed to provide any more Cheadles, which was in itself a blessing, though her husband was fond of reminding her that she was not worthy of the name 'woman,' for she had not proved herself as one by becoming a mother. My Mama is the elder of the two sisters, but though she had disapproved of the then-young Isobel's marriage to a wealthy brewer, her union would surely destine her to be more comfortably financed and placed in her widowhood than Mama was in hers. Our Papa had been a gentleman with only a tiny income but also expectations of inheriting a tidy fortune, and though when he was alive we lived quite simply, we were then far from being destitute, and when the occasional necessity arose, my father could always obtain credit quite easily, for it was well known that he was heir to a wealthy bachelor cousin. So from her position of gentility and a presumably assured future, Mama had viewed with dismay the liaison of her younger sister with an elderly brewer, no matter how successfully he ran his business. The fact that he was in business, a tradesman, was enough to make my mother view her brother-in-law with dubiety, and that was even before we got to know him! But positions were unexpectedly reversed. Papa's cousin, though well advanced in years, took to himself a wife and begot himself a son — at least he thought he did — and no sooner had that occurred than Papa's creditors began to dun us, and when he caught quite an ordinary chill, it was enough to make him take to his bed, never again to leave it whilst he lived.

So there she was, widowed, penniless, with her late husband's debts still to be settled, and with two daughters to support. That was four years ago, when I was fifteen and Tiffany eleven. Mama's parents had been dead for many years, so there was no help to be obtained from that quarter, and thus it was that we became the recipients of the Cheadle charity; and he who dispensed it never lost an opportunity to remind us of the fact. Mama was meekly grateful to be accepted into the brewer's household, more for the sake of her daughters than for herself, and Tiffany was even then a sunny-natured, lovely child who was ever eager to please and think the best of everyone; but I was not so biddable, and perhaps my five extra years of age made me more conscious of every snub, every slight, every derisory remark concerning so-called gentlemen who lived a life of ease, incurred debts, which was in itself a form of dishonesty, and then left other folk whom they had despised to carry their burdens for them, these burdens being Mama, my sister, and myself. Oh, we ate at the family table, but every mouthful was watched; and Mama was given a meagre allowance so that we might be clothed, but I did not fail to notice that shortly after our arrival the sewing maid was dismissed, for Mama was an excellent needlewoman; and the services of the under-housemaid were also dispensed with,

8

for Tiffany and I would be only too pleased to make ourselves useful, chiefly by doing the dusting and other genteel little tasks; and I was of course delighted to read aloud to the invalid for hour after wearisome hour during the course of his last illness: to read aloud until my throat burned and my jaws ached, to read to him even though he dozed, for at the slightest pause he would waken and take me to task for faltering.

'Laura, do hurry! The luncheon bell rang minutes ago!'

'Did it? I failed to hear it.'

'No, you were gazing at the ceiling as though expecting it to fall on us. And I repeat what I have already said. Are we to go down or not?'

'Why not? We always do.'

'Well, under the circumstances . . . '

'Oh, I take your meaning. There is only Mr Peppercorn and his clerk apart from the family, and I think the clerk will be directed to the servants' hall. So we shall go down to luncheon as we normally do. We can always withdraw if our presence is not desired.'

Tiffany and I had both been given black serge gowns to be worn as a badge of sorrow, but as mine was soaked and soiled I donned with satisfaction one of the three others I possessed. True it was grey, but when I made my appearance I should probably receive sour looks for choosing comfort rather than a display of respect for he whom we had only just buried.

'Are you ready?'

'Of course, I am. I have been waiting for you!'

9

Tiffany sounded justifiably pained. 'So do come on. They will be so cross!'

'I think not. He who always held his timepiece in his hand and lectured the tardy is no longer with us, praise be!'

'Laura! S-sh! What a thing to say!' Tiffany glanced apprehensively over her shoulder.

'Goose! I speak my mind, but only to you. Never fear.'

Cousin Albert now occupied his late father's chair at the head of the table and his body, though a shade less bulky than that of his deceased sire, just as effectively screened the sulky fire from the view of anyone else. Table talk was suitably subdued, but then it always was. I only caught remarks on those who were present at the funeral, and most of the names mentioned belonged to people of whom I had never before heard. But though the collation was cold and the occasion sombre, this did not seem to affect anybody's appetite overmuch. The knives and forks of both widow and heir were plied with gusto.

'May I trouble you for the mustard, Aunt Charis?' Cousin Albert addressed my mother, then, 'Ondine, my dear, do try a morsel of this veal and ham pie. Yes, and a little beetroot sets it off quite nicely. The salt if you please, Laura. And pass Mr Peppercorn the pickles!'

Tiffany choked on a crumb and was stared at, but sipped her water and recovered sufficiently to meet my look of concern with sparkling eyes brimming with mirth. However, nobody lingered over the pudding and presently Aunt Isobel rose and ordered, 'Judkin, we shall take our coffee in the library.'

This was departure from custom, but of course the library would provide a suitable setting for resolving the mystery that had occupied everybody's mind for a long time — who would receive what portion of the money bags that death had freed from the tenacious grasp of the 'dear departed.' This would not concern Mama, Tiffany, and me, so we lingered in the dining room until the solicitor's clerk was sent to summon us, and in those few moments the realisation dawned on me that, though I had disliked heartily my late uncle-by-marriage, he had provided for us, albeit in meager fashion. Whilst he lived, he had stood as buffer between us and the hostile world, if only for the sake of his own pride, but now that he had quit this earth, we had no protection at all!

'If you please, Madam, young ladies, Mr Peppercorn instructs me to tell you that they await your presence in the library,' the youthful clerk, with his pimple-adorned face and woefully large ears, flushed scarlet as he addressed us.

'Do they? Dear me, I had no idea. Thank you, young man. Come girls.'

Had Mama's thoughts marched along the same path as mine during those last few moments? Probably, but one never knew with Mama. Her carriage was always faultless. Not for her, the drooped shoulders and downbent head of despondency, and only before Tiffany and me would she betray any emotion other than that of genteel affability, and even those occasions were rare. So now with face devoid of expression, she led us to where we should discover whether or not we had misjudged he whom I, at least, had always regarded as a tight-fisted skinflint. And I was delighted at being so summoned, not because I had any great hopes of being revealed as an heiress, but so my vulgar curiosity might be satisfied by learning who was to get what.

The Cheadle family and we Lambournes sat on chairs; the solicitor took his place at the desk; and the upper servants stood against the farther wall, doubtless in high expectancy of just rewards for years of labour. Admittedly, they had always received their board and wages, but the wages had never been overgenerous, and to serve a master so hard to please as he surely warranted some gesture of appreciation for their forbearance and ofttimes sorely-tested loyalty.

Judkin and Mrs Monks, the housekeeper were each to receive forty pounds, a tidy sum but certainly not tidy enough to retire on; Lessing the valet would have his late master's wardrobe of clothes, but that did not include any article of jewellery, watches, chains, fobs, links or anything of that nature. Well, the sale of the clothes would surely realise several pounds, but, there again, if his master had lived the valet would in due course have received these garments anyway, for castoff clothes are always considered the perquisites of a personal body servant. The footmen were to have ten pounds apiece, Cook a similar amount, and so on down the scale of below-stairs hierarchy until the scullery maid was reached, her legacy being a single sovereign.

These lesser bequests having been settled to the recipients' obvious dissatisfaction, they were dismissed from the room so that the field should be left clear for the big guns to be brought into play.

'To my dearly beloved wife Isobel I bequeath . . .' Mr Peppercorn paused, as though he hesitated to put into words the esteem in which my aunt had been held by her late spouse. 'A-hem. To my dearly beloved wife, Isobel, I bequeath an article which I prize above all others: to whit, the gold ring she gave me upon the occasion of our marriage. I also charge my only son Albert to see that her dress allowance of two hundred pounds a year be continued until such time as she may wish to remarry, when it will of course cease. I further charge my son Albert to provide his stepmother with a home in his own household: to live on equal terms with his family and under his protection for so long as she wishes to do so and is agreeable in her manner.' Was there more? No, there was to be nothing more for poor Aunt Isobel!

'To my wife's sister, Charis Lambourne, I leave an annuity of fifty pounds a year, a further twenty pounds per annum to be added to it until my wife's younger niece, Theophania Lambourne, attains her eighteenth birthday. Upon that occasion the aforesaid Theophania Lambourne is to be provided with fifty pounds, this sum being of sufficient size to furnish her with a wardrobe suitable to the station in life in which she will earn her living. And to my

13

wife's elder niece, I bequeath a further fifty pounds, to be used in a like manner, that is, to equip Laura Lambourne to take up a suitable position that will provide her with the means of earning her bread.'

There were various bequests to charity, then, 'To my dearly beloved only son Albert Edwin Cheadle, I leave the residue of my estate.'

All eyes rested upon the new master, for master he was in truth; and, as if conscious for the first time of being completely free from his father's domination, he seemed to grow in stature even as we gazed upon him. Actually, there had always been quite a strong resemblance between his sire and himself; and, although Albert had always been the more restrained in his manner and behavior, now there was nobody to gainsay him, he was the cock of this his own particular dungheap, and he would be able to crow as he liked, flap his wings as he chose and, just like his father before him, bully into submission anybody with the temerity to say him nay. Now he rose abruptly.

'I take it you have reached the conclusion of the pertinent business, Mr Peppercorn? Then I must return to my office and doubtless you, Ondine, will wish to be driven home? Stepmother, be so good as to ring the bell. Mr Peppercorn, I desire that you come to my office tomorrow forenoon at ten o'clock. I should be able to spare five minutes or so at that time in which to discuss further matters, the sale of this house and the disposal of various other items I shall not require.' Then as if aware of the unseemliness of his apparent haste to step into his dead father's shoes, he turned to my aunt.

14

'Do not be alarmed, Stepmother. The sale of this residence will take weeks, even months, so there is no question of you being obliged to pack an overnight bag and coming to live with my family and myself straightaway! There is no hurry, no hurry at all! Actually it will suit me quite well for you to remain here for the time being. And we must take thought for your sister's future and that of the dear girls. No, there is no need for alarm. I am sure you and we shall get along famously, and I am only too delighted to abide by my late father's wishes, for I wholeheartedly agree with his opinion that it does not do for a genteel female to live alone or even in a solely feminine household, with no person of the stronger gender to guide her and guard her from any stray opportunist. Oh yes, this arrangement will be eminently suitable!'

'Yes, Albert, I am sure it will.' As Aunt Isobel had deferred to her late husband, so she now deferred to his son.

'Ah, Judkin, at last. My carriage, to be brought round at once. Ondine, my dear, you had best go up for your bonnet and wraps.'

'Certainly, Albert.'

'And, Judkin, Mr Peppercorn will probably desire a cab to be procured for him?'

'Indeed, I do, sir. I am most obliged to you for the thought.'

Oh yes, Albert would certainly be a worthy successor to his late sire, for his own vehicle could easily have carried the solicitor and his clerk to his place of business with only a slight deviation from its route, or the carriage that served this household

15

and now formed part of his inheritance could have been ordered to convey them to Mr Peppercorn's chambers, but that would have betokened an unwarranted consideration for people who were, after all, in a sense mere employees! We heard the footman blow upon the whistle that was part of the equipment of every hall in a respectable house, and kept for the purpose of summoning public transport. Two blasts: a single one would have summoned a four-wheeler, but that would have incurred greater expense than would the hansom cab that should presently arrive. Even the footman had gauged the status of the solicitor to a nicety, for though he would pay for the cost of his own transport, a hansom cab was quite grand enough to suffice for his needs.

'Yes, you may continue as you have been doing for a little while, at least, Stepmother. And there is no need for you to concern yourself with the dismissal of the servants or anything of that nature. And I, my wife, or Mr Peppercorn will take an inventory of the contents of this house, and I shall supervise the sorting of everything, at the same time making a selection of articles I wish to keep, before arrangements for the disposal of the remainder be set in motion. But there is ample time. Yes, you and your sister and her daughters are more than welcome to live here as you have been doing, for several weeks at least. And by the end of that time, we should have resolved what is in the best interests of everybody.'

Leave-takings were brief, for the horses must not be kept standing in the inclement weather, and soon they were gone. And then, as if we were automatons, my aunt, my mother, my sister, and myself continued to sit in the library, silent and motionless, the masterhand that turned the key that gave us animation having been withdrawn. The library was a gloomy chamber at any time, but, now in the gathering dusk with only a faint glow from its small fire, it seemed to be an ideal place to sit, thinking the thoughts that occupied my mind. A single thin spiral of smoke lost itself in the mysterious vastness of the chimney, and, as my gaze travelled on upwards, it rested upon the portrait of he whom we were supposed to be mourning. There was his likeness: actually it flattered him somewhat, for the artist had not caught the arrogant, self-satisfied look that we all knew so well; rather, he had made him appear dignified and slightly benign — but of course, by so doing, he had probably made certain that his fee would be paid. So there it was, gold watchchain very much in evidence, framed in an ornately carved and heavily gilded frame, the whole tastefully draped with swags of black crepe. Tiffany began to fidget, and, as though this action roused a spark of life in Aunt Isobel, she rose to her feet and crossed the room to the bellpull and, when it was answered, said, 'Judkin, we shall go up to the drawing room in ten minutes, and I wish for the teatray to be taken there. And will you tell Cook that I should like to see it especially well-laden? And for dinner I think we shall have something a little more appetizing than the dishes we have in the usual way, just in the nature of solace, so to

17

speak. I will leave it to Mrs Monk's ingenuity to think of something nice for us.'

For the first time, ever, I saw Judkin really smile!

'Certainly, Madam.'

'Oh, and I should be obliged if you will see that the dining room fire is a really warm one. It strikes me as being extra cool today, or perhaps it is just the somber occasion that makes it seem so. In any event, I should be pleased to see really good fires burning in the dining room and the drawing room, and I also desire that they be lit in our bedchambers too. Otherwise I fear we may well take a chill after being exposed to all that dreadful weather this morning.'

'Just so, Madam.'

'I leave it to your discretion to see that the servants are also warm and well fed, for even though this is a house of mourning, it is only wise to keep up one's strength no matter how melancholy one may feel. Indeed, it is one's duty!'

'If I may say so, Madam, that is a very sage observation.'

'And at table this evening, we shall all drink a libation to the late master's memory, below-stairs as well as in the dining room. I know little of wines, Judkin, so I leave it to you to select whatever you consider suitable. You have the cellar keys?'

'Yes, Madam. Will that be all?'

'For the moment, yes. I will ring if I think of anything else.'

Will that be all, indeed? Uncle Wilfred would be turning like a teetotum in his newly dug grave if he could hear his widow's reckless orders. And had Albert had the slightest suspicion that his stepmother would have the temerity to issue them, he could certainly have taken the cellar keys and probably those to the storerooms and pantry away with him, sending his wife daily to dole out the meager supplies that had hitherto been the lot of everyone in this house. Oh, now the mice could play for a while, until the new cat took an inventory. And though the time allotted the game might only be short, I resolved to wring every ounce of pleasure from it, and so as Judkin withdrew I approached the fireplace, took up the seldom used poker, and cracked the large lump of coal that had been barely smoldering, then raked at the embers until flames were leaping up the chimney and flickering their light upon the maroon papered walls.

'Laura, there was no need to do that. We shall be quitting this room in a few minutes, and that piece of coal would have done for tomorrow!' Mama evidently had not reacted to the new order of things so quickly as had I.

'Leave the girl alone, Charis. She may do as she likes! Let us make the most of our freedom for the little while we may have it!'

And like plants drawn towards the warmth of the sun, with one accord we gathered close around the fireplace for the few minutes that elapsed before the butler came to announce that our repast awaited our pleasure in the drawing room. The selection of dainties presented for our consumption made me wonder if the staff had always lived the same frugal existence as had we who ate at the

19

master's table? For, if so, from whence came the delicious sponge cake, light as a feather, where it was not weighed down with its dripping burden of strawberry conserve, the little cakes, stuffed with cherries and topped with pink frosting? The scones were ordinary enough, but the thick cream with which to smother them was a rare sight indeed, as also were the cucumber sandwiches and, as I had not heard the bell of the muffin man, I inferred that Cook must have made the ones that sat in a sea of melted butter beneath the cover of the silver dish!

'Thank you, Judkin. That looks quite tempting. We shall serve ourselves, and I will ring if I require anything further.'

'Very good, Madam.'

Oh, how content we were with no stern eye to quell any sign of enjoyment as we sat at our ease, Tiffany upon the hearth rug, me on a footstool, and Mama and Aunt Isobel in comfortable chairs.

'I shall never manage to eat any dinner later on,' said my sister, 'and I know I am being greedy, but please may I have another scone?'

'My dear child, you may have whatever you wish. Laura, will you be so obliging as to refill the cups?'

'With pleasure, Aunt Isobel.' I glanced at her curiously, wondering whether she had been as shocked as I had by the terms of the so-recently-read will. I had been quite confident that she would be left a comparatively wealthy widow, but though she would never have to live in want, it is a very different thing to have one's own establishment and the ordering of one's own affairs than to drag out the rest of one's life under the roof of another person and be dependent on their every whim! The wording of the testament was that she might continue to do so 'if she were agreeable in her manner,' and that could easily be construed as never raising her voice in protest at anything at all!

'After tea, I think we should all rest before dinner,' my aunt announced. 'We have all had a very long, tiring and unpleasant day, and when we are refreshed we shall be able to bring clear minds to the solving of the problems that confront us at the moment.'

'Well, I can feel myself nodding off already,' Mama agreed, though Tiffany and I were somewhat loath to leave the drawing room, which for the first time in its existence could be described as cosy. When we entered our small bedchamber we had reason to believe that somebody below-stairs actually liked us! For, yes, a fire crackled merrily in our grate; the plain cotton coverlet of the bed had been replaced with one of heavy damask; our lumpy pillows were gone, and, set in their place, were two plumply filled with feathers; and from somewhere had appeared a square of turkey carpet, which now covered a goodly portion of the bare floorboards.

'O-oh, look! Laura, just look!'

'I am. I have. But just now I am quite weary. I think I must be a little too tired to appreciate fully all this splendor. But I shall certainly do so when I waken. Yes, who is it?' as a knock sounded upon the door.

'If you please, Miss, Mrs. Monks sent me up with a warming pan,' the second housemaid stood with her burden poised ready to do its duty. 'And if you please, Miss Laura, can I take away with me anything you wish to be dried and brushed?'

'Yes, Mavis, thank you. Here are the things I wore this morning.'

'I shall bring up hot water and rouse you and Miss Theophania at half-past six, shall I, Miss?'

'Yes, that will do nicely.'

'It is like being Cinderella!' declared my sister when the maid had gone, and she had recovered her power of speech. 'Oh, why could it not always have been like this?'

'If it were not ordered otherwise, it probably would have been. And now I shall take a nap.'

'So will I. I know I did not go to the funeral, but I am not going to forego the luxury of getting between warmed sheets, just because of that! Besides, nobody can say that I was not willing to attend it!'

As my sister had observed, it was as though a spell had been put upon, or lifted from, the whole house; but instead of a fairy godmother waving her wand, it was the absence of the erstwhile master that was responsible for the generally lighthearted atmosphere. Oh, there were no shrieks of laughter or any other sign of jollity, for such behavior would not have been fitting under the circumstances: but after dinner, when the servants had left us with the coffee tray, we conversed as we chose without waiting first to be addressed, nor did we mentally weigh every word before we uttered it. Of course,

Judkin's choice of the wines that were served at table might have played their part in loosening our tongues, for as we started to lay the plans for our future we spoke without reserve.

'Well, I shall take the first opportunity to seek employment, Isobel.' Mama broached the subject. 'Perhaps in a dame school or something of a like nature, or I could always ply my needle. But I must say that for your late husband to make me an allowance was quite an outstanding act of generosity, and completely unlooked for!'

'Do you think so, Charis?'

'Indeed, I do. And to provide for the girls, too! That was truly handsome of him!'

'Have you any idea of the size of the fortune he left?'

'None. But I do think you deserved a trifle more.'

'A trifle?' Aunt Isobel almost shrieked. 'He must have left an estate worth thousands upon thousands! And after all the time I spent in thraldom to that, that, that . . . creature? Oh, if only you knew!'

'S-sh, Isobel! The girls!'

'Have no fear. I am not about to say anything unfit for their ears, but surely there is no need for me to tell you of the miserable years spent in this house? Of his parsimony, vulgarity, autocracy? His pettiness, his spitefulness, his slyness? Those are only a few traits in his character. I make no mention of repugnant habits!'

'Well, er . . . '

'Oh, you were so right. I will admit now that I did have my doubts before I wed him, and, just

23

so soon as his ring was on my finger, those doubts became certainties! Oh, he was pleasant enough during our courtship: eager to please, quite the doting suitor, and at that time I, in my youthful ignorance, though I could easily cure him of one or two of his shortcomings. Just little things, you know. But though he vowed he would give me the moon if he could, once we were wed it was a very different story! And it is typical that he should have placed me as he has. For the sake of his own good name he could not leave me destitute, but he has tried to make certain I shall not henceforth live as I have earned the right to now that my shackles to him have at last been struck off!'

This diatribe was indeed a revelation. Tiffany's eyes were like two blue saucers; Mama was gazing with needless concentration at the toes of her slippers; and I broke the ensuing silence by asking brightly,

'Would you care for more coffee, Aunt Isobel, Mama?' only to be ignored.

'For all these years I have lived in this hateful house, surrounded by these odious furnishings and in the company of that repugnant man, and for what? I was never truly mistress of this place. Every order I gave was issued first by his lips. I never had the choosing of so much as a pair of curtains! Every item in this house was either selected by him or his first wife, and neither of them had any idea of elegance. He did promise that it would be all redecorated and refurnished to my taste, but he never kept his word. No, once I wore his wedding ring, all pretence and pretty speeches and even the rudiments of good manners were forgotten, and he reverted to his true, coarse, domineering nature!'

'Speaking of rings, he bequeathed to you the one he usually wore, did he not, Isobel?' Mama reminded her. 'One that you gave him in the first place, and which he greatly treasured?'

'Yes, and is it not in keeping with all the rest? It was so firmly set on his finger that it was buried with him, so without digging him up again, I do not get even that!'

Mama suddenly buried her face in her hands, and I thought she was so overcome by the tribulations endured by her sister that she wanted to conceal her sorrow, but Tiffany had been doing her very best to stifle a giggle, albeit with indifferent success, and I must confess to an utterly inappropriate feeling of mirth which coursed through me, threatening to conquer the sympathetically mournful mold into which I was trying to school my features. My mother won her battle for self-control, and, though her shoulders had shaken just a little whilst her face was hidden, when she at last raised her head her tear-wet eyes could easily be attributed to commiseration.

'Well, look on the bright side, sister. You will never live in want for the rest of your life. You have a handsome dress allowance and you own a few quite valuable pieces of jewellery. Matters could be worse.'

'Yes, but they could be a whole lot better! We are just family now and I shall speak my mind freely, for any loyalty I once felt I should have for my late spouse, I can now see was wholly misplaced. He wed me when I was young, fresh, and innocent, but I very soon had a rude awakening to what he was truly like. During those first years I was ofttimes tempted to run away from him and seek sanctuary with you and your dear husband, but pride held me back. And just when I did decide that, scandal or no, I could stand no more, your dear husband died and your misfortunes fell upon you!'

'Oh, Isobel, you poor dear. You never said anything. And we never guessed that things were so bad,' Mama said.

'I know. It was my intention that you should not. And then when you and the girls came here to live, at least I had a target for which to aim. Wilfred was a goodly number of years older than I, therefore I knew it would be likely that I outlive him, and it has long been my wish to be in a position to do something really nice for Laura and Tiffany. To launch them into society in the proper manner and to make sure that they should meet eligible young men. And so I was biddable and meek, outwardly the ideal wife, foolishly hoping that in due course my patience would be rewarded with a handsome legacy. And God in His heaven knows how richly I deserve one!'

'Never mind, Aunt Isobel. The thought was lovely, and I want you to know we are all grateful for it, but we will manage, have no fear. I shall obtain a position and be able to help Mama who is herself a genius at making ends meet. And in time Tiffany will make a brilliant match, for a lovely creature like she is cannot fail to bring down a duke!'

'And be tied to such a person as he from whom I have only just been released? Never!'

'Well, that is for the future, anyway. And when we find a little place in which to live, you will be able to visit us often,' I enthused.

'Visit? My dear child, I shall be in residence, not visiting!'

'What do you mean, Isobel?' Mama questioned sharply.

'I mean, Sister, that I have no intention of going to live with Albert and Ondine. Ondine, indeed! What a name for her. Anyone less like a water nymph than that overweight young woman I have yet to meet.'

'Never mind the proportions of your step-daughter-in-law's figure. You must live with them. It is a direction of your late husband's will.'

'Ah, but only if I am agreeable in manner! And I am sure it would entail no great effort for me to prove to be one of the most disagreeable people who ever drew breath. But I need not put that to the test, for the will also directs that I am to receive my dress allowance until such time as I might remarry, and as I have no such desire, that will be mine to do with as I choose and cannot be taken from me. Now whilst I was dressing for dinner, I was also doing my sums. You, Charis, are to get an allowance of fifty pounds a year with an additional twenty pounds to provide for Tiffany until she is of an age to earn her own living, and you only get that petty amount so that it could not be said that my

27

husband left you entirely destitute! Well, add your portion to my two hundred pounds and I think you will arrive at a figure that should enable us to live in modest comfort. Independence, at least. True, we would all have to be careful, and each of us would have to help, for we could not afford more than one maidservant. But the important thing is we should be safe, and free!'

'No Isobel, I could not allow it. It would be neither right nor just,' Mama demurred. 'If I could offer an income to match yours it would be different, but not as things stand.'

'Do not be a fool, Charis. What does it matter who contributes what? It comes from the same source anyway, and both are only a form of pension, to which we are entitled. Yours is for all the duties for which you and your daughters were never paid, but mine is the greater for having to suffer extra indignities. And if I had been left better placed in a financial sense, I should have realised my chief ambition, which was to set up an elegant residence where we could all live in peace and happiness. And I will not be denied even now! We can take a neat little villa somewhere in the suburbs, or we could rent a cottage in the country if we chose. Or live by the seashore if the fancy so took us. And if you should continue to quibble over what you consider to be fair, we could even turn our minds to setting up a little business somewhere. An apartment house, or a genteel little teashop. And if we do, I promise you that you would have the running of it, for I should be hopeless at anything like that! Now, what do you say?'

'I do not know what to say,' Mama replied feebly. 'We must think about it.'

'Well, I have thought about it, and my mind is quite made up. And as you love me you had better say yes, for rather than end my days under the roof of abominable Albert, his dreary wife, and their obnoxious offspring, I shall set up an establishment of my very own. And then I am certain to meet with disaster, for I should have nobody at all to counsel me as to how I must go on.'

I could tell my mother was wavering and inwardly rejoiced, for it would be the solution to the most pressing problem, that of keeping a roof above their heads. For though I had every intention of entering enthusiastically into their plans and helping them to set up their establishment, I did not include myself amongst the future inhabitants of this proposed haven of peace. Aunt Isobel's idea was very practical, and it could be brought into being, but it would not be quite so easy as she thought. The day-to-day running of such a household on the income at their command should present no real problem once they were established, but first it must be set up, and the expense of that could be greater than she imagined. But the thought was warm within me that I should be able to help! Nobody seemed to have taken into account the fact that I would be able to contribute toward this intended new home. But was I not a young woman with intelligence, all of my faculties and in good health? And I should easily manage to secure some remunerative position and, by so doing, not only be able to earn my own living but also be able to furnish a steady stream of sovereigns which otherwise would be in very short supply. Yes, in the morning I should set out early and begin my search for employment. I would tell nobody of my intention so that their amazement should be all the greater when I returned home in triumph to announce that I had secured a prize position which would pay a handsome salary, bringing benefit to us all!

2

'Where are you going, Laura?'

'Just for a walk and a breath of air,' I lied.

'Good. I think I shall come, too.'

I loved her dearly, but Tiffany could be very trying at times.

'No, you had better not. It might start to rain, and you must not get a wetting. You have only just recovered from that cold.'

'Oh, I have quite got over that, now. I know! I shall ask Mama. If she says I can come with you, it will be all right, will it not? Wait for me. I shall not be more than a minute.'

The day was a cold one, but the sky was clear with not a cloud to be seen, and so I was forced to tiptoe down the stairs and creep past my mother's bedchamber door, through which I could hear Tiffany being instructed to wrap herself warmly and to keep on the move. And that accelerated my own progress, for I was out of the house, had traversed the portion of Grosvenor Crescent that must be trod, and had turned the corner before I had even fully decided where my steps should lead me; for I had only the haziest of notions on how to start my quest. Of course! I must find an agency! And once there, I should be able to make my selection from the vacancies they had to offer. It was simplicity itself to ask the police constable who was just approaching from the opposite direction, and, in less than ten minutes, I found myself climbing a flight of stairs covered with worn linoleum and opening a door bearing the request: PLEASE ENTER. The room beyond was small with a bare, grimy window and benches ranged against its dingy walls. Upon the benches were seated a dozen or so women, some young and timid-looking and others elderly and timid-looking, the only exception being one stout female who sat stolidly munching a pasty of some sort. All heads were turned in my direction as I entered, but she was the only person to continue to regard me, inspecting me carefully from the brim of my bonnet to the toe caps of my boots.

'Come in and sit down, girl.' she said. 'And shut that door! There's a draught!'

'If you please, may I sit there?' I asked, indicating a space beside a youthful fellow applicant.

'You can sit where you choose, my duck. So long as you do not try to go in out of turn.'

'Go in? In there?' There was a second door leading from the room. 'Oh, I would not attempt

31

to take the place of someone who was here before me!' I said.

'Well, there's some as would. First time here, is it?'

'Yes, indeed.'

'What are you trying for?'

'I do not really know. It depends on what is offered.'

'If you ask me, I think you've come to the wrong place. All of these here are domestics, but I am a cook!'

'Oh! Well, I do not mind what situation I take, provided it is genteel and well paid.' I replied.

'Have you been in service before?'

'Not exactly. Do you think we shall be kept waiting for long?'

I was becoming annoyed with her probing questions and had no intention of relating my life's history to satisfy her curiosity and maybe relieve the tedium of the time of waiting for the other people present.

'We waits for as long as it takes,' my inquisitor answered, but just then a gaunt, middle-aged woman emerged from the inner sanctum and said, 'The next is to go in,' and the cook rose, brushed some crumbs from her lips and departed, leaving behind her a welcome silence in which I could collect my thoughts.

Yes, probably I was in the wrong sort of agency, for I had no great desire to be found a place as a kitchen maid! I had envisaged something more along the lines of a governess or lady's companion. Well, I was here now and would await my turn, just to see how I fared, and that alone should prove to be a useful experience. It was indeed!

'Name?'

'Laura Jane Lambourne.'

'Age?'

'Nineteen.'

'Status?'

'Spinster.'

'Address?'

'At the moment, No. 19 Grosvenor Crescent, Mayfair.'

'You are employed there?'

'No, not quite. I just live there for the time being.'

This merited a sharp look from the woman who could make or mar my fortune.

'Experience?'

'Well, I do not actually have any, apart from dusting and tidying.'

'Can you sew?'

'Oh, yes, and I can darn beautifully.'

'I mean really sew. Make a blouse from an evening gown?'

'Er, no. Not exactly.'

'What exactly are you looking for, Miss Lambourne?'

'Oh, anything. I have never earned my living before, but I am very willing and can soon learn. And I am strong and healthy.'

'May I see your references?'

'References? But I do not have any. I have just told you, I have never before worked for anyone.'

'Miss Lambourne, I am afraid we are wasting each

other's time. You come to me with no experience or references and expect me to place you? Let me tell you that women call here daily, again and again, hoping that I may be able to find them employment, and they are all greatly experienced and have references that are impeccable, but still I cannot always help them! Have you any idea of how difficult it is to secure a position these days? For every vacancy that is registered in my books, I have at least a score of applicants! I bid you good day, Miss!'

And that was after waiting for almost two hours! But the time was not entirely wasted, I reflected as I made my way homewards so that I should not be late for luncheon, and I consoled myself with the knowledge that I had gone to a very unsuitable agency, anyway. For even if I had been able to give satisfactory answers to the questions asked, I might have found myself in an exceedingly uncongenial position. It was my own fault for not giving sufficient thought to the ways and means of realizing my ambition, and I recalled that *The Times* had a section wherein were advertised vacant situations and various agencies. So after luncheon I would try again, and this time be a little better prepared for the bombardment of questions I now knew I should have to face. Yes, this time I would surely meet with greater success.

'What previous positions have you held, Miss Lambourne?'

'None, I am afraid. This is the first time I have sought one.'

'So, naturally it follows that you have no experience?'

'Yes, that is so.'

'Perhaps we should then pass on to your accomplishments? You have languages?'

'Well, English, of course, but only a few French phrases apart from that.'

'Can you comprehend a French conversation? Make yourself understood in that tongue?'

'No, not really.'

'You play, of course?'

'Play? Play at what?'

'Not *at* anything. I mean musical instruments, Miss Lambourne. The pianoforte, the lute, the harp?'

'No, I am afraid I have no ear.'

'You can draw, perhaps? Are gifted with an artist's talent?'

'I used to sketch a little when I was younger, but my efforts could only be described as mediocre.'

'Pray forgive this observation, Miss Lambourne, and correct me if I am in error, but it appears to me that in every respect you are a very mediocre young female. And what it is you expect me to do for you, I cannot imagine! Tell me, is there anything you *can* do, really well?'

'It has been remarked that I have a very pleasing voice when reading aloud,' I replied desperately.

'My dear young woman, you cannot honestly think that anyone will employ you just to do that! Your education falls far short of that required from even a nursery governess, and as a lady's companion you would be quite hopeless. How

35

would you go on if your employer wished to travel abroad? For you would certainly be expected to make all the arrangements, and to speak fluent French is the minimum requirement. No, no! You have nothing at all to offer.'

'Only willingness, common sense, and a desire to please!'

'And then you could only produce character references, and even those I have not seen.' (We had already grappled with that problem.) 'No, Miss Lambourne, it will not do! I fear I can offer you no more than you can offer me or any prospective employer. Good afternoon, and, on your way out, will you be so kind as to ask the next applicant to step this way?'

During the rest of the week I pursued my course, making one excuse after another to try and deter Tiffany from wishing to accompany me upon these jaunts. I visited every agency that lay within my reach, and daily my despondency grew. To fulfill my fine aspiration to be the steadfast rock upon which my mother, sister, and aunt could cling, became as remote as the moon, for I was informed over and over again that I had nothing to offer. I even tried some of the larger stores where females were employed, for to work in an emporium selling gloves or hose was surely not beyond my capabilities, but there my advanced years were against me. Too old at nineteen! At that great age, I was expected to be an experienced saleswoman, for the shops would only consider such, or took girls of twelve or thirteen to be trained; and many such children were only too eager to toil for long hours with just their board and lodgings in exchange for this privilege. I trudged for miles, and my despondency gradually altered itself to resentment, chiefly directed against Mama! She should have made certain that I received a proper education! It was all her fault! She should not have allowed me to pick and choose the subjects I would learn. She ought to have made me pay attention to the long-suffering governess who was in our employ when Papa was alive! Even though in those days when it had never been envisaged that I should be forced to earn my living, she ought to have been more concerned with my total lack of accomplishments of any kind; and, indeed, Tiffany would be no better equipped than I was when the time came for her to step out into the unfriendly world about us and somehow extract from it a living. Despondency, resentment, uneasiness, despair, and eventually fear, in turn took hold of me. Until then I had never fully appreciated the shelter that had been afforded us by living under the protection of my late uncle-by-marriage. True his charity had been of the grudging variety and I had never been servile enough to please my benefactor, but I had never before been truly conscious of how important this gift was; and now the difference between my hitherto sheltered existence and the black prospect that lay before me brought me fully to my senses. And my total dejection must have become apparent to my kinfolk, for after a while Mama questioned me: 'Laura, you have not seemed your usual self for a day or two. Are you quite well?'

37

'Yes, thank you. Just a slight headache, that is all. A breath of air will soon blow it away.'

'Later, perhaps, but certainly not now. It is raining cats and dogs!'

'Oh, I can take your umbrella. May I?'

'No, you may not. Do not be so foolish, child. Whatever has come over you lately? You can go up to your room and lie down for an hour. Tiffany will not disturb you. She can keep herself occupied by tidying my workbox.'

'I have no desire to disturb her, nor for Laura's company at all!' my sister declared roundly. 'Headache or no, she has been nothing but a crosspatch recently. She takes umbrage over the merest trifles, and I am more than content to stay well away from her!'

'Now, girls, that is quite enough,' Mama said firmly.

'But I have not even spoken!' The injustice of it all brought me perilously near to tears.

'Laura, you go on up, and you, Tiffany, come with me.'

Well, at least I had an hour of complete privacy before me in which I could wallow in self-pity, and this I did. Oh, everybody was against me! Nobody cared! True, I could not expect anything else from strangers, but now even my own family had become hostile — my mother, whose fault it was that I could not obtain employment, my sister, for whose ultimate benefit it was that I had walked until there was a blister the size of a farthing on my left heel. Yes, those whom I loved so dearly were now regarding me with coldness, even carping at my behavior! And I was trying so hard, so very, very hard! O . . . oh! It was so unjust! Of course, during this fit of weeping, I quite overlooked the fact that nobody knew what it was I was trying to do. As I had confided in nobody, it was not so greatly surprising that I should have received no comfort nor words of encouragement concerning this enterprise of mine that I had kept quite to myself. And it was also more than probable that Tiffany was in the right of it when she said I had been intolerable to live with, moody, silent, disgruntled, and prepared to take offence at nothing at all. And so I wept. I wept until I realised I was beginning to suffer from the headache I had falsely claimed earlier, and then presently I dozed, to be awakened later by a very contrite sister bearing a tray of tea.

'Dear Laura, I am sorry I was cross. Are you feeling better?'

'Yes, thank you. And you are not the one at fault, for you are quite right. I have been horrid, I know.'

'No, it was me. And I must say, you look dreadful! I am going to fetch Mama.'

'Do, and I shall never speak to you again!' I said dramatically.

'Oh! Then if I do fetch Mama and you will not speak to me thereafter, I shall not speak to you. And that will be a shame, for I will not be able to tell you my news!'

'What news?'

'Well, it is not mine, exactly. And it is not really news. And it concerns you, not me.'

39

'Go on, do tell.'

'Your presence was required downstairs this afternoon, but Mama said you were indisposed and not to be disturbed.'

'Who? Who wanted me?' Instantly I was alert. Was this a lost opportunity? Had somebody after all needed the services of an ignoramus such as myself? 'Tell me at once!' I said sharply to my sister who stood looking upon me, on her face the smug expression that the informed bestow upon the unenlightened.

'If you ask me nicely, I might. Or there again, I might not. But I certainly shall not tell you if you command me in such a peremptory manner!'

I gritted my teeth. 'Dear Sister, pray do not be a tease. This might be important. So tell me, I implore you,' whilst beneath the coverlet my fingers itched to slap her.

'Oh, very well.' She seated herself upon the side of the bed. 'Though really I think it is so incredible as to be ridiculous. Yes, yes, I am coming to the point. Somebody has made you an offer.'

'An offer? What? Who? Where? What kind of offer?' There, I knew it! My persistence had been rewarded! Somebody must have been discerning enough to perceive the sterling qualities that lurked beneath my surface unsuitability to enter their employ!

'Do not be so obtuse, Laura. What kinds of offers are there? For girls like us? Why, marriage of course! And so now, you sly creature, we all know! You have an admirer, so you might just as well tell me who he is.' Tiffany was obviously prepared to be admitted to my confidence, awaiting expectantly the romantic story of my secret love.

'That is something I should very much like to know, myself. That is, if you are not making the whole thing up.'

'On my honour, it is true!'

'Then tell me what has occurred, for I am as completely mystified as you are.'

'You must know who he is. Very well, keep your silly secrets to yourself! I am sure I do not wish to pry into them!' She tossed her golden curls and prepared to rise.

'Somebody is playing a joke, and his sense of humour must be in the worst possible taste,' I said. 'Believe me or not as you choose, but I tell you I know nothing of anybody who would wish to make me a proposal of marriage.'

'Well, there is somebody. Mr Peppercorn said so.'

'The solicitor? He is old enough to be my grandfather!'

'Not for himself, you dolt! He came to speak for a client of his.'

'Are you trying to tell me that Mr Peppercorn has been here this afternoon, bringing with him a proposal of marriage between me and one of his clients?'

'Exactly.'

'But who sent him?'

'I have no notion. He called, was ushered into the drawing room where we were all sitting, and asked for you. Mama said you were unwell and asked his business, and he said that, as you were a minor, Mama must be consulted anyway and that he saw no harm in telling her. Then he did. He said somebody wanted to wed you.'

'Go on. You must tell me all.'

'That is all. All I heard, anyway. Even though I was sitting as still as a mouse hoping not to be noticed, Aunt Isobel said should she retire from the room and Mama said, no, but that I was to leave it.'

'I cannot credit it. It must be a hum,' I declared, my mind busily inspecting then discarding every acquaintance of the requisite gender who could possibly seek me as his wife. 'I do not know of anybody at all who would wish to become even affianced to me.'

'Oh, you are not so bad as that! When your nose is not so red as it is now, and your eyes are not puffed into slits as they are at this moment, there are times when you could be called quite handsome, attractive anyway.'

'Thank you very much. And so you do not know what reply Mama gave this offer?'

'No. I told you. I was sent from the room, and, though I lingered near the door for as long as I dared, I had to move away because one of the footmen was giving me most peculiar looks. Are you getting up for dinner?'

What a question! As though I could remain in bed with such a mystery unsolved.

'Indeed, I am. I have already told you I feel quite recovered.'

'Shall I help you to do your hair?'

'No, thank you. I feel strong enough to manage

that task unaided. You go now, and I shall drink my tea, and you may tell Mama I will be down presently.'

'Well, hurry then, for even if you are not curious as to the identity of your admirer and the outcome of this afternoon's conversation, I am. And Mama will tell me nothing at all!'

And when, after several hours, my mother had made no mention of the subject and I was forced to ask her what had transpired, she was hardly anymore forthcoming with me.

'So Tiffany told you Mr Peppercorn was here? What a prattler the child is!'

My sister flushed crimson, but I knew she would forgive my betrayal, for it seemed to be the only way to get Mama to speak.

'She only said the solicitor was here and desired to have speech with me, but that he did say something about a proposal of some kind.'

'Well, you may dismiss the matter entirely from your mind, Laura. Mr Peppercorn was here with a proposition that was extremely impertinent. Have no fear, I soon set him to rights and so we shall hear no more!'

'But I have not heard anything! You might at least let me know what he had to offer!'

'If you must know, it was an outrageous proposal of marriage, to a complete stranger.'

'What do you mean, a complete stranger? A person whom I have not met, but who has seen me and desires me for his wife?'

'Nothing so reasonable as that. The gentleman involved has never seen you. He just wishes to wed a healthy young woman of good breeding and character. Any female would do, so long as she met those requirements.'

'Then why should Mr Peppercorn choose me, rather than another?'

'I suppose he thought he was doing you a kindness. Yes, perhaps I was a trifle abrupt with him. The solicitor is aware of our financial position, and something he said about a handsome marriage settlement could have prompted his thoughts in your direction.'

'Money? There was money involved?'

'Yes. Mr Peppercorn did speak of money.'

'How much?'

'I did not enquire, and it pains me to hear you do so. I cut him short long before he had arrived at a figure! 'That, sir, is of no interest to us, whatsoever. We may be in straitened circumstances, but I am not so far reduced that I should even consider selling my elder daughter!' I told him. Yes, for that is what it amounts to. For you to go as bride to a total stranger and know that he only wants you because you are healthy, well-bred, and virtuous. It is like a farmer selecting his cattle for, yes, I say it outright, breeding! Well, this one can find himself another market!'

'I should still like to know who it was.'

'After my explaining to you how monstrous the whole scheme is? You amaze me, Laura. I should have thought you would have been as mortified as I, by the very idea! No, the matter is closed, and we shall hear no more from Mr Peppercorn regarding the Merricks, for I made my attitude very clear to him. Very clear indeed!'

Mama had put on her affronted-dignity expression, and I knew I would elicit no further information from her. She had let slip the name Merrick, but though Tiffany and I racked our brains later on as we made ready to retire for the night, neither of us could match the name to the face of anyone we knew.

'Anyway, Mama said we were not acquainted with him,' my sister reminded me. 'We may as well forget all about it, for it would never have come to anything. You could never have made a match of that nature!'

'It is not so very long ago that marriages of that kind were quite common. The bridal couple wed whomever their parents chose for them, and ofttimes they had never set eyes on each other before the ceremony. Especially where there was wealth or property involved.'

'Well, that hardly applies to you, now does it? Surely your legacy of fifty pounds is not sufficient inducement for a fortune hunter to seek your hand, enlisting the services of Mr Peppercorn to court you by proxy!'

These sage words from my little sister brought to my consciousness the humour of the situation, and we were both giggling helplessly as I blew out the candle and we lay watching the light from the flickering flames dance upon the walls, for, yes, a fire was now lit for us every morning and kept burning throughout the whole day. But when Tiffany slept and I lay silent, my mind would not be wrested away from the incredible conversation I had had with Mama. It was so incredible as to be intriguing, and, to me, it was like the promise of aid being offered to a drowning man! For I alone knew how good my chances were of obtaining employment. Nobody within the house but myself knew that I was virtually useless at anything, and for me to even acquire the position of scullery maid would be little short of a miracle. And though that miracle did occur, I did not want to be a scullery maid! I was poor but also suffered from the disadvantage of being proud! No, more lay behind this offer than was apparent at first sight, of that I was certain. If money were offered, it followed that the prospective groom was, if not wealthy, at least comfortably off. But why should he not seek and choose his own wife? Well, perhaps he was shy, or had commitments, things he could not leave behind when he went acourting? Perhaps he lived in a remote part of the country or was old-fashioned enough to approve of this method of selecting a wife that was practiced so long ago? List his requirements, state what he had to offer in return, and put the whole matter into the hands of a matchmaker, who in this particular case was Mr Peppercorn.

Mr Peppercorn! I would go and see him! He would tell. At least I stood a greater chance of learning what I wished to know from him than I did from Mama or Aunt Isobel, who would side with her. Yes, even though nothing ever did come of it, I would find out who had made this proposal. I must learn his circumstances, where he lived, everything I could, particularly the bride price he offered. That may sound mercenary, as indeed it is, but when one has nothing and wishes to do much, especially for loved ones, money can be of the greatest importance, as is also the opportunity to acquire it. And so I must discover what it was Mama was refusing on my behalf, for if I never did, the question would tease me for the rest of my days!

★ ★ ★

'You are not going out today again, surely.' Tiffany said, as she watched me kick off my houseshoes and put on my walking boots.

'Yes, I am.'

'But you are being most unfair, Laura. I have done your share of the dusting as well as my own for days now! You should really pull your weight a little more!'

'Why? Why dust? The furniture is soon to be sold, anyway. Let the dust lie and maybe everything bought will be mistaken for antiques and fetch a higher price. And that would please Cousin Albert inordinately.'

'Well, where are you going?'

'Promise not to let Mama know, and I will tell you. I am going to Mr Peppercorn's chambers, to see what I can discover of that secret affair of yesterday.'

'O-oh! You dare? I am sure Mama would be so cross if she knew.'

'That is why she is not to know.'

'Can I come?'

47

'No, better not. I will go alone, and, as you have just said, there is the dusting to be done.'

'But, as you have just said, Sister dear, why bother with it? And I think it would be wise of you to let me accompany you, or I might let it slip. When you have gone, I mean. Mama declared only yesterday that I was a prattler. Remember?'

'Yes, I do. But she did not mention extortion, and that is what this is!'

'Is it? You are so clever, Laura. I never know what big, unusual words mean. Now where did I put my gloves?'

'Then do you understand the meaning of the word sly?'

'Indeed, I do. It describes just such a thing as we are about to do at this moment. I am ready. Are you?'

Mentally, I shrugged. Why not let her come with me? After all, if it were not for Tiffany, I should not know anything about that offer that had led to this presently planned escapade, for my mother had obviously not intended to let me become aware that my hand had been sought in so unique a manner.

'Very well, but you must promise not to breathe a word of this to a living soul.'

'You cannot be serious, Laura. As though I would! I am not quite so foolish as that!'

'H-m. Come on, then. The sooner we get there, the sooner we shall learn more about my mysterious suitor.'

Mr Peppercorn's chambers lay within easy walking distance, and a scant quarter of an hour had passed before we stepped across the threshold, entered a narrow hallway, and tapped upon a sliding window of frosted glass that bore the legend PLEASE KNOCK. A short pause, then the window was pushed aside to reveal the clerk with the big ears, who respectfully asked me if he could be of service.

'Yes, young man,' I replied, in a tone as near to the one Mama used when wishing to give the impression of authority as I could imitate. 'I desire to have speech with Mr Peppercorn, concerning a matter of importance.'

'May I have your name, Ma'am?'

This I gave, reflecting that the young man could not have regarded our last meeting as being memorable, as it was not so very long since the day of the funeral at which he had been in attendance.

'And the nature of your business, Miss Lambourne?'

'That is not only important, it is also private.'

'You have an appointment, Miss?'

'No, I do not, but it is imperative that I speak to your master.'

'If you will please wait a moment, Miss?'

The small window was returned to its original place, and as we stood there Tiffany whispered, 'What if he will not see you?'

'Why should he not? And in any event, I shall wait here until he does.'

Wait, we did, though not in the draughty passageway, but in a small comfortably furnished room just a little further along it. And patience was

49

eventually rewarded, for we were ushered into the solicitor's presence.

'Good morning, Miss Lambourne, Miss Theophania. What a pleasure it is to see two such charming young ladies in this musty office of mine. A rare treat, I assure you. And may I ask what brings you here?'

'Good morning, sir. And what has brought us, myself particularly, is the strange business you discussed with my mother yesterday afternoon. For I would hear more of it.'

'Indeed? Well, I do not know whether it would be proper to disclose the whole of it to you, Miss Lambourne.'

'Is it so shocking?'

'No, no. You mistake my meaning. But as you are aware, you are a minor and must abide by your parent's or guardian's wishes, and Mrs Lambourne bade me say no more on the subject.'

'But you asked to speak to me in the first place! My sister told me so.'

Tiffany nodded agreement.

'There I fear I may have been at fault,' Mr Peppercorn smiled ruefully. 'Actually, I was a little taken aback by Mrs Lambourne's reaction to the proposition. I was merely a go-between, bearing an offer to be accepted or refused, or so I saw it. But I am afraid your mother took strong exception, and so I think it would be politic to forget all about it.'

'Mr Peppercorn, I may be a minor, but I am not a child. I am nineteen, almost twenty! Many women have married, run their households, and borne children along before they reach that age. And so I would address you as one sensible person would another. There is no need for me to pretend. You know the position in which we find ourselves, financially speaking, and that position is extremely precarious! Now, my mother, in the mistaken belief that she is protecting me, has rejected the proposal you made concerning me out of hand. She is a very proud woman, Sir, and I fear she took affront quite unnecessarily. Indeed, I feel that an apology is owed you, and this I now make on her behalf.'

'Not at all, not at all. The lady was surprised. Quite understandable, really,' he murmured, but looked gratified just the same.

'Now I am also proud, but I think I am a little more realistic. Mr Peppercorn, my education leaves much to be desired, I am not talented in any way, in fact my accomplishments are nil! For more than a week, I have trudged the streets of London, morning and afternoon, seeking employment. And nobody will take me!'

'So that is what you have been doing!' interrupted Tiffany. 'Why did you not tell us?'

'Because I wished to wait until I had something to tell. But there was nothing.'

'Your attempts were most commendable, if I may say so. But times are very hard and respectable positions few, I believe.'

'Yes, Sir, they are indeed, nonexistent, so far as I am concerned. That is the point I wish to make. If I have a long life ahead of me, have no private means and cannot support myself, what is to become of me? What is there, apart from the workhouse? And I should like you to know that I would not disdain to wed with a man, albeit a stranger, provided he were gently born, kind, and in possession of his wits, and that he would also agree to provide for my mother and sister to live in decent circumstances.'

'Oh, but he must not be too old, and he must be healthy!' my sister interposed.

'Does Young Miss here speak for you, Miss Lambourne?'

And, although I was glaring her into silence, I answered, 'Yes, for those are not unreasonable attributes, surely?'

'Well, the gentleman meets all of your requirements, but one. I fear he is in poor health. In fact, he is not expected to make old bones, as the saying is.'

'Yet he wishes to wed?'

'For companionship, only. That is all he desires. He is in his mid-thirties, not too great an age difference, I think you will agree. He is extremely wealthy and prepared to be most generous. He has a younger brother who is married, and this brother and his wife live at Merrick's Mount with my client, as also does his spinster aunt. But my client keeps mostly to his own chambers. He is very conscious that he might be the cause of restraint between his brother and sister-in-law, for they are not long wed. He fears that for them to have to study his health all the while might in time prove to be a trifle irksome for them.'

'You say it is his residence?'

'Yes, yes, but though my client is the most considerate of gentlemen, he is lonely. He lived abroad for a long while, but when his father died and he inherited, he returned home. During the years of his absence, he had lost touch with the friends of his youth. People's tastes alter and most of them are now family men, and, as I say, what he now desires is for a young gentlewoman in straitened circumstances to become his wife, merely for the sake of propriety. He stipulates that she must be able to hold a moderately intelligent conversation, be healthy, for he maintains that one semi-invalid in a household is quite enough; and he would greatly appreciate an ability to read aloud in a pleasing, coherent manner. I understand that the years spent beneath a semitropical sun have weakened his eyes.'

'Is he blind?'

'No, nothing like that. But small print can cause him some slight difficulty after a while.'

'Well, that I could do. And I believe I should not be totally useless in the sickroom. I helped tend Papa and my late uncle.'

Now that was an idea which had not occurred to me before, to try and become a professional nurse! Admittedly the two sufferers whom I had helped to care for had both died, but not through any fault of mine. And this sounded like a much more tempting and remunerative position, and I would not have to waste valuable time whilst I trained for it!

'Oh, you would not be called upon to anything of that nature. His valet attends to all of his personal requirements, and, I reiterate, he is in poor health but not bedridden. Occasionally he has a giddy spell and is forced to rest for a day or two, but that is all. No, Miss Lambourne, my client requires companionship. There are plenty of servants, of course, but they lack the qualities he seeks. No wifely duties, in the accepted sense of the term, are desired, even though he has this fancy to wed. Perhaps the sight of his younger brother's happiness has inspired this notion. His aunt is anxious to indulge him in all his whims for the time it is allotted him upon this earth, and it was she who came to me, instructing me to find somebody suitable, who would be pleased to become Lady Merrick, if only for a brief while. And let me assure you, Miss Lambourne, the young lady who consents to marry Sir Matthew will have a great deal to gain — a handsome settlement; an absurdly generous allowance, to be continued, no matter what, until her own death; position, for the family is an old and highly respected one; and the opportunity to be mistress of an establishment that is the envy of many!'

'To order the running of a large place would utterly confound me,' I observed.

'Not so, not so. His aunt would continue to see to all that sort of thing, and, as I have said, there is no lack of servants.'

'It sounds too good to be true,' I remarked in a wavering voice.

'It is exceptional, I agree. The chance of a lifetime, surely. But as Mrs. Lambourne has vetoed the idea of your considering this rare offer, there is nothing more to be said. There are several other young ladies with whom I have the honour to be acquainted, and doubtless I shall have no great difficulty in finding one who will be only too eager to leave penury behind her, exchanging it for a life of security and ease.'

'Did my mother know of all the circumstances appertaining to this offer, sir?'

'No, Miss Lambourne. She cut me short in midsentence once she understood less than the gist of what I was trying to say. She gave me no opportunity to speak fully. Most regrettable, but that leaves me no alternative than to seek elsewhere.'

'Mr Peppercorn, you have been so very kind, and please believe that I appreciate deeply the fact that you tried to give me the chance of the first refusal. But, Sir, I have not refused! The whole idea appeals to me strongly! And now I beg of you one more favour. Just a little time. Let me speak with Mama. Explain to her what it is she is refusing on my behalf. Let me reason with her, so that she will at least be prepared to hear from your lips the nature of the transaction that is proposed. For after all, that is just what it is. In actual fact, it is merely an unusual form of employment. Instead of going as a lady's companion, I should become a gentleman's companion, but to protect my good name and assure that my honor is not besmirched he is willing to let me share his name, and he will also reward me handsomely.'

'You have the whole matter in a nutshell, Miss Lambourne. How very remarkable!'

'Some females are capable of reasoning, sir,' I smiled. 'So will you allow me just a little time in which to persuade Mama not to dismiss, out of hand, what I at least consider to be a heaven-sent opportunity?'

'How could anyone refuse such a small and prettily-worded request? Allow me to say I shall let the matter rest for the remainder of the week. Then, if I have not heard from you by noon of next Monday, I shall take it that your powers of persuasion have proved to be unsuccessful. And Mrs. Lambourne might be reassured to know that my client's aunt is staying here in London at this moment and that a meeting could certainly be arranged. Miss Merrick will naturally wish to approve of the chosen bride of her elder nephew and will most probably have some questions of her own to ask. Questions, Miss Lambourne, which I know you will be able to answer more than adequately.' He rang the small bell that had been resting upon his desktop, thus summoning his youthful clerk. Then he rose. 'And now, young ladies, I will bid you good day and hope for a happy outcome of the business that presently concerns us.'

'Good day, Mr Peppercorn, and once again, thank you.' I was unaware that I had traversed the hallway until I stood upon the pavement outside, for I was completely dazed by the revelations of the past half hour.

'Well! Did you ever hear such a story? One occurring in real life, I mean? Oh, how romantic it is! It might be taking place upon the pages of a novel!' Tiffany exclaimed.

'Yes, it does sound remarkably like a piece of fiction,' I agreed slowly. 'That is just what I said before. It seems too good to be true!'

'If you really think that, why did you ask the solicitor to give you a little time in which to try and sway Mama? And why should it not be true? Indeed, how can it be untrue? The gentleman's aunt is here in London. Miss Merrick! And you would have to meet her before anything is finally settled. Just think, Laura, you would be Lady Merrick! Referred to as 'Her Ladyship,' addressed as 'Milady!' My stars, my own sister would bear a title, and so would my brother-in-law! Oh, when Mama hears that, it will surely dispose her to listen with a more sympathetic ear to what you are going to tell her. Oh, yes! How *are* you going to tell her?'

'In the usual way. No differently from how a person tells anyone anything.'

'But what will she say? For you must then reveal that we have been to Mr Peppercorn's chambers this morning!' Tiffany sounded more than a trifle apprehensive, and I could not restrain a smile.

'You see? Now you have your reward for making me let you accompany me! For if you had not, you would be sitting snugly at home and as astounded as anybody by my news — and by my daring to cross Mama. But, as it is, you are as guilty of disobedience as I am, and fear not, if punishments are to be meted out, you will get your share!'

'Oh, Laura! Perhaps it would be best to forget the whole idea! Say nothing. We have been walking and looking in shop windows, that is all. Yes, that would be best!'

'What a craven little creature you are! Anyway, I

have no intention of embroiling you in any trouble. I shall say, if asked, that you had no notion that I planned to do as I did.'

'Will you? Oh, you are the dearest sweetest sister anyone could have! Well, come on then. Let us make haste, for I cannot wait to see Mama's face when you reveal all.'

'All?'

'Not quite all. Not my part in it, you promised. But everything else!'

Cousin Albert had been taking one of his meticulous inventories that morning, and, as he joined us at the luncheon table, near-silence reigned in the dining room, as it had when his father was alive. Aunt Isobel had so far failed to enlighten him as to her future plans, and he therefore assumed she would soon be moving into his house, but no word was uttered as to what it was he intended to do with us, if anything. As though in unspoken agreement, all but he ate sparingly, as though to reassure him that he was not being called upon to feed an army, but I knew that the appetites we would bring to the dinner table later on, would more than compensate for this dainty, birdlike pecking during luncheon.

And, that same afternoon, Mama and Aunt Isobel had special plans of their own. They had made an appointment to view a villa in Bloomsbury! Could Tiffany and I also come and see it? No, we could not! Two people were quite sufficient to go all that way and inspect a house that was probably unsuitable, anyway! There were omnibus fares to be considered, and, as we girls had been wasting time on pleasure for all of the morning, we could employ ourselves usefully about the house during the afternoon. Should I tell them what we *had* been doing, there and then? Declare that there was now no need for Mama and Aunt Isobel to inspect a modest villa, for it was more than probable that I should be able to set them up, together with my sister, in a much more elegant establishment! No, better not. I could see Mama was in no humor to be delightedly astonished at such a prospect, for she was already drumming her fingers irritably upon a small table whilst Aunt Isobel wrestled with the buttons on her gloves.

'Isobel, do hurry. We are already late!' she said sharply.

'What of it? The agent will wait, and you surely would not have me leave this house in a state of undress?'

No, now was not the time. This evening, perhaps, when she was mellowed by the consumption of a good dinner and the prospect of an hour or so of sitting comfortably, then would be the time. And my task would be made easier if the villa they presently set out to view should be so shabby and small, and so badly placed, as to be quite out of the question.

'I thought you would tell them straightaway,' Tiffany said with a hint of reproach in her voice, when she and I were alone.

'Yes, and if I had Mama would have bidden me be silent, reprimanded me severely for disobeying her, and that would have been the end of the Merricks so far as we are concerned. You must have noticed that her temper was not at its best!'

59

'I suppose you are right. This evening, then?'

'If I think it opportune, then I will. But I shall not speak if I judge the moment is not right, for Mama would not only be vexed, she would be highly incensed. She would think I had challenged her authority. In a way I suppose I have, but only for the best possible reasons.'

'What shall we do this afternoon?'

'I do not know. I have not thought.'

'Well I have, and if you can propose nothing more original, I suggest that you and I darn some of the stockings that are awaiting Mama's attention in her workbox. That will surely make her appreciate what loving and dutiful daughters she has. Especially if she finds us busy with our needles when she and Aunt Isobel return!'

I regarded my little sister with admiration, not quite untinged with awe. Was she growing up to be a schemer? She must have sensed my reaction to this suggestion of hers, for she smiled and said, in a purely adult way, 'An element of slyness in one's disposition can sometimes prove to be useful.'

So my sally of that morning had been marked, and noted. But she was in the right of it, and the next hour or so was spent by setting the neatest stitches of which we were capable, into the heels and toes of Mama's woollen hose.

★ ★ ★

'You did what?'

I took refuge in silence.

'After I expressly forbade you to give that insulting

60

offer further thought, you demeaned yourself by actually seeking out the creature who dared to make it? Oh, the shame of it! Go to your room, Miss! And you will remain there whilst I consider what is a fitting punishment. Tiffany, you will share my bed tonight. I cannot have you led astray by the reprehensible influence of your elder sister.'

But, for the first time in my life, I stood my ground.

'Mama, pray do not be so melodramatic,' I said. 'I am not a little girl to be sent back to the nursery. I am a woman! And now I have started I shall tell you all, and nobody will stop me!'

Gradually I began to detect a slight thawing of the chill atmosphere, particularly when I averred, 'He is a respectable gentleman, plagued by ill-health, and I think it most creditable that he should wish to protect the reputation of some genteel female by offering her his name and rank, when all he requires is companionship. His aunt is here, and we should, of course, meet her, and she would explain more fully the duties that would be involved. And I should not be alone with him. She lives there, as too does a brother and the brother's wife.'

'H-m, well, on the face of it, the proposition sounds very fair, but life has taught me to regard with suspicion things that are presented in such pretty packaging! Yes, it seems to be an offer that can only be described as dazzling, but to be dazzled means that one is not able to perceive things as clearly as one ought.'

'Mama, I am almost twenty. Uncle Albert Cheadle left me fifty pounds, but I cannot live on that for the rest of my life, and I cannot obtain employment of any kind, no matter how menial! I am not qualified to do anything and am too old to be taken as an apprentice. I have tried so hard during this past week and part of the one before. I have walked for miles, visited one agency after another, but the answer is always the same. I am too old or too ignorant!' I paused to let this penetrate my mother's understanding, then continued, 'And now I have been given a chance. To acquire a position, to earn a good salary, and to have a pension to follow, when the position no longer exists. Yes, for that is all it is! You surely could not, would not, deny me that chance! After all, it may come to nothing. Miss Merrick may not think I am suitable, or we may not like her! But please, do not forbid a meeting. They say that everyone is given at least one opportunity to make something of their life whilst they are on this earth, and this could be mine, but it could also be my only one! Please Mama, give it further thought!'

'Where is this place? The one of which you speak?'

'Merrick's Mount? Do you know, I quite forgot to ask Mr Peppercorn that,' I confessed.

'It is in the West Country, if that means anything.' Evidently Tiffany now thought it safe to speak, then as though to gild the lily she rose, dipped me a curtsey and declared, 'Your ladyship. Lady Laura Merrick of Merrick's Mount!'

'Not Lady Laura, she would be known as Lady Merrick! The use of the Christian name betokens a higher rank than that held by this Sir Matthew, be he baronet or knight!' Mama corrected her musingly.

My sister and I exchanged glances, and then I held my breath until: 'Well, do not think I condone your action, Laura. It was willful and deceitful, all the more shocking because you coaxed Tiffany, an innocent child, to accompany you! But, upon further consideration, I will own that I may have been a trifle hasty in my judgement. Yes, we might be prepared to discuss it in more detail! Miss Merrick! Of Merrick's Mount? The name sounds good. If they are anybody of consequence they should be in *Who's Who*. Go to the study, Laura, and fetch your late uncle's copy of it, and we can look them up.'

Why had I not thought of doing that this afternoon? I must be extremely dull-witted, for it was the obvious thing to do. And I began to understand with a greater clarity, why it was that no agency was anxious to register my name upon its books! For I was a very simpleton!

Merrick: Sir Charles Pomeroy. Bart. only son of Sir James and Lady Merrick, b. 1796. Married Miss Marguerite Gillespie of Exeter 1825: issue, two sons, Matthew, b. 1826. David, b. 1832. Interests: limestone quarries, Devon; sugar and coffee plantations, Sandwich Isles. Clubs: Boodle's and The Portland. Address: Merrick's Mount, South Devon.

But that was all the information to be gleaned and obviously referred to my suitor's late father, though Mama's voice became almost respectful as she intoned the words.

'Well, if these are the people concerned, they seem to be quite creditable. But what puzzles me is why such a situation should have arisen? If they are all that it says here, why should Sir Matthew Merrick seek a bride in such a singular fashion? For according to this, to put it plainly, he appears to be quite a catch! And surely there must be gently-bred young females living locally who would not spurn the opportunity to be his wife!'

'But he does not want a wife, Mama. Not really. He wants a companion. And as Mr Peppercorn has told us, having lived abroad for so long, he has lost the close contact he once had with friends, even acquaintances.'

'Surely his brother could rectify that small matter for him? Or his aunt could invite people to Merrick's Mount?'

'Not if Sir Matthew's health prohibits much entertaining.'

'Abroad, you say? Probably he took an interest in his family's plantations.'

'That is indeed very likely,' I agreed.

'What do you think, Isobel?'

'I am not highly impressed, I must confess. It reminds me too strongly of my own unfortunate experience. As you have remarked, the proposal is so exceptional as to be almost bemusing. But I can recall being bemused, and a very rude awakening I got! And do not forget, the state of matrimony is very permanent. And if, as in my marriage, promises are not kept, there is nothing you can do. Once you are wed, you are tied to a man until one of you dies!'

'But if everything were drawn up in legal fashion? There could be no breaking of promises then!' I objected.

'Maybe not, but you would still be tied to him, possibly for longer than you might quite like!' was her indisputable answer. 'Yes, you might meet somebody and fall truly in love, and there you would be, already bound to another!'

'Well, I am not likely to meet anyone here in London. Nobody whom Mama would countenance, anyway. And anyone of whom she might approve, would certainly expect me to bring him a dowry! And I do not have a dowry, and what is more, in a very short space of time, we may not even have a respectable address!'

'Let me assure you, Laura, that your aunt and I will ensure that our future abode is in a respectable locality.'

'Yes, but probably peopled by artisans and certainly not so elegant as this one. Bloomsbury and suburbs of a similar status do not have eligible suitors growing upon trees, surely? A clerk, or perhaps a shopkeeper would be all that I could aspire to, and even they would look for a little nestegg along with their bride!'

'I shall sleep on it and let you know tomorrow at breakfast, Laura.' Mama's decisive voice brooked no further argument. 'If I do decide to accede to your desire to meet Miss Merrick, I shall send one of the servants with a message to Mr Peppercorn's chambers requesting that he come here. But let this be understood, Miss, that never again will you lower yourself so far as to go to the solicitor's place of business! I make myself clear?'

'Very, Mama.'

'I have your word?'

'Yes, Mama.'

Tiffany daintily patted away a yawn. 'Oh, I do feel weary! May I go to bed, Mama?'

'Certainly, my dear.'

'If you please, where am I to sleep?'

'Do not be absurd! Oh! Yes! Well, you may retire to the room you share with Laura, for I think we have now reached an understanding.'

'Are you coming, Laura?'

'A little later, perhaps,' I replied.

'Laura, go up with your sister. It is entirely your fault that the child is tired out. What with forcing her to go all that way this morning, then making her bear the burden of keeping your guilty secret until this evening, then constraining her to endure all this upset and excitement! Yes, you will retire with Tiffany now, and then you will not disturb her rest.'

Once we were quit of the drawing room, all signs of my sister's lassitude completely disappeared, and, bright-eyed as a robin, she chirruped gaily, 'Now we can talk! Make plans! Will you invite me to stay! May I be bridesmaid? What shall we wear? White for you, of course, and, as you know, blue is my best colour. Or pink. A pretty rose-pink? Or should I too wear white, with perhaps a pastel sash to match my posy?'

'Hush, you go too fast. I have yet to get Mama to even agree to a meeting.'

'Oh, have no fears on that head! Did you not remark how she read the description of the Merricks and their circumstances?' my sister said wisely. 'You know how snobbish she is.'

'Are not we all?'

'Yes, I am very pleased to say.'

'Even if it should come to anything, I doubt that the actual wedding will be of the type you seem to envisage. A very simple ceremony will be all that is required.'

'What could be more simple than having only one bridesmaid? And if it takes place in our parish, Sir Matthew cannot be all that poorly! Otherwise he could never stand the journey! It would be the greatest shame if he came to be wed and were buried instead! O-oh, that rhymes!' she giggled, heartlessly.

'You have a warped sense of humour, child,' I reproved, keeping my face as straight as I was able. 'Anyway, it is still only a proposal, and even that has not been confirmed by Miss Merrick, nor have I accepted it.'

'But you would? You will?'

'I do not know. For, foolish as it may now sound, I am beginning to have doubts.'

'About what?'

'Why, everything to do with it. The strangeness of the offer, made as it is by someone we do not know.'

'Then why did you tell Mama about it and make us endure all that fuss this evening?'

'Again, I do not know. Perhaps I was secretly hoping she would be adamant in her refusal.'

'So, this is where your brave talk brings us, is it? Feeling secure in the belief that Mama would forbid you, you were prepared to dare all! Laura Lambourne, you are all say and no do!'

'Well, it is a very great decision to make, especially so suddenly,' I countered.

'For you perhaps it is, but I should have no hesitation,' my sister said. 'I would be only too delighted to be in a position to help Mama and yourself, were you my younger sister! Oh, if only I were the elder! I would grasp the chance to marry the man and see Mama restored to her proper station in life, instead of having to be meekly grateful for charity during the rest of it. And I should ensure that you, as my younger sister, had the right clothes and mixed with the right people, so that you would be able to meet someone really eligible when the time came for you to wed. Oh, if only it were me, I would not shrink from such a veritable gift as this is!'

'I have not said I would. Only that I am still a trifle dubious.'

'Every bride is that! It is a well-known fact that every girl suffers from her nerves just before her wedding!'

'And how would you know that?'

'Because, even though I am treated like a child, I am not one. I am fourteen, almost a woman. And sometimes I think I am more of a woman than you are, dear sister. I observe things, things that would normally be concealed from a woman but that they think a mere child would not notice. I hear little things: things that are sometimes discussed in front of me because it is thought I should not understand them. And there I quietly sit, absorbing a great deal of miscellaneous information.' Then she laughed. 'What a deal of nonsense I am talking. Yes, I am more tired than I thought. So let us follow our esteemed mother's example. Let us sleep on it and then wait to see what tomorrow will bring.'

★ ★ ★

Tomorrow brought Mr Peppercorn who was close-closeted with Mama and Aunt Isobel for more than an hour. And they too must have been impressed by the reassuring way in which he acted as Cupid's messenger, for it was arranged that Miss Merrick should call upon us the following afternoon. There! It was done! But instead of reveling in my triumph, the doubts that had assailed me became even more insistent. It was all too swift. It seemed that my role of decisionmaker had been snatched from me: the whole matter had been taken out of my hands and now lay between Mama, Mr Peppercorn, and the unknown Miss Merrick! Yes, I had labored too successfully, been too convincing that to become Lady Merrick was only to cloak in respectability the fact that I was to enter the employ of a bachelor gentleman. And the arguments presented to me earlier, that

I had brushed aside as being of no moment, now took on the most daunting proportions. What if anything should happen? Anything I might not quite like? I should be miles from here, alone, amidst complete strangers! To whom could I turn for succour, or even advice? Oh, why had I ever been so foolish as to put myself in this position?

'Laura, you have dusted that chiffonier twice already! Pray do not start on it again.' Tiffany's plaintive voice brought me back to the drawing room on which we were lavishing extra care in preparation for Miss Merrick's visit. 'I wonder what she will be like? What will you do if you think she may prove to be a dragon?'

'I doubt that a lady who has gone to so much trouble just to please her sick nephew would be anything but kind.'

'I wonder if he will live for long?'

'Possibly for longer than either you or I!'

'Oh! Then you do not think you will be a widow in the very near future?'

'I am not yet a wife!' I protested. 'And do you think this conversation could become a little less morbid?'

'I should call it realistic, but as you please. Now what can we talk about that is cheerful. I know. Christmas! You will not depart before then, will you? It is only three weeks away, and you could not be expected to leave your family at such a time. If I were you, I should insist on waiting until Yuletide is over.'

'Yes, I intend to, if I go at all.'

3

There must be a contrary streak in my nature, for when I thought the position was as good as mine and I only had to declare a willingness to accept it, I had begun to waver. But upon learning that I was but one of three young ladies from whom Miss Merrick would make her final selection, I became determined that no other should win the prize I already considered my own.

'You see, Mrs. Lambourne, I find myself in some slight difficulty,' Miss Merrick said as she daintily sipped her tea. 'Your daughter is quite the most suitable of the three young ladies. Pray allow me to congratulate you on having guided Miss Lambourne into becoming the charming young person she now is. But there is the question of relatives.'

'I can assure you, Miss Merrick, that her father's people, and mine too, had unblemished reputations and were respected by all!'

'You mistake my meaning, ma'am. It is the fact that she is fortunate enough to have relatives living! Ideally, the young lady I had in mind would have no kindred. This may sound inhospitable, but I will speak plainly. Not much entertaining is done these days at Merrick's Mount. We live very quietly, for my nephew's state of health precludes that we should have guests. Now in every civilized household, when a young woman marries its master, it would be not only natural but also desirable that she invite members of her family to her new home! But here we have a situation that is different. Actually, although my nephew keeps to his chambers for the most part, the whole household revolves around him, which, as he is its master, indeed it should! And so whoever is chosen to become Lady Merrick must be prepared to sacrifice these privileges that are normally accorded the mistress of such an establishment. Particularly so far as entertaining is concerned.'

'May I speak?' for I thought I had been dutifully silent for long enough.

'Certainly, my dear. Please do.'

'Well, ma'am, I look upon this whole venture as the taking up of a unique position. As a means of employment, but nothing more. If Sir Matthew has the whim to wed his companion, so be it, but I should not look for anything other than that which would be granted me if I went into anyone's employ as a lady's companion. And whoever heard of a lady's companion inviting her friends or relations to become guests in her employer's residence?'

'What a sensible, reasonable young woman you are!' Miss Merrick smiled at me approvingly. 'And what a pleasant voice you have. Low and well-modulated. So different from some of the girlish twittering one hears these days! Oh, this is very perplexing! It is so very important that I make the right decision. You, Miss Lambourne, are the very epitome of the young lady I envisaged when I set out upon my quest, although the other two are also worthy, even if in a lesser degree. But they do merit consideration. One of them is in very dire financial straits but she is the one I favor least. A little too anxious to please, if you please, a trifle too biddable and meek, and I mistrust that, though she does hold the advantage of being completely alone in the world. The other is nearly so, apart from having a younger brother. But although he is now away at school, who knows, in time to come he could be an encumbrance. It is Friday today. Perhaps you will be kind enough to allow me to consider the matter over the weekend? And then on Monday I shall instruct Mr Peppercorn to visit all three applicants, of whom you are one, and announce my decision.' Miss Merrick rose, and so too did I, subconsciously trying to impress upon her that I knew my manners. 'You have been most kind to receive me, Mrs. Cheadle, Mrs. Lambourne.'

Mama reached for the bell.

'Oh, Mama, pray allow me to show Miss Merrick the way down,' I said, opening the door, then gently closing it behind us, 'This way if you please, ma'am.' But I was not too preoccupied to notice a mane of golden hair cascading from over the balustrade of the floor above. Tiffany peeking! And probably hoping that the visitor would glance up, espy her, be entranced by her beauty and state there and then that the matter could wait long enough for her to grow old enough to herself become the sought-for Lady Merrick. We were at the front door, and an attentive and highly curious Judkin was hovering. Miss Merrick took my hand in her tiny one gloved in finest kid.

73

'Good day, Miss Lambourne. It has been a great pleasure meeting you, and I feel almost certain that you and I are destined to become firm friends.'

I bobbed my curtsey.

'Thank you, Miss Merrick. I should consider myself most fortunate if this should be so. Good afternoon. Judkin, please escort Miss Merrick to her carriage.'

I stood in the open doorway and watched her enter the most splendid vehicle that had ever carried a passenger away from Grosvenor Crescent. It was varnished in so dark a green as to be almost black, and its brass accoutrements glittered in the wintry sunlight. The coachman and footman were also liveried in dark green, the latter servant leaping from his seat to open the door and let down the steps that Miss Merrick might enter; and once she was safely installed the door was closed to enable me to see, upon its panel, a coat of arms. But before I could study it, the two gleaming chestnut horses that drew this equipage were set into motion and rapidly clip-clopped away, leaving me to reflect that as it was privately owned it probably belonged to some friends with whom she was staying. I wished that I might have had more time in which to study their family crest, for from it I might have learned something if I had looked it up. Whoever they were, they must be gentlefolk at least, possibly even of the nobility! Those were the circles in which I should soon be moving, bearing a modest title of my own! Lady Merrick! I had the peculiar feeling that my physical stature had increased within the last half hour, and it was only fitting that I should now retrace my steps up the stairs in a stately manner instead of scampering up them as I was tempted. With studied dignity, I reentered the drawing room to be met with, 'The effrontery of the woman!' Mama was so angry. 'To come here, inspect you, and then to calmly tell us that you are only one of three, and that she will make her selection at her leisure! Just as though she were engaging a servant!'

'She is. A superior one, but nonetheless, a servant,' I replied. 'I thought that was understood.'

'Well, the solicitor certainly gave no hint that there were other aspirants.'

'I know. But it does not matter for I feel the lady has already made up her mind. She has chosen me!'

'Think you so, Miss? Well let us hope that you will not be too disappointed if her choice falls elsewhere.'

'It will not do that. She has already chosen me. And I am glad! I liked her. Did not you?'

'Not especially. She possessed a trifle too much of *la grande dame* attitude, for all her diminutive size.'

'Mama, I thought her demeanour completely natural. Obviously, she is *la grande dame* and acted and spoke as she always does,' I defended. 'What did you think, Aunt Isobel?'

'Principally, that her sable-lined cloak would cost my whole year's dress allowance several times over! And did you observe that rope of pearls she was wearing?'

'I thought they were beads. Were they indeed pearls?'

'Grey ones. Extremely rare and very, very costly!'

'She made no mention of money,' I said, 'named no specific sum.'

'My good girl, you would hardly expect her to.' Mama allowed herself to smile at my naïveté. 'Such sordid haggling she would certainly leave to underlings. In this instance, Mr Peppercorn.'

'She complimented Laura upon her speaking voice,' Aunt Isobel remarked.

'Yes, and I must admit that Miss Merrick seemed to be quite taken with her.'

'And on Monday I shall be proved right in my assumption that I have been chosen,' I asserted.

'You may be, dear. If so, all that will remain to be decided will be whether or not you shall accept.'

Saturday and Sunday dragged by on leaden feet, and when Tiffany learned that, in any event, there would be no forthcoming sojourns in Devon so far as she was concerned, she began to lose interest, declaring she had after all decided that the circumstances were all too peculiar for her taste, I should be too far away, and that it would be best to forget the whole thing. But I was now strongly in favour! I had met and liked Miss Merrick, so I would have at least one friend at Merrick's Mount, and then there was also the question of financial reward. For, surely, anybody who could afford to dress as she did and also wear such jewellery, was not likely to be the representative of a family that would prove to be niggardly! And when on that fateful Monday morning was disclosed the sum offered, the size of it was sufficiently generous to still any further real argument Mama was about to make.

'Miss Merrick has instructed me to make this proposal. She has Sir Matthew's written authority to make it, and she desires that the amount mentioned shall be considered as an annuity, not a salary nor an allowance. From the day she weds Sir Matthew Merrick until the day of her own demise, I am empowered to offer Miss Lambourne an income of one thousand pounds per annum, provided she resides at Merrick's Mount for all of her husband's lifetime. This shall be regarded as full recompense for the loss of the companionship of her own family during Sir Matthew's lifetime, and for any curtailment of freedom she be constrained to suffer whilst being in attendance upon her spouse. I am also instructed to say there is to be no bargaining. This is Miss Merrick's only and final offer.'

'Does she take us for hucksters at a fair?' My mother was deathly pale with anger.

'No, no, ma'am. I am but speaking in legal terms, and nobody even considers that you might. One thousand pounds per annum, to be paid quarterly into any bank Miss Lambourne cares to name. For her to put to whatever use she chooses.'

'You have documents to be signed?' I asked swiftly.

'Yes, Miss Lambourne. By you, and by your mother, as your legal guardian.'

'Then pray let us proceed,' I said.

But Mama was still not totally convinced, still seemingly hesitant, until I whispered, 'Mama, I cannot force you to sign, but believe me, if you deny me this chance, and such a one will never come my way again, I shall not forgive you for so long as I live!'

'Very well, let us get it over with and have done. One thing though, when is my daughter expected to travel to Devon?'

'As early in the New Year as it can be arranged. I am also empowered to offer an advance on the coming quarterly's allowance, if this should be desired.'

'Thank you, Mr Peppercorn, but that will not be necessary. I am not so impoverished that I cannot furnish my daughter with a wardrobe suitable for her new station in life.'

The solicitor bowed.

'I have taken the liberty of bringing with me the small legacy left Miss Lambourne by my late client Mr Wilfred Cheadle. That is yours by right, Miss, and I think the expenditure of it was envisaged to cover the expenses of just such an eventuality as this. Just sign here, Miss Lambourne, and here, and here. And now you, ma'am. Yes, that seems to be in order.' He stood up. 'I shall call again if I may on January 1st, next year, in the forenoon. I shall then be in a position to tell you what arrangements have been made for your journey to your new home. Good day to you, ladies.' And he was gone.

I do not think I was alone in employing the

ensuing short silence in a little mental arithmetic, then I took up my copy of the agreement. Yes, there it was. One thousand pounds, yearly!

'Well, what do you make of that, Isobel?'

'It matters not what I make of it. It is done. Signed and settled. It is too late now to have further thoughts,' my aunt replied.

'Why on earth should I?' I asked. 'Oh, just think of the difference this will make. Mama can now match your income and thus enable you, her, and Tiffany to live in a quite comfortable fashion. And Tiffany can go to school and be finished, even though she has never properly been started. And she can there meet other gently bred girls and their families. Yes, at last you will be able to move amongst genteel people once again.'

'Laura, you are mistaken. If you think your sister or I would wish to touch a penny — '

'Mama! Please! Say no more. The whole point of my taking this position was that it would enable me to be of help!'

'But the income is yours, child! We would not wish to profit from your sacrifice.'

'What sacrifice? To be Milady? To have servants, clothes, the use of carriages, and a fine establishment to live in? And what else should I do with all that money?'

'Your wardrobe will cost a fair amount.'

'Why? I shall not go avisiting, and we will not entertain. A basic collection of good, well-chosen garments will suffice me for years, and if I can dress half as elegantly as Aunt Isobel does on her allowance of two hundred pounds a year, I shall be more than content. So what would I want with the other eight hundred? Come Mama, do be reasonable!'

'There is another thing. We have to equip you for your new life, and even with that fifty pounds we shall find it rather difficult to manage.'

'With fifty pounds? That is a very large sum to spend solely on clothes,' I objected. 'I had thought to save some of that!'

'Laura, you have no idea! We cannot have you gaining the reputation of being nothing but a ragbag! You will need to be fitted out from top to toe. You must have costumes for every waking hour, and they must be good ones. I know! I shall sell that garnet and diamond brooch of mine, and with the money raised from that and what you already have, we should just about contrive,' said my aunt decisively.

'Isobel, you shall do no such thing.'

'Yes I will, Charis. I never liked the bauble, and it will be my contribution.'

'No, I cannot allow it.'

'Charis, you cannot forbid it. And the proceeds from the sale of the brooch will be my investment in my niece's future. For do not forget, I too will benefit! If Laura persists in her desire to provide you with an income that will be the same as mine, it will enable us all to live much more comfortably than we had any hope of doing previously. And I will freely admit, I am very fond of my comfort!'

★ ★ ★

I sat alone in my reserved, first-class compartment, watching the cheerless landscape flash by at an alarming rate. It was many years since I had made a journey by train but now, after staring at disconsolate bent-head cattle standing in wet meadows beneath lowering clouds for more than an hour, the novelty of it was beginning to pall. *The Ladies Journal*, with which I had been furnished to relieve the tedium, had no article within its covers capable of inspiring more than mild interest, and so I sat, not quite believing that this was really happening to me! It was as though I were still held in thrall by some dream and, in the moment just before waking, was aware that I was dreaming though still unable to bring myself back to full consciousness. I raised my hand to survey it neatly gloved in soft brown kid, I lifted the hem of my skirts fractionally to admire my new boots, also brown. Then my glance fell upon the topmost skirt, fashioned from the same material as my Zouave jacket, both of them made up in a brown and green tartan plaid not likely to be claimed by any true clansman. And over all was my traveling cape of beige merino, edged with bead embroidery and lined with quilted satin. To complete my ensemble I was wearing a bonnet of brown velvet with a beige silk lining that showed itself in gathered effect just inside the brim. Admittedly it became me well enough, though I had set my heart on buying instead a saucy hat with an artificial bird about to take flight from its crown, but this was denied me because it might be considered too fashionable for country wear, or even a little fast!

'Your clothes must be good, elegant, but not sufficiently *a la mode* to cause remark. After all, you are not setting yourself up as a leader of fashion!' Mama had seen fit to inform me.

But apart from regretting the loss of the hat, I was more than content with the purchase that had been selected and fitted and now lay snug between layers of tissue paper inside my three nearly new trunks reposing in the guard's van.

'It would look bad to have obviously new luggage and might give the impression that we do not already own some. Even though it would be true, we do not want the whole world to know it. Yes, we shall buy trunks secondhand but they must be in excellent condition and unadorned with the initials of a previous owner, unless their surname began with an L!'

Of course, all of this shopping had had to be done during the fortnight just before Christmas, when every shop and store was at its busiest, or immediately afterwards, when the bargain sales were in progress. This had necessitated a great loss of time whilst waiting to be served, crowded streets and omnibuses, bad weather and tempers to match. But at last it was done. I now owned more clothes than ever before in my life, all of them new and bought especially for me! Never again would I wear one of Mama's old gowns, shortened and turned; or even one of my own that was darned, patched, or inserted with a similar piece of material to make it encompass my growing body, the renovation always being glaringly obvious. Anyway, I was not fully grown, and the clothes I was taking with me to Merrick's Mount satisfied me completely. One dozen each of every article of nightclothes or underwear, and three each of everything else: morning costumes, afternoon gowns, dinner gowns, evening gowns; pairs of boots, shoes and slippers; outdoor apparel such as cloaks and capes; and two of the new patent crinolines that would collapse when one sat on them! I had also been well provided with accessories: gloves, hose, reticules, bonnets but no hats; and such fripperies as collars and cuffs of lace and cambric, and sets of inner sleeves to wear within the wide pagoda sleeves that were currently the fashion. I had an ebony toilette set, a daguerreotype of Mama and Tiffany that did neither of them full justice. I had proof of identity in the form of my birth certificate and my mother's written permission to wed Sir Matthew Merrick of Merrick's Mount. Mama had also presented me with her fob-watch, so that I should have the means to keep track of time. And, in the Berlin woolwork purse given to me by Tiffany at Christmas, lay riches, three whole golden sovereigns! And beside me on the seat was a packed luncheon that I was far too nervous to eat.

Yes, I was well provided for any eventuality, and now a glance at my timepiece informed me that soon my train would arrive at Exeter, and there I should leave it and continue my journey by the private carriage, which would have been sent from Merrick's Mount to meet me. But I had not expected and was therefore pleasantly surprised by the presence of Miss Merrick.

'Ah, there you are, Laura. I cannot continue to

call you Miss Lambourne for you are almost one of the family, and I should be pleased to hear you address me as Aunt Ruby.'

'What a pretty name,' I murmured.

'Do you think so? Personally, I dislike it intensely. It was chosen by my father. A gentleman of scant imagination, I fear. But he always considered me a gem, even though he was proved to be alone in that opinion.'

'Surely not!' What else could one reply to such a remark?

'Well, in any event, I remained a spinster. A jewel without a setting, so to speak.'

'I should wager that was purely from choice.' I felt on slightly firmer ground and was rewarded by a brief smile. 'And I am most grateful that you took the trouble to come all the way here to meet my train. I do hope that the double journey will not prove to be too wearisome for you. I believe you mentioned it was a distance of some sixteen miles or so between here and Merrick's Mount?'

We had left the station, emerging into the street, to almost collide with a gentleman in naval uniform who in a very mannerly way stood aside, raising his cap and bowing as we passed. Aunt Ruby seemed totally unaware of his presence, for she gazed through him as though he were invisible. But I thought his courteous gesture merited some small sign of recognition, so I smiled slightly and nodded as a wordless thank you. From the corner of my eye, I saw him straighten but instead of resuming his progress he stood where he was, staring after us, as my companion replied, 'Oh it is, but I came

84

up to Exeter yesterday. I did a little shopping and stayed overnight. Here is the carriage. James and John are seeing to your baggage. Here they are, now. Just the three trunks, are there?'

'Yes, that is all.' Suddenly I felt that I should have had more.

'Then we may as well get in, and once the luggage is secured we can set off without delay. Even so, I fear night will have fallen before we reach home.'

'It does grow dark so early at this time of year. But the shortest day is now behind us, and I always find that a comforting thought,' I said.

'Speaking of comfort, place that rug across your knees, Laura. It is quite cosy in here now, but when the footwarmers start to cool it will soon become chilly, and we shall have no opportunity to have them refilled with a fresh supply of hot embers between here and Merrick's Mount.'

This carriage was not quite so elegant as the one she had used whilst in London, but it was the finest I had ever ridden in, and, as I leaned back against the grey velvet upholstery, I realised how easy it would be to take to my new way of life. For though we should not entertain, it would surely be permitted that I take drives through the countryside surrounding my husband-to-be's home, and also it would be expected that I attend church with the rest of the family. And, as Lady Merrick, it would be only natural that I visit the poor and sick on the estate, dispensing the charity that was usually forthcoming from the master's residence. Yes, I could envisage myself quite clearly: calling

85

upon cottagers, doling out soup, jellies, and advice! The vicar's wife would rejoice at my coming, or, if Aunt Ruby already undertook these tasks, I should help her instead. Oh, I would soon be indispensable in a hundred little ways. I might even be the incentive that would make Sir Matthew recover from his illness! I had heard it said that sometimes the will to live, if it were powerful enough, could of its own accord defeat the most serious type of illness: that if the spirit were so inspired, it could conquer most ailments of the body! I might prove to be his salvation, and for the umpteenth time I wondered what he was like and if he were the kind of person who would respond to my efforts to play ministering angel, or whether he would be such another as my late Uncle Wilfred, querulous, impatient, suspicious, and irritable.

There had been a short silence whilst I pursued these thoughts, but instead of contemplation of the future, Aunt Ruby must have been preoccupied with memories for she suddenly said, 'No, I never married. And you were right in what you said, for I did have several offers. But I was needed at home and felt unable to accept any of them.'

'How sad. Your parents were in poor health?'

'No, no. My parents left this life when I was only a young girl, not yet out of the schoolroom. My brother was quite a few years older than I, and he, his wife, and I lived a very happy existence at Merrick's Mount until she died, shortly after giving birth to Matthew.'

'You speak of the present Sir Matthew Merrick?'

'Yes. And what a beautiful baby he was! But his

father was desolate at the loss of his lovely wife, and irrationally, he blamed the helpless infant for her death.'

'What a shame,' I murmured.

'Not permanently, I hasten to add. But he did become overfond of the bottle, shunning the nursery for more than a year, and during that time I lavished all of my love on the innocent mite. Yes, from when he was newborn, I have been the true mother of he who has now reached manhood. But so it was that, when he was little, no suitor could persuade me to wed and leave my baby nephew. No gentleman who ever came acourting caused my heart to flutter sufficiently to make me think of deserting little Matthew!'

'He was a very fortunate child to have such a devoted foster mother,' I remarked. 'But I was under the impression he had a younger brother.'

'A half brother. David is the son of my brother's second marriage,' Aunt Ruby said shortly.

'Oh, I see. And the second Lady Merrick? Does she still reside at Merrick's Mount?' I asked, for this might be something for which I was not prepared. A stepmother-in-law!

'No. She lost no time in remarrying. It was barely two years after my brother's death that she wed Lord Rowan and went up north to live near the Scottish border. But even though I should have appreciated that she show loyalty to her husband's memory for a little longer, I was not sorry to see her go.'

'You had a dislike for her?'

'As she had for me! I suppose I was partly to

blame. She was quite a pretty creature but certainly not of our social standing, and totally without the background or experience to enable her to be at ease in her position of being Lady Merrick. Actually, I found the woman rather plebeian, and there was always some slight mystery surrounding her. From whence did she come, who were her people, and so on. Well, during the interval between his marriages I had the ordering of everything at Merrick's Mount, and when he wed for the second time I was still young enough to be thoughtless in some ways. The servants would come to me for instructions, and I would issue them. Admittedly, my new sister-in-law declared she was pleased that I did, for she had no inkling of how the house should be run, but it was probably for that reason she came to resent me. Also she did not have the fondness for little Matthew that I did, and when she produced David, my brother's second son, poor Matthew could have gone to the devil so far as she was concerned. In fact, she would have been well content if he had!'

'She doted on her own boy, then?'

'Indeed she did and lost no opportunity to praise David and belittle Matthew, especially in their father's hearing. And that strengthened my determination never to leave the home of my birth, at least not until Matthew reached an age when he had no further need of me. I knew that if I did the poor little fellow would have a sorry time of it, with nobody to champion him.'

'Could you not have spoken to your brother? Made him aware of this unhappy situation?'

'I tried, but she held him in the palm of her hand, and he was quite besotted with her, for all her vulgarity. And I must confess that she was, and still is, an extremely attractive woman with the added advantage of being able to lie glibly enough to be believed by those who know no better.'

And I guessed that, if Aunt Ruby described her as attractive even though there was no love lost between them, the lady must be a rare beauty.

'I have a confession to make,' I said. 'We looked up your family in *Who's Who*, and no mention is made of Sir Charles's second marriage.'

'There is no need to confess to that Laura, for that was a most natural thing to do. And I must say, that does puzzle me. But no matter. It must be just an omission in the printing.'

She seemed to be once more lost in reverie, but presently a very gentle snore informed me that Aunt Ruby was dozing. Dusk was beginning to fall, but it was still light enough for me to see my traveling companion quite clearly, and whilst she was unaware, I was able to study her at my leisure. She was not very tall, but such was her deportment that it made her lack of height of small consequence. She was neat of figure, but though her complexion seemed quite youthful, her hair which had once been dark brown was now lavishly streaked with silver in the most becoming way. And by her appearance and by what she had previously told me, I judged her to be in her early to mid-fifties. And I also noted that she was wearing a hat! But hers was of a simpler design than the one that had been denied me, for the one I had coveted had a complete bird upon its crown, whereas Aunt Ruby's was decorated more modestly with just a single feather secured by a buckle, and her richly braided blue velvet gown with its matching pelisse was in the latest style and probably purchased during her recent stay in London. But though she was asleep, only her closed eyelids betrayed this fact, for she still sat almost erect. And as dusk deepened into nightfall, the swaying of the well-sprung carriage instilled in me an overpowering drowsiness, and presently I, too, slept.

For how long, I do not know, but I was jerked into sudden wakefulness by the crunch of the horses' shoes upon gravel and then the cessation of all movement, until lighted lanterns cast their radiance through the besteamed carriage windows.

'Ah, here at last!' Aunt Ruby exclaimed as the door was opened and the steps let down. 'Come, Laura, you have arrived at your new abode, so let us lose no time entering it. Good evening, Flint.'

'Good evening, Madam. I trust you and the young lady had a comfortable journey?'

'Tolerable. This person is Flint our house steward. Miss Lambourne has honoured us by becoming our guest, Flint.'

He bowed to me, then addressed his mistress, 'All is prepared, Madam. Will you and the young lady go straight up or shall I have a teatray brought to the little parlour?'

'We shall go up. Miss Lambourne will probably wish to freshen herself and we will take tea in her suite. I shall show her the way, and you may have the luggage brought up as soon as you are able, but her maid can unpack it later.'

Newly awakened, I was not fully alert as we entered the house, and at first glance the scene that met my slightly bemused senses was a conglomeration of white, black, crimson, and gilt: a marble floor, predominantly white, and with an elegant pattern of Greek key design picked out in black of the same stone and a crimson carpet to cover the central portion of it; white walls with panels edged in gilt, each one a setting for either a portrait or landscape; ebony furniture, the chairs and small sofas upholstered in black and white striped satin; and at the far end of this apartment, which was only the hall, a wide staircase of white marble also carpeted in crimson and with a black wrought-iron balustrade, ascending in an imposing curve to the floor above. Aunt Ruby ignored two footmen garbed in the brown livery evidently favoured by the Merrick household and led me toward the stairs, but not so swiftly that I failed to note a succession of neatly capped female heads showing themselves briefly from around the partially opened door at the far end of the hall. I realised that the owners of them were all taking a peep at me and rejoiced inwardly that my appearance at least would be able to withstand the scrutiny of the maidservants.

Up the stairs, we turned right along the landing, then left along another, passed three doors, and the fourth gave entrance to my sitting room. I was wakeful enough by now to take mental note of the location of my chambers, for I was determined that in the near future I should not betray the fact that I was not used to dwelling in mansions of a similar size by having to ask my way back to the main hall of this one! The landings were crimson-carpeted and also had white walls, but here we had niches containing bust-surmounted pedestals, busts of people whom I failed to recognize, but as some were bearded and others clean-shaven and crowned with laurels, I comforted myself with the thought that they were most probably of long-dead heroes and scholars with whom I should scarcely have been on nodding terms.

So far I had received the impression that the house had been built perhaps a hundred years earlier, for the dainty furnishings and decor of the hall and landings betokened the influence of the 1750s. But when my suite was reached, it was obvious that somebody with no taste added to a woeful sense of color had attempted, within the last twenty or so years, to modernise it. Dark brown flocked paper hung on the walls; a carpet of a blue and white tartan covered the floor and clashed abominably with an overstuffed horsehair sofa and two armchairs upholstered in a Royal Stuart plaid that was mainly scarlet, these pieces of furniture cravenly seeking the protection afforded by antimacassars with bobbled fringe. Two hideous bronze figures were displayed upon the mantelpiece that was itself covered with a brown velvet bobble-fringed drape, and, from above it, Landseer's *Stag at Bay* seemed to stare with bitter reproach down at the beholder. There were two tapestry-worked footstools, so placed as to trip the unwary; three small tables that looked as if they would spill any burden not placed upon them in the most careful fashion; and also for my use was provided an escritoire of mahogany, cumbrous and lavishly bedecked with brass knobs and handles. A whatnot reposed in one corner of the room and in another a chiffonier, both of them crammed with knickknacks. The most attractive piece of furniture in the whole room was the window seat, which was presumably a fixture. But even this had not been overlooked by the masterhand of mediocrity that had planned the decor, for the brown velvet with which it was covered was hardly visible beneath its load of puce satin cushions!

'Come to the fire, Laura, and warm yourself. I hope you will find your apartment comfortable, and if anything is lacking, please do not hesitate to say so.'

'Thank you, but I am sure that everything is already here,' I replied.

'Your bedchamber leads off, through that door yonder, and your bathroom and dressing room open directly from your bedchamber.'

'It sounds very cosy and compact,' I remarked, all the while listening for the tinkle of china that would herald the arrival of our tea, then for good measure, 'quite charming.'

'Does it please you? Personally I find this modern furniture ugly in the extreme, but I suppose one must move with the times. I suppose you being of a younger generation than I, will heartily approve of all things new, but I must confess to being somewhat old-fashioned. I think I must be the only female to visit the Crystal Palace when it was opened ten years ago and not find a single thing to my liking!'

'You did not plan this room, then?'

'No, I disclaim all responsibility. My brother's second wife is the genius who designed this bower. Fortunately she did not attempt the bedchamber until this room was completely to her taste. But she wearied of this hobby, and so it was left as it had always been, that is apart from a new set of hangings. Ah, here is Flint. Will you pour, my dear?'

That was a task I was eager to perform for I was extremely thirsty. I was also hungry, but only thin slices of bread and butter fashioned into dainty little rolls accompanied the beverage, and so I resigned myself to a further wait until my clamoring stomach should be satisfied.

'Tell me, Aunt Ruby, how is this household arranged? Do we all take our meals at the same table, or do Mr. David Merrick and his wife live separately?'

'No, they and you and I all dwell *en famille*. Only my elder nephew lives apart, for the sake of his health. And lest you are a trifle nervous about dining with David and Celia this very evening, allow me to set your mind at rest. They are away, visiting Celia's family until at least the end of the week. I expect their return sometime this coming Sunday or Monday, therefore there will be only you and I for the next day or so. And Matthew, of course. I planned it so, to lessen any feeling you might have of being quite overwhelmed by a sea of new faces.'

'How very thoughtful of you. And Sir Matthew? I shall make his acquaintance this evening?'

'I think it hardly likely. As a general rule, he retires quite early. Of course, it greatly depends on how well or how poorly he feels. In any event, he does not dine with us, though his valet, Virtue, always makes sure I know how his master fares. There will most probably be a message awaiting me in my rooms. Normally we dine at seven, but as we have nobody else's wishes to study and we are both of us tired, you I daresay even more than I, I suggest we take our meal at an earlier time and then get a good night's rest.'

'That sounds most pleasant. Yes, I must confess to a slight feeling of weariness.'

'Then I also suggest we do not trouble to change our attire. Anyway, your trunks are not yet unpacked. Your maid will show you the way to the small dining room. Shall we say in about an hour's time?' She rose and crossed the room to the bedchamber door, which she opened. 'There you are, Tansy. Come and meet your mistress. Laura, this young woman is to be your personal maid. She is not fully trained, at least not to fashionable standards, but she has a modicum of common sense, and I have found her to be a willing, cheerful, and neat creature. Tansy, as you know, Miss Lambourne is a stranger in our midst, and I want her to receive the impression that the house servants at Merrick's Mount are second to none!'

The girl was young, fresh faced, and sturdy looking, clad in a brown gown, though probably as a mark of her elevated position hers was of silk with cream muslin apron, collar, and cuffs, as too was her frilled cap set off with pink ribbons. She curtseyed to me with a reverence due only to royalty, and though almost overcome by the importance of the occasion and her obviously new station in life, she answered, 'Oh, Madam, Miss will lack for naught at my hands.'

'I am sure I shall not. Tansy? What a pretty name!' I remarked with a smile.

'She is niece to my housekeeper, Mrs Sweetbriar,' Aunt Ruby informed me. 'And now I shall leave you to refresh yourself.' She inclined her head and left me, who had but only recently aspired to become a lady's maid myself and had failed dismally, with one of my very own! And this brought me no little satisfaction, for though I had no real need for a body servant, I certainly desired to obtain information, and as she was niece to the housekeeper, Tansy should be in a position to give it. But in time I recalled the saying 'A bird that fetches will also carry,' and so I made my queries in as devious a fashion as I could devise.

'You must know all about this lovely house, Tansy. Were you employed here before you were engaged to serve me?'

'Oh yes, Miss. Stillroom maid, I was, at first, and then I was put in the laundry, and when my aunt saw how fine a hand I was at starching and how well I could use the goffering iron, after a while she took me out of there and put me in the sewing room so that I could learn fine work. She said then that, if I worked hard, I might one day become a lady's maid, and that, if I applied myself, she would help me to get a start.'

'Well, she has kept her word, has she not? I think I shall just rinse my face and hands for now and have a thorough wash later, before I go to bed.'

'Then you will take your bath in the morning, Miss?'

'Yes, that is what I prefer,' I replied, as though it were a normal daily occurrence instead of the weekly Saturday night ritual I had been used to. In the Cheadle household, hot baths had been considered an extravagance, necessitating the costly consumption of fuel to heat the water.

'Everything is in readiness now, Miss. Will you come this way?'

'In a moment or two, Tansy. I wish to look about me, first.' And look I did, with delight, to find the bedchamber in complete contrast to the sitting room. Here, everything was dainty, elegant and restful, the main feature being a large half-tester bed, its hangings and coverlet of ivory brocade. A similar material curtained the two windows and encased the cushions upon the rose silk covered daybed, this being so placed that during the hours of light a person reclining on it could gaze out of the casements to admire the view, if there were one of note. It did occur to me that though the furniture was delicate and in exquisite taste, there did not seem to be a great deal of it; then I remembered mention of a dressing room, which would probably contain wardrobes, presses and a toilette table, and in this assumption I was shortly proved correct. And the glow from the oil lamps I found most pleasing, for they were shaded with pink glass engraved in a floral pattern, and the carpet on the floor was of ivory hue and bedecked with garlands of roses. A fire was burning in the white marble-enclosed grate, and on either side of this was an easy chair upholstered in the same stuff as was the daybed, and there were little tables set at convenient places. Yes, in here I should be quite at ease, and there and then I decided that the sitting room would see but little of me, for almost everything I should require, even in the daytime, I would find here in my bedchamber.

'Here is your bathroom, Miss. There is no running hot water, only cold. I bring your heated water up from the kitchens. The bath is set in though, and so is the basin and the W.C., but the mistress said it would be too costly to have hot water piped all over the house, as well as cold.'

'I should think not, indeed. Anyway, there is no real need for that,' I asserted, for I should not be required to carry it.

'No, Miss, I just thought you might be used to having it.'

'Well I am not. Few people are. This will suit me very well.'

'And the lamps, Miss. We only have oil or candle-light, here. I expect you are accustomed to gas?'

'Only in main rooms. Most bedchambers, even in London, are still served as you are here.'

'I have seen gaslight in the streets of Exeter, but never in a house!'

'Well, it can be convenient I suppose, but I prefer the old-fashioned means of illumination.'

'Shall I dress your hair afresh, Miss?'

'No, not now. You may tidy it and tuck in any stray wisps.'

And so soothingly did Tansy wield the brush that I almost dozed beneath the gentle strokes until, 'If you please, Miss, if you are ready, I think it is time for me to show you the way downstairs.'

'Very well,' I agreed, although at that moment I would far rather have succumbed to the inviting promised embrace of the plump, feather-filled mattress that I guessed was hidden beneath the coverlet of the half-tester bed. But first I had to endure the ordeal of consuming dinner! I must rouse myself sufficiently so that I should not be disgraced by falling asleep over the soup or using the wrong cutlery for some unfamiliar dish. But all went quite well. The small dining room was, to my standards, a vast apartment. It contained two fireplaces with glowing log fires, and the table was of a size to accommodate a couple of dozen diners comfortably, but Aunt Ruby took her place at one end, and, as I was seated next to her, we could converse quite easily as we ate. True we each had a deft footman behind our chairs, and Flint, whom I would describe as butler but Aunt Ruby referred to as house steward, hovered discreetly in the background, and, although four courses were presented for our delectation, each with its attendant entrees and removes, there was nothing with which I

99

could not cope, and hunger helped me overcome my
initial shyness. Once I had blunted the edge of this
somewhat, I began to cast approving glances about
the chamber, to silently admire the snowy damask
napery, the heavy, crested dishes and candelabra
of solid silver, and also to resolve at some time in
the future to inspect the huge tapestry that almost
completely covered the far wall of the room. I had
no need to concentrate too closely on what I was
saying to Aunt Ruby, for as there were servants
present, we were only discussing table generalities,
and so I was comparatively free to imagine the
reaction of my mother and sister if they were
suddenly placed in such a setting as this. Oh,
how they would enjoy it! How Mama would revel
in this atmosphere of genteel, graceful living, and
Tiffany would take to it as readily as a duck did
to water. I could envisage them both making their
wishes known in gentle yet authoritative voices to
the staff of well-trained servants who ministered to
the needs of the people who dwelt at Merrick's
Mount. And Mama would appreciate in greater
measure than even did I the fineness of everything
within the walls of the mansion. If only she could
see it! Well, why not? Admittedly it had been agreed
that they should not visit me, but why should they
not? If as Aunt Ruby averred, Sir Matthew kept
to his own apartments, how could they disturb
him? It was unreasonable to require this of me.
Surely in a house this size, it would be possible to
have several guests, particularly one's own kinfolk,
without causing a catastrophe! My mother was a
lady and, of course, knew how to conduct herself,

and my sister, though young, was not a hoyden! Why should they not come, if only for a short while? Just to see the state in which I should now live. Yes, I should let the matter rest, and, at a later date, perhaps in the spring, I would voice my plea. By then I ought to be on friendly terms with Sir Matthew, and if I applied to him, as he was master here, and if he granted my request, there would be none who could say him nay! Not even Aunt Ruby! And upon this pleasant reflection, I presently bade her good night and was escorted back to my suite of rooms by one of the footmen.

The luxury of having one's personal maid can be agreeable but also irksome, as I soon discovered when met by a waiting Tansy who helped me to disrobe and put on my nightrail and wrapper, unpacked in my absence. She then wished to trim my nails and polish them, to take down my hair, which was a task that had to be done, brush, and then braid it.

'Oh, leave it as it is. I am so tired I am already nearly asleep.'

'It will be woefully tangled come morning, Miss.'

'Then we shall worry about that when the time comes. Put out the lamps please, and you may go.'

'What will you wear, Miss? What am I to press for you to put on when you rise. I will do everything later, of course, but I must have the garments you choose to wear first thing, crisp and ready.'

'Prepare whatever you like. Anything suitable will

do. And now pray leave me.' I mumbled the reply for, as I had anticipated, my bed was blissfully comfortable, the pillows just right, and the smooth linen sheets warmed to perfection. At last I have found my niche in life, I drowsily thought in the moment between sleeping and waking. Yes, this would do very well! But though I slept almost instantly, I dreamed, at least I thought I did. In my troubled sleep, I dreamt, or I became aware, I knew not which, of a low voice saying, 'She is very young and very fair.' And also that someone was carrying a candle with a shaded flame and moving softly about my bedchamber. Or could that have been an illusion caused by the last feeble flickering of the dying fire within the grate? And in my dream I can recall starting up, crying, 'Who is there? Step forward so that I can see you!'

And from the shadows emerged the trim figure of Aunt Ruby. Silently she approached my bed, then whispered, 'S-sh, child. Did I alarm you? I am so sorry. I only wished to ascertain that you were comfortable.'

But there was somebody else there as well!

'Who is that behind you?'

'There is nobody here but me, Laura,' she stepped to one side, thereby blocking my view of one shadow that seemed to loom blacker than the others cast by the furniture.

'Look! Just behind you. I am sure there is someone there!'

'Where?' Swiftly she turned, so swiftly that the flame of the lighted candle she bore, brushed against the elaborately carved footboard of my bed and was instantly extinguished, plunging the room into nearly complete darkness.

'No, dear, there is nobody here but just we two. Hush now, and go back to sleep.'

With no light to guide her, a lifetime's familiarity with my room must have enabled her to find the door without hesitation, for I heard it open and then close, but she must have lingered on the threshold for just a moment and that would explain why the brief time that elapsed between the two sounds was of a sufficiency to enable two people to cross it, and not only one!

Fully awakened now, I could not rest easy until I had made certain I was alone, and remembering the candle and Lucifers on my bedside table, I struck my own light to behold the chamber empty of any person other than myself. But still not content I must leave my warm bed to peer under it, look behind the daybed, which afforded scant place for concealment, then go to the dressing room and inspect the wardrobes, ridiculously to even lift the lids of my still partly filled trunks, and for good measure, peep into the bathroom lest somebody should be lurking in there! No, all was as it should be but nonetheless I slid the bolt on the door leading into the sitting room and also locked my bedchamber door, which gave onto the passageway, and Tansy could think what she liked when she came to awaken me in the morning. And before I again entered my bed, I cast one more glance underneath it, just in case someone should have doubled back and was hiding there. Idiot! Fool! Pull yourself together and stop this nonsense. How could they? You would have seen them. Not if my back were turned. If they were in the bathroom whilst I was looking in the dressing room, they could have guessed I would search in there next! Had I not better take one more swift look in there, just to make certain? And then again under the bed? Dolt! You could continue this senseless circle until the dawn breaks! Get back into bed and do not be so stupid! But my nerves must have been strung taut as a bowstring, for, though I resolutely blew out my candle and tried to once again compose myself, for many hours I lay wakeful, tense, and alert, and only when I heard the stirring of the housemaids as they went about their first daily tasks, did I feel safe enough to unlock my door and then doze fitfully until Tansy came to again awaken me.

How thankful I was that nobody had witnessed my inane behavior during that night, for later in the morning I realized I had been the victim of nothing but a particularly vivid nightmare, or not even that! Yes, it was only a dream, for when I apologised to her the first moment that was opportune, begging her pardon that I had challenged her in such an abrupt fashion the night before, Aunt Ruby did not at once understand what it was I said. Then she smiled and told me there was nothing to forgive, for quite definitely she had not entered my bedchamber at all, and so it therefore followed that I was completely mistaken and, indeed, most certainly must have dreamt it!

4

'If you will allow me an hour in which to see Mrs Sweetbriar my housekeeper, give her my instructions, and then attend to some urgent correspondence, I shall then be happy to acquaint you with your new home, Laura,' Aunt Ruby said as we finished breakfast. 'As the day is so fine even though it is cold, we can, if we wrap ourselves warmly, go into the gardens, and you will be able to see the outside of the house and the direction in which Sir Matthew's residence lies. We can leave the interior of Merrick's Mount until another day when the weather is too inclement for us to venture forth.'

'Thank you. Yes, that sounds most interesting. Was I mistaken, or did you imply that Sir Matthew does not actually live here?'

'No, he does not reside here. This house was built a hundred and twenty years ago or thereabouts, but before then we Merricks lived in a manor house on a nearby site, and that had a dower house, attached to which was our private chapel. Although the old residence is now little more than a ruin, when the family moved up here, the dower house and the chapel were kept in a reasonable state of repair, and a covered walk, a type of cloister, was constructed to run from the west wing of this house to the chapel. And in the dower house adjoining this, Sir

Matthew chooses to live.'

'Oh? He is a very pious gentleman then, wishing to spend his life so near to the chapel?'

'The chapel is no longer used, and Matthew is no more pious than most folk, if as much. It is not the proximity of a place of worship that attracts him so much as the compactness and solitude of the dower house beside it. But do not think he stints himself in any way, for though the building in which he lives is far older than this, he has had it so altered to suit his convenience that I daresay the former occupants would not recognise it. Actually, he sent his own designs and had the place made to suit his taste before he even returned home to take up his inheritance! Oh, he has it furnished and equipped to a nicety, and nothing is lacking that could afford him the slightest degree of comfort!'

'But why? I do not mean to pry unduly, but it does seem strange!' I exclaimed.

'His health, my dear. There are days when he wishes to be completely alone, in utter silence, and in a place the size of this, there is always the coming and going of servants. True they are trained to carry out their duties in a quiet and orderly manner, but occasionally a little noise is unavoidable: the clatter of a coal scuttle or of water cans, the sound of the gong that summons us to meals, or even the peal of the main doorbell. Such trivial sounds can so grate upon his nerves when he is having one of his poor days, and he himself says he does not wish for the whole household to have to creep around just on his account!'

'Poor gentleman! But how very, very considerate

and unselfish of him. Just fancy studying other people to such an extent as that!'

'Yes, he is a dear creature.'

'What about the servants in his own establishment? Are they especially trained?'

'There is only one. His manservant, valet, call him what you will. He sees to all of my nephew's needs. Matthew brought him back with him when he returned from the Sandwich Islands.'

'Oh? Perhaps he is also skilled in nursing?'

'He is. Yes, Virtue is aptly named for he seems to have his full share of them. And now, my dear, if we are to leave this house and return before luncheon, I really must get on with my tasks.'

'Certainly. And please let me find my own way back to my suite, for I am sure I will be able to do so. In one hour, then?'

'Yes. Come down to the main hall and be sure to dress warmly.'

As Aunt Ruby had remarked, the day was fine, and, although it was chilly, the light frost that had covered the land that could be seen from the house was already being dispersed by the sun's rays, so they must have warmth in them. The morning room and breakfast parlor were swept and furbished, and so too was hall and staircase, so it was that not until I ascended these and was making my way along the landings did I encounter any of the housemaids. Neat in brown and white striped poplin gowns with crisp linen caps and aprons, each of the five young women whom I passed paused in her task to drop me a curtsey, return my murmured 'Good morning,' and then flatten herself against the nearest wall as I went on my way. My bedchamber too had been set to rights and from the dressing room came the sounds of activity as Tansy pressed my clothes on the table set within it, heating the irons on the trivet beside the grate in which a small fire was burning.

'Will you be going out, Miss?'

'Presently. Miss Merrick and I intend to walk in the grounds.'

'You will need a cloak then, Miss. This one of bottle green will go best with the gown you are wearing. Shall I set it to air?' And without waiting for an aye or nay, she proceeded to do so. 'And the gray velvet bonnet, Miss? And your black walking boots. Gloves! Gray or black? Gray, I think. Black ones are more for mourning.'

'I shall put on the black ones,' I said, for though it did not matter in the slightest. I thought it time to issue an instruction. 'And have a care with that bodice. That type of fabric scorches very easily.'

'Yes, Miss.'

'Have you come across my writing case yet?'

'Yes, Miss. I have put it on your escritoire in the sitting room.'

'Thank you. How does one despatch a letter from here? Is there a nearby village with a post office?'

'Just put any letters you wish to send in the post bag in the main hall, Miss. One of the footmen goes to the village twice a day, to fetch the mail and to send it.'

'Excellent. Then I shall pen a note to tell my family of my safe journey and arrival here. I will have time to do that.'

'Yes, Miss.'

I did not care to remain in the sitting room, and, as there were fires burning both there and in my bedchamber, I fetched my writing materials and returned to the latter room. I could not resist the temptation to bring with me from the escritoire a sheet of the household notepaper headed by the Merrick crest of a head-rearing, coiled serpent pierced by a sword, surmounting what looked like a chaplet above a motto, the Latin of which defeated me. Resolving to ask Aunt Ruby its meaning, I settled myself before the fireplace, writing case upon my knees, and proceeded to assure my kinfolk that all was well and that I should write again in the very near future, when I had a little more time at my disposal. I used one of my own plain envelopes, for though there were crested ones aplenty, I did not want to be thought overbold by the staff who would see my missive. Then, glancing at the mantel clock, I saw it was almost time so I readied myself for my tour of the grounds. The view from my chambers had given me no inkling of what I might expect for though there was a close-shaven lawn immediately below my casements, this very soon ended when it reached a small wood comprised of pine trees. Ah, yes, and I could see the beginning of a roofed, colonnaded walk that left the house and also disappeared amongst the trees. I smiled as the thought came to me that it looked a little like the setting for a fairy tale.

But my smile froze on my face, for upon passing the foot of my bed, I happened to glance down, and there, plain to see, was a dribble of hardened candlewax! So Aunt Ruby had been in here! The wax was in the very place where her candle had caught against the footboard and been extinguished by it! Why did she lie? What possible reason could she have to do so? And if she had lied so glibly once, could she also have been telling an untruth when she had assured me she was alone? Was there someone with her? That shadow that had seemed to have more substance than its fellows? And if so, who? And why? Numbskull! You probably did it yourself! If you recall, you were waving a lighted candle about whilst you conducted your idiotic search of the apartment! And quite possibly there is more proof of your inanity, if you seek diligently enough beneath the bed, for an instance. And if the housemaids find candlewax there, it will certainly make them wonder about the peculiar creature calling herself Miss Lambourne!

'A letter to post, dear? Just put it in that leather satchel. Are you ready? Then we shall set off.'

The steps were shallow and wide, ending beneath a pillared porte cochere. Before us was an almost circular lawn with a fountain at its center and the carriage sweep as its boundary. There were two pairs of high wrought-iron gates, each with an attendant lodge or small dwelling of some sort, and a stone wall between them.

'Actually, the land on the other side of the wall also belongs to us, or I should say to Sir Matthew, so its only real purpose is for neatness of design.'

'What lies beyond?'

'Nothing of any great interest. Just the clifftops and the sea.'

110

'The sea?' I must have squeaked. 'We are so near the ocean?'

'Oh, yes. Did I not mention it?'

'I have not seen the sea since Papa took us to stay in Margate! That was during the summer before he died.'

'I am not acquainted with Margate, but I do not think you will find much similarity between there and this coastline. Just here the cliffs are too precipitous to allow a person to descend to the beach, presuming that anyone should wish to. Further along it is not quite so forbidding, but neither is the view so spectacular. That is where the old wharfs are, or the remnants of them is a better description. Disused now, I fear they have become rather an eyesore. I tell my nephew something should be done about them, and he keeps saying he will when he has the time to arrange it.'

'Wharfs owned by the family?'

'Oh, yes. It was from there the stone was transported from our quarries, you know. Limestone. It used to be very busy down there when I was a young girl. But my father was the last Merrick to have the quarries worked. Actually, he only did so to give employment to the local people for we had no need for the revenue acquired from the limestone. And when my brother inherited, eventually he stopped it altogether.'

'But what about the people who had worked there?' I asked.

'He helped them to find other employment, well, some of them, anyway. And folk can be quite resilient if forced to fend for themselves! Probably there was a little hardship, but I do not believe anyone actually died from want through any action of his!'

'How comforting to be able to think so.'

Aunt Ruby glanced at me sharply, as though aware of the dryness of my remark, but merely said, 'If we walk towards the fountain for just a few paces, the house can then be seen to greater advantage.'

'Ah! That is very unusual!' I exclaimed, for as we neared it I could perceive in the middle of the fountain bowl a stone serpent, coiled, of course and with its head high as though to strike, but its mouth ejecting only harmless sprays of water.

'Oh, that. It forms part of the Merrick arms. Granted to a long ago ancestor who saved his sovereign from a snakebite. He was knighted, too, for in those days we were only yeomen.'

'How interesting. Where did this take place?' I asked politely.

'Somewhere near Acre, I believe. During one of the crusades. I forget which one.'

'As long ago as that?'

'We are a very old family though ancient records show us to be very modest at the outset of our history. We have suffered reverses, as well as some success. There have been fortunes made and also lost, advantageous marriages and some that were quite disastrous. The last beneficial one brought us the plantations on Maui. Sugar and coffee. My grandmother brought one of them with her as her dowry and then inherited the other two. She was Spanish.'

'That is where Sir Matthew spent his time abroad? Looking after the family interests?'

'Yes. There, now, what do you think of Merrick's Mount?'

For a moment, I gazed as if silently admiring, then I lied, 'Very elegant. Quite charming,' for, truth to tell, it reminded me too strongly of a public building to appeal to my taste. Yes, the Pantheon Museum on a slightly smaller scale! Palladian in style, built in grey stone with a pedimented roof that echoed the one that topped the porte cochere. Sash windows interspersed with venetian served the ground floor, and sash windows with mock balconies adorned the story above. There were smaller versions of the same immediately beneath the roof, and the level parts of that were edged with a balustrade that put me very much in mind of the Embankment that ran beside the River Thames!

'There is this main front, which faces south, with the west and east wings forming half a square and enclosing a courtyard.'

'How very compact,' I murmured.

'My chambers and those of David and his wife are in the main front. Yours are in the west wing, and in the east are the domestic quarters, kitchens, offices, and storerooms. Come, this way. There! Those are your chambers.'

'I see. I am alone in that wing, then?'

'Yes. I put you there as it is nearer to Matthew's domicile than any other part of the house.'

'I saw a roofed pathway when I was gazing out of my bedchamber window. Yes, there it is.'

'We find it invaluable. When I visit my nephew

or his servant comes to me, we usually walk along it. It was originally constructed to shelter the family from the elements when they went to worship in the chapel, for, as you perceive, it leads from the end of the west wing. The chapel itself is much older than Merrick's Mount. It was built at the same time as the old manor house and served the family in the days when they resided there. But our ancestors were hardier creatures for they never thought to pamper themselves by having a similar structure erected from there to the chapel, even though it lies farther from the old house than it does from this one and they attended services with great regularity! Much more often than did my parents or even grandparents, though they, of course, worshipped at the village church. Yes, nowadays those who are so minded attend St. Margaret's in the village, though I must confess that none of us are regular worshippers. Are you?'

'I do not think so. Not really. I went to church whenever the rest of the household did, but there were daily family prayers conducted by my late uncle-by-marriage. On Sundays he gave extra time to them, but he preferred the sound of his own voice to that of the local vicar, and his own sermons he judged to be superior, too.'

'Oh, dear! Do I detect a note of derision in your tone?'

'Perhaps. Well, my sister and I in particular did find his eloquence rather tiresome upon occasion.'

'Matthew's house is just beyond those trees.'

'Are we going there now?' Nervously I touched

my hair, lest any stray strand should have escaped its rightful place.

'No. Later you will meet him. If we turn this corner here, you will perceive that the narrower path leads down to the lake, but we shall follow this one that will bring us to the steps and the terraced garden. Over to the right lie the kennels, the stables, and the kitchen gardens. We do not have orchards here, for they form part of the home farm. Do you ride, Laura? If so we must find you a suitable mount.'

'I am afraid I do not, though I would very much like to learn.'

'Oh, I think we should be able to arrange for that. We can discuss it at a later date, for it is a little too cold at this time of year.'

'Are you at home in the saddle, Aunt Ruby?'

'In my younger days, but now my bones are set in their ways, I prefer to drive. Do you do that?'

'Drive myself? No, I fear I do not.' And as I answered, I was reminded ·of another lady's impatient observation, 'Is there anything you can do?' It seemed I replied to every query in the negative. Could I do this, or that, or anything? No and no and yet again, no! But fortunately my companion did not appear to think any the less of me, for she said, 'Of course, brought up as you were in the capital, you would have had no opportunity. Well not much, anyway. Now, from this parapet, I maintain, can be viewed a vista that will rival, indeed, outshine, any other in Devon!'

I caught my breath at the unexpected panorama that lay spread before me, for though the house behind us stood at a slightly higher level, in front of me and at either side it followed a downhill course so that it was as if one stood on a mountaintop and could literally see for miles! The parapet itself was stone-slabbed with a balustrade atop of which there was a wide stone ledge, and immediately beyond, it was what could be described as a ha-ha, whether man-made or as nature intended, I do not know, but I leaned over to see a sheer drop of some forty feet that fell to a rippling stream with boulders at either side. My gaze traveled on, over meadow and heath, farm and hamlet, to a winding river in the distance that gleamed palely in the weak sunlight. And beyond that, there was a sudden splash of bright moving colour that seemed to crawl toward the horizon, though in reality, to its hapless quarry, doubtless the pink-coated riders that comprised the hunt moved at too fast a pace for comfort.

'It is a pleasing point of vantage, is it not?'

'I should describe it in more enthusiastic terms,' I replied. 'It is absolutely wonderful!'

Aunt Ruby looked most gratified.

'Of course, the house being so situated, gives it its name. Merrick's Mount. We live on one of the highest points of the coastline. You remark how the ground drops away, especially on your left, and then rises slightly? Over the rise, although one cannot see it from here, is our old manor house, empty now and falling to pieces, as are the wharfs. In the days when the quarries were the main source of income for members of the family, they used to live near them and the wharfs so they could see what was going on. And there is very little idling amongst workers when their masters can catch them at it. But times change, and most people now choose to live a comfortable distance away from their businesses, though very often sloth amongst the employees is the result.'

'There is nobody there at all, now?'

'No. All are gone. It is a deserted hamlet. The manor house was used as offices and a counting house when the family moved up to the Mount, but it has stood empty for many years, as have the cottages in which the workers were once housed.'

'May I go to see?'

'There is nothing to see. Only ruins! No, you had better not. It could be dangerous. A falling roof, a rotten floorboard. No, it is wiser to keep away.'

'Oh. Very well. I expect you are right.'

'Dear me, that cannot be half-past twelve!' as a clock chimed the half hour. She opened what I had thought was a locket, to reveal a tiny timepiece. 'It is, you know. How times flies! That was the stable clock striking. Luncheon is at one o'clock, so we had best return to the house. Come, Laura. I wonder if Cousin Richard has arrived?'

'You are expecting a visitor?'

'Not a very important one. A distant relative of Matthew's Mama. We make him a small allowance, and, in return, he occasionally proves to be useful.'

'He is a neighbor?'

'No. He was curate to the vicar of some parish near Ludlow, but he has recently left that position to realize a private ambition. He and his wife shortly intend to open a boarding school for the

117

sons of gentlemen, and though they have not yet settled upon a property, they have decided that Yorkshire would be an excellent place to sustain such a venture.'

'Is his wife coming to Merrick's Mount, as well?'

'No. Only he.'

'Will he stay for long?'

'Just overnight. I expect him to depart first thing tomorrow morning.'

But Cousin Richard had not put in an appearance, so just Aunt Ruby and I sat at table, to be served in stately fashion with a meal that was only a little simpler than that of the evening before.

'And what do you intend to do this afternoon, Laura?'

'I have not thought. Perhaps explore the house a little, if I may?'

'No. Wait until I have the time to show it to you properly. Tell me, do you care for books?'

'I am an avid reader whenever the opportunity arises.'

'Then after luncheon I will take you to the library. You should be able to find something of interest in there.'

This prophecy was amply fulfilled, for there was such a profusion of volumes that I did not know where to start.

'Never before have I seen so many books in a private collection!' I exclaimed in what must have been a voice filled with awe.

'Well, child, stay in here for as long as you like, and you may take whatever you choose to your suite, though I would appreciate it if when you have done with them you return the books to the places from whence you took them, for the servants have no idea when it comes to such things.'

'Yes, certainly. I shall be very careful to do that.'

'I will not see you at teatime. You may take yours in here or in your chambers, as you wish. And if you require anything, the bell is over there by the mantel. Oh, and of course we always change for dinner, which is at seven.'

'Of course.'

'What do you intend to wear?'

'I have not decided. Why? Will there be more company?'

'In a sense I suppose you could say that. So put on your nicest gown, and have Tansy dress your hair with extra care, as it will add to your confidence to know that you look well. For it is only natural that you should be nervous, and, like every young maiden, you will wish to look your very best for your wedding!'

'My wedding?' I squeaked. 'When?'

'This evening. After dinner. Cousin Richard will officiate, for as an ordained minister of the church he is empowered to tie the knot!'

'But does one not need a licence to be wed?'

'That has been obtained. A special one, with a dispensation from the archbishop to permit the ceremony to be conducted in a private residence if Matthew's health does not permit for it to take place in the chapel.'

'But does not Sir Matthew desire his half-brother

119

and sister-in-law to be present? Cannot it wait until their return?'

'Why should it? It is no concern of theirs, and, anyway, Cousin Richard departs in the morning.'

'But Sir Matthew and I have not even met, yet. He might not like me!'

'I seem to be hearing a lot of 'buts,' my dear.' Aunt Ruby smiled thinly, her lips compressed. 'Why should you wish to hesitate? The position has been made clear to you, the terms agreed, and the contract signed!'

'But witnesses? Who will stand?'

'I will, and Matthew's valet Virtue will be the other. For as he is a Christian, he is quite eligible.'

'Are not we all? Christians, I mean?'

'Oh, yes, but Virtue was not one from infancy. In actual fact, he was only baptised into our faith shortly before coming to England with his master.'

'What was he before that?' In reality, I did not care a row of pins and realized that I asked the question with the stupid notion at the back of my mind that, if I could keep Aunt Ruby in conversation, somehow it would avert, or at least delay, my impending nuptials.

'Nothing in particular, if you discount the island's fire god who dwelt in a volcano. I think he used to worship that in some peculiar way. Oh, of course you have not yet seen him, have you?'

'That pleasure, like that of being introduced to his master, has yet to come my way.'

'Virtue was born in the Sandwich Islands, though

he is of African descent. His parents and he are negroes. Slaves, you know.'

'I thought slavery was banned.'

'Importing new ones, yes. And in the midst of the Pacific Ocean, old customs die hard, especially as the influence of Spain is still very strong. But Virtue is not a slave now, for though Matthew purchased him, he gave him his freedom long since.'

'How creditable.'

'Yes Virtue is a free man, but with no real desire for freedom. He would lay down his life for his master and only lives to serve him. Oh, it slipped my mind. Matthew desired that I should give you this before you meet him this evening. He also sends his compliments.'

Beholding the small, square, jewellers' box, I inferred it contained my wedding band and that I was to put it on to ensure it would fit. But, no, within, on its pad of velvet, rested a golden ring set with a solitary diamond that even outshone any I had seen upon the fingers of Aunt Ruby! Or upon those of anyone else! It was oval, its length equaling that of my thumbnail, and so expertly cut was it, that from its many facets were reflected the leaping flames of the fire and the shaft of sunlight that fell upon it. Glittering as though it were imbued with life, it held me in thrall.

'Try it on. It is not newly purchased. It is Matthew's mother's betrothal ring. But when she died, I took it into my keeping, and my brother's second wife never wore it, dearly though she would have liked to. The stone is a fine one, is it not? I had it cleaned during my recent visit to London.'

'I fear it may be too small for me,' I said prematurely, for I did not really want to put it on.

'Nonsense. Of course it is not. Here, let me!'

And Aunt Ruby was proved correct, for it was not too small. In fact it was a trifle too large for the third finger of my left hand, where she desired it should go.

'Try it on the first finger.'

'Yes, it fits that.'

'Well, you will have to wear it there until we can get it altered. I must say, it does look quite well!'

'Do you wish for me to wear it?'

'Naturally. Does one not usually wear one's betrothal ring?'

'Am I to have a wedding band as well?'

'Of course, child. But we shall find no problem there, for Matthew told me to purchase several in different sizes, and there is one that is slightly smaller than your betrothal ring. Good! Now we have that settled. Until this evening, then.' She smiled, nodded, and left me to my thoughts, for any inclination to inspect the bookshelves had quite departed from me. Oh, what had I done? And a question of even greater moment, what was I about to do? Things were happening much too quickly for my liking, and I was powerless to call a halt! I knew next to nothing about these people whom I had come amongst, and the little knowledge I was beginning to acquire was far from reassuring. There was the half-brother and his wife, strangely absent; a reputedly trusted body servant who had been a heathen worshipping a fire god, only lately becoming a Christian but really setting Sir Matthew up in the place that should be occupied by the Holy Trinity. Now there was talk of a clergyman, conveniently related to the family, but whom I had yet to meet, arriving one day and conducting the wedding ceremony, then departing the next, whither I knew not, and despite the fact he was a relative, and therefore might be expected to stay on for at least a little while. And then there was Aunt Ruby, autocratic, sweeping aside any opinion or desire that could run counter to her own. And Sir Matthew? Living a mysterious, hermitlike existence, and not even in his own house! What was wrong with him? He might have two heads, and I was to marry him, sight unseen! He could be a monster! And I was committed! I was pledged to wed him. I was bought and paid for, and I could not retract now, even if I wished, for Mama and Tiffany were almost solely dependent on my purchase price!

But presently basic common sense came to my rescue, for after all, the situation had been fully explained to me before I had set my hand to the agreement. And had I not secretly been pleased with the thought of becoming Lady Merrick, 'Milady,' especially as it was to be in name only? As for any forebodings that Sir Matthew might be demented or grotesque in appearance, they were soon dispelled when I thought of his sojourn on the other side of the world and that he had taken an active interest in the source of the Merrick's income, for no moron would be capable of such work, and nobody who was deformed would have been able to undertake such a long, arduous journey and then live abroad for any length of time! I regarded my ring, practicing graceful gestures and admiring the rainbow sparkle emitted by the costly jewel. Well, and so I was to be wed! A little sooner than I had envisaged, but the matter was already agreed and, as Aunt Ruby had said, why dally?

What to wear? I could choose from six dresses, for though my wardrobe was comprised of but three costumes for every occasion, Aunt Isobel had maintained that I must have dinner gowns as well as slightly grander toilettes for an unexpected special event. And, if my so sudden wedding were not one of those, what was? My dinner gowns were long-sleeved with modest vee-shaped necklines that followed the pointed dip of the waistline, tight-bodiced, and full-skirted to fall pleasingly over my crinoline petticoats, a gown of crimson velvet, a tawny brown silk, and another of deep blue brocade. The more elaborate ensembles were *décolleté*, with small cap sleeves, fuller flounced or draped skirts, tighter bodices, and more trimming. There was a pale-blue watered taffeta, with ecru lace-edge frills; a dove-grey *Gros de Naples*, its draped skirts held in place by posies of silk violets and a corsage of them to enhance the bodice; and there was another of coffee-colored lace, its skirt a cascade of flounces from waist to hem, with a bodice beautifully cut but severely plain. I did not possess a white one and wondered if I should have heeded Mama's exhortations to purchase pastel muslins, 'Much more suitable for a young girl,' but disdained by me as being quite unfitted for my new station in life, in fact, positively juvenile! I would wear the coffee lace and my bronze kid slippers. I owned no jewellery other than the diamond ring, though I did not consider that to be really mine, but that alone was more than fine enough to compensate for my lack of other embellishments. And after spying a small volume of *The Book of Common Prayer* and reading the marriage service several times so that I would know what to expect, I considered that I was as ready as I should ever be and in a comparatively composed frame of mind. I then made my way to my apartment, where I ordered tea and then gave Tansy my instructions.

★ ★ ★

In answer to the summons of the dinner gong, Tansy led me downstairs and to the *petite salon*, where the family would gather before the meal was announced, and as I followed in her wake, I wondered if Sir Matthew would leave his retreat, just for this once, and dine with us? After all, it would be but common courtesy on his part, if only to make the acquaintance of his fiancée before making her his wife! And, as Aunt Ruby had asserted that he was not bedridden, it would be a thoughtful gesture on his part if he made the effort, if only to reassure his future bride. But obviously he did not consider it to be necessary, for the gentleman whom I judged to be in his thirties clad in well-worn black apparel relieved by rather limp falling bands could only be, as Aunt Ruby named him, the expected relative.

'Laura, my dear, pray allow me to present the

Reverand Richard Garfath. Cousin Richard, this young lady is Matthew's affianced wife, Miss Lambourne.'

The usual courtesies were exchanged, and, as we sat at table, I had leisure to observe the thin, angular clergyman who only picked at his food even though he looked in dire need of a spate of good meals to fill his bony frame. But perhaps he was the type of man who believed in self-denial, this being an exercise of mind over matter? Whatever the reason, this abstinence did not appear to be of benefit to his nerves, for he was startled out of all proportion by any sudden movement of the servants and also kept glancing furtively at the gilt clock upon one of the mantel shelves. Aunt Ruby ate heartily, but, in common with the cleric, I had little appetite, accepting a morsel of this or that, but merely toying with my viands, for I felt the veriest crumb would choke me, although nourishment in liquid form did not seem to present my gullet with the same problem. Yes, I realize I paid far more attention to glass than to plate, and Aunt Ruby made certain the former was kept well charged. I remember wondering how it was that so apparently shabby a gentleman could have acquired the wherewithal to set up his own school; perhaps his frugal way of life had enabled him to save it? Or possibly a recent inheritance was allowing him to realise this ambition?

'Miss Merrick tells me you plan to venture into the field of education, Mr Garfath?' I said.

'Ah, yes. Only on a very small scale you understand, Miss Lambourne. Small, but exclusive.

I intend that, in time to come, my establishment will be recognized as one of the finest in the land, and places sought accordingly.'

'How very interesting. You have experience in this type of work?'

'In my younger day, I used to go as tutor during my vacations, and it always gave me the greatest satisfaction to impart knowledge to eager young minds. Yes, to give a child the will to learn, to make him regard it as a pleasure and not a duty! That, Miss Lambourne, is my aim.'

'What fortunate scholars they will be, who come to you!' I remarked, for as we spoke of his plans, Mr Garfath had become quite animated, and he seemed to have forgotten his former nervous demeanor. But Aunt Ruby, as though thoroughly bored by the subject under discussion, made some observation on the weather, and once again Mr Garfath found it needful to steal a glance at the clock. When the cloth was drawn and dessert placed before us, Aunt Ruby too became conscious of the time for she said to Flint, 'Do not take the teatray to the drawing room until I ring for it. And you may go now and clear presently,' then when the servants had departed, 'I think you will need a cloak, Laura. I shall too, so we will call in our chambers for them on our way, and then descend again by the stairs at the end of the west wing. Richard, Laura and I will meet you there in a few minutes. You know your way? Good! Come, child, it is almost fifteen minutes after eight, and we are expected on the half hour.'

Suddenly Aunt Ruby seemed much more

approachable than I had hitherto thought her for, like a companion of my own age, she linked her arm in mine, and I found her friendly gesture comforting and also rather useful, for being held by her in this fashion meant that I did not have to pay too much attention to my own movements, particularly those of my legs, which had developed a most peculiar buoyancy! Of a sufficiency to project me into the air? But anchored firmly to Aunt Ruby as I was, this I was unlikely to discover unless I took her with me. The absurd thought of the two of us floating to the ceiling gave me cause to giggle, and, like a conspiratorial schoolroom miss, my companion giggled too. Then when we reached the stairs she declared roguishly, 'Laura Lambourne, you strike me as being a trifle tipsy!'

'No, no. Indeed, I am not. I just feel a little strange, that is all,' I protested.

'I am but funning, child. It is nerves, I know. Come into my apartment whilst I get my cloak, and you can take a drop of a restorative I have made up to my own recipe. Just soothing herbs. A thimbleful of that will settle you in a trice.'

I sipped from the cap of a small flask, one and then another, and as the fiery liquid coursed down my throat, I thought it had a vaguely familiar smell. Of rum? Whisky?

'Never mix grain and grape!' I heard myself assert pompously.

'Of course, Laura. But camomile tea is made from neither. Come, now.'

A cloak had been placed around my shoulders,

and I was being guided along the landings and down stairs.

'Let me put up your hood, my dear. The wind is quite fresh, but the night air will soon revive you. Cousin Richard, you take the lantern and walk ahead. Laura and I will follow.'

Hugging my arm once again, she propelled me onwards. The fresh wind of her description I thought could better be named as a gale, tossing the branches of the trees on either side of the roofed path we took, causing the flame within the lantern to flicker and cast ominous shadows. He who bore it, whose cloak being whipped by its force seemed to float from his shoulders like unto the wings of some great, evil bird of prey, and it would not have greatly surprised me to see him take flight! Foolish, nonsensical thoughts, purest fancy! Well, it was, was it not? Purest fancy? For I was not really here at all; I was but dreaming it. It was not a nightmare, for I was not in the least alarmed; I was detached, as though I viewed the spectacle from a safe distance. I found it interesting, even faintly amusing, but certainly not frightening, for as I was not actually here, why then, nothing could harm me!

We came to a clearing amidst the trees and the bulk of a dark building, the pointed steeple of which was outlined against an only slightly lighter sky. No moon, no stars, just one blackness against another a little less dense. Skirting this building, we came to another; this was bigger and had a doorway through which we entered, but still it was so dark that even the immediate steps we must take were almost invisible. To me, at least!

'Ah, Virtue! Where is Sir Matthew?'

'In his chambers, Missus. Master is poorly and has gone to rest.'

Suddenly I found my voice.

'We are so sorry to hear that. Please tell him we called. We shall come again another day.'

But, as though I had not spoken, Aunt Ruby said, 'You may show us up. Is everything in readiness?'

'Yes, Missus. All is prepared.'

I had seen a negro before though never at such close quarters. But now one stood immediately before me, an immense man of about six and a half feet in height. That I could easily perceive, but his features were quite blurred, only his gleaming teeth and the whites of his eyes being clearly discernible in the gloom that surrounded us. Cousin Richard's lantern had been extinguished as soon as we entered the house, and now the valet Virtue, carrying a single candle, ascended the stairs. But he was so far ahead that the light he bore was of no use to me, and if it had not been for Aunt Ruby's support and guidance, my stumbling steps would probably have resulted in my being the victim of a nasty fall. But it was all part of the dream, for of a surety Virtue truly belonged to a world of fantasy, not fact. Did he live in a bottle? Was he a Genie, emerging from his residence when the cork was drawn, to flit across the pages of the *Tales from the Arabian Nights*?

'Where is Mr Garfath?' I enquired.

'I am here. Just behind you, Miss Lambourne,' came a voice from that direction. By now we had survived the peril of the unlit stairs and were walking along a corridor. A door upon our left was opened to reveal a dimly lit room, which at first seemed brilliant in contrast to the rest of the house. It was a large chamber with a welcoming fire within the grate and on the mantelpiece a candelabra holding three lighted tapers.

'Go to the fire, Laura. Take off your cloak and warm yourself. You too, Cousin Richard,' Aunt Ruby bade us, though she did neither but walked to the far end of the room, where stood a huge four-poster bed. I heard her speak in a low voice, though her actual words escaped me, and I did not attempt to hear them, for I felt completely incurious as to their meaning or to whom they were addressed. Yes, rather than eavesdrop, I was quite amenable to do her bidding and warm myself, for suddenly I was aware of being thoroughly chilled. Mr Garfath relieved me of my cloak and laid it with his own on a nearby table. Then he stirred the coals within the grate and said, 'Will you not take that chair, Miss Lambourne? We may as well sit at our ease whilst we warm ourselves.'

'You still have your gloves on, sir!' I remarked, then had to sternly repress a rising giggle at the absurdity of his absentmindedness.

'So I have. How forgetful of me.' But I do not recall seeing him take them off.

A moment or two elapsed while in silence we contemplated the flames, then Aunt Ruby rejoined us, and Virtue busied himself at his master's bedside. I was perfectly aware that the sequence of events was only part of a dream, but despite that it did seem rather less than accepted social behavior to invade the privacy of a gentleman's bedchamber, particularly as he was a total stranger to me, and poorly into the bargain!

'Do you not think we had best depart?' I asked. 'Leave cards perhaps, and call again when our host is in better health?'

'Oh no, my dear. Matthew is more tired than unwell. He begs you to excuse him and craves your indulgence for the niggardly fashion of his welcome, and that he has not been able to be presented to you in a proper manner. As I have already told you, there are times when his eyes trouble him greatly. He then cannot bear to have a light anywhere near to him, but if some form of illumination is a certain distance away he can be comfortable and still see quite well. He has asked me if I will request you to stand so that your face is fairly lit by the light from these candles. If you would be obliging enough to do so, it will then enable him to perceive what a lovely young lady you are!'

'You are most kind to name me so,' I replied. 'And I shall be only too pleased to comply with the unfortunate gentleman's request. Like this? Can he see me clearly if I stand thus?'

'Indeed, I can. And I have the greatest difficulty in crediting my good fortune. That you should have left the gay life of the metropolis to become immured in this isolated place! Aunt Ruby, you are not guilty of exaggeration in the slightest degree. Miss Lambourne, good evening. I am deeply honored to make your acquaintance, and even more so that you have consented to become my wife!'

It was eerie, being inspected and spoken to by this unseen person. The curtains of the bed were drawn in such a way that only a small gap was left at the foot and also at one side, through one of which the occupant must be viewing me. But the voice of the semi-invalid was not what I had expected, faint, weak, and even imbued with weary petulance. No, the tones I heard sounded more as though they came from the throat of a hale and vigorous man, for they were deep-timbred and full, even if they were a trifle hoarse. Not knowing how to reply to him, I took refuge in silence, merely making my curtsey to the bed and he who was concealed within it.

'Then you are content, Matthew?' his aunt asked.

'Much more than that. In this instance, at least. And now, if everyone is quite comfortable, I suggest that we should proceed. Richard, my dear fellow, it is long since we last met. And is it not fitting that we should come together once again in such happy circumstances as this? Have you not brought vestments?'

'No. A simple private ceremony, such as I was told this was to be, did not seem to require them.'

'Ah, well. Perhaps you are right. Virtue, you may bring the trappings forward and then escort the ladies to their places. Where would you have everyone stand, Richard?'

The valet was drawing aside the curtains on

the near side of the bed, the lower one to its foot and the other until it reached the banked pillows, but no further, and thus it was that the head and shoulders of Sir Matthew Merrick were still shielded from our gaze. Virtue then set at the bedside a small round table upon which was resting a massive family Bible, a prayer book, a tiny cushion on which was a plain golden ring, pen, ink, and sandtray, together with a folded document and a tissue wrapped package. I became conscious that I was moving toward this piece of furniture as were the others. Cousin Richard arrived at the table first and obviously preferred to use his own prayer book, even though when he produced it from the pocket of his frock coat it looked sadly tattered in comparison to the elegant, new one that had been provided.

'Will you take your place next to Sir Matthew, Miss Lambourne? And, Miss Merrick, you at her side if you please and, Virtue, just a little behind the ladies?'

We would and we did, then Aunt Ruby took the tissue wrapping from the package to reveal a single glove, which she bade me put on my right hand.

'But why? I have never before heard that this is a part of the marriage service,' I said wonderingly.

'No, dear, it is not. Call it rather a local custom. Just an oddity of this district. You do not have to, of course, but it will please us greatly if you will.'

'If you say so, ma'am.' I drew on the white cotton glove, which though obviously new, had a strange-smelling aroma. And then I stood awaiting whatever would happen next. There was a very short silence, then Cousin Richard cleared his throat nervously and intoned, 'Dearly beloved, we are gathered together before God and in the sight of this congregation . . . '

The curate had a monotonous voice, and even though this was my very own wedding, after a while I began to lose interest and, instead of paying attention to his words, allowed my mind to wander. I felt drowsy; my thoughts were confused. I wanted to go to sleep and the droning of Cousin Richard affected me in the same way as would a lullaby. Oh, dear, what a very long time it was taking, but I was jolted back to my surroundings and the matter in hand by the sound of Sir Matthew's voice replying, 'I will.'

Where were we? How far had we got?

'Laura Jane, wilt thou have this man to be thy wedded husband, to live together after God's ordinance in the holy estate of matrimony?'

'I will,' my reply sounded high, reedy. Then suddenly my gloved right hand was grasped by Virtue and, outraged by his temerity, I was just about to jerk it free, when the minister asked, 'Who giveth this woman to be married to this man?'

The valet answered, 'I do.'

My hand was transferred to Cousin Richard's, and then he placed it in the clasp of Sir Matthew whose right hand, also gloved, had by now appeared from around the curtain.

'I, Matthew, take thee, Laura, to be my wedded wife . . . '

And then I said the fateful words, 'I, Laura, take thee, Matthew, to be my wedded husband, to have and to hold from this day forward, for better for worse, for richer for poorer, in *sickness and in health* . . . '

'With this ring I thee wed.'

I stood there petrified as the ring was placed upon my finger. I wanted nothing so much as to take to my heels, to flee this place and the strange people within it, for it was only then that the enormity of what I was doing truly registered on my mind. I had just given my troth to a gloved hand! Had vowed to remain with its owner until death parted us! I had not yet set eyes on him, but I was fettered to him until either one of us died. And judging by the firmness of the hand's clasp and the resonance of his voice, he could well outlive me! Panic began to rise within me as the minister droned on, 'I pronounce that they be man and wife together, in the name of the Father, and of the Son, and of the Holy Ghost. Amen.'

As though she sensed my new awareness, Aunt Ruby edged a little nearer to my side. I glanced over my shoulder to see the valet directly behind me. In front of me was the table and the curate and, to my other side, my husband. My husband! A stranger! And now I was virtually his chattel, subservient to him in all things. Everything I owned or acquired whilst he lived was legally his! Even the staggeringly extravagant allowance that had baited this trap into which I had just fallen was still his! To cancel whenever he chose, for every woman's property upon her marriage became her husband's! The blessing was being intoned, but I paid scant regard to that, for now one idea only occupied my mind. To see, once and for all, who or what it was I had just married. Man or monster, whatever it was I must know, and suddenly. To catch everyone by surprise and before my determination left me, I attempted to twitch aside the concealing curtain. But now that our hands were no longer joined, my new spouse was using his to hold the bed hanging securely in place, as though he anticipated this movement of mine. However, nothing was said, and as I stood there, hemmed in from all angles, Cousin Richard closed his prayer book and returned it to his pocket.

'S-surely there is more?' I stammered.

'In the full length marriage service, yes. But that of you and your husband was the shorter version. Though there is no need to concern yourself, Lady Merrick, for it is quite legal and equally binding! And now if you will be kind enough to sign this affirmation?'

'The light is too dim for me to read it,' I faltered.

'You may take it across the room and there peruse it if you wish, but it is a declaration that you have just become the wedded wife of Sir Matthew Merrick, nothing more. When all present here have signed it, I shall take it to the proper place and register the marriage.'

Wordlessly I took the proffered pen and, for the very last time, inscribed my name, Laura Jane Lambourne, then Sir Matthew's gloved hand once again appeared to sign his. Aunt Ruby affirmed in a neat hand that she was witness, and, though Virtue made rather heavy work of it, he eventually declared in quite legible scrawl that he too was in that happy position. And Richard Joseph Garfath, D.D., confessed in writing that he had tied the knot.

'I do not think we need dispense with the toast as well as the usual prayers and injunctions,' Sir Matthew said. 'Virtue, please bring forward the wherewithal.'

The valet removed the small table and, from the shadows, brought forth on noiseless wheels a trolley laden with decanter and goblets.

'I beg you to excuse me,' Cousin Richard said. 'I am not very fond of strong liquor, and I am in haste to depart. May I wish you every happiness, Lady Merrick, and, Matthew, pray accept my congratulations. Miss Merrick, I shall be on my way. I can return to the house without a light to guide me, and I will probably be gone by the time you reach it.'

He bowed to the company and was already donning hat and cloak when Sir Matthew said, 'And I may leave the registration of the marriage to you, Cousin?'

'Certainly. Immediately I reach Exeter, I will see to it.'

'Excellent. And just so soon as I receive the certificate of registration, I shall instruct my bankers to transfer your fee to your account.'

'Farewell then, and may God be with you all.' Swiftly and with only a slight click of the door handle to mark his departure, Cousin Richard was gone.

'I thought he was staying overnight!' I remarked.

'I too assumed that he would, but if the man

chooses to make a fool of himself, that is his affair,' Aunt Ruby replied. 'And what the head coachman will think when told to harness up and drive to Exeter at this time of night, I cannot imagine!'

'I can, vividly.' A chuckle came from behind the curtains. 'Ladies, are your glasses charged? Yours too, Virtue? Then see to it. And now let us drink to the continuing health and happiness of my lovely bride.' Just in time, I restrained myself from drinking, although I was greatly tempted to down the contents of my goblet with one gulp, so direly did I feel in need of a restorative.

'And now to you, Matthew. You and Laura. May your marriage bring you both fulfillment and whatever it is you seek.' A rather ambiguous wish, and once again I was not in a position to drink. My mouth felt dry, and therefore I was quite happy to oblige when encouraged by Aunt Ruby: 'And now let us drink to absent friends and relatives. In different circumstances, they would have been with us on this joyous occasion, but as they are not, let them not be forgotten.'

'Virtue, Lady Merrick's glass needs refilling. Perhaps, my dear, you would like to return to the fireside to sip your wine, whilst I have a quiet word with my aunt?'

So he could see me, even though I could not perceive him! Perhaps he was looking at me through a strategically placed mirror? I glanced around swiftly for if I could spy it, it would perform the same office for me, and enable me to see his face reflected in it. But if it existed it was too well concealed for my purpose, and so I said dutifully, 'Certainly, sir,' as I was quite content to obey this his first command, if such it could be described, for it was voiced in a pleasant manner and fell in with my own wishes. To sit in warmth and comfort, imbibing my wine. 'Sip your wine,' he had said. Did he think I was a tippler? Probably, for the rate at which I had emptied my first glass could be reason enough for him to entertain that suspicion. But why worry? He could soon be disabused of that idea if he should think it, and anyway, I had something else to ponder. For just before his so-abrupt departure, Cousin Richard had told Aunt Ruby he might be gone by the time she returned to the house. She! Not she and I, but just she! Was I to deduce from that that he assumed I was to remain here at the Dower House? With just the unseen person whom I had newly wed, and his servant, the latter possibly having cannibalistic tendencies? These only thinly covered by his recent veneer of professed Christianity? Surreptitiously I reached for my cloak, though I was somewhat reassured to hear Sir Matthew say, 'Virtue will light you and Laura back to the house. I am very tired now, so please forgive me for saying I wish to rest. Good night, Aunt. Good night, Laura. And thank you both for coming and making this one of the most pleasant evenings of my life.'

'Thank you having me, sir,' like a child at the conclusion of a tea party, it seemed the appropriate thing to say. 'And good night to you, Sir Matthew.'

'I am Matthew to my wife, if she will so honor me.'

'Then good night, Matthew.'

I made my curtsey and then was ushered out into the still boisterous night, where it seemed the strength of the gale had intensified, tossing the treetops and moaning through their branches, and the cloak I wore afforded but little protection from its icy blast. Aunt Ruby too was shivering by the time we reached the main house, and, instead of the postprandial tea we had neglected to sup before setting out, she called for a steaming bowl of rum punch to be brought to us.

'For Matthew would never forgive me if I allowed you to catch a chill! He is quite taken with you, child.'

'Is he? I am so pleased. But he would not think very highly of me if he came to hear that I was an habitual toper!'

'Nonsense! This is purely medicinal! Do you not care for it? Still, one is not supposed to like medicine, is one?'

But I thought it most agreeable! The promise of the spicy, fragrant cloud hovering over my silver tankard was amply fulfilled by the sweet, fiery liquid sliding smoothly down my throat and on until it reached my very toes!

'I find it quite pleasant,' I confessed.

'Sensible girl! And it is a complete nightcap. It wards off chills as well as bringing sweet dreams and tranquil rest.'

Tranquil rest, certainly, sweet dreams, perhaps; but if there were any such I cannot recall them, for so soon as my head touched the pillows, I slept like a log!

5

Next morning I awoke to see the fire in my bedchamber grate well-established and the chinks of light from between the still-drawn curtains bright enough to proclaim the day was well-advanced. I became aware of a slight sound of movement in my dressing room and feebly called, 'Tansy, are you there?' thereby discovering that at first my tongue had cloven to the roof of my mouth.

'Yes, Milady, I am coming.'

Her initial task was to fling back the curtains, and I winced at the unbearable noise their rings made as they moved along the supporting rod, and I blenched as daylight came flooding in and closed my eyes against its blinding brilliance. My head felt as though it were twice its normal size and within it a hammer was being struck with steady rhythm.

'What time is it?'

'Almost eleven, Milady. I have your teatray ready in the dressing room, and the kettle is only just off the boil. I shall fetch it straight away.'

'Why did you not call me? I should have been up and about long since.'

'Madam's orders, Milady. She said to let you lie until you woke of your own accord. And I am to bring up your breakfast when you are ready for it.'

'No breakfast, Tansy, just the tea. As quickly

as you can,' I said, for the thought of food was antipathy to my wilting frame, though I craved liquid in any shape or form.

Did a slight smile hover on her lips as she replied, 'Yes, Milady, I will fetch it instantly.' And was she eyeing me with more than her usual curiousity? I felt too unwell to care, and it was not until I was trying to drink as speedily as possible the scalding hot beverage that the reason for my queasy state dawned on me. For the unaccustomed fragility on my part could be described well enough as a classic example of 'the morning after the night before!' What had I had, and what had I done? There was the wine at dinner, far more than I was used to having; Aunt Ruby's camomile tea, 'to revive me'; two large trumpet-shaped goblets filled with sparkling wine, probably champagne; and then to crown all, two brimming tankards, each charged with strong, steaming rum punch! 'We may as well drink it while it is hot, dear. Otherwise it will only go to waste, and I cannot endure any form of that!' Aunt Ruby had encouraged. I could not recall coming to bed nor making ready for it. But though I did try to shrug aside other recollections, they would not be denied, for there, for all the world to see and mark, was a plain golden band upon the left-hand third finger! Milady! Lady Merrick! Wife to Sir Matthew and, if I chose to assert myself, mistress of this house and of all those who served within it! And how outraged Aunt Ruby would be if I took advantage of this unique situation, demanding her keys, the household books, and bidding the servants that in the future they must look to me for their orders! But I knew that, even if I felt so inclined, I would never dare, and anyway, I had no desire to.

'If I were you, Milady, I should rest for another hour or so at least. Madam said that, if you did not feel quite yourself, you were to spend the whole day in bed and that she would look in on you later.'

'That will not be necessary. But I will lie here for a little while longer, and you may bring my bathwater, together with another teatray, at noon. And I shall go down for luncheon.'

'Yes, Milady. I will give your orders to that effect,' Tansy replied, as though to remind me that, as lady's maid, she did not demean herself by toiling up the stairs with heavy cans of water.

'And now leave me. But partly close the curtains again before you go.'

Her curtsey was a little deeper than it had been yesterday, and that had struck me as being over-emphatic, and I now wondered if all the other servants had been apprised of my rise in status. Probably, for now I was indeed her ladyship, a pleasurable thought, but what exactly would it entail? For though my headache was still with me, it was not of a degree to dull my wits more than they had been heretofore. Memory of my confused though brief thoughts of the previous night returned to me: that, now I was legally wed, I was totally subservient to my husband; and that, in the sight of the law, my every possession was now his. And another thing, I had understood he wanted to marry me so that my good name would not be sullied by being employed by a bachelor and dwelling in his establishment. But though he owned this place, it was not his residence! He lived elsewhere, so why be so careful of my reputation? Indeed, it would have been quite proper for me to retain my single state as, presumably, we were to dwell under separate roofs. My headache grew no easier as I tried to answer my own questions. Perhaps the key to the problem would reveal itself if I remembered every detail of what had so far transpired. That was not too difficult, until dinnertime of yesterday, but after that one thing merged with another, giving just the impression of a stormy night, a house so dimly lit that one had to grope one's way about it, and of being joined in holy wedlock by a man I did not know to a man I could not see, the former departing immediately after the unusual ceremony, whither I knew not. I must be out of my mind! Oh, then a happy thought: Was it but a dream after all? But reluctantly I was forced to face stern reality, for there could be no denying the wedding ring that adorned the appropriate finger on my left hand!

Never before had rising, bathing, and dressing entailed such an effort, but, with Tansy's help during the last stages of my toilette, I managed it and eventually tottered into the small dining room just as the luncheon gong was being sounded with enough clamor to awaken the dead, or so it seemed to my fragile nerves. But to protest Aunt Ruby's action of seating herself in my former place at the side of the table and insisting I sit at the end was hardly worth the argument that might ensue and which, in any event, I would surely lose.

'You poor dear child! Tansy was quite right, you

do look a trifle unwell today. And so pale! Foolish girl, you should not have come down at all! I would have understood.'

'I shall feel better soon,' I replied without conviction and waved aside the soup.

'Of course, you will. But fasting will not help, and so I will not take soup either and we shall pass on to the fish. Now a morsel of this poached salmon and just a sip of light white wine should settle any slight queasiness.'

And though it was all I could do to partake of any form of sustenance, presently Aunt Ruby was proved correct, for I did feel a little more like my usual self. Nothing impaired her appetite, for she proceeded to eat a hearty meal and then said brightly, 'Now, if you should like me to, I will show you over some of the house.'

'This one, or the dower house?'

'I mean Merrick's Mount, dear. Even I do not go to the dower house uninvited.'

'Oh? I was under the impression that you called there frequently.'

'That I do, but never without Matthew first sending Virtue across to ask me to.'

'I see,' I said, although this was a monstrous untruth, for I did not see at all.

'And Matthew is resting today. He was so delighted with you and with the wedding and everything, but I am afraid the excitement of it all has taken its toll on him and left him more weary than usual.'

'How sad. Poor gentleman, and yet do you know, to hear him speak, a total stranger such as myself would never think he was a semi-invalid, unless they were, as I was, told otherwise.' I observed.

'He will be pleased when I tell him you said that, for he does so abhor being thought of as a weakling. Now here is the grand dining room. Is not the size of it ridiculous? I can only recall it ever being brought into use for the most splendid occasions, for it is much too large for a normal dinner party of a dozen or so couples, and nowadays we do not even have those! The library you saw yesterday, and here is the ballroom. Ah me, I broke some hearts in there when I was young and thought it clever to make a man fall in love with me, only to spurn him.'

'I am sure you were never so unkind as to do that deliberately,' I said, summoning a smile.

'Well, perhaps not too often. I did not make a habit of setting out to do that, but when one is newly fledged one is inclined to try one's wings. Test one's power. And it is a heady sensation to discover that one has it!'

'Is it?'

My dubiety must have been apparent, but my guide only laughed and said, 'Ah yes, indeed it is. And here is the music room. Did you say you played?'

'No, I fear I am not so gifted.'

'Do you play other things? Chess, perhaps?'

'No.'

'Backgammon?'

'I am afraid not.'

'Cards?'

'Playing cards? No. They were forbidden where

147

I used to live. 'Fifty-two soldiers in the Devil's army.' ' I quoted in a voice as near as I could get to the pompous tones of my late uncle.

'I shall teach you. It will be something for us to do during the evenings. And David and Celia will return tomorrow, so you will have a little more company than just that of an old woman.'

'That is the last appellation I should apply to you!' I answered dutifully.

'Now here is the green saloon, and just across the passageway is the rose drawing room, and then we enter the west wing, where there are the gunroom, the muniment room, and various others that are not in the general way used for entertaining.'

'Perhaps we can leave those until another day?' I was prepared to admit defeat, for to sit at my ease did at that moment hold far greater attraction.

'Certainly, Laura. I have been very thoughtless. I know! Let us go up to my suite, and we can sit cosily and have our tea brought to us there.'

'That sounds delightful.'

'Or would you rather rest?'

'No, no. To sit and talk would give me far more pleasure than to retire again to my bed.'

'I agree it will be better for you. Otherwise, you may not sleep a wink tonight.'

I had been in her bedchamber the previous evening, but I would have been hard pressed to describe it, for the memory of that was one of the more vague parts of my recollection. However, she led me to her sitting room, which was as prettily furnished as mine was ugly. Pink and grey, with furniture as comfortable as it was elegant, and it seemed that everything contained within it was of a bygone age, the only concession to the nineteenth century being a pair of small daguerreotypes each framed in silver. She must have seen me eyeing them for, as she rang the bell for tea, she handed me the nearer one. The likenesses of two figures were captured and held upon the slightly blurred print. A younger version of Aunt Ruby sat upon a straight-backed chair, on her face the expression of one who is ready to run for safety and behind her stood, with his hand resting lightly on her shoulder as though to prevent any sudden movement on her part, an extremely handsome young gentleman. Tall, slender, clean-shaven, with dark wavy hair, and dressed elegantly in a fashion of perhaps twenty years ago. He stood not only unafraid, but from the mischievous half-smile on his lips and the laughter lighting his eyes, quite enjoying the tense situation and the apprehension of the lady beneath his hand.

'You, of course,' I remarked. 'And one of your suitors?'

'Good gracious, Laura, I was never constrained to steal from cradles!' Aunt Ruby replied. 'That is Matthew! When he was up at Oxford and sometimes had a short vacation from his studies, I would travel to London, and he and I would meet and have the greatest fun. And that portrait was taken during one of those visits. It was all quite new then, and one never knew exactly what to expect. We passed this studio, and Matthew urged me to go in with him. Dared me to! The imp knew I would never refuse a dare!'

'So that is why he is smiling,' I said.

'Yes, he was enjoying himself hugely, but I was rather less so.'

'How handsome he is! And he looks quite tall. Is he really?'

'Of course you have not seen him clearly, have you, Laura? He is six feet two inches in height and one of the best looking young men whom I have ever encountered. Beautiful teeth, lovely eyes. Oh dear, it makes me want to weep every time I think of how he was and then of how he is now!'

'Thank you for showing me his likeness. This may seem foolish to you, but I must confess that until I saw it I was a little afraid.'

'Why so, my dear?'

'Well, as you know I have not seen him clearly. Indeed, I have not really seen him at all! It was most worrying, especially with that bed curtain veiling him completely, and the most absurd notions have been plaguing me.'

'I do not follow your meaning?'

'I feared he might be grotesque. Monstrous to look upon. Anything.'

'Matthew does have a heavy cross to bear, Laura. There is his illness, which has had some effect upon his eyesight and as well as that, as though it were not enough, his face is scarred!'

'An accident?' I asked.

'Yes. Actually he regards it with far greater abhorrence than it merits. I do not even notice it when I see him, but Matthew shrinks from the gaze of strangers for fear they may find it repugnant to behold!'

'But I am not like that!' Tears stung my eyes. 'Please! Tell him! Tell him I am no fainthearted young woman, to swoon at the sight of a little disfigurement!'

'Later, perhaps. When you know each other a little better, but not yet. He might find it hard to forgive me for betraying what he likes to think is a well kept secret. But you have the right to know and, thank you, Laura. It lifts a great weight from my mind to hear you speak those compassionate words.'

'Any young woman with only a streak of sensibility would echo what I say.'

'Oh no, some would not! And anyway, Matthew would writhe at the thought of incurring the pity of a lovely young girl. He is so terribly proud! But now, even though he is especially dear to me, I think he has been the subject of our conversation for long enough, so let us talk of other things.'

'As you wish. Oh, look! It is snowing!' My torpor forgotten, I ran to the window. 'Is it not a pretty sight? Do come and see!'

'Pretty sight, eh? Probably I thought so too when I was your age, but not now. My eyes find much more pleasure when viewing the glow from these coals! And now come back to the fire, Laura, for I can hear the approach of our tea. Did I remember to order the muffins? Ah yes, there they are! Flint, be so good as to have the curtains drawn and the lamps lit. Then you may go and we shall serve ourselves.'

'What are they like? Mr and Mrs Merrick, I

mean?' I asked when once more Aunt Ruby and I were alone.

'David and Celia? Well, er, average people, I suppose. I have never given the matter a great deal of thought. David is twenty-eight, favors his mother in most ways and is a great one for outdoor pursuits, hunting, shooting, and things of that nature. Celia is nearer your age. She is twenty-four. Her people are merchant bankers, and she is the only daughter, although she has four brothers. Her family is not too *nouveau riche*. They are established long enough to have acquired a civilized veneer and are accepted in all but the very best society.'

'But you yourself have certain reservations? And as you say David strongly resembles his Mama and you have already told me you did not care for her, it is likely to follow that you are not over-enchanted with him!' I remarked.

'A sharp little puss, are you not?' Aunt Ruby gave a short half laugh. 'Well, I suppose it is pointless to pretend to an affection where none really exists. But we tolerate each other and live side by side amicably enough. And they must accept the fact that, while Matthew lives, with his authority I rule this house. But I do not flaunt my position and try to make the situation more awkward than it already is.'

'Why do they not set up their own establishment?'

'Well, David has an income, but it is not large enough to enable him to live as he does here, freely. A residence that would lie within the scope of their present finances would certainly be much more modest than Merrick's Mount! And so they wait for 'dead man's shoes,' so to speak.'

'That sounds horrid! But if Sir Matthew and his half brother do not have an amicable relationship, does it not occur to Mr. David that Merrick's Mount might fall to somebody else? Be inherited by another?'

'No, it cannot. The whole estate is entailed to the nearest male heir. It must come to David, and so he waits.'

'It makes him sound like a spider,' I said.

'I am very fond of spiders! They are useful creatures, which he has never been nor is likely to become. A leech, perhaps, though even they perform some service to humanity. No, let us leave it, and him. You will be able to judge for yourself soon enough.'

'I am not greatly looking forward to that.'

'Oh, you mistake me if you think he may be an uneasy gentleman to get on with. He can be most charming, especially if it will benefit him or if the observer of his behavior is female, young, and has a pretty face! Believe me, you will like him well enough, and soon you will begin to wonder about me! That I misjudge him, am prejudiced against him because I did not like his mother, that he is misunderstood.'

'I am sure I shall not,' I protested.

'We shall see. Actually, I am quite looking forward to your meeting. For your presence will undoubtedly be a belated New Year's gift for him.'

'Did they not know it was arranged that I should come here?'

153

'No. Why should they? What is it to them?'

'But surely it would have made the coming situation much more easy if they had been told!'

'They are not in a position to make it uneasy! Now that you and Matthew are wed, you have more right to live in this house than they do. Or even I, if it comes to that!'

'But even so — .'

'Do not concern yourself, Laura. And surely you would not deny Matthew the little pleasure of giving David's tail a gentle twist? Poor Matthew has so few pleasures!'

'Far be it from me to even question Sir Matthew's wishes, but the gist of this conversation has told me quite clearly that I can certainly expect a constrained atmosphere within this house, even if there is no open resentment at my being here, and of my position,' I said straightly.

'That is most unlikely, but if it should occur I am sure we will be able to survive the situation. And now my dear, I have a few little things to do so I pray you to excuse me. Shall you be able to occupy yourself agreeably until dinnertime?'

'Yes, I will write a nice long letter to my Mama, aunt, and sister, for they will want to know that everything is well with us here in Devonshire.'

'Ah! Us, you say. That sounds well. Us! Yes, we Merricks stand together, and now you are truly one of *us*!'

Was I? Did I want to be? That was certainly open to question I thought, as I left Aunt Ruby's sitting room to emerge into the corridor outside and find to my surprise that it was still only dusk. We had been sitting in lamplight with curtains drawn to shut out the sight of the snow, and now I hurried to the nearest window, hoping to see a world covered in sparkling white. But no. The fascinating descent of the snowflakes must have ceased almost immediately, and, apart from just a light sprinkling here and there, the landscape remained the same, desolate and grey beneath a sky heavy with lowering cloud.

It took much careful thought to compose a missive that would not bring Mama hasting to Merrick's Mount as soon as she was able. What to include and what to omit? Safe journey and arrival; kindly reception and having been given my own personal maid; and the wedding that made me Lady Merrick and not some deluded girl whose reputation was now lost to her: Yes, those things I could write about. But I would certainly draw a veil over my inebriation, the fact that I was high-flown with wine when I made my sacred vows, that I had not yet set eyes on my husband, and that he lived in near darkness in a place apart, with only a semi-heathen emancipated slave, elevated to the position of valet, to tend him. I would make no mention of the other members of the family, for, having yet to meet them, there was not much I could say apart from the fact that they were not likely to take too kindly to my sudden appearance in their midst. And so with the letter written, signed 'Laura Merrick,' and sealed within a crested envelope, I had leisure to think very seriously about my future.

And the thought that was paramount was more

akin to suspicion. Suspicion that Aunt Ruby had led, was leading me by the nose! What game was she playing? In the first instance, I had been led to believe I was merely being engaged to allay the boredom of a semi-invalid, to read to him in dulcet tones, perhaps converse with him, and in exchange for this be paid an exorbitantly high salary and have my reputation preserved by becoming his lady wife. A quiet wedding I had certainly envisaged, but not one so quiet or peculiar as the one that had taken place. And now to crown all the rest, I had just been told that the remainder of the family knew nothing of me, or the wedding plans, or that upon their return from a visit they could expect to find a new, completely strange Lady Merrick taking her seat at the foot of the table! Presumably the head of it remained vacant for Aunt Ruby would never countenance David Merrick taking Matthew's place whilst the latter person lived! And yes, nasty thought, but I had to face it: How long would he live? Not very far short of the allotted span, three score years and ten, or I should be very much surprised, and a little swift mental arithmetic soon informed me that, at the end of that time, I should be approaching, if not actually past, sixty summers! Oh, what had I done? What had I done? And then I began to grow angry. That woman had made a fool of me! Had played me like she would a fish on a line: the bait, money and position; but the actual fate, loss of liberty, the company of my own family, and the prospect of living the rest of my life with uncongenial people, amongst whom she might well be counted! She had mentioned the heady feeling having power gave her, and as things now stood she ruled this house, its lands, and quite probably the sugar and coffee plantations from whence came the family income. Yes, it would be very far from her liking to have this power snatched away, as it surely would be should David Merrick step into his half brother's shoes. But what place did I have in all this? What did she want from me? To annoy, possibly even to alarm David and Celia? Would she take all the trouble she had done, just to do that? No, there was more! Then I realized with some surprise that, since I saw the daguerreotype of Matthew and his aunt and thereby learned that he was not a freak, that he did not have three legs and two heads and was at least a normal, albeit scarred man, my mind had been free to pursue other channels than those that led to dreadful fears of being wed to a monster! Yes, he seemed to be normal enough, but now it was the other people who answered to the name of Merrick with whom I must chiefly concern myself!

A further flurry of snow had fallen by the time I went down to dinner, but though I felt quite out of charity with my hostess at the outset of the repast, she proved to be an amusing enough companion to temporarily dispel the resentment I felt at her high-handed attitude in arranging my life for me. And after the meal the evening passed pleasantly enough, by my allowing myself to be further debauched by being taught to play piquet. Foxed one night, playing cards the next, even though the stakes were only comprised of mother-of-pearl counters. Yes, I was well on the road to ruin, and a remark made once by my late Uncle Albert that had deeply affronted me at the time — 'That girl is a pert piece and should be kept on a tight rein!' — now seemed to have acquired the significance of deep insight into my flighty character.

Yes, the hours passed swiftly, and it was almost midnight when in nightgown and robe I stood at my open casement gazing at the world of whiteness that lay outside the house. The snow would only be about an inch in depth, but quite sufficient to transform the scene before me, and, as I watched, for a brief spell the moon won its battle with an almost cloud-filled sky and in triumph cast forth its beams to light the fairy world that lay all sparkling and new before my enchanted eyes. The conifer trees wore glistening caps; the lawns lay covered with a pristine blanket; all was still, as though waiting for further proof that the might of Mother Nature could obliterate, with no effort whatsoever, any attempt that puny man could make to combat her strength. I had dismissed Tansy and put out my lamp before opening the window, and now after gazing my fill I intended to kneel in front of my still glowing fire for a few moments, to banish the chill, before snuggling into my well-warmed bed. I was just about to close the window and draw the curtains once more, when suddenly my movements were arrested. For all was no longer still! Two horsemen emerged from amongst the trees at a gentle trot, then as they reached the snow-covered lawns they urged their beasts to a canter. Who were they? Were they coming here? But they were heading away from the main door of the house and taking the direction that Aunt Ruby had told me led to the old abandoned manor house and the deserted quarries. Who could they be, from where had they come, and whither were they bound? They had not been near enough for me to discern their features, and their progress had been so swift that I could not even describe the clothes they wore. All I had received was the general impression that they were both large men, well-mounted, and adequately cloaked against the elements. And they had come from amidst the trees, and beyond the trees lay the dower house! Certainly Virtue could be one of them, he was of sufficient stature, and the other? Sir Matthew? He was tall, Aunt Ruby had said so! No. Impossible. He was a semi-invalid, resting after an exciting event, and must surely be snug and warm beneath the bed covers on such a night as this! If marrying me constrained him to keep to his bed for all of the next day, it was certain that to ride forth and risk being caught in a blizzard would undoubtedly kill him! Or would it? Or could it be a lesser feat of endurance than the wedding ceremony? No, it could not be Sir Matthew, but I had not imagined it for there in the moonlight, plain to see, were the two sets of hoofmarks that the horses had left behind them.

★ ★ ★

'Well you should be quite a contented young lady today, Laura,' Aunt Ruby greeted me next morning. 'But I fear the menservants do not share

159

your enthusiasm for snow. They are still clearing a passageway down the drive!'

'Yes, the fall has been rather heavy,' I replied. 'And by the look of the sky, there is yet more to come.'

'Then if you are proved right, we shall have to be content with each other's company for some time. For David and Celia could not possibly travel from Exeter in this!'

'Oh? How unfortunate,' I said, although this piece of news did not disturb me unduly.

'You are not in London now, my dear! For there the traffic clears the streets quite quickly, but here we can become completely cut off from the outside world, sometimes for weeks on end!'

'I suppose we could be if the roads become impassable,' I agreed.

'I think they are already that. A sudden thaw is the only thing to clear them properly, and more snow will only aggravate this vexing situation.'

'Will we suffer from a shortage of supplies?' I felt a show of concern was expected of me.

'Dear me, no. I always prepare well for any eventuality. Actually, we are almost self-sufficient, if one reckons on the produce supplied by the home-farm.'

'Can that be reached?'

'The servants will make certain of that, for if they do not, they know they will soon find themselves on very short commons!'

'What about the mail? Can we still send and receive letters?'

'One of the footmen can make his way to the

village immediately after breakfast. He can take any letters you wish to send, but I am afraid that days may pass before we receive any correspondence. I know that here the snow is less than two feet deep, but inland the drifts could have formed higher than a tall man. We shall just have to be patient.'

'Then I am indeed thankful I wrote to tell my family I had arrived safely as soon as I did! To receive that short note will put their minds at rest, for a little while at least.'

'Yes, that was a deed well done.'

'Oh, I meant to ask you. I saw two horsemen late last night. They came from the direction of the dower house and rode as though they intended to pass near where you said lay the old manor house. Who could they have been? Do you know?'

'Not off hand, but they could hardly have been people of good sense, unless their journey were imperative.'

'Two quite large men, or so I thought at the time. I wondered if one of them could be Sir Matthew's valet?'

'Virtue? It is possible. Yes, it is probable. They often turn night into day at the dower house. They have only themselves to consider, so it does not matter or discommode anyone. It could have been Virtue exercising Matthew's horses before the imminent snowfall confined them to the stable.'

'The stable? But surely the grooms would see to the animals' welfare?'

'Matthew keeps just a small stable of his own at the dower house. He likes to be completely independent of us up here at the main house.'

'Oh? Then he must employ other servants besides his valet? Grooms, for instance.'

'Only one man. I think he is a little simple, and I believe he is also mute. Matthew has a penchant for employing the virtually unemployable, but the man seems competent enough. Yes, it must have been he and Virtue whom you saw. And now I am afraid I must leave you to your own devices until luncheon, for I have much to do and have spent too much time in gossip as it is.'

She rose from the breakfast table abruptly and left the room in the same manner, thereby causing me to wonder if I had offended her in some way. And had she hinted I was a gossip? Hardly, for it was only from her that I could acquire any information unless I sought it from the servants, and she would surely not approve of me doing that! Well, gossip or not, I was learning a little something every day. Now I could add to my stock of knowledge that my unseen husband was not only served by a semi-heathen, but by a man who could not speak and might be mentally retarded, and I wondered if any more unusual people inhabited the dower house and, if there were, what ailments or disadvantages they suffered from? A slight cough behind me indicated that I had lingered over my coffee for long enough, and so, leaving the servants to clear, I made my way to the morning room. Once there, I sat thinking of Mama and Tiffany, wondering if any further progress had been made in finding a new address, and then the thought struck me that, if they moved to one, I would not know where they had gone, not until the weather improved and their letters could reach me. And until then I could not even look forward to those! I would not know how they were faring or even where they were! Restlessly I returned to my suite of rooms to find Tansy busying herself in the dressing room.

'Oh, Tansy, what sort of winters do you usually have in this part of the country?'

'Why, Milady, we just has winters,' she looked justifiably puzzled.

'I mean, are they of short duration? Are they mild, or are they prolonged, with much ice and snow?'

'They varies, Milady. One never knows what to expect, but we always prepare for the worst!'

'Thank you.'

I left her and went into my bedchamber, noticing as I did so that the trail of candlewax was now gone from the footboard of my bed, then I passed through to the sitting room where, for want of something better to do, I examined the ugly miniatures on the whatnot and then the contents of the escritoire, which revealed itself as being quite unremarkable, nothing having been left behind by previous users, everything being fresh and new. Downstairs again to the library, but I could not settle with a book even though there were some new novels, probably brought back by Aunt Ruby when she returned from her recent stay in London. Utter boredom assailed me. Was this to be the pattern of my future days, roaming from room to room, seeking for some means to occupy the dragging hours? I might as well be in prison! Of course, I had no conception of what prison was like, otherwise I should not have drawn the comparison, but here I was certainly immured within the house. I could not even take exercise in the grounds, explore the home farm or stroll to the village, though really only the weather could be blamed for my incarceration. And my childish delight to see snow fall began to change into a purely adult attitude, for I was beginning to realise it was not so attractive as I had hitherto thought.

With mixed feelings, I learned that I should take up my duties that same evening.

'Sir Matthew is a little better, then? I am pleased to hear that.'

'Yes, he feels a lot stronger than he did yesterday.'

'Will I be able to get there?'

'Certainly,' she looked at me as though I were the veriest fool. 'I should not ask you to go if it were otherwise.'

'At what time does Sir Matthew expect me to go to the dower house?'

'After dinner. I shall take you there this first time, and I suggest you dress warmly, though you can put on suitable footwear just before we set out.'

'Shall I take anything with me? A book to read aloud or something like that?'

'If you wish to. But do not be surprised if Matthew is still confined to his bed, for in this type of weather he takes a chill so easily that his physician advises him to avoid all draughts if he possibly can.'

'Of course. I understand.'

'I mentioned a scar upon his face yesterday. If I recall correctly I told you then that he is very sensitive about it, and so if he should keep his face averted from your gaze or even go to the extremity of wearing a light mask to hide it, do not be alarmed. I am sure it will only be a temporary measure, until he gets to know you. He never troubles to conceal it from me, but after all you are comparative strangers even though you are wed. And manlike, he will surely want a pretty girl like you to think well of him. Ah, vanity! I wonder who first attributed that failing to females? For I have always found that gentlemen are equally guilty of it, if not more so!'

'Well, neither by look nor word shall I show a consciousness of its presence if Sir Matthew should choose to don one,' I said. 'And let us hope I can relieve his ennui, if only for a little while. Tell me, is he a garrulous gentleman, or does he just prefer to listen to others?'

'He has been a chatterbox all of his life! To me, that is. But at first you may find him fairly silent, though that is often so when people are newly met. They take each other's measure for a short while, then if they find they have something in common with a person, the promise of a sympathetic companion, they will lower the barriers of reticence to become their normal selves.'

That evening Aunt Ruby only accompanied me so far as the front door of the dower house, which upon her tug of the bellpull was immediately opened by Virtue to admit me into the hall that I instantly noted was lit well enough for me to

165

perceive where my next steps would take me.

'I will see you later, Laura, but do not stay for too long and overtire Sir Matthew, will you, dear?'

'No. I shall take great care, I promise you.'

'This way, Ladyship.' Virtue had evidently been primed as to the form of address that was now my due, even though he had not got it quite right.

'Lead on, Virtue. I will follow.' My tread was firm on this occasion, for, apart from the fact that complete sobriety steadied my feet, there were lighted oil lamps spaced at intervals which not only enabled me to see my way, but also that this house was vastly different from the one I had just left. This was much older, with carpeted oak flooring and paneled walls, and though the casements were close-curtained, I guessed from their size and shape that they would be of the small latticed type that would be all of a piece with a house of this apparent age. However, Sir Matthew's bedchamber was much more dimly lit with, as on the previous occasion, just one candelabra with three lighted candles set on the mantelpiece above the fireplace. Of course, his delicate eyesight would be the reason for that. And the brazier burning a not unpleasing aromatic incense in the far corner of the room was probably there to aid the breathing of the semi-invalid, for at our last meeting it had registered on my befuddled brain that Sir Matthew's voice was a trifle hoarse, as though he also had trouble with his throat. Somewhat apprehensively I entered, to be greeted by my host, husband, employer, saying quite matter-of-factly, 'Good evening, Laura. How very nice of you to come. Now it will please me greatly if you go straight to the fire, divest yourself of your cloak, take a seat, and warm yourself. And pray forgive me for being the cause of your having to expose yourself to the elements on this bitterly cold night.'

'Good evening, Sir Matthew. Actually, it is not so cold as one might suppose. Crisp, you could say. And the few minutes spent in walking from the main house to this, I found most exhilarating.'

'The servants have made sure the pathway is quite clear?'

'Indeed, they have, and there is no fear of slipping, for they have also strewn gravel. Yes, the short walk was most pleasant. You would like me to sit here?'

'Yes. Perhaps if you will be so very obliging as to draw your chair just a shade forward, I could see you with greater clarity. Or is it too heavy for you to move? No, do not trouble yourself. I will ring for Virtue to do it.'

'Sir Matthew, it is done. I am not made of thistledown, you know!'

'Are you not? From here you look completely ethereal. The candlelight shining upon your golden hair gives you a truly angelic halo. Tell me, are you an angel come down to earth to cheer a sinner like me?'

'No, sir, I am not. I am a very mortal young woman with her full share of human faults.'

'Tell me of them. What are your chief besetting sins?'

'Pride is one of them, I know. I have my share of vanity, I suppose. A little greed, perhaps. What are the others? Oh, sloth is one but I have never been accused of that!'

'So we have a proud, vain, greedy, yet industrious Lady Merrick? An honest one, too, by the sound of it.'

'And a rather uncomfortable one at this moment. If I were a Catholic, I should think I was in the confessional!'

A chuckle came from behind the partly drawn bed curtains.

'No, Laura. I am no priest, nor in a position to absolve anyone.'

'Well, having established some of the flaws in my character, what shall we do next? Shall I read to you? I have brought several quite new novels with me.'

'I would rather talk. I should like to know of your life before you came here. And why you came here. Of your family, friends, interests, and aspirations. Tell me of the things that are happening in London. Tell me about people whom you know, the things they do that amuse you, or of things that make you sad. Just talk to me, Laura, and bring the outside world into this gloomy chamber of mine.'

'First of all I will introduce you to my family, and, as you are so very kind as to liken my appearance to that of an angel, you should behold my little sister Tiffany . . .'

The minutes flew by. To speak of Mama, Tiffany, and Aunt Isobel seemed to bring them so much nearer. I told him of the more recent events that had led to my coming to Devon, of how my aunt's late husband had left his fortune, and of her chagrin that she could not even retrieve the ring he had left her as it was already buried with him. This Sir Matthew thought particularly amusing, for he laughed aloud at her indignation at being so misused, and I too chuckled at the memory of it. I told him of my sister's loveliness and of her stubborn insistence that she accompany me when I went to see Mr Peppercorn about acquiring my present position, and of her trepidation at the thought of braving Mama's wrath when she was told of what I had done. I described the foibles and the mannerisms of my loved ones, made them come alive. And though I pleased myself whilst talking of them as well as entertaining Sir Matthew, also there existed the barely half-formed thought that, if I aroused his interest in them, at some time in the future when as I had already determined I made my request that they should be invited to Merrick's Mount, that request might well receive a favorable reply.

Quietly the door opened, and Virtue announced, 'It is ten o'clock, Master. Does Ladyship go back now?'

'Gracious heavens, is that the time? And I promised Aunt Ruby I would not stay for too long on this first visit. I do hope I have not wearied you, Sir Matthew.'

'I have told you before, Laura, I wish you to address me simply as Matthew, if you will. And no, I am not in the least tired. But Virtue is right. You had better go now, or Aunt Ruby will be anxious. And thank you, Laura. Thank you for the most pleasant evening I have spent in a very long while. Will you come again? Soon?'

'Tomorrow? Shall I come again tomorrow, Matthew?'

'If you will honor me with your company once more, I shall be delighted. Farewell until then, Laura. And good night, my dear.'

'Good night, Matthew.'

The snow lingered for almost three weeks, supplemented by several further light falls, and during that time the regular after-dinner visits to the dower house, instead of being a tedious duty, became the highlights of my days. For that space of time, Merrick's Mount was almost cut off from the rest of the world, as also was the village to which a very indifferent path had been cleared and kept open, so that one of the menservants could walk there daily to enquire as to whether the mail coaches had managed to bring any post. But the answer was the same, day after day. Heavy drifts making the main roads impassable lay all the way between the village and Exeter, and until a thaw set in, bringing with it possible flooding, conditions would remain the same. And so one must, as Aunt Ruby regularly told me, just be patient.

Therefore, I repeat, my visits to the dower house were the times around which each day was centred. I had Aunt Ruby's company at mealtimes, but she always seemed to have something that needed her attention when we were not actually at table, and I had nothing much else to do but think. Sometimes of my dear ones in faraway London, wondering if they were anxious about me and if they still occupied the same address as heretofore. But more often I thought of Sir Matthew, of what I could tell him to make him laugh, of how his sense of humour matched mine, and I triumphed in the knowledge that he seemed to look forward to my visits, for he would greet me as would a person who was eager for my company. And I began to grow quite fond of him! Or was it just compassion? They say that pity is akin to love, and I would not deny it. But never did I actually see him! Whether he was masked or not I had no means of knowing, for always he was abed with its curtains partly drawn, so that he could see me but himself remain invisibly in the shadows. But now that I knew he was normal even though he was disfigured, all my fears had left me. The daguerreotype of the youthful Matthew had shown him to be tall, well-formed, and extremely pleasing to look upon, and though he was now scarred, the marring of his features was not a thing to be regarded with abhorrence. At least, not by me! And I began to wonder! Was his illness so serious after all, or was it merely used as a cloak to cover his reluctance to show himself to others? For that would account for many things. Living in shadows as he did might be caused by bright lights being uncomfortable to his vision, or it could be just to excuse him from being seen by other people. And it would also account for the way in which he dwelt apart, instead of taking his rightful place in his own mansion! On the occasion of our marriage, his hand's clasp had certainly not been such a one as to be expected from a frail, semi-invalid, and though his voice remained husky, that could always have been so.

171

And the way he laughed and the vigorous way in which he spoke, joined with his alert, inquisitive mind, gave me good reason to believe I had guessed the true reason why he shunned the light and all but the company of a mute and a person who, though legally emancipated, was still to all intents and purposes little more than a slave!

So I began to dream. And my favourite daydream was that, in time to come, I should prove to be his salvation. The hand of fate had led me to this place so that, with my patience and gentle reasoning, I might release from his self-imposed captivity the prisoner whose bonds existed only in his own mind. But I must not attempt to hurry him. Slowly I would gain his confidence, and then one day he would reveal his face to me, and I should gaze unflinching upon whatever disfigurement I beheld and thus begin to heal the spirit which, I by now had convinced myself, was the only part of him that truly ailed. I knew I must tread very warily, must never try to surprise him into a confrontation, for on one occasion I had risen from my chair and approached his bedside as though to illustrate by gesture some remark I was making, when he had halted me by saying abruptly, 'Stay where you are!'

Then in more amicable tone. 'Now please return to the fireside. I like to see you, Laura. And I cannot do so when you move away from the lights.'

And the burning incense? Probably a liking for its aroma was acquired whilst he lived abroad, for though he would not permit me to see him, he talked to me as one would to a friend. He told me of his life spent in the Sandwich Islands and was revealed to be a most entertaining *raconteur*.

'The family of which you are now a member, Laura, has business interests there. In fact, it is from there that our chief source of income is derived.'

'Yes, Aunt Ruby told me. You own some plantations, I believe?'

'Sugar, with a little coffee. Well really it was by purest chance that I was sent there at all. I will not bore you with the details, but the domestic situation at Merrick's Mount was not exactly ideal when I was a young 'un. I seem to have been born with an especial gift for annoying my father, for somehow everything I ever attempted to do to please him always ended in disaster, and finally I gave up trying. I was sent to school and then on to Oxford, whereas young David was considered delicate and was tutored at home. And when the time came for me to return here permanently, the question arose as to what was to be done with me. This was still being mooted when once again I upset my father. Indeed, I incurred his displeasure to such an extent that as a form of punishment he shipped me off to the other side of the world to teach me a lesson, presumably of good behavior.'

'Rather a drastic punishment, I would say,' I observed. 'Whatever had you done?'

'Ah, well! That is another story. But to remain with this one, this desire that I should thereby be chastened was also thwarted, for once arrived there, and the journey took months, I became so enamoured of the place that I would willingly have stayed there for the rest of my days!'

'Oh? Aunt Ruby did say that you remained there until you became master here.'

'Yes, it was a real wrench to come home to England again, but it had to be done, and so here I am.'

'What is it like there?'

'If you can imagine everyone's conception of paradise, that is the place on earth where they are most likely to find it. Ah, the islands! Where the sun is hot, but the breezes are cool. The skies and seas are always a heavenly blue by day, and at night the stars are so brilliant and seem so near at hand that one could reach up and touch them. There are palm-fringed golden beaches, creamy surf, and coral reefs. And in the ocean, there is such an abundance of fish of beauteous color and design as would amaze you. And upon the land, amidst the trees, fly birds of such gaudy plumage that they give the impression of bewinged jewels, flashing from bough to bough.'

'Yes, it does rather sound as though you quite liked the place,' I said.

To be rewarded by one of his rare chuckles and the remark, 'Laura Merrick, you too are a gem! And of a quality to deserve a setting such as the one I describe, instead of this mundane one in which you are now placed.'

'It suits me very well here, Sir. But tell me, what did you do when you got to your paradise?'

'Firstly I damned myself forever in the eyes of the

other white men, by freeing the slaves that worked our plantations.'

'Your father gave you permission to do that?'

'Eventually, but I had already done it by then. But really it was little more than a gesture, for the poor devils had nowhere to go, once they were free men and women. They were glad to remain in their compound, live in their huts as they had always done, and continue to work the cane fields as they had when they were slaves.'

'But they could have left if they had wished to, surely?'

'Oh, yes, but practically all of them stayed, for I paid a fair wage for their labor, and, as free people, they were socially superior to the blacks on the other plantations. And that alone gave them no small cause for contentment, believe me!'

'Indeed, I do. And that was when Virtue entered your service?'

'He was with me from the very first hour I set foot on Maui. An agent ran our plantations until I went out there, just as another one does now. But upon my arrival the agent announced that as he was ageing, he wished to retire and come back home, so after he had told me what little he knew about the running of the place, he took ship, and I was left to do more or less as I liked. But before he went he made sure I was well served and comfortably housed, and thus I came by Virtue. He would have been about sixteen at that time.'

'But you encouraged all of your slaves who were not already to become Christians?'

'No. I took no hand in it. But once they were

175

free, their Sundays were their own to do with as they pleased, and after a while they mostly gravitated toward some chapel that American missionaries had set up. They liked the lusty singing and the Hallelujahs, to wear their finery, and to meet others. It was a place to go, to gossip, exchange their masters' secrets, make assignations. Oh, everything was arranged on Sundays! But, to go to chapel, one must first at least profess to Christianity, and so they were baptised, but basically they still mostly worshiped the old gods that their parents and grandparents brought with them. These people are mainly of African stock, and the religious cult of voodoo has a much stronger hold on them than anything they are likely to acquire from the so-called civilized world.'

'And what is voodoo?'

'It is an evil, nauseating form of worship as old as time itself! Its origins lie in the Dark Continent, but wherever you may find Negro slaves in any great number you will also find that they or their ancestors have brought their cult with them.'

'What is it? A type of witchcraft?'

'I suppose one could say that, though it is of a particularly evil variety. I see you smile! Well, my dear, let me assure you it is nothing to smile at! In these reputedly enlightened times, we deride the notion of witches and magic spells, but those who have seen what I have seen are not amongst the ranks of the scoffers!'

'You mean that there is really a power of some sort attached to it?'

'Oh, yes there is a power! Such a power that,

if one is wise, one has a very great respect for it, if not actual fear! Sacrifices are involved, sometimes human, and there are other equally revolting practices!'

'Did you say that Virtue was, and maybe still is, one of these people?'

'Well, he is, but he stands in the greatest fear of me. The chief deity of this cult is the snake god, Damballah. And as all of my luggage and most of my personal possessions were imprinted with the family crest of the coiled serpent when first he saw me, he is utterly convinced that I am Damballah in human form and that he is highly honoured by being privileged to serve me. In actual fact, he worships me!'

'What a shame! How can you so deceive him?'

'He deceived himself! Many times I told him I was just an ordinary white man, but he merely grinned and prostrated himself before me. For every time I tried to disabuse him of the notion he was standing in the presence of a god, he simply thought I was testing his faith! He even sacrifices cockerels to me. Black or white ones!'

'Not in here?'

'No. By now he knows I am better pleased if he does that outside. Then he tells me of his offerings, and I accept them gravely, and then I instruct him as to whether I wish them to be broiled or roasted for my dinner!'

My face must have been a study for from behind the bed curtains came a great shout of laughter, and I coloured at the thought of my gullibility.

'Thank you for telling me your most interesting

177

fairy tale, sir,' I said in a voice that expressed my deep affront.

'It is true. Every word. I swear it!'

'Upon the sacred book of Damballah?'

'I do not believe he has one. Very well. If you doubt my word just mention that name to Virtue and observe his reaction,' I was invited, but having no desire to make a bigger fool of myself than I had already, I just smiled in a frosty manner and changed the subject.

But I could not be cross with him for long, for he always greeted me with such eagerness, and if I were ever a minute or so later in my coming than was usual, when I did enter his chamber, it was almost pathetic to witness his concern that all might not be well with me and to see his relief when I assured him that this was not so. He never asked me to read to him, and I suppose it was understandable that his chief desire should be for conversation, and sometimes I would be tempted to try and give him cause to reconsider his life of self-imposed seclusion. Oh, I never even hinted that I suspected if he chose he could live normally, but I would ask him what springtime was like in Devonshire, whether he had used to go riding or sailing along the coast. I coaxed him to speak of his boyhood and of one close friend he had had until their respective fathers became enemies, but even after that they would still meet and talk of how they would reshape the world, and this particular part of it, when they reached full manhood themselves and became masters of their families' estates.

'Seth Quillian is about the same age as I and as

lads we were quite inseparable. That presented no problem until our fathers disagreed, though even after that we used to meet on the sly whenever we could.'

'And why was there a disagreement, or should I not ask?'

'Oh, it is all long past and almost forgotten. It was to do with the quarries. The Quillians owned a small part of the business, and as they were not so nicely placed, financially speaking, as we Merricks, they depended on their share of the profits for their income. Whereas we had our overseas source for ours, and the quarries were not yielding a sufficient sum for my father to consider it would pay him to keep them open.'

'On whose land do they stand?' I asked.

'Today it is all Merrick property, but at that time the Quillians owned a small proportion. Their estate used to adjoin ours, and, when eventually they were forced to sell and move away, we acquired their land at a very reasonable price. Well, my father did, for I was up at Oxford then, and my opinion was neither sought nor desired.'

'Could not this family have kept the quarries open on their own account? As your father presumably had lost interest in the business, could they not have run it themselves?'

'No, they did not have the capital. It needed quite a lot of money spent on it at that time, and my father decided not to make any further outlay on the place. Why should he? He would not suffer from its closure!'

'But others did? Aunt Ruby told me there was

a little hardship among the workers when it was abandoned,' I remarked.

'A little? Laura, you can have no idea! There was nothing for them to do, nowhere for them to go. Folk whose families for past generations had laboured at hewing and shaping the stone, suddenly found themselves with no means of earning their bread and also without a roof over their heads!'

'There was nothing else?'

'Not for many miles, and even then work was scarce. Then it was that Seth and I made a pact that, when the time came, we should reopen the quarries, and things would be the same as before.'

'And yet you did not?'

'It was only an adolescent dream, after all. We both thought of ourselves as youthful knights in shining armor, riding forth to right the wrongs of the world. In those days the Quillians were still our neighbors, and hungry men wandering the lanes were a common enough sight. But everything is now changed. The workers have long gone their separate ways, and Seth and his family settled in Plymouth. Seth himself went to sea. He and I chanced upon each other years ago when his ship took him to Owhyhee, whilst I happened to be visiting there. But although I invited him to Maui he never came, and that was the last I saw of him.'

'What of your other friends?'

'He was my only close one. Those whom I met at Oxford are probably all settled in staid professions and have numerous progeny by now.'

'Poor Matthew! And so now you rely on the company of a stranger!' I said unthinkingly.

'Do not call me 'Poor Matthew' '!' he replied sharply. 'I seek nobody's pity! And as to being a stranger, are you not my wife? And, as such, a person upon whose company I could call twenty-four hours of the day, if I so desire?'

I felt my face flush crimson as the implication of his words penetrated my understanding. For he was right! He could command me to remain at his side, be subservient to his every demand, and the law would uphold him if he did! Fearfully I glanced towards the door. What if he should suddenly conceive the notion that he wished to exercise the rights to which every husband is entitled? I could not refuse him! For one cannot cry 'Rape' against one's husband! The ensuing silence was becoming oppressive, for I did not know how best to end it and he seemed to have lapsed into a speculative study of me, when suddenly he said in a voice more hoarse than usual, 'Unpin your hair, Laura.'

'I beg your pardon?'

'Laura, it will please me greatly if you will let down your hair.'

Now this I was extremely loath to do, not so much from a sense of modesty as from fear as to what thoughts such an action might inspire. If he were regarding me as a man would his true wife, to comply with his request would probably make matters worse, for was not the sight of a woman's unbound hair supposed to inflame the baser masculine instincts? Was it not for this reason that, upon reaching the state of nubility, a young girl was bidden to put up her tresses lest they should tempt the stronger gender to forget its present-day chivalrous attitude and revert to the uncivilized ways of long ago?

'Have no fear, Laura. I have no intention of molesting you. But for once, just this once, indulge my whim. And that is to see your golden hair, flowing freely. Please, Laura! Let me see your hair!'

With trembling fingers, I slowly removed the pins that held my chignon in place, and the heavy massed coil tumbled and fell to almost touch the floor as I sat in my fireside chair.

'Stand up, Laura. Oh, a lock of your hair is caught up at one side. Shake it loose, if you please. Ah, yes! Just as I imagined it would be! Will you turn around? Slowly, if you will be so obliging. And thus I shall be able to perceive the full glory of it!'

Slowly indeed, for, as I reluctantly did his bidding, I was wondering what further requests he might make of me, but when I was once more facing the direction from which the hoarse-toned instructions were coming, Virtue quietly entered the chamber with his usual reminder, 'It is ten o'clock, Master. Does Ladyship go now?'

I held my breath until, after a short pause, came the reply, 'Yes, Virtue, damn you! Her ladyship is going now. Thank you, Laura. You have made me very happy by pandering to my foolishness. I cannot say I am sorry for I am not, but you have my word that I shall not cause you confusion in a like manner, ever again! Good night, my dear.'

'Good night, Matthew.'

Although I did not actually hasten to leave the dower house, I did not dawdle either! For people have been known to change their minds! Therefore I was relieved to reach the main house with no further loss of composure than having tumbled hair, but though a safe distance now lay between me and the recent scene of my embarrassment, my thoughts were in a turmoil for a considerable while after this alarming experience. Would anything have happened if Virtue had not come into the room when he did? Matthew had declared he would not molest me, but would he have abided by his word? On a former occasion, he had described me as being lovely, and he must have been thinking about me in quite an intimate way, otherwise he would never have imagined, as he confessed to doing, what my hair would be like when I was in a state of undress! What other imaginings did he have? Admittedly my thoughts were running along most immodest lines, but though my upbringing had been comparatively sheltered, I was no fool and was fully aware of what normally took place between a healthy man and his wife. And that was a point in question. How healthy was Matthew? Much more so than the frail, sickly semi-invalid whom Aunt Ruby had described to me. That was very apparent! But what could I now expect upon future visits to the dower house? And how should I react if the worst came to pass? Would it be so very dreadful? I liked what I knew of Matthew Merrick, could even secretly confess to a fondness of him, and he had made it crystal clear that he liked me! Perhaps more than liked me? I

183

knew it must have been in his thoughts that he had the right to demand of me what he chose. Would he have made those demands if his servant had not appeared at that, in my view at least, opportune moment? Matthew found me desirable, and that is a thought that must surely please any woman, to be regarded as attractive. But how strong was his desire? Was it powerful enough to thrust aside the barriers of self-control? To insist upon its dues and to brook no denial? And would I, really and truly, be so utterly desolate if it did?

6

Though glancing at me curiously, Aunt Ruby had passed no remark when, pleading a headache, I retired straightaway to my chambers. I felt I could not face the probing questions that doubtless would be asked if I removed my hooded cloak in her presence and revealed my disheveled appearance, and anyway, I wanted to be alone with my tumultuous thoughts. And later I dreamed of him! An older, more mature version of the youthful Matthew in the daguerreotype stepped out of the silver frame and came to me. With words of love, he came to me! He was tall and strong and manly, comely to look upon, his voice eloquent though husky and throbbing with passion. And in my dream, he took me in his arms, with his own hands he unbound my hair, to nuzzle his face in it, all the while whispering endearments until I felt as though I would melt in his embrace. And though I feebly struggled when his kisses, light as a summer shower began to rain upon my modestly bent head, his arms, albeit gentle, were like steel bands enfolding me. And therefore what could I do but raise my face to his? With eyes closed in rapture, I awaited the moment when our lips should meet and our love for each other would silently be declared. But the kiss for which I was all athrill never came, and I opened my eyes to stare up into the grinning countenance of Virtue! Pure horror assailed me, and somehow I broke free from his clasp and ran, and ran, and ran. With feet fettered to invisible leaden weights, I ran over marshy ground. Monstrous black or white birds, with beaks and claws poised to rend, flapped and whirled about my head, and behind, close on my heels, came a horde of malevolent, hydra-headed pursuers! And then I fell, down, down, down, and just as I was becoming resigned to being dashed to pieces upon whatever lay far below me, I awoke. I awoke and lay petrified with fear, until gradually I became aware of bright moonlight piercing the chinks that edged the drawn casement curtains, and, though snug between the bed covers, I found myself bathed in the icy perspiration of unadulterated terror!

Perhaps the dream, nightmare, was sent to me as punishment for my shameless thoughts! Yes, I must indeed be a depraved hussy, for my salacious suspicions and speculations were entirely unfounded, as was vouchsafed to me the next

185

evening. As the day had progressed, I had spent the passing hours in wondering how best to deal with the situation. I was embarrassed, unsure as to how I should greet Matthew when the time came. To completely ignore his startling request during our last meeting seemed the wisest course to take, but what if he chose to do otherwise? What if he demanded a repeat performance? And if he should make advances, how should I receive them? Or should I take to my bed and thus avoid the after-dinner visit to my husband? But I would have to face him again at some time, and to delay might only make the situation more awkward. And though I knew I was playing with fire, and though I inwardly squirmed at the secret knowledge within my heart, I was aware of a strong desire to see him again, to find out just how deeply my nearness did affect him, to discover whether the sight of me would make him forget his former promise. Could I stir his senses so deeply that despite his good intentions, he would succumb to temptation? And by yielding, could I wean him away from the solitary existence he led? It would be like the story in a romantic novel, the beauty of a virtuous and understanding woman inspiring a love so great that it conquered all!

But when one has mentally prepared oneself to play the part of the sacrificial lamb it is more than a little aggravating to be informed that one's offering is neither expected nor greatly desired! For after dinner, Aunt Ruby said quite casually, 'Oh, I meant to tell you earlier, Laura. Matthew begs you to excuse him this evening. He is suffering from headache and says he is not fit company for anybody. You will understand, I know, for you too were a victim of the same complaint only last night.' She glanced at me slyly from beneath lowered lids.

'Yes, mine came upon me quite suddenly,' I replied. 'I am so very sorry to hear that Matthew is unwell, but he is most wise to keep himself quiet until its effects have gone. My mother, too, is often prostrated by migraine, and then there is nothing to be done but for her to lie in a darkened room and just wait for it to depart.'

'Anyway, it will be a little respite for you, my dear. From your regular visit to the dower house, I mean.'

What else could she mean, I wondered, but merely smiled and said, 'I do not regard them as uncongenial, Aunt Ruby. And therefore I do not consider a respite needful, nor even welcome. I just hope that Matthew will feel in better health and spirits as soon as may be.'

'So do I, of course, but I must confess to a purely selfish pleasure in the thought that you and I can spend a cosy evening together. Lately we have seen little of each other. When I am free from my duties, you are about to start yours! And *vice versa*. And I think your coming to Merrick's Mount has made me aware that I too can be lonely upon occasion.'

This was a thought that had never occurred to me, for Aunt Ruby always seemed so entirely self-sufficient.

'In what way has my coming here made a difference?' I asked.

'Only in a small way. For obviously I do not spend so much time at the dower house as I used to, but apart from that, it is possible that my recent trips to London and then to Exeter have unsettled me a little.'

'Why do you not come with me when I go to visit Matthew?'

'No, child. That I know would lessen his pleasure. And why should he wish to see an old woman like me, when he can feast his eyes upon a fresh, lovely young creature like you?'

'Could he not enjoy the company of us both?'

'Hardly! For what gentleman welcomes the presence of a third party, especially that of one whom he regards as his mother, when it spoils a *tête-à-tête*, no matter how innocent? Tell me, does he try to flirt with you?'

'No! What a strange question!' I exclaimed as I felt a crimson flush emerge from the bodice of my gown to creep relentlessly upwards until it suffused my face. 'Actually, we talk mostly about his life on that island, and mine whilst I dwelt in London.'

'Hmm, sounds like dry stuff to me! Anyway, it is none of my business what you discuss though, whatever it is, I am sure Matthew derives more enjoyment from it than he would if I were sitting there, playing chaperone!'

I could have then easily changed the subject, but could not resist saying, 'In any event, a gentleman in a poor state of health does not usually even wish to indulge in flirtations.'

'Poor Matthew! If that is true of him, he must be much more debilitated than I thought! For let me tell you, before his illness he was regarded by the ladies as quite a rascal! A delightful one, but a rascal nonetheless!'

'And yet he did not marry?'

'Well, this may sound a trifle indelicate, but there was never any real reason why he should wish to! And placed as he was on the other side of the world, he did not even have to watch his manners as a gentleman has to who resides here in England! Besides, eligible young women do not abound in the Sandwich Islands, but dusky beauties are in plentiful supply, and by just crooking his little finger they were his for the taking!'

'Oh? Then how did he acquire this reputation for gallantry?'

'He has always been an imp. Just for amusement he would dally with the planters' wives and sometimes even their pudding-faced daughters. They were all bored and very ready to fall in love with a personable, wealthy young man, but he was wise enough never to get totally enmeshed by any one of them.'

'But why did he not look about him for a wife when he first came home?'

'Oh, he was busy. And his illness was beginning to discommode him even then.'

'He told me he would have been happy to stay where he was, instead of coming back to England.'

'Pure foolishness! He is master here, and it is only right he should return to the place of his birth and to claim his inheritance.'

'True, but if as you have told me his illness is

terminal, it might have been for the best if he had stayed where he was. He was happy there, he told me so. And his half-brother will inherit anyway, eventually. So why not sooner than later?'

A silence fell upon the room, then Aunt Ruby pronounced as though after deep consideration: 'Not necessarily! I believe that Matthew is still quite capable of fathering a son if he were so minded!'

'But he is no longer free to marry!' I exclaimed. 'Unless of course, this union of ours is dissolved.'

'Why should it be? He has assured me several times that he is more than content with it.'

'This is a very strange conversation, Aunt Ruby. I am beginning to feel a trifle uneasy,' I said. 'You told me I was to be a companion, nothing more.'

'Well, are you anything more? Is there something you have not told me? Something which has passed between you and Matthew of which I am in ignorance?' she sounded quite eager.

'No. It is just all this talk of fathering children that makes me feel uncomfortable.'

'Oh? That is all? Then you may be easy, for the occasion is never likely to arise. I said that I believe Matthew is capable, but not that he intends to. Quite the reverse, in fact, for his physicians have advised him that his illness is of the type that can be passed on to future generations.'

'What is it? From what does he actually suffer?'

'Oh, some obscure tropical disease. Very rare in Europe.'

'Like malaria? I have heard of that!'

'Something of that nature. I declare, Laura, we

seem to talk of nothing and nobody but Matthew! How his masculine heart would be flattered if he could hear us! And now let us discuss something else. And I do believe I hear the approach of the teatray.'

'Well, probably our conversations will cover a wider range of subjects when some news reaches us from the outside world,' I replied. 'For, I must confess, I would dearly like to hear from my family.'

'Ah, yes. Your mother, sister, and aunt. Tell me, is there anybody else from whom you may expect a letter?'

'I cannot think of anyone. What sort of person?'

'Oh, friends, acquaintances, even erstwhile beaux! Thank you, Flint. Leave it, and we shall serve ourselves.'

'I possess no friends, and any acquaintances I do have are not likely to write to me! I doubt that anyone, apart from my kinfolk, even knows where I am! And beaux? I have never had one,' I answered after the servants had gone.

'Never? Are you telling me in all seriousness, Laura, that you have never developed even a secret fondness for a young gentleman?'

'Indeed, I am. I do not know of one. For never in my life have I met anyone whom I could think of on those terms.'

'You poor dear child! No beaux? No sweethearts? Not even an admirer?'

'Not to my knowledge, but I do not think being so neglected has done me any harm,' I replied cheerfully.

'Ah, Laura. You do not know what you have missed!'

'From what I have read on the subject of romance, I can only guess that I have missed a great deal of anxiety, frustration, and possibly heartbreak. And if I were already attracted to a young gentleman in London, I should never have applied for this position, met you, nor come to Merrick's Mount. So I would have missed that instead.'

'Yes. What a wise young woman you are! Indeed, as you so sagely say, you would have missed that and all that the future here holds for you.'

'I wonder just what it does hold?' I replied musingly.

'Well, you are assured of financial security and of a comfortable home, though whether or not you find the company of us Merricks congenial as the months pass, only time will tell. Unfortunately you have come amongst us when the weather and the scenery are at their worst, but there again, in that direction matters can only improve. For when we can once again get about, go driving, and you acquire some equestrian skill, life here will be far less boring.'

'Yes, in the springtime it must be lovely here in Devon!'

'Indeed, it is. But though we may make you come to regard us with even a small degree of affection, in one way we cannot compensate. For now I have had leisure to think about your position here, I am assailed by a feeling of guilt!'

'Oh? I do not grasp your meaning.'

'Well, you are wed, yet not a wife. And though I am aware it is my doing, or let us say chiefly my doing, you are so placed, and even though you yourself were willing, it nags at my conscience that you should be so deprived.'

'I am quite content with the terms of my contract and with the conditions of my marriage,' I answered flatly.

'Oh, I do not suggest that you should desire more from Matthew than just his company, but every woman has the right to have children! For that reason we were fashioned as we were, and a childless woman is a sad, unfulfilled creature! To hold a baby in one's arms and then as the years go by, to have little fingers clutching at one's skirts is every woman's due!'

'You did not and seem none the worse for it,' I remarked.

'Ah, but I did. I did! I had little Matthew! He was mine! For though I neither conceived nor bore him, he was nonetheless mine. I was his mother as he was, is, my son. And the joy I felt when tending him, guiding him, was such that I shrink from the thought that by an act of mine, another woman is forbidden the joy that motherhood brings.'

'Aunt Ruby, I cannot imagine you shrinking from anything, particularly a thought!' I replied. 'And obviously not all females are blessed with such strong maternal instincts as you were, are! In actual fact I am not greatly concerned if I never mother a child, so I pray you to set your mind at rest. For the plight in which you believe you have placed me does not affect me in the least!'

'Oh! Well, though I am very happy to hear you say that, I was about to suggest a solution to the problem.'

'There is none. Problem, I mean.'

'I was about to suggest that you and Matthew adopt a child.'

'No, I think not.'

'There are so many poor innocent, orphaned mites in this world, yearning to be loved. To be cared for.' Her eyes were moist, whether through concealed annoyance at my lack of cooperation or from pity for the parentless babes, I could not tell.

'Then why do you not adopt one? Several, even? If it gave you satisfaction, it would also be the answer to your feeling of loneliness, as well as being of benefit to the children.'

'Oh no, it would not serve. I am too old, now. I get cross too easily these days. My patience is not what it was!'

Was there a double meaning to those words of hers?

'Besides, I might die,' she continued, 'leaving the little ones bereft for a second time. And at my age one must be prepared to be suddenly called.'

'By whom?'

'By the Lord, child! It is as well to have one's house in order when that dread day comes!'

'Aunt Ruby, I feel quite certain you will outlive us all. So make your plans I beg you, and I promise here and now that, if you should be snatched away from us, I will continue to care for your orphans until they are of an age to care for themselves.'

'So you do not welcome the idea on your own account?'

'No. I am afraid I do not!'

'Tut-tut. Just look at the time! How it flies when one is engrossed! I will bid you good night, Laura.' With startling abruptness, she rose from her chair, and though she nodded graciously, the smile she bestowed upon me was brief and forced, and her eyes, though bright, no longer glistened moistly but sparkled with anger.

'Good night, Aunt Ruby. I shall sit here for just a little while longer,' I answered. 'You go on up.' And with no further word, she did.

Although I now lived a life of complete ease, every day passing in idleness, the happenings and conversations here at Merrick's Mount were of sufficient import and of such variety, that my thoughts alone were quite enough to occupy my hours, waking and sleeping. It was as though I were set a puzzle to solve with, at the start of my task, only a few of the pieces. And gradually more were given me, but still I did not have the requisite amount to enable me to see the picture clearly. However, the cosy chat Aunt Ruby and I had just enjoyed was now beginning to fill quite a number of the blank spaces, for though she had disguised her latest proposition in sentimental terms, the issue had emerged very clearly. She wanted me to have a child! Apparently she did not care overmuch whether it were the progeny of Matthew and myself or an adopted baby. And her lighthearted, casual questioning about the existence of any former beau, also gave me cause to wonder if she would turn a blind eye if one such did come avisiting, and I had a lapse from virtue resulting in a pregnancy! Undoubtedly a child was strongly desired, although I did not imagine that to hear the pitter-patter of tiny feet was the only reason for Aunt Ruby's recent suggestions, veiled and otherwise. No indeed, for such sentimentality was quite out of character for one whom I judged to be almost ruthless. Miss Ruby Merrick wanted an heir to the Merrick estates, and he could be anyone other than David Merrick! It seemed she was obsessed with the desire to thwart him of his expected inheritance. Anybody could have it, so long as it did not fall to him! Was this the reason I had been engaged in the first place? Not to read aloud to Matthew nor to entertain him with my brilliant conversation, but merely as a cloak to cover the arrival of a new heir! And to get one should not present insoluble difficulties to such a person as Ruby Merrick! There must be scores of young women who would gladly sell an unwanted babe. Yes, that would surely be a buyer's market. Aye, money could purchase most things, and there would be many who would eagerly sell a bastard male child. And this I should be well aware of, as I was no better, for had I not sold myself?

And Matthew? How would he receive the news of his aunt's little schemes? Or was he already involved in them? Was this all planned even before Aunt Ruby had set out for London to find such a female as myself? One who was willing to comply with any trickery provided the price were right? But on the other hand, Aunt Ruby had asserted that

Matthew was capable of fathering his own child, so if he desired one so greatly, why did he not? Not with me, of course, but it would not have been impossible to find some young woman who, for a certain amount of monetary inducement, would have been willing to be his true wife in the accepted sense. Or perhaps he did not like women in that way. There were such men. No, for then he could not have acquired his former reputation of being a gentleman who was regarded by the ladies as rather a rascal! And he did like feminine company, for he had always received me with courtesy and made my visits most enjoyable for both of us.

Though what about the last one, for that had certainly been different from the others? Had he decided to satisfy his aunt by exercising his connubial rights but wanted a better look at me before he definitely committed himself? Perhaps he was very particular when it came to a choice of feminine partners? Had his vast selection of dusky beauties made him so difficult to please that only after the most careful of inspections would he bestir himself sufficiently to father a child? And I could not deny that I had been inspected, even if it were in a lesser degree, but how far would his appraisal have gone if his valet had not entered when he did? Though Matthew *had* let me go without demur, and surely he *could* have sent Virtue away, telling him to return later. And then a thought struck me, making me positively bristle with indignation. Perhaps he had seen enough, enough to decide that I did not reach his high standards of womanly perfection? Who did he think he was? What right had he to deny me the opportunity of showing him that, even if I were not what was considered a classical beauty, I was not ill-favored and, with the freshness of youth, could compete with other females, even dusky ones!

Laura Lambourne, no Merrick, whatever next? Are you becoming as odd in your behaviour and notions as are the other members of this family you have entered? Can you actually be aggrieved that the chance to flaunt yourself before an almost completely strange man has been withheld from you? Are you demented? Or shameless? Or both? And does the fact that you are no longer a Lambourne, but now bear the name Merrick, answer for this strange change of outlook of one who was brought up to be modest to the point of bashfulness?

Stop it! These are completely nonsensical thoughts! Matthew is not like that. Has he not always been most considerate and courteous in his speech and manner toward you? He is in utter ignorance of these hopes of his aunt, for he could certainly never countenance such deceit. Why should he? For when the time comes for this Merrick inheritance to fall to another, Matthew will be far above and beyond earthly cares. No, this is a maggot in Aunt Ruby's brain, alone. Or had I misjudged her? She had not actually said in so many words that it was in her mind that an adopted child should be passed off as a true Merrick. Anyway, that would be impossible for were not Mr. and Mrs. David Merrick expected to return here just so soon as the weather permitted? And would they be stupid enough to just stand tamely by and let themselves be tricked out of their expected fortune? Of course not! And thus it must follow that Aunt Ruby meant nothing more than she had openly declared, that as she was the type of woman who was dedicated to rearing infants, she imagined that all others were cast in a like mould. My contentment was all that she desired, and it was shameful that I should harbour such unworthy suspicions against an elderly lady who had never shown me anything but kindness! It must be my nerves that fed my mind with these fantasies. Yes, being confined as I was with no outside interests and only my vivid imagination for company, I was allowing it much too free a rein!

But even though I had decided it was only my own foolish fancies that plagued me, once I was snug between the well-warmed sheets I forced myself to lie wakeful for fear the torment of nightmare would again return. And I had no recollection of falling asleep until a sharp, staccato noise like pebbles from a gravel path being flung up at my casements awoke me to a by now almost familiar feeling of apprehension. Who was it? What did they want? Was I to get no peace in this damned house? Tensely I lay, waiting. Waiting for the action to be repeated so that I might be sure I had not dreamed it. Wide-awake and alert for the slightest sound, my patience was rewarded in a very short while by hearing it again. And then again! I was just about to rise and fling open the window, when the realization came to me that it was naught but flurries of hailstones! And as I pulled the covers even higher about my shoulders and nestled deeper into the feather mattress beneath me, I heard the rattle of hail upon the glass panes being replaced by the steady, drumming rhythm of driving rain! Glory be, it was raining! A veritable torrent, betokening that the blanket of snow that had covered the countryside, imprisoning us and depriving us of all communication with the outside world, would soon be gone! I should get letters from my dear ones, meet my half brother-in-law and his wife, and be able to walk abroad freely for the first time since my marriage. I could even go to church! Make myself known to the villagers and possibly indulge in some charitable works. For was I not Lady Merrick of Merrick's Mount? And, as such, to undertake these tasks would be expected of me. Ah, how welcome was the rain! The snowdrifts would soon disappear and then, almost before we were aware, spring would be here! Mother Earth would don fresh finery; everything would be new, including the way of life it was now my duty, nay privilege, to lead!

★ ★ ★

But first there were floods which must be endured, and so it was a further ten days before I met the rest of the Merrick family, and during that time I made no visit to the dower house! Firstly migraine was the excuse, and when that became too protracted to be credible, Matthew was stricken with a heavy cold with which he was reluctant to infect me. And when he recovered from that, a fit of dire depression

200

descended on him, and he was best left alone whilst in this state of mind.

'But surely, if I visit him, it will help him to combat it?' I said.

'No, better not. When one of these black moods is upon him it is well to leave him alone, for he does not welcome any company. In actual fact he shuns it, and even I would hesitate to invade his privacy at such a time,' Aunt Ruby answered, thereby making me feel that she thought I was being too forward.

'I did not think that a friendly visit might be construed as an invasion of privacy,' I retorted, much nettled. 'And I certainly have no desire to thrust my company where it is not wanted!'

'Do not take offence, my dear. I beg your pardon if I gave you to understand that your presence would be especially unwelcome, for that is not so. No, this is a symptom of Matthew's illness, and when it comes upon him, he is like a crustacean who wants nothing but to retire into its shell and be left completely alone. When it has passed, he will emerge, but he must be allowed utter solitude until then.'

'How is he served during these times? Is Virtue with him?'

'Of course, but the fact that he is there is quite different. For Matthew can order or ignore him as he chooses and has to make no effort to be even civil for the benefit of his servant!'

'Very well, but if you do communicate with the dower house, I beg you to convey my good wishes and hopes for Matthew's speedy recovery.'

'Certainly, Laura. If the opportunity arises, I will do that.'

And so I was left in a state of quandary, for though Aunt Ruby could have been speaking the truth, she could also have been lying in an attempt to save me from the embarrassment of learning that Matthew no longer desired to see me. But why? What had I done? In his presence my last action had been to let down my hair, but he had bidden me do it, and it is a wife's duty to obey her husband. Or had he expected me to refuse? As he was not really my spouse, had he been testing me? Simply desirous of discovering how strong was my sense of what was fitting? And how far his commands could go before he outraged my modesty? Well it had not taken him long to find out, for after merely the slightest hesitation I had complied with his request. Only a little urging had been required before I did unpin my tresses, and by so doing, had I forfeited his esteem? And this thought once formed, rarely left me. He had been shocked by my swift, obedient reaction to his unusual request. Yes, I had made a grave mistake. I should have been strong in my denial, gentle but firm. I should have refused calmly, glanced at the clock and said it was time for me to depart. And now he held me cheap! Well, never again would I do it, no matter how hard he pleaded. In future I would preserve my dignity, and having resolved this course of action, I waited for the chance to prove to him that I did not make a habit of such goings-on. So as each dinner hour approached, I always dressed and had Tansy tire my hair with the greatest care, for I must be ready, elegant, and coolly confident when Aunt Ruby at last said that Matthew desired my company. But the summons did not come and my usual query of, 'Have you heard how Matthew is today?' was invariably met with, 'A little better, but still not quite himself.'

If David and Celia had shown themselves to be a disagreeable pair, I should not have been too greatly affected, for I was rapidly reaching the stage when to converse with anybody during the daylight hours came as a welcome relief from sheer loneliness. But I was pleasantly surprised. Aunt Ruby's remarks and adverse comments regarding them whilst they were absent had led me to believe that their return would bring an atmosphere heavy with constraint, but they were not like that at all! I thought they were nice! David was very handsome, with dark, waving auburn hair, hazel eyes, and a finely-cut countenance. Actually, he was the epitome of what I considered should be the model of an aristocrat, broad of shoulder, lean of waist, with beautifully shaped hands, and though I judged he would not match what I guessed would be Matthew's stature, he was tall enough to be well above average height. His clothes were fashionable and elegant, and he wore them with the air of carelessness that only an assured income can afford. And Celia? Obviously she adored him, and I could quite see why, for even though her family were reputedly wealthy, she was almost nondescript in appearance, and the fact that she had snared him for her husband in the face of extremely probable rivalry from other females gave her cause to wonder how she did it. This I know, for she confessed as much to me at a later date, for although she was pleasant to look upon, she was certainly no beauty! Her hair was light brown and given to frizziness where her maid's application of the curling tongs had been too enthusiastic. She was plump enough to at first make me wonder if she were *enceinte*, but I soon learned she was not, even though it was her chief desire to be so. The poor dear also was myopic, ever peering shortsightedly at distant objects because she disliked to wear her spectacles. And upon their return to Merrick's Mount, David and Celia did not treat me with even a hint of coolness, nor look at me askance.

'Ah, here she is! Look, my love, is she not a charmer? Trust Matthew to win himself a beauty!' David said, and Celia came towards me with outstretched arms.

'Oh, how wonderful it is to find you here. A sister-in-law! I have a sister at last! I thought I never should, for I was brought up with only horrid brothers, but we shall be sisters, you and I. Shall we not?' She clasped me warmly, and I was a trifle nonplussed by this apparently genuine show of affection from a complete stranger.

'Er, certainly. Thank you. I hope we will be friends,' I replied.

'More than that! And though I could be quite vexed at finding you so handsome, I will not be. For I own that I am as plain as a boiled pudding, and as the thought of attempting to vie with you is utterly ludicrous, I shall be content to merely admire.'

'You do not mind my presence here?' I asked diffidently.

'Mind? Of course not! Why should we?'

'You do not even seem surprised to find me here.'

'We are not. Oh, you are thinking that being stranded in Exeter as we were, we should not have heard. But we did, almost at once. Did we not, David?'

'Indeed! It is rare for such good news to travel so fast, but you will come to learn that here in Devon we have our own secret means of communication.'

'Like drums in a jungle?'

'Not quite. Possibly a servant here is related to a villager who knows a packman whose distant cousin works on the railway and who is also kin to an innkeeper who served ale to another servant who has a position in Exeter and who is acquainted with . . .'

'Pray stop. You lost me with the packman,' I said with a laugh.

'Where is Aunt Ruby?'

'She is here in the house, somewhere. But often I do not see her until the evening, apart from at mealtimes.'

'I expect we shall see her at dinner. And how is Matthew?' his half brother asked.

'Not too well, I am afraid. Nothing serious, though. He did have a nasty cold but recovered from that, but it has left him in a rather depressed state of mind.'

'I hope he will soon return to his usual self. May we call you Laura?'

'You know my name? How very well informed you are! Yes, please do.'

'Are you busy?' Celia enquired.

'No, not really,' I replied with truth.

'Then will you come up with me whilst I supervise the unpacking? We can then have tea, just you and I, and David can take himself off somewhere.'

'In actual fact, I must go to the stables. I want to see Cobweb's new foal.'

'That man and his horses!' Celia exclaimed when he had gone. 'He has been positively fretting to get back, just to see his favourite mare! But I must say, my chief desire was to set my eyes on you! And what a relief it is to find someone who is genteel and yet not an affected creature with her nose permanently in the air!'

'You thought I might be?'

'It was possible. As you are a protégée of Aunt Ruby's, it was more than probable you would be like her. For she can be almost snobbish, you know.'

'Can she?'

'Oh, yes. She regards me with a certain amount of disdain, for I am very ordinary, even though I am rich.'

'Well, I am also very ordinary, but I cannot claim your distinction, for I am poor.'

'Ah, but you are lovely, and that makes a difference. Come on, let us go up, and you can tell me what you think of some of my latest purchases, and I will show you my new ruby pendant. Papa gave it to me as a gift for

New Year, and it will make Aunt Ruby green with envy.'

'I have seen her wearing some very fine pieces,' I remarked.

'But nothing like this, I assure you.'

Even my inexperienced eye could tell at a glance that this gem was quite extraordinary, though its very size did not commend it to my taste. 'Vulgar and flashy,' Mama would have described it, but Celia seemed delighted with her acquisition if only as a means to vex her aunt-in-law, if there be such a form of relationship.

'Are you and she at odds with each other?' I was emboldened to ask.

'No, not exactly. But we are so polite to each other that it sometimes becomes a bit of a trial, especially when I am but freshly returned from visiting my family in Exeter. For there, although we can be dignified and formal when the occasion demands, in the normal way we are not! We laugh aloud, sometimes even shout! And when we are all together, we can be very noisy indeed! I have four brothers. Two are married with little ones of their own, and the other two still live with Mama and Papa when they are not away at college. Yes, after being amongst all of that boisterousness in Exeter, coming back here is just like returning to a morgue!'

'I admit that I, too, find it rather quiet.'

'But so far as I am concerned, it will be better now that you are here. And tell me, do you have a family? And though I know I risk being thought rude and inquisitive, do tell me, for I have been in an agony to know, for ages now. What is Matthew like?'

'You do not know?'

'No, I have never met him. Never even laid eyes on him! Well, not close to!'

'How strange,' I observed. 'Not ever?' whilst I was wondering what reply would be best.

'Well, once I did, but only at a distance. And such an aura of mystery surrounds him that I have sometimes wondered whether or not he is mentally unstable?'

'Why ever should that thought cross your mind?'

'Oh, the way he lives in such seclusion. And on the only occasion that I did see him, he was mounted upon a great black horse and riding it like the veriest madman, and his valet Virtue was in close attendance.'

'Are you sure it was he? Matthew, I mean?'

'It must have been. There are only three of them at the dower house. Matthew, Virtue, and the stableman who is almost a dwarf, as well as being quite mute. I am short-sighted, I know, but I am not blind! And the rider with Virtue could not have been Matthew's stableman, for he was much larger than that person!'

'Oh! Well, so far as I am aware, my husband does not venture from the dower house. Not these days, anyway. His health precludes it.'

'Do tell me what he is like!'

How vulgarly curious she was! But so must I be, for Celia was only asking the questions to which I too would dearly like to learn the answers.

'Well, he is taller than David. In fact, he is a

larger person altogether. And he is dark-haired with brown eyes, and his countenance, to my mind, is quite pleasing to look upon. His voice is deep, and he laughs often, for he has a very keen sense of humour.'

'Then he *is* sane?'

'Of course, he is. He is a highly intelligent and rational gentleman,' I declared emphatically. 'What an absurd question!'

'Yes, it is, and I beg your pardon for asking it,' Celia replied. 'For it has only just dawned on me that I have insulted you by implying you would marry an imbecile. Oh, what can I say? I am so sorry, so very, very sorry! But how did you happen to meet him?'

'Oh, Aunt Ruby and my Mama were friends long ago,' I lied. 'And I have known Matthew since I was a very small girl, and he and his aunt used to visit London during his vacations when he was at public school, and later when he was at Oxford.'

How very remiss of Aunt Ruby and of me not to have foreseen this quite natural inquisition and prepared a story to satisfy the curiousity of my sister-in-law, who would doubtless repeat my words to her husband. But I was rather pleased, for I thought I had acquitted myself well under the circumstances, though I knew I must inform Aunt Ruby of the gist of my tale so that our explanations would not contradict each other.

'David and I had only been married for six months when Sir Charles Merrick died, and then when Matthew returned home from abroad, he moved straight into the dower house. It had been

209

prepared for his coming, and though at the time I did think it quite strange behavior, I did not refine upon it too much for I had concerns of my own to occupy my mind. Being a new bride, as I was, my thoughts were chiefly centred on my own handsome husband.'

'Very right and proper,' I approved.

'But Matthew was in poor health even then! Does it not distress you to be wed to a recluse?'

'He is hardly that! And he is a very charming person, so I am perfectly happy. Our marriage is the fruit of a long-standing arrangement between our respective fathers, Sir Charles and my Papa.'

Dear Papa, please forgive me my lies!

'How quaint! Then tell me . . . '

Laughingly I rose to my feet.

'How many confidences we have exchanged in so short a time!' I exclaimed. 'But I must go, now. There are some letters I really must write today. I expect I shall see you at dinner.'

'Oh, yes. And keep a close eye on Aunt Ruby if you wish to be entertained, for I intend to wear my pendant.'

With a thankful sigh, I escaped and lost no time in seeking out that lady, to tell her of the questions that had been put and the answers given. And when I had done, she said, 'That was capital, Laura! Allow me to congratulate you, for you are becoming almost as good a liar as I am! Yes, you acquitted yourself admirably, at such short notice. And I apologize for not having some sort of tale prepared, for by not doing so I put you in an awkward position. But, there, who would guess you would be faced with such an interrogation at a first meeting? I do declare, what a middle-class young woman she is! For I think you will agree that no female of good breeding would be so *infra dig* as to probe and pry in such a manner.'

'I confess I should not have been quite so forthright,' I agreed.

'No lady would. Not unless she were questioning a servant, and even they have some rights to privacy. But as I say, the explanations you gave are credible and certainly good enough for her!'

'Perhaps, but what about David? He will surely know that a long-standing betrothal between Matthew and myself is nothing but a piece of fiction. And Celia is sure to tell him what I told her!'

'She may well do so, but even though he might have his doubts, he will not be certain. Matthew is eight years his senior and was mostly under my wing during David's boyhood. Only I ever went up to London and met Matthew there, so nobody can say with sureness that we never met you and your Mama at the same time. Also my brother Charles was not likely to discuss with his younger son what plans he had made for the elder! Why should he? And even if he had, that kind of information would be hardly likely to register upon the mind of a mere boy!'

'Well, we shall just have to hope that he is satisfied with my story,' I said.

'It is all the same if he is not. Oh, tarry a moment, Laura. Here is something I should like you to have.'

211

I took the proffered leather-covered jewelers' box and opened it to reveal a *parure de diamants*, a ring in the centre flanked by earbobs, surrounded by a necklet and underlined with a bracelet, and every piece made up of diamonds set in daisy shapes. One for the ring and another for each earbob, and the necklet and bracelet were each a single row of them. It was so dainty and exquisite that I caught my breath in sheer delight.

'Oh, how lovely! How pretty! And how valuable! No, Aunt Ruby, I could not possibly!'

'Huff puff, and tarradiddle! Of course you can, my dear! They are mine to give, and I have not worn them in years. They are much too young in style for me, now.'

'But they could be reset. They must be worth a great deal of money!'

'It would be a shame to break them up. They belonged to my mother. She was called Marguerite, and her father had them made for her especially as a compliment to her name. And now they are yours!'

'I am sorry but I cannot take them.' I was steadfast, though reluctant.

'You are Lady Merrick, child. You must have jewels. It is expected! David and Celia have never seen them, so you need not feel embarrassed to wear them whilst in their company, and it will please me if you will put them on this evening.'

'Why?'

'I hear we are to be favored with the sight of a new piece, bought by Celia's father for his commonplace daughter. And she thinks to dazzle us, me in particular! Yes, though she does not intend to, she can be quite amusing!'

'How did you know?'

'Her personal maid is quite friendly with yours, and as you are aware, Tansy is niece to my housekeeper.'

'Ah, servants' gossip,' I said.

'Which should never be discounted nor disdained. I acquire some very useful information by being interested in what my upper servants have to say.'

'So you wish me to put on these jewels this evening in an attempt to compete with Celia's finery?'

'You think such a desire unworthy of me? How right you are. It is! But I cannot resist making that young woman sit up and take notice. Have you seen this bauble of hers?'

'Yes. It is very large and must have cost a fortune,' I replied. 'And do you intend to wear anything extra special? For I know you own some extremely nice articles of jewellery.'

'You have only ever seen me wearing my favourite pieces, and though they are quite ornamental enough for my taste, they are certainly not exceptional. But the family jewels, you have yet to see! So too has Celia! They are all safely in my keeping and well tucked away, for as you know, nobody adorns themselves with aught but simple items whilst in the country! Not unless they are attending a ball or dining en *grande tenue*!'

'Of course,' I agreed, as if I were fully aware of this fact.

'Nobody who is anybody, I mean. How typical

213

of Celia to flaunt a monstrous ruby at a family dinner table! She has not an iota of taste, and the gew-gaw is probably flawed, anyway. She would never see it!'

'I think not. To me, it looked quite perfect,' I answered, reflecting privately that Celia had been right in her assumption that Aunt Ruby would be quite put out.

'You wait here for just a moment, Laura. I wish to show you something.' She disappeared into her bedchamber, closing the door firmly behind her. Then after a short interval she returned, bearing with her a small chest that enclosed a dozen or so drawers, each with an important-looking lock, and these she turned one by one with a diminutive key, worn with others suspended from the chatelaine belt at her waist.

'Now, Laura, these are what I really call jewels!'

Slowly she opened the bottom drawer and gave me ample time to gasp my admiration and awe before passing on to the one above it. Everything was there, every type of rare gem I had ever heard of, and some that I had not! There were bracelets and rings, necklets and pendants, tiaras and brooches, there was a ponderous gold cross set with enormous diamonds and looking as if it were medieval; and there were other costly ornaments so clumsy in design as to give the impression of great antiquity.

'This thumb ring was given to one of my ancestors by Henry V.' A huge sapphire winked its blue fire at me. 'And this diamond tucker belonged once to Dame Alise. Not for long though, for she

214

came to a sudden end.' Aunt Ruby held up an article shaped rather like a baby's bib and fashioned from hundreds of tiny sparkling diamonds made up in an open trellis pattern. 'She caught the eye of Henry VIII when he was down this way inspecting the *Mary Rose* at Plymouth. The affair was only of brief duration, however, and when it was over, she was left with two mementoes: this, and a steadily increasing waistline! And though her husband had not dared to protest when the monarch was still nearby and had received a knighthood for his complaisance, he wreaked his vengeance upon his erring wife once King Hal had returned to London. He kept the knighthood and the diamonds, but her he 'put to cliff'! A pleasant lot we Merricks, were we not?'

'What do you mean? What did he do?'

'He pushed Dame Alise over the cliffs, to fall upon the rocks below and either be dashed to pieces or drowned. It mattered not. That was the usual way to dispose of living creatures, animals or people, in those days.'

'Another local custom?'

'Yes, you might say that. Of course, those items and others like them are never worn. They are kept as part of the family history and purely for sentimental reasons. Actually, very few of these pieces have been seen for many years. David's mother was the last person to adorn herself with anything contained within this jewel chest, and one or two of the articles she tried to take with her after my brother's death, when she left here to marry Lord Rowan. Ah, but I was ready for that

215

and soon put a stop to her attempt to pilfer.'

'And you never wear any of these things?'

'In the ordinary way, I have no desire to, but this evening I think I shall put on this emerald set. What do you think? Will it be in good company with Celia's ruby?'

'Well, if the object is to outshine her, you will certainly achieve that! For I should imagine those emeralds would almost vie with the crown jewels!' She gave a crow of pleasure.

'You may be right. You have a discerning eye, Laura. Of course, we Merricks have quite a start on people like Celia and her folk. For we have been amassing our collection for nearly seven hundred years! So take your little diamond daisies with a clear conscience. You are depriving nobody, certainly not the family, and wear them if only to please me!'

'Thank you, but I still do not think I should.'

Sharply she clapped her hands.

'Get along with you, Laura, and take your baubles with you. Be off, for I am a very busy woman. And so, be gone!'

I chose my crimson velvet dinner gown to complement this new finery, but the necklet and bracelet were the only items I wore; for the earbobs were designed for pierced ears, which mine were not, and the betrothal ring on my finger I thought quite sufficient ornament for my hands. And after Tansy had dressed my hair, helped me into my gown, and fastened my jewels, I dismissed her and stood admiring my reflection in the pier glass. And what I saw, I liked well!

Penniless Laura, so accustomed to wearing shabby, ill-fitting clothes made from the cheapest materials, and now gowned in costly fabric and bedecked with diamonds! Oh, if only Mama and Tiffany could see me now! I could well imagine their reaction, for though my sister would exclaim her admiration unreservedly, my mother would appraise me with critical eye before pronouncing coolly, 'Yes, my dear, you really do look quite nice.' But my real desire was for the approbation of another person. Matthew! I wanted him to see me as I looked now, not with tumbled hair and a face probably contorted by embarrassment, but elegant, dignified, and confident, with my lovely dress softly draping my body, my tresses freshly coifed, and myself all aglitter with precious stones. If he had thought me lovely before, he would certainly do so if he saw me now! Would he see me? Would he send for me this evening? He might. He had probably heard of David and Celia's return, and it was possible that he would wish to learn any news they had brought with them from Exeter. For, yes, ridiculous as I admitted it to be, I wanted to be summoned once more to the dower house! And that I could be playing with fire, if and when I went, did not seem to be a deterrent. No, on the contrary, I had to confess to myself that it was an added attraction!

Aunt Ruby was attired in bronze hued brocade when next I saw her, and though to my mind she looked a trifle overloaded with emeralds, they were set off very well by the shade of her gown even though there were too many of them: twin bracelets, the necklace, a brooch, pendant earrings, and two finger rings. But even she must have become conscious of the bizarre effect created by this plenitude of gems, for she had left the matching tiara behind in its case. Yes, she did rather resemble a Christmas tree in its full splendor of brilliant, gaudy trinkets. Celia was the last person to join the company before we went in to dinner. Perhaps she was desirous of making an entrance, and if so, she succeeded, for all eyes were upon her as she approached us.

'Ah, my dear, how very nice it is to have you and David returned to Merrick's Mount again.' Aunt Ruby cooed. 'Surely that is not your wedding gown you are wearing, is it? Is it? For you look positively bridal!'

'I wish it were, for if it were, it would mean I had not put on any more flesh during the last three years. Yes, I much doubt that I could still get it to fasten around me,' Celia replied quite cheerfully.

'Well, the one you are wearing looks to be rather tight! Are you quite comfortable in it?' Aunt Ruby was all concern.

'Yes, thank you.'

Evidently Celia had selected her gown for the same reason that I had put on mine, to show off her newly acquired jewel; and I must declare it did look most effective as contrast, the glow of the eye-catching ruby against the sheen of pure white satin. But tight white satin was not the happiest of choices for a young woman who is decidedly plump!

'We are all very grand tonight,' Celia broke the following silence, all the while staring fixedly at

Aunt Ruby's emeralds.

'Yes, I thought it would be rather nice to dress up for a change. And I have ordered your favorite dishes for dinner, thinking we would have a little welcome-home party, just on our own.'

'That was a very kind thought, Aunt Ruby,' David said.

'Think nothing of it, dear boy. And what a very pretty necklet you have on, Celia. Is it part of a set?' Thereby she dismissed, with a few well chosen words, any high esteem with which Celia might have regarded the pendant.

'No. Papa gave it to me just as it was.'

'Ah! Then I should imagine he intends to follow it with others, at later dates. Perhaps when happy events take place? That would be a very pretty conceit.'

How skilfully Aunt Ruby was baiting her, not only dismissing the gem as being of no account, but also reminding Celia that so far no 'happy event' had occurred. And that it should I later learned was Celia's secret hope, dearest wish, and utter frustration that so far, it had not. I felt quite sorry for my new half sister-in-law, even though I realized that Aunt Ruby was merely toying with her in playful manner, as a kitten would dab at a ball of wool with its soft paws. For I also suspected that she was just as capable of unsheathing the claws of a full grown shecat, and anyone who was the recipient of their attentions would best have a care for their safety. And during the conversation at the dinner table, I wondered if David had been as unaware of his wife's discomfiture as he had

219

seemed to be, or whether he was now indulging in a game of tit for tat, for he said quite casually, 'Oh bye the bye, I ran into Seth Quillian whilst I was in Exeter. I did not recognize him at first, for it is a considerable time since last I saw him, and he has aged considerably. But he made himself known to me, asked after you and Matthew, and told me he probably would call. Has he?'

'No, he has not!' Aunt Ruby's voice did not encourage further probing.

However, David continued unconcernedly, 'Oh, then I expect he will. Of course they were much older than I, but I can recall that he and Matthew were very close at one time, and now that the latter's health seems to be improving somewhat, I am sure he will be delighted to talk over old times with Seth.'

'And what gives you the impression that Matthew's health has improved?' Aunt Ruby asked frostily.

'Why, his marriage to Laura of course! Nobody at death's door enters into the state of matrimony, now do they? And I think that Matthew has immured himself in that gloomy old house for so long that he is now reluctant to leave it. So we shall have to set about prising him out of it, and Seth says he will be pleased to help in any way he can! And that also he would be honored to meet Matthew's new lady wife!'

'What does he know of that?'

'My half brother's wedding? Well, as you and he set about it in such a sly way, for an instance waiting until Celia and I were absent and then making no formal announcement, you can hardly wonder that when the secret became known, as it very shortly did, it became the *on dit* of Exeter, until Lady Shawcross eloped with her footman!'

'Has she? Really? I always knew that Julia Shawcross had the worst possible taste!' Aunt Ruby chuckled, and I sensed her mood had abruptly changed for the better. But why? She had seemed most displeased when David had mentioned the name of Seth Quillian, and I was fully aware that, if this man should decide to call upon Matthew, problems might arise. Or would they? For I too had wondered whether Matthew's illness were more psychological than physical, so perhaps a visit from his old friend would inspire him to bestir himself. And though our marriage had indeed been conducted in a most extraordinary way, one could even call it underhanded, Aunt Ruby did not seem in the least put out that it was now common knowledge. Was it that? Or was it the fall from grace of the unknown Julia Shawcross that had put her in such good humour again? And was this what I could now expect? Challenges being subtly issued every day, accepted and returned. Undercurrents, crosstalk, and constant battle of wits? And wills? And was my role to be the bone over which these skirmishes would be fought? Must I ally myself with one side or the other? To please Aunt Ruby, must I live in enmity with David and Celia, and had Celia been so friendly towards me expressly to woo me away from Aunt Ruby's influence? And had this lady given me the diamonds I now wore to ascertain

221

that Celia did not succeed in this endeavor? If all this were not a figment of my imagination, I could envisage that the coming days, weeks, months would find me in a completely unenviable position, pulled one way, tugged the other, and closely watched by all!

The lengthy meal progressed, ended, and as we adjourned to the drawing room, where tea would presently be served, the minutes passed. And as they added themselves into hours, I knew that once again my presence would not be sought by the occupant of the dower house.

7

Every morning now saw me up betimes, and I was always the first person to enter the breakfast parlor. Not because my body craved sustenance, but because my mind did; I was hungry for news. What was happening to my family? How were they faring in far away London? There must surely be quite an accumulation of mail, and there was now no reason why it should not be delivered. Indeed, it was, for on most days there were letters for Aunt Ruby and David, and sometimes there was one for Celia, but there were never any for me!

'Do not fret, Laura. Most of the missives beside my plate are from local people, and some roads may still be in a sorry state. And do not forget, any that you may expect have much farther to travel,' Aunt

Ruby said in an attempt to cheer me.

'But letters posted in London would come by train as far as Exeter!' I objected. 'And there is no difficulty to be overcome, so far as transport is concerned, from there to here!'

'True, true. Did you not tell me your people were thinking of making a change of residence, though?'

'Yes, I did, and that is what worries me. For if they have already moved, I have no idea where they may be!'

'I do not think that is very likely. To remove house is not the work of a day, you know! So many things must be arranged first. And surely, if they had accomplished all with the speed of lightning, they would have left a forwarding address?'

'Of course. Yes. How silly of me,' I agreed.

'Then if I were you, I should again write to your mother. And I suggest you tell her that although you are fully aware that she is extremely busy, nonetheless you are anxious as you have heard no word from her. And that even just a short note would put your mind at rest.'

'Yes, I shall do that. Directly after breakfast, I will set pen to paper.'

'Then it will catch the midday collection, for though I also have letters to write, mine will not be ready until this afternoon. But I shall send one of the footmen to the village especially, just with yours. Give it to me when it is written, and I shall speed it on its way.'

'Thank you. You are very kind.'

When this was done, Celia sought me out,

inviting me to take a stroll with her.

'Now that will give me the greatest pleasure,' I replied. 'I have hardly seen the grounds here, so perhaps you will show them to me?'

The morning was dank, with dripping trees and a slightly misty atmosphere. The lawns and bare flowerbeds were sodden, but we kept to the gravel paths where walking was not too uncomfortable. Our steps eventually led us to the terrace Aunt Ruby had shown me on my first day at Merrick's Mount, and despite the mist, we could — or at least I could — see quite a long way, but we did not linger there long as the prospect that lay before us was too dismal to merit admiration.

'Where is David?' I asked.

'Probably at the stables. Have you been there yet?'

'No. Actually I am not too knowledgeable when it comes to horses or anything of that nature.'

'Neither am I, but as we have nothing better to do, let us go and take a peek at David's pride and joy.'

'The new foal?'

'Yes. I expect it is quite pretty, for all creatures are when they are tiny, even though some may grow into the most unattractive things later on.'

But if the foal grew up to resemble its mother, it would indeed be a handsome animal. The mare was dapple-gray with a flowing white mane and tail, and she nosed her baby gently as, on ridiculously long legs, it took faltering steps about the sweet-smelling stall carpeted with fresh straw. Yes, David was there, discussing the finer points of Cobweb and what might be expected from her offspring, though as soon as he saw us he welcomed us warmly.

'There! What do you think, ladies? Is he not a rare beauty?'

'Is it a he?'

'Yes, just what I hoped for. Ah, he will make me the envy of the county when he is grown! I intend to leave him entire, you know.'

'I beg your pardon?'

'Never mind. It is of no consequence to anyone but himself and me. Have you seen the rest of the horses, Laura?'

'No. This is my first visit to the stables.'

'Then come with me, and we shall select a mount for you for when the weather improves sufficiently to make riding pleasant.'

'I must learn first, sir. For the saddle and I are not even on nodding terms,' I replied.

'That we shall soon put to rights. And the sight of you rapidly becoming a horsewoman *par excellence* may inspire my dear wife to follow your example.'

'I think not,' Celia swiftly rejoined. 'I will take the reins of a neat little gig or trap at any time, but with that accomplishment I am more than content.'

She and I were in most amicable mood as he left the stables, and our path led us past the kennels.

'Do you know, I have never heard the bark of a dog since I came here,' I said. 'Their keepers keep them remarkably quiet, do they not? Shall we go in and see what is inside? I like dogs!'

'I do, too, but the kennels do not house any

dogs. They are empty.'

'Oh? Then it is not surprising they are so quiet.'

'Did you own a dog in London?'

'No. My late uncle, with whom I lived, did not care for them.'

'I was brought up with them when I was a girl. Pets, I mean. Papa still has two terriers at home.'

'Why do you not have one of your own, here? Actually it is strange that a house the size of this does not keep at least one.'

'Well, I did say once that I should not dislike to have a spaniel, but though the idea was not exactly vetoed, it was not encouraged either, so I did not persevere. Does Matthew own a canine companion?'

'Not to my knowledge, for I have never seen a dog at the dower house.'

'Then he cannot, for you would surely be aware of it if he had!'

In leisurely fashion we progressed back to the house, and as we went I let Celia chatter on unheeded, for my mind was now occupied with something else. Yes, another hurdle had presented itself, and if I were not to be utterly confounded, I must find a way of taking it smoothly. For it would certainly not be long before Celia's inquisitiveness would lead her to ask me when it was that I saw my husband! When a man is sick, no matter how many servants and nurses he has about him, if he is married, it would be extremely strange if his spouse did not venture near enough to his bedside to see how he did! So as I was no longer summoned to the dower house, I must resort to subterfuge. I must go into hiding for part of each day, pretending that during these times I had been to call upon Matthew. This suggestion I put to Aunt Ruby, when next I had the opportunity of a private talk with her.

'Yes, Laura, you have hit upon a neat solution which will solve the problem,' she said. 'Actually, the presence of the dilemma had also occurred to me, and I did intend to speak to you about it. And I have true cause to congratulate myself, for I chose better than I knew when I decided that you should become Lady Merrick. Your common sense and agility of mind does you great credit!'

'Thank you, but I fear it could also be described as deceitfulness,' I answered.

'Diplomacy, child. That is the word we will use. And surely, to absent yourself from the company of Celia for a short while every day is worth the exertion of telling a little white lie? For do you not find her prying questions and general inanities rather wearing?'

'Well, er.'

'And you do not have to keep to your chambers whilst you are presumed to be at the dower house. When the days are fine, you can always slip outside discreetly and go walking.'

Well, there was nothing wrong in either keeping to my chambers or going for solitary walks, but the thought came to me after this conversation with Aunt Ruby: Why did I need to do one or the other? Why should I not simply tell Celia and David the truth? That I was only a paid companion,

Lady Merrick by name but not Matthew's wife in fact? And it had not even entered my mind to do so! I was rapidly becoming as devious as was Aunt Ruby, but I much doubted that my brain could ever match hers for reasoning. For though she seemed quite pleased that I had entered into the spirit of her plotting, I was very far from understanding it! For my marriage to her elder nephew had been conducted with the greatest secrecy, but now that she had learned it was a secret no longer; indeed, that it had become common knowledge almost immediately, she seemed to be delighted!

And now that spring was approaching, I adopted my new routine. After luncheon, I would declare it was time for me to visit my husband, and though on one or two occasions Celia expressed a willingness, nay an eagerness, to accompany me and be introduced to Matthew, my gentle albeit steady refusals and the quelling stares of Aunt Ruby at last caused her to desist. And even though this may sound unsociable, I must confess I was glad to be relieved of her presence for some part of the day, for apart from these interludes she seemed to cling to me like a limpet!

I found it quite a simple matter to leave Merrick's Mount unobserved, for as Celia's and David's rooms were in the main part of the house and I was the sole occupant of the west wing, I could descend the stairs at the far end of this and be entering the covered walk in less time than it takes to tell. I always went that way but I would leave the walk when it became shielded by the encompassing trees, either just walking amongst them or returning in a half circle to the cliff tops a little further along the coastline, although I heeded Aunt Ruby's words well, never going too near the edge.

'Whole stretches of the cliff face have been known to fall, my dear. And especially after this recent bad weather, the slightest weight put upon the cliff edge can cause it to crumble completely, with no warning whatsoever!'

Then one day I walked a greater distance than I had before. Spring was well upon us, but my mind was troubled, for still I had received no news from my family. My steps led me on unaware, until I stood gazing down at what once must have been a busy landing stage for the now disused quarries, and beyond, I could just glimpse the tops of some chimneys. The old manor house! I had never before been so close to it, and though Aunt Ruby had told me that to enter it might well be unsafe, at least I could view it from the outside. A glance at my fobwatch informed me I had time enough, for nobody would expect me to return to Merrick's Mount at an exact hour, so I started to negotiate the steep descent that lay between me and my goal. It stood there, empty and forlorn, and as I stared upon the dilapitated dwelling, I knew that I wanted it! It was of the same period though larger in size than I guessed the dower house to be (for that I had never seen by the light of day, always avoiding it when I took my afternoon walks, lest I should be seen from its windows and thought to be spying on the occupant). But I had become conscious of the fact that the dower house, like this one that lay before me, was commonly known as a 'magpie house,' with white plaster walls supported by a timber frame, usually of oak. These I gazed at were black with age, and some of them were set into an intricate pattern, but the plaster between them was weathered to a dirty grey colour. It was customary for the roof of this type of house to be of red tile, but these roofing tiles were a muted green, and gaping holes showed where they had been allowed to fall away and had never been replaced. The windows were small and latticed, and though seemingly sound, were thick with the grime of ages, and the shallow steps leading up to the great iron-studded main door with its massive hinges, were broken and grass-grown. But as if to compensate for the careless neglect of man, Mother Nature, with lavish hand, had starred these same steps with the sweet freshness of primroses!

Oh, how Matthew would delight to see them. There they were, unobserved and unadmired by anybody but me, gleaming palely in their loveliness. The very epitome of spring! And why should he not see them? What was to prevent me from gathering a posy of them, and (daring greatly) leaving them upon the steps of the dower house? His valet would surely find them and carry them up, and Matthew would know from whose hand they had come. For who but a simpleton like me would do anything so nonsensical? And, an underlying thought, such an action might remind him of my existence, and he would send for me once again! A minute or two of undignified scrambling down the slope saw me in what remained of the garden, and just a few more minutes passed before I was ascending the steps.

And then I was sharply arrested by the sound of a man's voice, 'Please, ma'am, do not enter the house! Part of the flooring is not to be trusted.'

I whirled about to face the direction from which the warning came and perceived a gentleman standing a dozen or so paces from me, the very same gentleman whom Aunt Ruby had ignored, despite his mannerly behavior outside Exeter Station, on the day I had arrived. But now he was clad in ordinary attire, whereas I recalled the last time I saw him he had been wearing naval uniform.

'Pray forgive me for startling you so, but you seemed so engrossed with the old house that I did not wish to disturb you. But when I saw you were about to go inside, I knew I must.'

'There is nothing to forgive, for you were doing me what you thought was a service. Though I did not intend to do anything but gather some of these lovely flowers,' I replied.

'Oh! Then I alarmed you to no purpose!' He sounded rueful. 'I beg your pardon, ma'am, and I shall take myself off without delay and leave you in peace.'

'No, please! You are not disturbing me, but who are you?'

'Seth Quillian at your service, ma'am. An erstwhile mariner, captain of his ship, but now retired from the high seas and intending to lead the rest of his life in contemplation and utmost ease.'

'Ah, you are Matthew's old friend!' I exclaimed. 'I am delighted to meet you. I am his wife, you know.'

'I did not know, though I did wonder. There

have been rumours but, as you are doubtless aware, rumour can be a lying jade. But when I saw you with Miss Merrick a little while ago, and then heard the unlikely news that Matthew had married, I did not know whether to give credence to the tale or not.'

'Then you need be in doubt no longer, Captain Quillian,' I said with a smile. 'In actual fact, it is for Matthew that I intend to pick these primroses.'

'What a fortunate fellow he is! So for some time I have pitied him quite needlessly, I can see that now. So his malady is not what was at first feared?'

'I do not take your meaning, sir.'

'Oh, er. Well, um. I do not mean anything in particular, only that the state of his health has given his friends cause for concern for some while, but now it appears he is not so poorly as was at first feared,' he answered lamely.

'Evidently not, sir. And what are you doing here?'

'Conjuring up old memories. This place was a favorite haunt for Matthew and me when we were lads. Forbidden, of course, and all the more attractive for that reason. I wonder if he would feel well enough to receive a visit from me? For I should dearly like to see him and talk over old times!'

'I do not know.' I felt myself color with embarrassment. 'Perhaps if you were to write, first?'

'I have. Twice. And have received no reply.'

'Now that I cannot understand. I shall ask him about it.'

'And will you give him my felicitations on his astounding good fortune in winning such a kind and lovely bride?'

'You are too kind, Captain Quillian. Yes, I shall tell him of our meeting and ask him to reply to your letters. He has your address?'

'Yes, indeed. And will you also be gracious enough to ask him to cast his mind back through the years? To try and recall our boyhood plans? That we should reopen the quarries?'

'Oh, I know about those! He has told me. Indeed, Matthew often speaks of you!'

'He does? Ah, now that is a heartwarming thought.'

'Well, I must start on my return journey now, before dusk falls.'

'Your flowers, Lady Merrick!'

'I will gather them on another day. It is too late now.'

'Oh dear, I have delayed you.'

'It does not matter in the slightest, and it gave me great pleasure to make your acquaintance, sir.'

'May I walk with you? Escort you back to Merrick's Mount?'

'No, I thank you.'

'Then at least allow me to aid you back up that difficult slope.'

Smilingly I nodded, for if I had refused it was quite likely that he would have remained to watch me ascend it, and such an exercise could not permit any great degree of graceful deportment. So when, though a trifle breathless but with my dignity still intact, I stood upon the cliff tops once again, I extended my hand and said, 'Thank you, Captain Quillian. That was most kind of you, and I shall look forward to meeting you again at some time in the future.'

'Good day, Lady Merrick, and pray take care upon your walk homewards.'

Daylight was fading quickly, and I knew I must hurry if I were to reach Merrick's Mount before darkness fell upon the land. There was no pathway along the top of the cliffs, but the coarse grass was quite short and springy underfoot, making my walk pleasant and easy. As I stepped out briskly, my mind fully occupied with the surprising encounter with Captain Quillian, I decided I liked him and that it was quite incomprehensible to me and reflected no credit on them that he was being treated so shabbily by the Merricks. Matthew was ignoring his letters, and with my own eyes, I had seen Aunt Ruby look straight through him as if he did not exist in Exeter. Yet he spoke of them in the friendliest of terms, of Matthew at least, but it seemed he was unaware that Matthew did not reside at Merrick's Mount, for he surely assumed I would live with my new husband and had offered to escort me back to there and had made no mention of the dower house! But how could I tell Matthew of my meeting with his boyhood friend, when I did not see him? And why did I not see him? For weeks now, my presence had not been desired at the dower house. Not since that night . . .

I had felt quite cheerful when I left Seth Quillian, but now the desolate world through which I trod seemed to enter my inner being. All was grey!

The skies above were heavy with cloud, and in the twilight, the very turf upon which I walked took on the same dismal hue. I could hear the soughing of the waves on the pebble beach far below, and the raucous cries of the gulls circling overhead grated on my nerves. And then some instinct older than time itself told me I was not alone! Someone, somewhere, was watching me! A prickling of my scalp warned me of danger, but from whence it would come I knew not. Behind me? But only Seth Quillian could possibly be behind me, and I had no fear of him. And ahead of me lay the trees through which I had intended to walk and thus reach the mansion. Dare I? But if I did not I should be very late, and questions might be asked. Ah, but to make up the time I would lose if I skirted the wood, I could run! And as I took to my heels the knowledge came to me that I was no heroine, for the gained minutes themselves seemed of far less importance than the fact that I might — though it was only a might — be running for my life!

It was several days before I plucked up sufficient courage to tell Aunt Ruby of my meeting with Matthew's friend, for I guessed she would not be overjoyed to hear of it.

'And pray, what were you doing there? I believe I told you it was most unwise to venture near the place?'

'But I did not enter and had no such intention. The captain seconded your warning, for he too told me it was unsafe.'

'How very kind of him, but the reason for him

being there also quite escapes me.'

'He told me that he and Matthew used to play there.'

'Well, even if he were not trespassing then, he certainly is now! Impudent fellow!'

'He wants to see Matthew,' I said. 'He was almost insistent.'

'What right has he to be insistent? He is an interfering, inquisitive individual. I never cared for him! Did you not tell him that to visit my nephew was completely out of the question?'

'I did not know what to say. He seemed to think that if Matthew were strong enough to marry, he would be strong enough to receive callers. And I also believe he infers that Matthew lives here and not at the dower house.'

'It is no business of his where Matthew chooses to live. I hope you gave him a sharp setdown?'

'To be truthful, I did not know what to do. And do you not think a visit from Captain Quillian might help Matthew shake off this depression that seems to be affecting him so deeply?'

'No, I do not! I think only harm could come of it, and if, as you say, Matthew has ignored the man's letters, then he cannot wish to see him.'

'But did he receive them? For surely they would be addressed to this house?'

'And do you not think they would reach him if that were the case?'

'Of course, they would. How stupid of me!'

'If I were you I should forget the whole incident, and also I would stay well away from that derelict ruin.'

'Yes, I intend to,' I agreed, for after my fright of the evening when my visit there had taken place, any desire to return to the old manor house had quite left me, at least until such time as the days lengthened sufficiently to enable me to walk there and back again while the sun still shone. Then I might go there occasionally, just to see what was by then flourishing in its long-neglected garden.

But whether or not Matthew received his mail became of far less concern to me than the fact that I did not receive any myself, for still I heard no word from Mama and Tiffany. So eventually I made a tentative suggestion that I should make a journey up to London, to learn for my own peace of mind what was happening.

'I could travel up one day and return the next,' I said. 'For I must confess, I am terribly worried about them.'

'All of them? Your aunt, too? My dear child, what could possibly have happened to all three of them to prevent them from writing? They could not all have been smitten by some dire illness! And if, as you suspect, they have moved house, how would you set about looking for them in such a short space of time? And though this may sound quite heartless, especially as you are so worried about your kinfolk, the terms of your contract clearly state that you must reside here at Merrick's Mount permanently, during your husband's lifetime! So therefore you cannot go trotting up to London, possibly to stay there for an unspecified length of time, just when the fancy takes you! It was with such an eventuality as this in mind that I did initially say I preferred to engage a young lady with no near relatives!'

'Yes, you are quite right. In what you say, and also that you feel I might think you are heartless to say it,' I answered shortly.

'Now, my dear, do not imagine I find any pleasure in baulking you of your desire. And there is a far simpler way to solve this problem of yours. You are not without means and are therefore in a position to hire somebody to make enquiries on your behalf. I suggest you write to Mr Peppercorn. Tell him of your concern and instruct him to seek out your family!'

'Aunt Ruby, if I knew you better, I should be tempted to hug you!' I declared.

'If you knew me better, I very much doubt it,' she laughed. 'Now get busy, my dear. Pen your letter without delay and then let us see a smile upon your face once more.'

So again I resigned myself to being patient, for it would be foolish to expect a reply from the solicitor for at least a week or maybe two, apart from an acknowledgement of my request, and as time passed, it began to dawn on me that I was not to get even that. And in the meantime, each passing day presented fresh, though minor irritations, the chief of which was Celia! At our first meeting, she had told me of her long-standing desire to have a sister, and now that she thought she had one, she seemed determined to make up for the length of time that she had been without! From breakfast onward, I was bombarded with her confidences, all trivial. She sought my opinion on matters of dress, coiffures, what colors to set into some seemingly interminable piece of embroidery, and, this decided, where to set them. She wanted to know about every moment of my history, and also that of my kinfolk, where I had been and what I had done prior to coming to Merrick's Mount. She inspected me carefully every time she saw me afresh; she admired my hairstyles, my hair itself, my gowns, my slippers. Every article of apparel I put on received some comment of her approval. And daily she paid particular attention to my waistline! Indeed, once she was brazen enough to say, albeit in gushing manner as though she were embarrassed, 'Other girls of my acquaintance tell their sisters everything, simply everything! And I can quite see why, for it is so comforting to have a real confidante. Someone with whom you can share your secrets, and knowing that you are so honored as to be told theirs!'

'But there is always a small degree of reservation, even amongst the closest people,' I replied. 'For I would not bare my very soul to Tiffany. Not entirely. And I should think that to place such a burden upon her would be quite unfair!'

'Ah, but you have told me of the age difference between the two of you. She is so young, little more than a child. But you and I are women. Married ladies! Wives, but alas not yet mothers. Tell me Laura, do you too long to hold a baby in your arms? As much as I do?'

'I have no idea. How can I measure the extent of your feelings regarding such a matter?' I hedged, though suddenly wary.

'Surely you can imagine! You must be able to.

And apart from the actual joy that motherhood in itself brings, to be able to whisper to one's dear husband that a little stranger is on the way must be one of the most precious moments of one's whole married life!'

'I daresay. Provided of course that he shares one's enthusiasm for parenthood.'

'What man does not? Every man is vain enough to wish to father an exact replica of himself, so that his image may be perpetuated throughout eternity.'

'You surprise me, Celia. I had no idea you were capable of such profound reasoning.'

'I am not quite addlepated, you know. And I also know it is David's dearest wish, to father a son. The more the merrier, so far as he is concerned.'

'What a typically masculine attitude! For he does not have to bear and birth them!'

'He is well aware that I should only find happiness in doing both. And fashioned as I am, it should not be too much of a hardship for me. But you, Laura, are a trifle narrower at the hip than I am.'

'Er, yes. That is true.'

'And do you not think Matthew would rejoice to learn he was to have an heir?'

'So far as I know, he already has one. Your husband David!'

'Laura, do not tease. I am being serious. A child of his own loins, flesh of his flesh, a son of his own making!'

'Celia, you sound positively biblical!' I exclaimed. 'And how could he have a son that was not of his own making?' Then I bethought me of Aunt Ruby's half-forgotten suggestion that we should adopt one.

'Well, he is not in the best of health, I know. But just how poorly is he? Does it prevent him from . . . ? Can he . . . ? You know!'

With averted gaze, she awaited my reply, which consisted of my saying with an air of utter finality, 'Let this be understood, now and for all time. There are some things I do not choose to discuss! Amongst them are those of a particularly private and delicate nature! Such matters are strictly between my husband and myself, and possibly my physician. But certainly nobody else!'

'I beg your pardon, Laura. I did not mean to offend.'

'I am not offended. I am merely amazed that you should have broached such a purely personal subject. And now pray, let us speak of something more fitted to genteel conversation.'

So Aunt Ruby had been correct in her assessment of David's and Celia's reaction to my becoming Lady Merrick, and I guessed by her attitude and the devious way in which she had tried to cozen me into confiding in her that Celia had been set the task by her husband. Of course, she too would wish to know how matters stood, for it concerned her just as closely as it would any child she might have. But I did not think that even she would have had the temerity to ask me outright, if it were not for some very insistent prompting. Well, once again I had defended my invidious position with some credit, as Aunt Ruby told me when I repeated the gist of this inquisition to her later in the day.

'So they are becoming worried, are they?' she chuckled. 'Well done, my dear! You are keeping them guessing nicely!'

'But what is the point? And I must confess that I find it rather a strain, being constantly on my guard as I am. Why do I not just tell them the truth?'

'Perhaps, because it amuses me that you should not. But I had no idea Celia was making such a nuisance of herself. The trouble with that young woman is she has nothing better to do.'

'Well, there is not a great deal to do! There is one thing that might keep her occupied though, if you would allow it.'

'And what might that be?'

'A dog. She has expressed a desire for one, and if she could have a puppy, it might serve to take her mind off me!'

'There has not been a dog in this house for several years,' Aunt Ruby replied slowly.

'I have noticed that. Surely country houses of this size usually keep at least one, unless somebody has a particular aversion to them,' I said.

'Actually, Laura, you have touched upon rather a sore point.'

'You do not care for the creatures?'

'On the contrary, but one can care too much. And that makes a person vulnerable.'

'In what way?'

'I will tell you of an instance. It is not a pretty story, but it is only right you should know, and it will perhaps explain my attitude. Now I am not a sentimental person, but I do dislike intensely needless cruelty. Especially toward children and animals! All of our family have the same feelings upon that score, that is all of us except one! David! He was the kind of child who took delight in pulling the legs off living spiders. He liked to stick pins in butterflies and watch them writhe in agony. To cut open a frog whilst it was still alive, just to see what was inside it.'

'How revolting! How hateful small boys can be!'

'Not all of them. Matthew was just as different when he was little. He cried bitter tears once when a mouse was caught and done to death with a swift blow. He would hold converse with the worms in the gardens, and as he grew older he was always rescuing something, a bird with a broken wing, an injured otter, or a motherless leveret. And he would nurse them back to health and rear the helpless little ones, and then he would release them to live their lives in their true environment in the open countryside.'

'How delightful! I do not wonder that you took such joy in him!'

'Do you remember me telling you how he and his father, my brother Charles, had a disagreement and Matthew was packed off to the other side of the world?'

'Indeed, I do.'

'Well, that was rather an understatement, and I will now tell you all. Matthew's education was almost finished. He was to return to Oxford for just one more term, and then he would be free to

243

take up a career. And he wanted that career to be here! He wanted to reopen the quarries. He wanted to be put in charge of everything to do with them, and he was full of plans and ideas for making them thrive. And I am certain he would have done so, if he had been allowed.'

'But the answer was 'no'?'

'It was. But Matthew persisted until eventually his father lost his temper, and then there was a full scale quarrel.'

'And that is why he was sent abroad?'

'Partly, but chiefly for another reason. My brother owned a pet dog. A beagle. Oh, there was a whole pack of them in the kennels, but this one was different from the others in that he was a housedog, regarded almost as a member of the family, especially by my brother. At the time of which I speak, the creature was ageing, though still healthy. Herbert, we called him. Ridiculous, was it not? And he would follow Charles wherever he went about the house and farther afield too if he were permitted. Or he would sit with his head resting upon my brother's knee, gazing up into his face with his canine eyes filled with adoration.'

'He sounds nice. I like dogs!' I said.

'Well, there was this quarrel, and Matthew was sent to his rooms, and then later we all retired for the night. But in the morning, poor Herbert was found hanging by his neck from one of the wrought-iron bannisters that edge the staircase. He was quite dead, and I fear he must have suffered, for his face was so contorted it was pitiful to see!'

'Oh, how could anybody do such a thing? It is positively nauseating!'

'And Matthew was blamed! In vain he declared his innocence, and I knew he was telling the truth, for I also knew he was quite incapable of such an action!'

'Your brother believed Matthew had done it to spite him?'

'Exactly, and nothing anyone could say would make him think otherwise. In actual fact though, nobody but Matthew and myself did say anything. And there in the background was David, smirking complacently when he thought nobody was looking.'

'But why should he? He could not then have been very old, himself.'

'Old enough. To my mind he was never really young! He was always a sly, calculating child, and he was thirteen when this event took place, with almost the stature of a man. So physically, he was quite strong enough.'

'So that is why there is this ill-feeling between you?'

'It stems from that. And now in time, he will inherit, for if it were not for his dastardly act of so long ago, Matthew would never have been sent to the Sandwich Islands and would not then have contracted the ailment from which he now suffers and which will bring an untimely end to his dear life.'

'Oh how sad. How very, very sad! And so there are no hounds kept here now, at all?'

'No. Matthew sailed, and it was not long afterwards that my brother sold the whole pack

245

to a knowledgeable friend of his. He almost gave them away.'

'I can quite understand why.'

'And so be warned. Never trust David, and if you can possibly avoid it, never put yourself in a position where he can strike at you through some creature that you love!'

Thenceforth I began to view David with fresh, more observant eyes. But though I did notice one or two things about him I did not quite like, they were trivial and could, if one wished, be accounted for fairly easily. He could be brusque with Flint, even high-handed, but the house steward was Aunt Ruby's man and seemed well aware that his position was secure, and perhaps he was not as deferential towards David as he might be! Then my half brother-in-law could make extremely cutting remarks regarding his wife's skill at the card table, and at one time I had thought Celia to be prone to colds for sometimes in the mornings her eyes would be red-rimmed and her lids puffed, but the head colds did not seem to actually develop, and though she would say in an explanatory way that she felt one was coming on, I began to suspect that in the privacy of their chambers, she ofttimes wept! But there again, Celia often stretched my patience to the limit. Indeed, she would sometimes have tried the patience of a saint, and David, although I could not discover any actual evidence that he was a sadist or anything of that nature, in my opinion certainly did not qualify to wear a halo!

Though when I told Aunt Ruby that I thought she might have assessed his character too harshly, she answered me by saying,

'Laura, I have known him for all of his life! Just lately he has been very pretty-behaved, I will admit that. Celia must be greatly relieved and more than thankful for your presence here.'

'Why so?'

'Oh, because David's party manners are very much to the forefront these days. He would not wish for you to see some of his little tricks. Not just yet.'

'But why should my being here have made any difference to him?'

'Who knows? He may have taken a fancy to you in his own peculiar way and perhaps wishes to make a good impression. For after all, you are a very personable young woman and a complete contrast to the one whom he calls wife! But he can be so cunning and calculating that it would be a grave mistake to even imagine that one knows what he is about.'

'If he is not happy with Celia's appearance, why did he marry her?'

'Because she was the best bargain on the marriage market at that time. She has a neat little fortune, and do not forget, when they wed he was a younger son with no prospects. A good name admittedly, but there was no thought that he would inherit, for Matthew was healthy and likely to remain so, then.'

But he did not seem so intent on impressing upon me that he flinched from crossing verbal swords with Aunt Ruby, and I must own that I found these mental contests rather amusing for they were a well-matched pair, both of them having the wit and skill to insult each other in the nicest possible way. But I was aware that Celia would be quite defenceless against her spouse's caustic tongue if the occasion should arise, and I did wonder that, if I were so unfortunate as to have David's ironic, rapierlike sallies directed against me, would I fare any better, myself?

Now that Aunt Ruby had made me sensible of the kind of person he really was, or could be, I developed a watchful attitude toward David, suspecting even his slightest courtesy. And as he was always pleasant to me as I was to him, I wondered if he regarded me in a similar light but concealed his feelings for me as successfully as I hoped I did mine? But all he had to do was wait, wait until poor Matthew died, and then the title, the riches, and the lands would be his! Through a single adolescent act, despicable in the extreme, he would reap such a reward! Oh, it was monstrous! For as Aunt Ruby had told me, if it were not for Matthew being so falsely accused, judged, and sentenced to what was virtually banishment, he would be as hale and hearty as he had always been. He would most probably have married an acceptable young woman in the normal fashion and have had a quiver full of little Merricks by now. And he would have been able to look forward to many more years of freedom to live a full life, instead of being a prisoner until the closely hovering hand of death at last released him! And when it did, what would happen to Aunt Ruby? For when Merrick's Mount was David's, I doubted very much that she would be begged to make her home there for the rest of

248

her days. And knowing her as I did, it seemed highly unlikely that she should want to. So there she would be, cast adrift at her age and having to set up a lonely establishment on her own, away from everything she had known and loved. She had never lived anywhere else but in the house where she was born. She had spurned offers of marriage and sacrificed her youth for the sake of Matthew, and though she could still possibly have married when he had grown out of leading strings, she had not, rather staying on at Merrick's Mount to guard his interests. And then when he had been sent to the family's plantations she had yet remained, awaiting his eventual return and envisaging how it would be. And how heartrending it must have been for her to receive the dreadful news that he was smitten by an incurable ailment and that his span of life upon this earth would only be of a short duration! Gone was the hope of any future family happiness she may have joyously anticipated, gone the possibility of seeing Matthew's children daily, of watching them grow, and of counseling the wife of he whom she regarded as her own ewe lamb! It was all gone! There was nothing to look forward to apart from the sight of David slipping neatly into his dead half brother's shoes! Was it any wonder she was so chagrined? Would I have felt differently had I been in her place? And therefore it was hardly surprising that her agile brain had ingeniously conceived such a solution to her problem as she had once put to me? Probably I too would have been tempted to deprive David of his ill-gotten inheritance? Yes, as fair means had not been employed on a previous occasion, foul ones could continue to serve! True, Matthew would not benefit, but Aunt Ruby would have the satisfaction of knowing that neither should David and that she herself could remain where she was until the end of her days! And I? Why I, too, could remain at Merrick's Mount for so long as I chose and she also wished me to, for if I fell in with her whim to introduce an imposter infant into the house, I would not quarrel with her over the rearing of the child, for that would be in her hands entirely. And then I could go where I liked, live where I pleased, and in the fullness of time, I might even think about marrying again. There was nothing in my contract to forbid it.

Suddenly I felt a little giddy, a trifle faint, for in a flash of inspiration I became fully aware for the very first time that they were all *in my power*! At a mere nod from me, Aunt Ruby would transform her outrageous plans into outrageous actions. It might be a difficult undertaking, but if she thought it could be done, it was as good as an accomplished fact. And then she could queen it here at Merrick's Mount for as many years as would matter to her and be revenged upon David at the same time. But if I continued to stand fast against her, eventually everything that she held so dear would be his! Presumably she already had her own income, but apart from that she would have nothing but a burning resentment, bitter grief, and memories. Irreverent as I owned the thought might be, it did occur to me that I was in a unique position, in a very small way akin to that of Almighty God! What should I do? Try to right one wrong by being party to another? And to whom would the wrong be really done? I thought about it carefully, over and over again. True I knew what was right, but I also knew it would not only benefit a wrongdoer, but also bring deep distress to she who was, in a financial sense at least, my benefactor. What would Mama have done if she were in my place? Just the thought of it was ludicrous, to imagine my mother, so dignified and discreet, yet so upstanding in character, being faced with such a dilemma! No, a thing like this could never happen to a person like her, for she would never have arrived at such a situation as this in the first place. And though I was quite bewildered by the maze of indecision that confused me, there were three invisible mental cords I could follow along its tortuous paths. The first being that it did not affect me in any way who it was who won the prize; the second, that Aunt Ruby had my sympathy and understanding; and the third, that anyone who had acted as David had toward a defenceless creature, even if it had happened a long time ago, need not expect any support from me!

8

'Oh, Aunt Ruby, I beg your pardon for disturbing you, but I was wondering if you would be so kind as to do me a favor?' After much hesitation, I had chosen the hour just before dinner to knock on her sitting room door.

'Come in, child. Do not stand there with the door half open. There is quite a draught! And what can I do for you?'

Although not entirely welcoming, she was not in a particularly forbidding mood either.

'The beautiful set of diamonds you gave me. I was wondering if you would lock them away safely? And just let me have them to wear on special occasions, if there should be any such? For I have nowhere really secure in my chambers.'

'And you fear they may go astray? I think not, my dear. Tansy is the soul of honesty, and so are the other servants.'

'Oh, yes. I did not mean to imply anything different. But it does not seem right that jewels like these should be left lying around,' I said.

'Very well, if it will set your mind at rest, I will put them away for you.'

'Thank you. Thank you very much,' but still I lingered.

'Was there anything else?'

'Well, yes. But I do not quite know how to broach the subject.'

'Is it important?'

'I do not really know. But once you gave me the impression that you thought so.'

Yes, she was being decidedly difficult!

'Indeed? Then whatever it is must be of the greatest moment. Sit down, Laura. I think I can spare you five minutes or so.'

And as I took the seat indicated, the heart-stopping thought struck me: What if I had been wrong? What if I had quite misunderstood that previous conversation of ours?'

'I have been thinking,' I began.

'Oh, yes? Not an unusual exercise for you, surely?'

'No, but my thoughts have been following a rather unusual course!'

'Say on, my dear. I am all attention,' though she glanced at the clock.

'Do you recall the two of us once discussing adoption . . . ?'

Ah, she was very attentive now, 'all ears,' as the saying goes.

'Vaguely. Yes, I do believe that once we did discuss its merits. Why?'

'It was just a thought I had, but to put it into actual words makes me realise how nonsensical it is.'

'Perhaps talking to Celia as you have been doing has awakened a latent urge in you? Regarding motherhood and things of a like nature?'

'I do not know,' I faltered, then irritation got the better of my temper, for why should I be made to feel uncomfortable when I was considering doing her a great favor?'

'We seem to be getting nowhere, Laura.'

'Oh, very well then, I shall speak out. Not so very long ago I received a strong impression that you were eager for Matthew and me to adopt a nameless child of the masculine gender. And to put it bluntly, to cozen the world, David especially, that it was born to us naturally. And by so doing, to settle old scores. Now tell me, was I mistaken?'

'No, you were not. But you are rather inclined to handle the subject a little less than delicately!'

'Probably my embarrassment is the cause of that. I lack your finesse, Aunt Ruby.'

'Well, having established the point of our previous conversation, where does that bring us now?'

'I have had a lot more time in which to consider. I have thought the whole thing over very carefully, and I am not so rigid in my attitude as I was a short while ago.'

'And what has changed your mind so drastically?'

'Does it matter? Of course, if you too have had second thoughts and wish to forget that unspoken proposal, I am quite amenable. I just had the notion you might like to pursue it further. I am sorry I have occupied your time for such a triviality,' and utterly confused although smouldering with resentment, I rose.

'Oh, sit down, Laura! You have taken me completely by surprise, that is all. Of course I want a child to come here! Any child other than a brat of David and Celia's. But I had become quite resigned that your straitlaced attitude would preclude any possibility of that! In fact, I can still not really believe I have heard you aright.'

'Well, you did, but I have no idea of how it could be done. And there is one stipulation.'

'Ah, now we come to the meat of the matter!'

'It is this,' I said, completely ignoring her almost triumphant exclamation. 'That nothing is done without Matthew's consent. He must be apprised of our plans, and even if he does not totally approve them, he must not actually say them nay!'

'Is that all?'

'That is quite all. And any suspicion you may have that I seek to gain from entering into such an undertaking, you may dismiss entirely from your mind. I want nothing more than what I have already been granted.'

'Oh, Laura! I do not know what to say.'

'For you that is most unusual, Aunt Ruby.'

'Do not serve me with sauce, Miss! I mean, your ladyship,' she replied with a short laugh. 'But I must confess I am almost bereft of words, even though I am aglow from top to toe with excitement. And I took you for such a bread-and-butter miss! Well, whoever would have thought it?'

'Or of you!'

'O-oh, we are going to have such fun!' she chuckled. 'Just as I was beginning to get thoroughly bored with life, in you come with an utter thunderbolt like this. Ah, just wait until I tell Matthew!'

'That is something else I should like to discuss. Why do I never see him these days? What have I done, for there must be some good reason why he does not send for me like he used to?'

'Not now, dearest child, for it is long past time we started to change for dinner. After the meal, if you plead a headache and retire to your chambers, I will join you there shortly afterwards. I need no excuse to quit the company, for I have always come and gone as I pleased. Yes, I shall come up to your suite, and we can have a nice cosy chat, and make plans. Such plans! Oh, you have made me come alive again, Laura. Indeed, I feel positively vibrant!'

'I am very pleased to hear it,' and for the life of me I could not refrain from returning her infectious smile.

'Until later, then. And thank you. Thank you, my dear!'

Well, I had done it now. Through the door I had just closed behind me, I could hear Aunt Ruby humming a merry tune, and I knew full well that if I faltered now, had another change of heart, the melody would swiftly become a lament, and that I also could be one who sorrowed!

The positive vibrancy of Aunt Ruby was quite unapparent as we sat at dinner. Indeed, I had nothing but admiration for the way in which she passed the most commonplace remarks in the most natural way possible, whereas despite my reservations regarding the deception she and I were considering, I must confess I felt a certain excitement. Could we do it? And why on earth should I even attempt to do it? There must be a streak of complete lunacy running through the Merrick veins, and even though I was not born one of them, their madness must be contagious for I was fast becoming just as much a candidate for Bedlam as they were!

'That was neatly done, Laura,' Aunt Ruby said approvingly as she joined me in my bedchamber. 'But why are we not in your sitting room?'

'I prefer this one,' I replied. 'I find the decor much more to my taste.'

'Oh? Well I cannot decry that, for mine is in complete agreement with yours. Now that is a thought. We shall have your sitting room redecorated and refurnished just to please you.'

'Perhaps one day, but just now we have other matters to discuss,' I said. 'And I think you must be the person to decide how and when, for I am quite ignorant of the ways and means we shall have to employ. Or even if it is possible at all.'

'Where is Tansy?'

'Having her supper. I told her I should not need her again before half-past ten. That should give us ample time . . .'

'To confound the enemy? Just so. But, of course, eventually she will have to know.'

'I suppose it will be necessary,' I agreed doubtfully. 'Can she be entrusted with the secret, though?'

'Oh, yes. Tansy knows on which side her bread is buttered. But the less people who do know about it, the better.'

'And how can it be accomplished?'

'With the greatest of ease. As the days advance you can feign symptoms of pregnancy, your waistline can be increasingly padded, and when the time is ripe you can retire to your chambers and there be brought to bed of a bouncing baby boy!'

'And from where will he come? Under a gooseberry bush?'

'You forget, Laura, I have lived in this district for all of my life and am also well acquainted with the City of Exeter. And there, there is a House of Refuge for Destitute and Fallen Women! That also has links with The Orphanage and Home for Waifs and Strays, and I am a patron of both these institutions!'

257

'But the risk of discovery, of somebody talking?'

'If there is enough of it, money will always buy silence!'

'And what will Matthew say to all this? For, as I have said, I will enter into no undertaking without his approval.' And the notion came to me that I wanted to actually hear him voice it! For to do so, I must be summoned to the dower house once again, and I wanted that! I missed him, and I wanted him to miss me! Oh, why did he never send for me?

'How seriously you take your wifely obligations,' Aunt Ruby observed. 'Of course he will agree. It will amuse him vastly, and he does get rather bored, as you know.'

'I do not know! I thought I did, but now I wonder! He seems to have shut me out of his life completely, and I cannot understand why. I did rather hope that he liked me. We seemed to have quite a lot in common, even laughing at the same things. At least that was the impression I received. Then suddenly, it is as though I was dismissed!'

'Well, he can be a tiresomely obstinate creature. Unyielding in some respects.'

'What respects? And tell me, now that we are being so frank with each other, what was the real reason for which I was brought here? Just to account for the sudden appearance of a new heir? Or was there any truth at all in the explanation you gave me initially? That Matthew wanted a companion?'

'Oh, dear. I had hoped to avoid this but now I see I cannot. No, I did not set out to deceive you. I truly wanted a young, female person to take Matthew out of himself a little, to relieve his ennui. For this idea under discussion only came to me later.'

'But everything went so well at first. Did I offend him in some way?' But even as I spoke a dreadful suspicion occurred to me. 'Oh, no! He cannot be . . . ? He is not already . . . ?' For it would not be beyond Aunt Ruby's capabilities to conceal the death of even one whom she loved as dearly as she did Matthew, if such an act should suit her purpose!

'Laura! How can you even think such a thing? Oh, I take your meaning well enough, although why you should entertain the thought for even a moment quite escapes me!'

'Why, indeed?' That I was watching her narrowly seemed to suddenly amuse her, for her face relaxed into a smile.

'*Touché*,' she replied. 'No, there has been no great change in Matthew's health, lately. And no, you have not offended him. On the contrary. An unwelcome element has intruded into my so successful plan to keep the poor boy occupied. For the poor, silly creature has fallen in love with you! He is smitten with a quite hopeless passion for you! There! So now you know. I set out only to please him, and the outcome has been that I have done him one of the greatest hurts possible!'

'And that is why he will not even see me? I do not understand.'

'He fears he may pass his ailment on to you! Strange, is it not? He does not even seem to consider that he might infect me. And I see him almost every day!'

'So that is why he would never let me approach the bed where he lay?'

'You attempted to? Shameless hussy! Fie on you!'

'No. This is not a subject for jest. But are you certain that what you say is correct?'

'Oh, indeed. He left me in no doubt on that score. He is over the worst of his depression now, but at its height he accused me of the most dreadful things! Of destroying what peace was left to him, of inflicting constant torment upon him! And in a way he was right, for I might have guessed how it would be. From the very moment he first saw you and stood there as though transfixed, just staring, I should have been warned.'

'Stood? What do you mean, stood? For I have never seen him out of his bed!'

'He took a peep at you on the night of your arrival. Childlike, he could not wait to see you. His excuse was that he did not want to be saddled with a wife whose looks did not please him, and that a preview would enable him to retire gracefully from the marriage lists without causing the young woman too much hurt, if such should prove to be the case.'

'So you did come to my room that night?'

'Yes, I confess it now.'

'But that means Matthew can leave the dower house when he wishes to!'

'Well, he can, but not for very long periods of time, and then only upon rare occasions. For if you recall, he was confined to his bed for the whole of

260

the next day because the exertion was really too much for him.'

'And yet he goes riding?' This was purest guesswork on my part, but any attempt to trick her into further admissions was a failure.

'Does he? Dear me, I had no idea! No, I think you must be mistaken. Now, let us leave Matthew's little peccadilloes and return to the matter in hand. When shall we make our move?'

'Whenever you please. It is not of any importance to me.'

'Oh come on, Laura! Enter into the spirit of the thing. I said we will have some fun, and so we shall. And I think a change of scene would not come amiss. We can go to Exeter for a day or two, stay at a hostelry, do some shopping, and perhaps enjoy an entertainment of some sort. And whilst we are there, I will be able to make a few discreet enquiries.'

'But I thought I was not allowed to leave Merrick's Mount,' I demurred.

'There is no reason why you should not if you are accompanied by me. For you will be under my chaperonage, and it will be my responsibility to return you safe and sound, back to your husband's house. And be sure, I shall now make certain of doing that!'

'I do not doubt it,' I replied dryly.

'Let me see. It will be Easter in a fortnight's time, so I think we should wait until just after that, and then we can go. Oh yes, everything will fit in nicely! Before we set out, we can hint at a visit to a physician, and you may be as coy as you

261

like over that but, in actual fact, say nothing. And in the meantime, I shall let a smug expression be seen upon my face occasionally, as though I find it impossible to wholly conceal my joy.'

'That will not demand pretence, surely?'

'No, it will not. Whilst we are in Exeter, we can select the stuff for some casual summer gowns, muslins and other light materials, for they can be made up in the sewing room here. But we shall also visit the *modiste* I patronise, for it is time that both of us had some nice, new garments. And you must have some loose ones, and all-concealing robes for the coming months when your proportions become more, er . . .'

'Hefty?' I suggested helpfully.

'No, Laura, you are not a haulier! Say rather, ample.'

'Aunt Ruby, you and I are sitting here concocting this most fantastic plan to defraud, but in my heart I feel it is doomed to failure. For nothing so flagrantly deceitful as this could ever be really accomplished.'

'That is why it will be so easy. Whoever would suspect it? Oh, David and Celia will fret and fume, but there will be nothing they can do! And as all along you parried Celia's probing, personal questions so cleverly, why should they not believe that you and Matthew have become parents in the usual way? Many a semi-invalid husband, or even a wife in ill health, can do their share in producing a new life!'

'If you say so, ma'am.'

'I do, so you need have no doubts on that score.

Now, everything is decided apart from one thing.'

'And what is that?'

'Well, you have already told me you want nothing for yourself in exchange for becoming my accomplice, so to speak, but I truly wish to reward you in some way. The contents of the Merrick jewel chest you have seen, and I should like you to select whatever takes your fancy. Anything within that chest is yours.'

'Thank you, but no. You have already given me a beautiful set of diamonds, and I wish for nothing more. I suppose I am not a great one for decking myself out with gems, and those you gave me appeal to me more for the sake of their daintiness than their actual value!'

'What a peculiar young woman you are!'

'I am. I agree. For who but a complete oddity would even countenance the dire deed we plan to perpetrate?'

'True enough. But you must have something. Anything! For I too admit to being an oddity, and one of my especial foibles is a strong sense of independence. I intensely dislike being under an obligation to anyone. It makes me feel most uncomfortable. Surely there must be something you would like to own? Something you have seen since coming here, and upon viewing it, you have thought: I would like to own that!'

I smiled. 'One thing only has inspired that thought, but I know I cannot have it.'

'Name it. Just name it.'

'Very well, but it is hardly likely to appeal to your idea of what is appropriate.'

'Give it a name, girl!'

'I should like to own the old manor house.'

'What? You cannot be serious!'

'I did say, I knew it was out of the question.'

'But why would you want that worthless old ruin?'

'Because I liked it. I saw it only once, but I thought then of how it would be if it were restored to its former beauty.'

'Now, Laura, I know you are jesting, for nobody could even think it had ever been beautiful!'

'I do. It is the type of house that appeals to me. Homely and comfortable, not too big and certainly not grand. But let us say no more, for I repeat, it is the only thing I have seen that I would take great delight in calling my own, but I am aware it is quite impossible.'

'But what would you do with it?'

'Live in it. For some part of the time, anyway. I have not really thought about it and to answer your question is in itself pointless.'

'Not entirely. And you have aroused my interest.'

'Well, just supposing you and I do somehow produce this longed-for new heir. In time to come the child will, if all goes as we plan, inherit.'

'Yes? Pray continue.'

'When that time does come, though I sincerely hope it will not be until many years hence, if that child should still be a minor, you will have authority over him. You will from the very start, of course, but when in the eyes of the world I become a widow, I think I should like to retire to a small place of my own. It would cause less complications regarding the upbringing of the child if I had departed from under this roof. People may say I am an unnatural mother, but I will not care greatly if they do.'

'There is a lot of sound sense in what you say. But why the old manor house?'

'Aunt Ruby, this is no well-thought-out plan of mine. I am but answering your questions as well as I am able, without having had any time in which to consider the whys and the wherefores. I just like the old house, nothing more. And I am well aware I cannot have it.'

'Well, I cannot see any reason why you should not have it. Of course, to set it to rights could cost a fair amount,' Aunt Ruby said musingly.

'It would depend on how sound the structure still is,' I replied. 'And to furnish it, I would think along the lines of chintzes and cretonnes, old-fashioned oak furniture and just rugs upon the floors, all quite unlike the silken hangings, satin upholstery, and deep-piled carpets of this mansion.'

'We will hear what Matthew has to say about it.'

'No, please do not trouble him. It is a foolish idea, anyway.'

'Yes, and just such a one as he would take delight in, if it were at all practicable. He has always had a fondness for that old place. I think perhaps that is why he ever had more important things to occupy him whenever I approached him with suggestions to demolish it. And he knows it better than anyone, for he and that friend of his were the last people to set foot inside it to my knowledge.'

'I wish I had not mentioned it at all, now. I would not, if I had thought for a moment you would even consider it,' I said.

'Why, to furnish it to your liking does not sound as though it would cost us a fortune,' Aunt Ruby answered.

'But I want it as it is! As it stands now! That would be the whole point, and to restore it would become my hobby. Gradually, room by room, until it was finished.'

'What a very unusual pastime! It would be so much easier to call in a professional person to do it.'

'You can surely see there would be no personal satisfaction in doing that! Anyway, the basic structure may be riddled with dry rot or anything. And that would render the whole idea an impossibility.'

'We shall see, and when I go to see Matthew tomorrow, I will tell him of all we have said this evening, and that in itself will give him something with which to occupy his mind for a long time to come. Bless you, Laura. Until you came amongst us, our days were very dull, and now it seems that everything is happening at once. You have brought us to life again!'

'Let us not lose sight of the fact, Aunt Ruby, that you, and you alone, are the initial instigator of our planned wickedness! Your brain conceived the notion, and your scheming and knowledge will actually perpetrate the deed!'

'How generous of you to give me all of the credit, Laura! But I must own that the thought warms me thoroughly, for is it not delightful? And so to bed. Good night, my dear.'

Oh yes, I was adapting myself with the greatest of ease to the manner in which these people lived, and I do not just mean their elegant life-style and the leisurely way in which they passed their days! It is ironic how country girls are reputed to be dazzled by the sophistication of the metropolis, and there meet their doom. But this was the situation in reverse: a city-girl coming to the country, but instead of finding a peaceful, bucolic environment, she was caught up in a secret game of bluff! No, be honest just for once, Laura! Underhanded double-dealing is a more descriptive word than bluff is for what you are about to do. And it was far from being a game, for this was to be done in earnest. But it seemed as though I was caught up in a whirlpool! At first I had simply dipped my toes in what looked to be a placid pond, and as all appeared serene, I had been tempted to wade into the shallows, but now I had got out of my depth and could see no way of freeing myself from my own folly. The maelstrom was all about me, and the only thing I could do was to cling to Aunt Ruby for support. Yes, I must! For of my own free will I had gone to her, for although she had first broached the subject, when I had refused, she had not pursued it. I must be completely out of my mind! No, I was not at fault, not to blame; it was the influence of the people whom I had come amongst! Living with them had changed me. I was beginning to think as they did, to plot and scheme as they did! My sense of values had changed, and it did not greatly surprise me to realize that I was not even ashamed of myself, for my paramount thought at that moment was not that I was about to cheat somebody out of his rightful dues but that I might get caught in the act of doing so! And then came another, and this one was much more to my liking. It was more than probable that I should receive the old manor house! And that would be nice! I could occupy myself in making it my very own home, and when all of this fuss and bother was over and I only had myself to please once again, I should live in it, and there would be nobody to tell me what I could or could not do. My family could live with me as well or stay for lengthy periods of time. Yes, and I should have earned it! Aunt Ruby was right when she had said I deserved some recompence for my trouble. I did. Indeed, I did! I had been an utter dolt to deny it. Well, no matter, for it seemed very unlikely that I should get the old house after all!

And what about the most startling revelation? That Matthew was in love with me. Could it be true? Did I want it to be true? And could I return that love? I liked him well enough. No, more than that, I had become quite fond of him. It seemed an age since I had visited the dower house, and I truly missed those visits. My every waking hour had revolved around them. I must remember to tell Matthew this, or that, or ask him something else! Would this amuse him? Would that cause him to chuckle or even laugh aloud? Like a squirrel I had hoarded pieces of useless information, items of gossip, or delved deep within my memory for little things to make him smile, although I never actually saw that smile! And now he no longer sent for me, my days had become empty, my reason for being at Merrick's Mount at all pointless. Or it was until I had entered into collusion with Aunt Ruby! Was that why I had done it? To justify my presence here? To please her? Or to please Matthew? Or simply to bring myself to his notice once again?

★ ★ ★

It became a source of wonder to me that so many people did manage to remain honorable and upright in character, for now that I was rapidly becoming steeped in sin, everything seemed to start going well for me. For just a few days after my momentous conversation with Aunt Ruby, I received a letter from my mother! Actually it was rather a strange letter, for it gave me the impression that she thought I had received others, but the most important facts emerged clearly enough. They were all well, and it appeared they were doing very nicely! There were references to 'Cook,' a 'tweeny,' and somebody else named Ivy, whom I presumed was house-parlor maid. The choice of the Misses Beddoes's Seminary for Young Ladies had been a most fortunate one, for though Tiffany was considered to be quite a dunce, as she was so amiable and pretty, nobody minded, and she had made so many charming friends there. Mama and Aunt Isobel too had become acquainted with an elite little circle of most genteel people, and they gave little supper parties and were themselves invited out in return for their hospitality. (Yes, I could just imagine, could almost hear, Mama casually making mention of 'my elder daughter, Lady Merrick,' or of 'Sir Matthew, my son-in-law.' There was a carriage rank on the corner of the next road, so it was simplicity itself to procure a vehicle at any time they wished, and every house in the square had its own key to the gate of a private piece of ground laid out like a park, on which every house fronted. Mama ended her epistle by enjoining me to take good care of my wrist, but not to neglect to exercise it (she obviously was getting me muddled with somebody else, which was most unlike her), and reproaching me for failing to tell her if I knew the whereabouts of Papa's japanned cigar box, despite her many times of asking. (Truth to tell, I had it here with me and kept my ribbons in it, but fancy her wanting that!) But that was of no great moment, for now I could write to her regularly. I could even send them each something nice when Aunt Ruby and I were in Exeter! No. 4, Eustace Square, Kensington! The address sounded as though to live there would be agreeable, and I could envisage them, leading their pleasant uncomplicated lives amidst their congenial neighbours, and the thought of that seemed to make my own trials and tribulations well worthwhile. For if it were not for me and how I was placed, the life-style of my loved ones would be very, very different!

Aunt Ruby herself had brought the letter up to my chambers, having laid it upon a salver and presented it to me deferentially as would a footman, but later she had said, 'Pray do not think me too much of an interfering busybody, but if I were you

I should be rather circumspect when writing to your family in reply.'

'To be circumspect in everything I say or do has become second nature to me since coming here, but which direction are your thoughts taking on this occasion?'

She glanced around to be sure that we could not be overheard, then whispered, 'I am thinking of our forthcoming happy event. I do not judge it to be wise to make an announcement to your Mama just yet!'

'Aunt Ruby, please give me credit for a little sense! True, Mama would be overjoyed at the prospect of becoming a grandmother. So much so that it would be virtually impossible to keep her away! But there is a small matter that would need to be explained, for how could I account for being in an 'interesting condition,' as under the terms of my contract I am merely engaged as a paid companion?'

'I just thought I would mention it.'

'Then let me assure you, Aunt Ruby, there was no need at all.'

'Good girl! Oh yes, I meant to tell you. I was talking to Matthew about your interest in the old manor house.'

'How is he?'

'Rather bad tempered, I regret to say. That is, he was until I started talking to him, and then he seemed to forget his own woes. He asked after you and appeared to be wholly taken with this ridiculous notion of yours. Look, he described how the interior of the house is designed and had me make a rough

271

sketch, so that you would have some idea of what to expect.'

'How thoughtful of him. Oh, I wish . . . I do so wish . . . ' I bit back the words that would have expressed my desire that he too should be actively involved in this project.

'If wishes were horses, beggars would ride! I shall leave you to study the layout of the old ruin, then. Oh! Yes! Do you want to attend church on Good Friday? That is the day after tomorrow.'

'That would be most pleasant. Yes, I should like to exceedingly.'

'Very well. And I shall go too. Actually, I think you and I should start to attend church regularly. People would think that your influence for good had brought me back into the fold! And an aura of pious respectability cannot do us any harm! Indeed, it could one day prove to be an asset!'

As she left me, I was reflecting that this was hardly the proper spirit in which to attend church! Admittedly one did like to wear attractive clothes and also meet people, but one's principal aim should be to give thanks for blessings received and to worship one's Maker, and never before had I entered God's house with such a guilty conscience as I would take with me on Good Friday. And I was not even a repentant sinner! For my wrongdoing was still only in embryo stage. Aye, that was apt! But as the coming months passed, so it would grow, become undeniably real, and only if our plotting should fail would it be stillborn. Otherwise it would at last take its wrongful place and remain there, lusty and strong, changing the lives of all those concerned, probably for generations to come! And then my gaze fell upon the sketch in my hand. Ah, there lay food for much more pleasant reflections. Yes, I would think about that instead!

Maundy Thursday, and during the afternoon I decided to go and see 'my house' once again. I had not returned since that day I had first set eyes on it, met Seth Quillian, and received that nonsensical fright on the way home, the last probably being entirely due to my own vivid imagination. Though perhaps not, for on several occasions the feeling had come upon me that unseen eyes were watching my movements when I walked alone in the grounds, but I admitted to myself that my nerves were not so steady as they used to be, and this alone could account for the fact that I found myself keeping to open spaces during these perambulations. Anyway, the days were now lengthening and there was no reason why dusk should overtake me before I returned to Merrick's Mount. So as the day was fine and mild, I followed my usual route when leaving the mansion, made my circuitous way through the pine trees, and emerged once more upon the cliff tops. And now that I had a definite destination in mind, it seemed to take me hardly any time at all to reach it.

Yes, there it lay below me, and I gazed down upon it with the new, possessive though critical eyes of near-ownership. Would I be able to match the remaining tiles exactly, for I did not wish for the roof to take on a patched up appearance? And if I could not, would it be very costly to retile the roof completely? Mmm, red would be nice for a change.

Whilst I was in Exeter, I must make enquiries. I peered down into the tangled garden, for though it was most unlikely that Seth Quillian would be there yet again, I did not wish for him or anyone else to witness the undignified scramble I was about to make down the steep incline that lay between me and the house. This I had no intention of entering, but as I had plenty of time at my disposal there was no reason why I should not inspect it thoroughly from the outside, and I mentally berated myself for not thinking to bring pencil and paper on which to write the most glaring repairs that would have to be made, so my memory would have to suffice. I soon discovered that at one time part of the garden had been sunken, but now it was so overgrown that this was not apparent to the casual eye, and I only became aware of it by almost falling headlong into the depression in the ground, but having staggered, recovered myself and established the cause of my near downfall, I pressed on to the manor house. Up the steps I went, avoiding the broken ones, using both hands to try and turn the rusted handle, and being utterly delighted when the door swung wide after a determined though far from hopeful push. Tempted as I was, I knew I would be most unwise to cross the threshold, but I could stand where I was and look! I saw a hall, grey flagstone-floored and with walls of paneled oak. A solid refectory table stood in its centre and there was a high-backed, wooden armchair and several joint stools, some intact but others broken. At the far end was a fireplace into which I could have walked whilst keeping upright, and on either side of that were inglenook seats. Wide stairs ascended to the next storey, but these were without a handrail and did look as though they might be in a dangerous condition, and at the foot of them, on its side as if kicked away in a fit of impatience, lay a spinning wheel. And upon everything lay the dust of ages! I walked all along the front of the house, rubbing patches of grime from the casements, that I might see what lay within. The chambers were all low-ceilinged, some with paneled walls and others lined with crumbling plaster. And then carefully watching where I trod, I made my way round to the back.

When at first sight the place had affected me, I had only viewed 'my house' from the front; but now that its hidden side was revealed to me, I was utterly enthralled! For if it were set to rights, it would vie in charm with any illustration of a child's storybook. A cobbled courtyard and in its centre, a well. A real one! I had only seen pictures of them before, but here was the actual model from which all others were drawn, with a low circular wall and a little tiled roof atop of it. There was a stone seat nearby and a short distance away, what looked like a horse trough. There was a stone dovecot, seemingly intact and ready to receive new occupants, though I would keep the lovely birds just for the pleasure of looking at them and certainly not for the table! And when I crossed the courtyard and skirted a thicketlike hedge, there lay the remains of the hen-houses, pigsties and stables, with what were probably the one-time herb and kitchen gardens beyond. And just past those I could glimpse the gleam of something golden! No explorer in search of El Dorado could have fought his way through a jungle with more determination than I brought to bear whilst crossing that densely overgrown piece of land, and there, in a small sheltered hollow, a glorious carpet of daffodils spread themselves before my delighted eyes! I stood there for a while, just drinking in the wonder of their beauty, and then the notion came to me that I pick some. For countless years they must have grown, bloomed and died, with no human eye to marvel at their loveliness, but this year at least two people would be witness to their beauty. Yes, I would take some to Matthew! The primroses had been denied him by my being delayed by Captain Quillian, but daffodils he should have! I gathered a great sheaf of them until it seemed my arms were filled with living gold, and then I lost no further time in hurrying back the way I had come. By entering the pine trees at a point a little nearer than the one where I had left them, I should only be a short distance from the dower house, and then I intended to lay my flowers on its steps, ring the bell and hasten away. I did not wish to embarrass Matthew by my unexpected and possibly unwelcome presence, but if I did not summon Virtue to the front door, the blooms might lie there unnoticed until they withered and died. Or what could be even more unfortunate, be seen by Aunt Ruby! For I did not think she would like that!

Guilty conscience, nervous tension, or was it just the gloomy atmosphere amidst the pine trees? Whatever the reason, I had only taken a few paces amongst them when the unpleasant sensation came upon me once again. Suddenly, for no real reason, I suspected I was not alone! And I had not even been thinking of that previous occasion, for just a moment before then I had been feeling quite pleased with myself, my burden of daffodils, imagining Matthew's delight when Virtue carried them up to him, possibly increased by the certain knowledge that my hand had plucked them and my mind had thought of him as I did so.

'Is anyone there?' With the scent of pine needles heavy in my nostrils I stood there, hoping that somebody would answer, though fearing that that same somebody might be bent on doing me a mischief. Otherwise why would they not show themselves? That is, if there were anybody there. A hardly audible rustle, the snap of a twig, the sighing of the breeze amidst the branches, that was all. Nothing more. This time I did not run, but as I hurried on, the suspicion that I was being followed left me. Had my challenge frightened away some vagabond, or possibly a poacher? Or had nobody been there in the first place? Or in this, the second? Ah, there was the dower house, and though I should have liked to take a closer look at it in daylight, for I had only ever before seen it at night, I did not linger. I just carried out my plan and then took the covered pathway back to Merrick's Mount, for fear that somebody might be looking out of a window in the dower house, espy me, and think I was trying to solicit an invitation to enter. And I should have hated for anyone to think that! But one day I would return this way and visit the chapel. That I could do without incurring anyone's displeasure, and I would walk in its graveyard and inspect the ancient, crooked memorial tablets to long-dead Merricks. Morbid curiousity? But I liked old graveyards, in particular those which could contain quaint and sometimes quite hilarious epitaphs to their occupants.

★ ★ ★

'Church? You and Laura? Tomorrow?' Celia seemed completely surprised. Then, 'Can I come too?'

'Certainly, my dear. Why ever not? Surely everybody is welcome in God's house?' Aunt Ruby replied unctuously. And so the three of us entered the carriage next morning and were driven to the little church of St. Margaret, which lay beyond the village. This itself would be more accurately described as a hamlet, for there was just a double row of cottages, each fronting the only street along the side of which ran a miniature stream, and a series of tiny bridges had been placed across this at intervals so that access to some of the cottages might be gained. There was a single shop that sold everything the local people were likely to require for their everyday use, this serving also as a post office, a blacksmith's forge, and, of course, an ale and cider house.

The family pew was a private one and once we were inside we were boxed in by its high sides and back and completely concealed from the rest of the congregation. This was not overlarge, but I

278

was very conscious of a score or so pairs of eyes fixed upon the back of my bonnet as I preceded Aunt Ruby and Celia (this, as the former lady said, being my right) down the length of the aisle. After the service, only three people were considered worthy to be noticed by Aunt Ruby, two elderly spinster sisters who resided about a mile distant, whom she made then known to me as Miss Faulkner and Miss Frances, and the vicar himself. I did silently wonder where his wife might be, but learned later that he had the livings of both this and the next parish, dividing his time between the two, and residing in the other one because it was the larger. The rest of the worshippers filed past us as we stood in the porch chatting to the Misses Faulkner and the vicar, but we were the only members of the gentry, the rest being simple folk who bobbed their curtseys or tugged at their forelocks as tokens of respect, in return for which they received condescendingly gracious nods from we vastly superior people!

But during luncheon Aunt Ruby was not again quite so welcoming when once more Celia proposed to join us, this time upon our planned trip to Exeter.

'When do you plan to set out?'

'Oh, we have not yet decided on a definite day. Probably on Tuesday or Wednesday. I must send one of the grooms first, to bespeak our chambers.'

'Where do you and Laura intend to stay?'

'At the Blue Boar, where I usually do.'

'But why do you not stay with my people? There

is plenty of room, and they would be only too pleased to entertain you. Yes, and I could come too! I do feel in need of a change of scene,' Celia declared.

'My dear young woman, you have not long returned from there! Surely you cannot think it fitting to crave their hospitality again? Not quite so soon, anyway?' Aunt Ruby replied.

'What stuff! You make them sound like mere acquaintances instead of my own kindred! After all, it is my home.'

'I was under the impression you regarded Merrick's Mount as your home. Oh, I see! Yes, I suppose it is understandable that you should have had second thoughts about that, lately.'

'Why? Why should I?'

'Well, of course, the former situation has now become quite changed, has it not?'

'In what way?'

'If I must speak plainly, I will say that, now Laura has become Matthew's wife, David is no longer the obvious heir apparent, so to speak. For now the future ownership of this place and everything pertaining to it may in time become the property of a little one who has not yet come amongst us!'

'Oh, Laura, are you . . . ?'

'No, no, Celia! But such joyful news might one day delight our ears, and I quite thought you would be aware of that!'

David was tranquilly sipping his coffee, seemingly unconcerned by this feminine chitchat.

'Well, one day such a thing may come to pass, but until then there is nothing to prevent you,

Laura, and myself from enjoying a short stay with my family in Exeter!' Celia was obviously not a person to accept defeat easily.

'Thank you, but no. I much prefer to put up at a hostelry, and they know me well enough at the Blue Boar. They should do, for I have been patronising that place since I became mature enough to make it perfectly proper for me to favour them so.'

'But a common hostelry!'

'You have never questioned my staying there on former occasions, so why now? And I prefer it. One pays one's bill, and then one can please oneself as to times of rising and retiring, going out and coming in, and when to take one's meals. Instead of having to study one's host and hostess and the habits of the rest of the people beneath their roof!'

'Oh, very well. I can see you are quite determined. You two stay at the Blue Boar then, but that will not prevent me from traveling with you. I can stay with my family and meet Laura sometimes and show her the city.'

'No, I would rather you did not! I think it is a grave mistake to live in each others pockets for all of the time. You remain here, Celia, and I am sure that both Laura and I will enjoy your company much more when we return, after a brief respite from it.'

Later when Aunt Ruby and I were alone, she referred to this conversation.

'That young woman reminds me most strongly of a burr! Irritating, and quite difficult to rid oneself of! I almost had to be rude to her!'

'What do you mean, almost?' I said and realised

as I spoke that, now she and I were conspirators, I no longer stood in awe of her as I had formerly. Yes, the unapproachable *grande dame* of our first acquaintance had now revealed to my certain knowledge that she had feet of clay!

'What is 'quite' to you, Laura, my dear, is a mere 'almost' to Celia! A hint is useless against a person so thick-skinned as she, so only a positive rebuff will serve. And speaking of hints, did you remark the one I made regarding the possibility of a 'little stranger' arriving one day?'

'I could hardly fail to, for it had about as much subtlety as a pickaxe striking a rock!'

But though it was not my intention, this observation of mine made her chortle with laughter.

'As I have said, it is useless being too devious with the likes of her! And a thought has occurred to me. I think it would be amusing if you should absent yourself from the breakfast table, occasionally for the first week or so, and then with greater regularity. Tansy can bring yours up to you, and as time passes it will become the accepted thing for you to lie abed in the mornings. And if that does not make them wonder, nothing will!'

'Why should I do that?'

'Such is the recognised behavior of an expectant mother.'

'It is? You seem very knowledgeable for a spinster lady, Aunt Ruby!'

'I can still recall David's mother's histrionics when she was pregnant, as though it were yesterday. Such a fuss as you would not believe, and her will

282

must not be crossed in any way lest she should become upset!'

'Oh? Then I can look forward to being indulged in all things for the next few months?' I asked lightly.

'Ah, ha! When we have an audience that may be so, but you and I have a deeper understanding, have we not? But referring to your earlier remark, I am not so knowledgeable as I would wish, so I must make it my business to discover certain things whilst we are in Exeter. And was it not fortunate that I was able to shake Celia off? For how we should have contrived with her about our heels every day I cannot imagine! Now before we set out we must make lists, of articles to be purchased, information to be gleaned, and arrangements to be made.'

'Does Matthew know of our plans?'

'The outline of them. And let me assure you, he is inordinately amused.'

'Does he know too that we intend to go to Exeter?'

'Oh, yes, he is fully aware of that. And do you think you can manage without Tansy's services for the day or two we are there? For if you can, I think it will be best to leave her and my personal maid here at Merrick's Mount.'

'Having never had a maid before I came here, that should present no great problem for me,' I answered. 'Is there anything we can get for Matthew when we are there?'

'One or two little things. I have already made a note of them. Oh yes, I was discussing your absurd notion to set the old manor house to rights with him yesterday.'

'What did he say?'

'He is as addlepated as you are, for he gives your nonsensical idea his wholehearted support. He asked me to tell you that you can have the place with his blessing, provided that you will agree to two conditions.'

'And what are they?'

'He said that you do as you please with the interior of the house, but he insists that before it is legally transferred to your ownership, he is permitted to make it structurally sound. The roof, outside walls, joists and inner flooring. Those sorts of things.'

'No! That would be too costly! Far too great an expense for him to undertake,' I objected.

'My dear Laura, do you think he is a pauper? And as you seem really interested in making the old place habitable once again, it would be a kindness for you to allow Matthew to have a finger in the pie too! To start with, anyway.'

'What is his second condition?'

'Merely that you should tell him what you are doing.'

'You mean he wishes to see me again, at last?'

'No. Not exactly. What he means is that he be shown samples of fabrics you choose, and simple sketches of how you intend to set out the rooms, and the type of furniture that you select.'

'I will comply with that request with the greatest of pleasure if you are sure he will not be bored by that sort of thing.'

'The poor man is bored to tears already, and this project of yours will give him something to think about for all of the summer months! He has always been of an inquisitive turn of mind and this would occupy his thoughts for many hours, just imagining the improvements you were making. He has long had a fondness for that ruin, you know.'

'Then let us hope I do nothing of which he would disapprove.'

'You accept his conditions, then?'

'Yes, and will you thank him for me?'

'I will. And he also desired me to give you the same message.'

'The same message?' I repeated stupidly.

'His last words to me upon my visit to him yesterday were, 'And when you see Laura, will you thank her for me?' For what, do you suppose?'

'Oh, probably for giving him something different to think about,' I replied, but though Aunt Ruby was apparently satisfied with this answer, I guessed it was not the true one. I hoped it was not the true one, and that in actual fact he had been thanking me for his daffodils!

9

Poor Celia looked so disconsolate as she stood on the steps waving us off that my conscience smote me.

'We could have let her come with us,' I said.

285

'For surely we could have managed to evade her when we wanted to?'

'Nonsense. Do not be so softhearted. This is primarily a business trip, even though nobody knows it but we two, and of course Matthew. True, we may enjoy ourselves a little whilst we are there, but we can execute our tasks with far greater despatch alone than we should be able to if we had to watch every step we took, lest Celia should espy us in places where in the ordinary way we should not be found,' Aunt Ruby replied.

'I suppose you are right, though it does seem a shame. She has simply nothing to do at Merrick's Mount!'

'Well, upon our return, she will acquire a very interesting occupation. That of counting her fingers until the total reaches nine!'

'The time of the supposed birth?'

'Yes, and to my mind, the month of October will be about the best date. The end of it. You can then be up and fully recovered from your 'lying-in' by Christmas. And I think, for the first time in years, we shall give a party. A big one. Maybe even a ball!'

'I have never been to a ball.'

'Have you not? You poor child! I wonder if there will be a public one held at the Guildhall whilst we are in Exeter? Or a concert? There may be, for though some of the inhabitants can be quite straitlaced during Lent and then there is little in the way of entertainment, now that Easter is behind us there should be something in the way of amusement taking place.'

'I would like to attend a concert, but not a ball. For I should only be embarrassed, as I cannot dance, you see.'

'Yes, I agree that that would present you with some slight difficulty. But even if you could, perhaps it would not be wise, for we have your delicate condition to study, have we not? And you must be seen to avoid all unwarranted exertion at this most interesting time!'

The city of Exeter lay inland some ten miles or so, but as Merrick's Mount lay to the southwest of it and not directly south, we had five or six miles further to travel to reach it, as we did in the late afternoon. And I soon saw why Aunt Ruby favored the Blue Boar as she did, for she was accorded the reverence due to the Queen herself. Though the hostelry had been an old coaching inn and no attempt had been made to modernise it, all was scurry and bustle when our carriage drew into its cobbled yard. Flunkeys and maidservants hovered near, each anxious to be the first to satisfy any whim of Milady and Miss Merrick, whilst our host made his bow so low that I thought he would experience great difficulty in rising from it. He then conducted us to the very best chambers, two bedchambers with a private sitting room linking them, which proved to be cosy and comfortable, with attendant service of the very finest.

'We did not stop for luncheon, so Lady Merrick and I desire that a substantial repast be brought up to us straightaway. It does not have to be hot. A cold fowl and a savory pasty of some sort will do for now.'

'Yes, Madam. At once, Madam.'

'Oh, and, Pearson, we did not bring our personal maids, but I am sure you will be able to arrange for our trunks to be unpacked and our garments pressed? But there will be time enough for that later on, for once the remnants of our meal have been cleared, we do not wish to be disturbed.'

'Certainly, Madam.'

And as we partook of our meal, Aunt Ruby announced the intention of going out, whilst I must stay behind, resting.

'Where are you going? And cannot I come with you?'

'I am going to visit the institution of which I told you. Just to make various tentative enquiries you understand, for it is far too soon yet for any definite arrangements to be made. But I should be able to ascertain what will be possible and what will not.'

'That can wait until tomorrow, surely?'

'It could, but we do not have too much time at our disposal. Today is Tuesday, and that is almost gone, so there remains only two complete days, for we are to travel home again on Friday. And it may well be necessary for me to call once more at this place I intend to visit now, before we go.'

'And you insist on going there alone?'

'Not exactly, but I would rather. For the less you know about my little dealings, the better it will be for all concerned.'

'Very well, but surely I can take a look at the shops whilst you are gone?'

'My dear, you forget your position! Lady Merrick

does not walk the streets unaccompanied, without an older lady or even a servant in attendance! Especially not in your delicate condition!'

'So I am to be in leading reins for the next few months?'

'No, Laura, but during the time we are here we must preserve your image. This may be a city, but it is quite a small one, where people of our class know each other very well! Tomorrow we shall call upon some of my friends for it is high time you were introduced into local society, and be quite sure you will cause a great stir! The new Lady Merrick! The lovely young wife of the mysterious Sir Matthew, herself equally mysterious! People will fall over each other just to be made known to you!'

'Indeed? And will that suit our purpose?'

'Of course. And then there is our shopping to be done, and Matthew has desired me to instruct the builders who renovated the dower house so satisfactorily that he wishes to have an estimate for the outside work to be done on the old ruin that has become your little hobby. And then doubtless you will wish to acquire fabric samples to inspect at your leisure once we return to Merrick's Mount. Then we must see what the mantua-maker has to offer, also the modiste and the milliner, choose our purchases and place our orders. So you see, there will not be a great deal of time to spare!'

'Oh I do. Already I feel weary at the very thought of it. Yes, I think I shall have a little lie down.'

'Wise young woman! I will not be long gone and whilst I am out I shall make enquiries as to what is available in the way of entertainment.'

As Aunt Ruby had said, the city was a small one having only two main streets, but these were lined with shops that were as well stocked as many were in London, and prices were much more favorable so far as the customer was concerned. Our personal wardrobes were our first consideration, for some garments that we wished to take home with us could be ordered, fitted, and finished in time if the seamstresses persevered at their tasks for 'just a few extra hours,' so Aunt Ruby informed me. And of course, any order with the name Merrick attached to it must take precedence over anyone else's! On then to the linen drapers and the silk mercers, the haberdashers and the bootmakers, then back to the Blue Boar for luncheon. And in the afternoon we went avisiting.

'That is another thing we must not forget. We must order your personal cards from the printers, Laura.'

But Aunt Ruby's card alone was like the key that would open all doors, for we called at three very grand residences, being admitted into each one, to be greeted gushingly by their respective mistresses.

'Ruby, my dear! Where have you been this long while? Oh Lady Merrick, I am so happy to make your acquaintance! May I present so-and-so, or such-and-such?'

And wherever we went Aunt Ruby made a small show of ascertaining that I was comfortably seated, with a cushion at my back, and well clear of any possible draught, and I also heard her murmur archly to one elderly female, 'Well of course, Beth, you are my closest friend, and as such will be the first to know when we are really certain! But it is still a little too early to be absolutely sure! Not just yet. Though nonetheless, we are taking every care! Although this is just between we two, for I know I can rely upon your discretion!' And her smile was particularly smug as we departed from that lady's house.

'What were you saying to that woman?' I asked, as if I did not know perfectly well.

'I was making a public announcement of our future hopes. For Beth Manning is the biggest gossip in Exeter, even Devon!'

Aunt Ruby was in the highest of spirits, and her mood was infectious, but not sufficiently so to banish the suspicion — no, the knowledge — that if I had not fallen in with her wishes there would have been no trip to Exeter, nor to anywhere else! For I was well aware that I was 'up for show.' In a small way at first, by being taken to church and introduced to the vicar and the Misses Faulkner, and now here.

'There is a musical evening being held at the assembly rooms tomorrow, and I have had Pearson procure tickets for us, but we cannot get into the Guildhall at all this evening, as every seat has been taken a long while since.'

'What is on there? Anything of especial interest?'

'Not really. Just that man Dickens giving one of his readings.'

'Is he? Oh, I should have liked to attend that, for I am a great admirer of his work,' I said somewhat wistfully.

'The work of that overrated scribbler? You surprise me, Laura! Well, everyone to his own taste and as you have been a very good girl I shall see what I can do. Let me think. Ah, yes! I do believe that one of my acquaintances is a relative of the Lord Mayor. I shall pen a little note and Pearson can have it taken by hand.'

The Guildhall had a capacity audience, but Aunt Ruby and I were nicely placed, having by some inexplicable means acquired seats in the center of the third row from the front, and as the evening progressed, I sat there enthralled, completely under the spell of this most ordinary-looking man, who could weave words into a magical carpet on which one could journey far afield upon flights of fancy. One could have heard the fall of a pin, and even Aunt Ruby soon ceased to fidget. Towards the close of the recital, when Mr Dickens was reading a passage from his novel, *Oliver Twist*, in which Nancy was being brutally slain by Bill Sykes, one lady in the audience had hysterics and another swooned clean away, and the ensuing disturbance quite spoiled the tense atmosphere and brought us all back to our surroundings with a jolt!

The next morning saw us up betimes for we had another very busy day ahead of us. Even during breakfast Aunt Ruby was crossing items off her lists and adding comments beside those that remained.

'Yes, two bolts each of red and white flannel and one of finest lawn for the layette, various muslins for the cradle drapes, and soft cotton for diapers. All of these we have obtained from the linen drapers. Ah, our needles will be well employed during this coming summertime, Laura.'

'I can darn and mend as well as the next person, but Mama was the accomplished needlewoman in our family, not I!'

'Then it is fortunate we have a sewing room staffed by three sewing maids, is it not?'

'Very true, and perhaps we can prevail upon Celia to add little touches of her never-ending embroidery here and there?'

'Callous creature! That would be adding insult to injury!'

'And who is instrumental in inflicting the injury? Certainly not I!' But Aunt Ruby only thought this remark amusing.

'Oh, now that was a foolish thing to do! I have only bought blue ribbon, just as though I knew without doubt that the baby would be a boy! I do, of course, but I must remember to buy pink even if it will not be used.'

Meticulous planning: no detail escaped her eagle eye, and shortly after this we set out to make more purchases amongst which were a Kashmir shawl for Mama, a dozen pairs of silk hose for Aunt Isobel, and for Tiffany, a taffeta petticoat heavily encrusted with lace, the garment designed to rustle importantly when she walked. Oh, I knew it was unsuitable for her, being fashioned for a grown woman to wear, but for that very reason I also knew she would take great delight in it. The luncheon at the Blue Boar, two more social visits during the afternoon, and after these Aunt Ruby absented herself for another mysteriously employed two and a half hours, during which time I remained at the hostelry to pack and have despatched the parcel to my family. Upon Aunt Ruby's return, we just managed to change, dine, and walk the short distance to the assembly rooms, where our ears were outraged by an indifferent orchestra playing a mediocre programme of uninspired music. During the interval, my companion whispered to me much to my relief, 'Do you wish to be in at the kill?'

'Oh? So that is what happens to the orchestra when they have finished?'

'It is a fate they deserve, but do not take me too literally, Laura. I mean, shall we go now?'

'If you are sure it will not spoil your entire evening,' I replied, rising from my seat with alacrity, closely followed by Aunt Ruby. As we were about to collect our wraps, who should be in the foyer of the building but Captain Quillian? Now this might enliven the rest of the evening a little I thought and wondered what would happen, but Aunt Ruby, having seen him as soon as I, had advanced toward him, saying in a voice lilting with delight, 'I do declare, Seth! It must be goodness knows how many years since I last saw you! How are you, my dear boy?'

'I am very well I thank you, Miss Merrick, and all the more so now that I have been fortunate enough to meet by purest chance a charming friend of long-standing and an equally charming more-recent acquaintance. Lady Merrick, how do you do?'

'And what are you doing here, Seth?'

'I live here, ma'am.'

'Of that I am aware, but I do not mean in this city, I mean here!'

'Oh, just making enquiries about some future program.'

'Then let us hope that if you do attend it, you will enjoy yourself more than we have this evening, for Laura and I have decided that our time will be better spent in returning to where we are staying and having our supper. And a lovely thought has just occurred to me! Why do you not come with us? And whilst we partake of the meal, you can tell us of your travels, for I am sure Laura would be as interested as I to hear of them.'

'That is most kind of you, Miss Merrick. Where are you ladies staying?'

'Where I always do. At the Blue Boar, and I can remember the days when you always addressed me as Miss Ruby, so why so formal?' Playfully she tapped his arm with her fan. 'Just allow Laura and me a minute or two to collect and don our wraps, and we shall rejoin you. And there is no need to call for a conveyance, for as you know, our destination is little more than a hundred yards away.'

'Why did you do that?' I asked her as soon as I could. 'I thought you did not like him?'

'Neither do I, but I think I have made a wise decision, and if you let me take the lead during the coming conversation, all should be quite well.'

'When do I ever do otherwise?'

'Exactly! Sensible child that you are!'

Her mood remained gay as, with each of us taking one of Seth Quillian's proffered arms, we strolled back to the hostelry. As we nibbled our way through a pair of cold capons, a venison pasty, oyster patties, and a syllabub to follow, the wine flowed freely and reminiscences became rather merry. Indeed, the atmosphere grew so convivial that Captain Quillian insisted on my calling him Seth, so what could I do but invite him to address me as Laura? And once we were on such a friendly footing, what more natural than that he should confide, 'I could not understand it when you walked straight past me earlier in the year, Miss Ruby.'

'But why did you not step forward, Seth? Laura did tell me of how she had met you at the old house and said she had seen you on the day of her arrival in Exeter. I realized then that somehow I must have missed seeing you, and the only explanation I can give is that I was so full of meeting Laura's train, I was oblivious of all else. Forgive me, please!'

'No, it is I who must crave your forgiveness. For I should have known it was not deliberately done! We have been friends for too many years for me even to suppose it for a moment!'

'Ah, that is settled then. And do you know what notion Laura has taken into her head? To restore that old place, no less! And Matthew is just as foolish for he has given the project his blessing!'

'Has he? Are you, Laura? That is capital news! And what do you intend to do with it when it is habitable once more?'

'We have not even considered that,' I answered swiftly. 'There is a great deal of work to be done first, before we even think of anything of that nature.'

'Well, when that time does arrive you will surely

want someone to live in it, otherwise it will only fall into decay again. So what do you say to leasing it to me?'

'Oh, that would be Matthew's decision entirely,' I replied. 'But I was under the impression that you already had a residence, here in Exeter?'

'I have, and though it is small, it was of sufficient size to accommodate me for short stays. But now that my days are my own, I do want somewhere larger, and I should prefer it to be within sight of the sea!'

'Are you a family man, Seth?'

'No, Laura, I have just myself to please. My parents are dead, God rest their souls, and my only sister is now married with a family of her own, and they dwell near Lincoln.'

'That is a fair distance away,' I remarked. 'And were you the guest of friends on that day when I saw you at the manor house?'

'No, I just came to have a look at it. To see if it were still standing.'

'What? All the way from here just to do that? And back again the same evening?'

'Ah, but to travel as I did is not such an undertaking as you ladies have to endure. I have a small sloop that I berth here in the harbor. In it, when the tide is right, I can slip down the River Exe and be in the open sea in very little time. And from the mouth of the river to where it was we met, is hardly any distance at all!'

'By yourself?'

'No. Usually my manservant comes with me when I go asailing. He was my bosun during our seafaring days and came ashore with me when I retired.'

'Retired? At your age?' Aunt Ruby enquired with suddenly renewed interest.

'Yes. A series of extremely fortunate ventures has enabled me to do so, but although it is not needful, I must look about me for something useful to do with the rest of my life.'

Leave-takings were cordial, Seth entrusting many messages to Matthew into our keeping, each of these received by Aunt Ruby with an assurance of prompt delivery. But when he had gone, she exclaimed heatedly, 'That damned man! Did you know he had retired?'

'I believe he did say something along those lines at our former meeting.'

'Then why did you not say?'

'Probably because I attached no importance to it. For what has that to do with us?'

'Only that he now knows work is to start on the old manor house, and he will be 'slipping down the River Exe in his small sloop' probably quite frequently, just to see how it is getting on! We shall have the confounded creature under our feet for all of the summer!'

'Yes, that is likely. Perhaps it was unwise of you to tell him about the house,' I agreed.

'I never should if I had known he had nothing better to do than make a thorough nuisance of himself!'

'Then perhaps it would be as well to defer that visit to the builders, that one you intend to make to give them Matthew's instructions?'

'I called upon them this very afternoon, during the time I was out alone and you were here. And I cannot go there again tomorrow morning and cancel, now can I?'

'Hardly. Well, the damage is now done, and we shall have to make the best of it,' I replied.

She glared at me, her mind most probably seeking some acid remark with which to wound my feelings, but if she found one, she must have thought better of it, for she only said, 'Well, I do not know about you, but I am for my bed.'

'Yes, I too am quite weary. So good night Aunt Ruby, and sleep well.'

★ ★ ★

Summer came early that year, and as May melted into June, I began to find my cumbrous extra petticoats irksome, for the serious business of padding my figure had not yet started, and I wondered how I would be able to tolerate it when Aunt Ruby decreed that the time was far enough advanced. But in all other respects, everything else seemed to be going quite well, at least so I thought. I was pampered to a ridiculous degree: I lay abed until late each morning, and my breakfast was brought to me on a tray, despite the fact I should have much rather been out and about on such fine, bright days. My slightest whim was indulged, but this did prove to be a blessing, for I could escape Celia whenever I wished, pleading fatigue. She would gaze after me with her bovine, mournful eyes when, upon these occasions, I left her to make my way up to my suite, for yes, Aunt Ruby had joyfully announced the expected coming 'happy event,' and though Celia and David had both of them shown every sign of being delighted, Aunt Ruby had remarked to me privily, 'Making the announcement was almost as enjoyable as I trust the actual 'birth' will be! And now I will wager there will be some home truths spoken between those two!'

'Actually, I thought they took the news quite well. I must admit to being a little surprised though, for from what you had said previously, I had feared to encounter a small amount of unpleasantness,' I retorted.

'Now, Laura, do use your wits! How could there be anything but apparent rejoicing? Admittedly Matthew is poorly, but the world will say he was not too ill to wed you and the marriage is registered at Somerset House for all to see, so there can be no question asked in that direction. All Exeter is aware of that, and if I know Beth Manning, everyone who matters is also fully aware of your 'delicate condition' by now! So what can David and Celia do but put on a show of glad anticipation just like the rest of us?'

And it was all so easy: too easy! The coming infant's layette was well begun and ofttimes Aunt Ruby would bring a finished, tiny garment to be admired, never neglecting to show it to Celia. The builders were busy working on the old manor house, for though I had not been to see what was taking place there, Matthew had sent me a message to the effect that the first thing he had ordered done was for it to be completely reroofed in red, yes, red, tiles, as the old ones could not be exactly matched. And letters now came regularly from Mama, Aunt Isobel, and Tiffany. Their gifts had arrived safely, and they were all very well and happy, though Mama wrote rather wistfully, I thought, that London was so stifling in this heat, but placed as I was so near to the ocean, I must be a little more comfortable than they, owing to the sea-breezes, though she herself had almost forgotten what it was like to be really cool! She was right, for now that summer was upon us, I had developed quite a liking for the blue, blue sea with its frills of creamy surf, so different from the cold, gray menacing appearance it had had during the winter!

'Perhaps next year, we could stretch a point and invite your family here for a visit,' Aunt Ruby said. 'Yes, I am certain that could be arranged, and with the use of a little ingenuity, the presence of the baby could somehow be explained. But we cannot have them here this summer, Laura! For at the moment, you and I have too much in hand!'

I glanced down at my falsely protruding stomach.

'Yes, there too!' she said laughingly. 'Especially there!'

'Well, Aunt Ruby, I am perfectly aware that agility of mind is your forté, and so when the time does come, I shall leave all of the explanations to you. But I will await, with the utmost interest, any tale you may devise that will inform my Mama that she is a grandmother when it is an accomplished fact, when my position here is of merely being a paid companion to a semi-invalid gentleman!'

'You think that is beyond me? Child, it will be simplicity itself! As you have just said, a semi-invalid gentleman. And 'semi' is the key word! I will only have to say that Dan Cupid loosed his arrows and they found their targets, and that is true enough at least as far as poor Matthew is concerned. Anyway, the two of you are man and wife in the eyes of the church and the law, so even though your mother may frown, I do not imagine she will be too irate! And neither do I think she will disdain to claim the new Merrick heir as her grandson! Especially if we invite her to come here, and during her stay, to stand sponsor for him when he is baptised!'

Oh dear, so now even my irreproachable Mama was being enmeshed in our web of deceit! And what a formidable woman Aunt Ruby was. She had an answer for everything, although some of the questions might escape her notice. For she had never even asked me if I felt a fondness toward Matthew, or if I ever thought about him. And perhaps this was just as well. For I did think of him — often — being all alone in the dower house, apart from his valet, during this lovely summer weather. But poor soul that he was, the brightness of the sunlight would be sheer torment to his sensitive eyesight, though perhaps the warmth of the evenings might tempt him from his self-imposed imprisonment? And had not Aunt Ruby once told me that they led an almost nocturnal existence at the dower house? And did he truly love me as she said he said he did? Was that the real

302

reason he denied himself my company, so that no harm might come to me through being in the same chamber as himself? And therefore running the risk of being infected by the same ailment that affected him? His aunt had informed me once that it was something akin to malaria, and espying a complete encyclopedia in the library, I looked it up, but it said nothing about it being contagious, a fact which I reported to her when next we met.

'Oh, those volumes are far from up to date, Laura. And anyway, I only said it was a tropical illness, something not unlike malaria. No, it has some utterly unpronounceable name of its own! Why are you so interested?'

'It just happened to catch my eye,' I replied lamely.

'Then let this catch it, instead. Is it not delightful?' She opened a package wrapped in dark blue paper and revealed the gleaming whiteness of a tiny lace robe, reeking with the aroma of mothballs. 'I wore it; so did my brother Charles. Matthew did not for he was a great hulking creature even when he was a baby and was too big for it when the time came for him to be christened. David was the last person to have it on. Ah, Celia, there you are! I do not believe you have seen this before? Do you not agree it is absolutely exquisite?'

It was midsummer day, and then July was with us.

'Only four more months to go,' Aunt Ruby whispered to me. 'We are more than halfway toward our goal!'

She was brisk, birdlike, with her bright observant

eyes and her quick movements, for the temperature of the hot, hot summer days did not seem to affect her in the least. But it affected me! It was as though I were really *enceinte*, for I became increasingly irritable, prone to headaches, and weary unto death of the padding within my loosely laced stays, which was in itself my chief torment, causing me to perspire copiously after only the slightest exertion. And so to be free from its cumbrous weight I began to spend more time alone in my chambers, for in the privacy to be enjoyed there, I could rid myself of it and be comfortable by slipping on a loose teagown or a cool negligee. And the more time I spent in my rooms, the more I thought of Matthew, for I began to realise how it must be to live as he lived, for he and I both were virtually prisoners, his sentence imposed by purest misfortune, mine by my own crass folly! We both of us had everything most people crave: a title, wealth, security, position. But we were denied our freedom, and without that, all else seemed utter dross! And then, on one of the hottest afternoons, such a feeling of restlessness overcame me that I thought if I did not leave the mansion for only a little while, I should go insane! To walk in the full glare of the strong sunshine would be unpleasant in the ordinary way, but especially wrapped as I was, like a fragile figurine ready for despatch protected with layers of padding, it would be unbearable. However, if I kept to the shaded spots I might be able to find a breath of cool air somewhere, and the shadiest place was amidst the trees that lay between Merrick's Mount and the dower house. I left the house the way I usually did and was soon in the covered walk, and I was right, for under the closely standing pines, the air if not exactly cool was certainly more tolerable than it was within the house, and with every step I took, the fragrance from the pine needles assailed my nostrils in a most pleasing manner. Aimlessly, I wandered on, until I espied the little chapel, and recalling that I had once promised myself that I would inspect the memorial stones that lay around it, I decided that now was the time.

Apart from a few loose lying blocks of unmarked stone, I could see nothing to define the boundaries of the graveyard. Had it ever been encompassed by a wall? If so, it had long since fallen and was now probably covered by the close-growing brambles and bracken. But somebody had been busy with a scythe upon the coarse grass that surrounded the most recent-looking graves, and this area I presumed was reserved for the actual family. When I had first approached, I had thought by the number of markers that the Merricks must have been a remarkably virile lot. Then I noticed that some of the less ornate headstones that still bore decipherable inscriptions carried other surnames, some being adorned with such legends of approbation as: WELL DONE, THOU GOOD AND FAITHFUL SERVANT. Yes, of course, the remains of the family retainers must lie here too, and there in a small spot apart from the others were even more diminutive slabs of stone, very plain these, and the only one I could read had TANTIVY chiseled inexpertly into its weathered surface. A much-loved family pet of long ago, perhaps, though I could see no sign of where the other dog, Herbert, had been laid to rest. The hand of Father Time together with exposure to all kinds of elements during hundreds of years prevented me from reading the inscriptions on many of the gravestones, though those that were still legible caused a mood of deepest melancholy to come upon me, particularly as there were many marking the spot where little ones lay! And then there were others for those cut down in the springtime of their youth. SACRED TO THE MEMORY OF MELISSA MERRICK, CALLED TO HER MAKER, 27TH NOVEMBER 1792, AGED 15 YRS. Presumably a daughter of the house? The most recent grave was that of Sir Charles, and I saw also where Harriet, Lady Merrick, lay. There too was the last resting place of her mother-in-law, Marguerite (she of the diamond daisies). And as I stood there staring at these memorial headstones, some of them pathetically tiny, I felt as though I too were one of this family, who had come here to shed their tears of grief and mourn the departure of their loved ones. Yes, I felt I was of them! True I sailed under false colors, but I was a Merrick despite that. And the least I could do as a mark of respect was enter the little chapel and pray for the sweet repose of these long-dead kindred of my husband.

Within it was so cool, so peaceful, and though a thick film of dust lay upon everything, it was not in so parlous a state as I had anticipated. Actually it was a little larger than it had appeared from the outside, with a dozen plain pews at either side of the aisle and set apart and to one side a special pew reserved for the immediate family, with a coiled serpent surrounded by other rich carvings adorning the front of it, on its seat the remains of velvet-covered cushions, and upon its floor hassocks to match, all in a similar state of decay. The whole of it was set in such a position that the entire congregation could be viewed by their master, lest any should dare to doze during the sermon! Near the altar a stone crusader lay atop of the original's tomb, and there were niches in the walls containing effigies of ladies and gentlemen clad in medieval garments and being prayed over by the little stone likenesses of their dutiful children. Upon the walls at a greater height were battle honors, standards, shields, pennants, all sadly discolored and some of them in tatters, and there were tablets, some inscribed in Latin, but others telling in brief though stirring English of exploits of those Merricks who had gallantly lost their lives on land and sea in the service of their God, their King, and their country. And everywhere, upon everything, was the name Merrick. And I too was a Merrick! And a proudness surged within me that I should be so honored to bear the same name!

Ah, yes, but what would they think of me? Of what I had done, of what I was doing, and of what I intended to do? From the time when the family surname was spelled Merycke, they had been masters of these lands, had lived their lives hereabouts and died, most of them anyway, in this vicinity, and now their bones lay below where I trod. And here was I, a penniless nobody, a nothing, a stranger without even a sense of honor, a veriest opportunist, come to stealthily substitute into the rightful place of the last true Merrick heir, a nameless male bastard! And I had had the temerity to enter their very own chapel to pray for their souls! Me! My very presence must be an abomination to them. Were their shades clustering there in the shadows, regarding me with reproach, with scorn, with utter contempt? And there, before the altar, I sank to my knees and whispered to Whoever, Whatever might be listening, 'Forgive me. Please! I am sorry. No, I will not do it! I cannot do it!' But I was not so intent upon my apology, prayer, whichever it was I was voicing, that I did not hear the creak of the chapel door as it closed softly behind me. And the day was still, with no hint of a breeze to blow it shut! And I was still on my knees as I turned my head to behold David standing there, hat in hand, watching me.

Then he bowed toward either me or the altar and said, 'You have finished your devotions, Laura? Then pray allow me to aid you to your feet.'

I smiled my assent and thanked him politely whilst my mind was occupied with the questions: Had he heard my words? What exactly had I said? If he had heard, would he put two and two together and arrive at the correct sum of my deceitfulness? But as we emerged into the sunshine, he merely said, 'I never thought to find you in there, Laura. Do you make it a habit?'

'No, that was my first time. And you?'

'I was only passing and saw the door ajar, and I must have a tidy nature for instinctively I went to close it.'

Slowly we sauntered back to the mansion and

though we chatted pleasantly as we went, I thought it prudent to keep at least a couple of paces away from my companion of the moment, for I did not quite like the way he had appeared so suddenly in the chapel! For only the creaking of the closing door had apprised me of his presence. He must have entered silently, for he had pushed the door to behind him. And why had he done that? So far as he knew, I was carrying within me the child who would probably deny him what he had presumed would be his inheritance. But if anything should happen to me and the baby he thought I bore, he could be assured of eventually stepping into his half brother's shoes. And many people have slain others for far less reason than that! I felt faint as the notion permeated my brain, but I forced myself to walk and speak quite naturally, aided by the knowledge that every step I took brought me just that little bit nearer to safety!

That evening I dined alone in my suite, for I was too beset by worries to rouse myself sufficiently to make the effort of changing my attire and joining the others in the dining room. For, yes, there I had been, in the abandoned chapel, all alone and on my knees, an easy prey for anyone wishing to harm me. And what had David been doing there, apart, as he had somewhat lamely explained, from coming to close the door? To do that he would not even have to enter the little place of worship, but he had and then stood there in silence watching me. Had he truly been surprised to find me there? Quite unprepared to snatch at the golden opportunity my averted, down-bent head had presented to him?

And had he been swiftly formulating some plan of dreadful action, just before I espied him? Or had he known I was there? Were his the eyes I had felt were watching me upon former occasions? Watching and waiting? But if that were so, why had he not struck this afternoon? For when he was little more than a child he had cruelly killed a pet dog, and as he was capable of such wicked callousness, surely now that he had reached maturity he would be even more so, especially as the incentive was so much greater!

Oh, definitely, it was high time I told Aunt Ruby I had changed my mind! She would be most displeased, but nonetheless, I should tell her tomorrow, sooner if possible, and to the devil with the consequences! Admittedly my guilty conscience might have made me extra susceptible to the atmosphere of sanctity and family tradition that the very stones of the chapel had exuded, but my decision then to do the right thing at last had since then received an added reason. The most powerful stimulant of all! The awareness that, by doing so, I could be saving my own life!

* * *

'Oh no, Laura, I am very sorry, but I am afraid that will not do! It will not do at all!'

'Well, I am equally sorry, but I am afraid it must,' I replied doggedly.

'No, Laura, our plans must go forward. All the arrangements have been made, and to do so, I have incurred a great deal of expense,' Aunt Ruby retorted.

'Then the arrangements must be unmade. And all of the expense must be deducted from my allowance. That I insist upon!'

'Come, child, come! Let us not quarrel. We have worked together so well, you and I. Just like a team in harness. And the aplomb with which you have carried off this very delicate situation fills me with boundless admiration! Nobody, but nobody, suspects a thing!'

'But I cannot go through with it. It is wrong! Utterly wrong! I should never have another easy moment knowing that I had been party to perpetrating such a wrong!'

'It is your nerves, my dear! They are fraught with anxiety, when there is no need, no need at all! Everything has been settled and paid for well in advance. The monthly nurse, the physician, and you know the nursery suite is all ready and waiting, and even the layette is practically finished. Obviously it is too soon to have procured the infant, but we shall find no problem there I assure you!'

'I know. I know all of this, but now I cry a halt!' I said. 'I should never have agreed to it in the first place.'

'Ah, but you did! And how can you now cry a halt. What could we say? How could you explain it away? As a phantom pregnancy?'

'No, there is a much simpler way. I shall keep to my chambers and have a 'miscarriage'! And nobody will question that, either. For they are common enough, are they not?'

'What do you really want? More money?' This was asked in such a tone of withering contempt that I felt my face crimson with humiliation, but I answered in a steady voice, 'I do not. I do not want anything but what I have just stated. To abandon the whole iniquitous plan!'

'And what do you suggest I tell Matthew?'

'The truth. That is all you can tell him. I will tell him myself, if I am permitted to.'

'And the house? What about the old manor house? After he has gone to all of that trouble and expense!'

'Indeed, I am very sorry. For that, and for everything. But my decision will stand, no matter what anybody might say. Persuasion is useless. Promise of reward is more than useless. And seeking to make me change my mind by telling me of Matthew's possible disappointment, is useless. For I am firm in my resolve and no argument will sway me!'

'Yes, I perceive you are not in a reasonable frame of mind,' Aunt Ruby answered. 'I think we had better sleep on it. Let us not be hasty in anything we say or do.'

'There is no reason for undue haste, but sleeping on it will not make me decide on a different course. I was never really happy about what it was we planned to do. I was foolish and weak, but now from somewhere I have found the strength to say no before it is too late.'

'I think something must have upset you, but we shall talk again, and by then you may have had yet another change of heart. Good night, my dear. Sleep well, and the dawn will bring a new day when everything may appear in a completely different light.'

After she had departed from my chambers, some few minutes passed before I felt myself relax, for I had been sitting tensed, ready to do strenuous mental battle with this redoubtable woman. But although she had been far from pleased, the encounter had not been so disagreeable as I had feared, though it would come as no surprise to find her attacking the more tractable side of my nature again and again, hoping that by sheer persistence she would wear away my resolve. Therefore I decided that my 'miscarriage' should take place as soon as may be, for once it was a *fait accompli*, I might be able to look forward to a little peace. From Aunt Ruby's pestering and from David's probably sinister intentions! And with this latter reason particularly in mind, I kept close to my apartment for all of the next day as well, thus letting it be known that Lady Merrick was not feeling her usual robust self, so that any sad tidings resulting from this indisposition would perhaps be half expected and would not cause such shock and lamentation as they would if no groundwork had been done first. But when Aunt Ruby came to visit me during the evening on the day after I had upset all of her plans, although she did try to draw me into them once more, she was not so vindictive as I had suspected she would be when she found she could not.

'Well, if you will not do as I ask, I cannot nor

wish to try and force you. But it does seem such a shame! I am bitterly disappointed, and so too is Matthew!'

'You have told him? Already?'

'Yes, I always make it my business to let him know what is happening around him, for incapacitated as he is, I think it only fair! And, after all, he is master here, even if he does not exercise his right to issue orders!'

'Well, even he could not order me to do this!' I said, ready for an assault couched in different terms from those I had already heard.

'What a singular young woman you are! You are as defensive as would be a cornered wild beast, with fangs bared ready to bite the hand that is nearest. The hand that feeds you, I might add. But no, Matthew has no desire to coerce you into doing anything either against your will or your conscience.'

'Did you tell him I was sorry?'

'I told him you said you were.'

'What did he say?'

'Not a great deal. Actually, he was more than a little puzzled, for he knew that this business would never have been entered into had you not come to me in the first place!'

'Yes, I know. I am sorry.'

'So you have said. And so now we must plan afresh, seek the best way to extricate ourselves from this ridiculous predicament. And decide what is to be done about the old manor house.'

'Lease it to Seth Quillian,' I suggested.

'You must be quite demented, child. To have

him under our noses for years to come? No thank you!'

'What then?'

'I do not know, now. For truth to tell, I was about to surprise you yesterday, before you surprised me! Mine was the nicer one I think, though. But you confounded me so completely that I forgot what it was I had intended to tell you, and when I thought of it later, I was, I confess it, so out of charity with you that I have said nothing until now.'

'Well, if it is a pleasant surprise, I agree with you. I do not deserve it,' for now that the worst seemed to be over, I could afford to be a little less wary and admit that it was all my own stupid fault.

'No, you do not! You are a very naughty girl, and you have made me extremely cross with you. But that was yesterday! And as I said to you then, a new day began with the dawn, and one cannot remain at odds with someone indefinitely!'

Could one not? But this query of mine remained unspoken.

'In actual fact, I came to your chambers to tell you that the builders had almost finished their work upon the outside of the manor house, I mean of course the work that Matthew commissioned them to do. All apart from one or two little details, and they cannot proceed further without instruction as to how you desire they should be done.'

'They have been very quick,' I remarked.

'Well, of course, they have had nothing to hinder them. The weather has been so fine, the days so long, and now the roof is completed as is the interior woodwork, floors, staircase, and such things, and the outside plaster has been renewed and whitened. Just the things Matthew insisted on having done when we set all of this unfortunate business in train, and I came so excitedly to tell you. I wanted you and I to go there and see it. Together! And I so wanted it to be nice, for you to be pleased. I wanted to hear you exclaim with delight and then be able to feel that in some small measure you had been rewarded for the boundless pleasure you had given to me. To us! To Matthew and me! And now it is all spoiled!'

'Oh, Aunt Ruby, what can I say? I am so truly, terribly sorry!'

'If I hear that word again, I shall box your ears!' But she smiled as she spoke. 'Perhaps in years to come, I may thank you for making this decision of yours, even if it is then rather belated. For time may prove that you are the wise one and that I am just a silly old woman living in a world of make-believe.'

'No, never that!' I demurred, uncomfortable at this unusual humility on her part.

'Anyway, Matthew says that you are to have the old manor house, no matter what.'

'But that is impossible. I could not take it now!'

'You can, and you must. You have already denied him one source of amusement, and he does so want to know what you will be doing to the old place now that it is no longer a ruin. He will take a vicarious pleasure in its refurnishing and may well have some suggestions of his own, which

I will pass on to you. And I must admit, I should very much like to see what has already been done there!'

'So would I. But I feel that everything about it has only been executed under false pretences.'

'Well, it would be arrant folly to let it moulder away again, now that the initial work has been carried out.'

'Yes, there is that!' I agreed.

'Then I suggest that we do this. We shall go and take a look. You can give the final instructions to the builders and so set them to work once more. And then during the time you are confined in here having your 'miscarriage,' you will be able to put your mind to what further work you want done there. The inside walls, for an instance. You have not yet been within the house, have you?'

'You know I have not. You yourself told me it was too dangerous.'

'Ah, yes. So I did. Well I should imagine that the kitchen alone will need a certain amount of attention! For I would think that all cooking was done by means of an open fire, with possibly an antiquated oven attached to it and probably a roasting spit either turned by some unfortunate small boy who had to sit so close to the fire that he burned his knees or a dog in a treadmill.'

'And I think you may well be right.'

'Shall we go tomorrow afternoon? Just you and I?'

'I should like to very much.'

'Do you intend to keep to your rooms for the earlier part of tomorrow?'

317

'I had thought to. In view of what is about to happen regarding the 'expected event,' I judge it to be best. What do you think?'

'Yes, I think you are right. Oh, I must tell you, Celia is very worried about the state of your health! She wished to come up and pay you a visit.'

'How very kind,' I murmured.

'How very inquisitive, you mean. But so far I have managed to fob her off by saying the heat has exhausted you and that you are resting. And I shall not tell her of our planned excursion of tomorrow afternoon, for she would then be very suspicious that you should even wish to walk so far on the first day you had left your rooms after being a trifle poorly, and she might insist on accompanying us, unless of course you wish for her to?'

'No, I think not. Another time, perhaps.'

'Then you do still have a grain of sense left! Until tomorrow afternoon, then. Good night, my dear.'

10

I lay abed until the clock hands had almost reached noon, for this had become my usual practise of late. By doing so, I lessened the number of hours during which I had to wear my padded stays, but on that morning I had lain between the sheets reveling in the knowledge that only once more should I be forced to endure them. Although Tansy never passed any remark upon the unusual clothes I had recently worn, for that very reason, I knew she must have been admitted into our erstwhile conspiracy. No, she had never actually said anything as she dutifully stitched within my corsets one layer of padding over another progressively as the weeks passed, nor when she let out my crinoline petticoats to the utmost of their adjustability. But though to hear her voice her thoughts might have been embarrassing, I would have preferred that to the sly looks and barely concealed smirks with which she managed to convey her opinions instead. Oh, there was nothing about her general demeanor that would warrant complaint or even rebuke, but I realized full well that she held me in some small degree of contempt, and though she did execute my orders, she never leapt to do my bidding with the same alacrity that Aunt Ruby seemed to inspire in her. Yes, it was evident Tansy was well aware that my pregnancy was false, just as she would also soon be aware that either I was too craven to let the matter progress to its logical conclusion — or too honorable, depending on one's point of view. And idly I wondered how much my personal maid was being paid for her silence, and when it became known there was nothing to be silent about, whether she would reap her reward or not?

And so at last I rose, bathed, and had Tansy help me dress in the complicated cumbrous harness that created the illusion of burgeoning motherhood, then my under and over petticoats, and finally my gown, and then I ordered my luncheon to be brought to me.

'You may come to clear in an hour's time,' I

319

told her. 'And after that I shall not need you until this evening.'

'Yes, my lady. Thank you, my lady.'

I was spooning my lemon sorbet when Aunt Ruby's head appeared around the door.

'You are still at your luncheon? Perhaps it is as well. You take your time, and I shall either meet you on the cliff tops or at the house itself, for I will go on ahead. It is most unlikely that Celia or David should espy us, but if we should be seen together, they would know that something had been planned between you and I, excluding them. And they would be certain to take umbrage!'

'Very well. You go on, and I will follow in about a quarter of an hour.'

I put on a light, all-enveloping cloak, and instead of one of my usual dimity sunbonnets, I donned a fashionable, elegant leghorn hat. For I was Lady Merrick, was I not? Come to inspect the work of the builders, express my approval or voice my criticism, and give them their final orders, and to do so, I must look the part! But gloves I could and did dispense with. Tansy had not been to take away the remains of my midday meal even though more than an hour had passed since she brought it to me. Yes, she was getting decidedly lackadaisical in her attitude toward me, and I resolved to make her sit up and take notice of my orders when everything was back to normal once more, and I did not feel at such a disadvantage as I had lately.

As I left the house, I took the greatest care not to be seen, for Aunt Ruby's words were still fresh in my mind, and although not quite so fresh, but much more worthy of note, was my uneasiness incurred by David's unaccountable presence in the chapel. For that, together with my reawakened sense of what was right and what was wrong, had been the cause of my braving Aunt Ruby's wrath. And had also implanted the idea in my mind that it might be in the best interests of my health to stay safely in my chambers until it became known that I had lost the expected though not yet born babe. And now here I was again venturing forth! All alone once more, and totally defenceless against any possible devilry planned to do me hurt. But soon I should be in the company of Aunt Ruby, and then all would be well, and after that, when David was informed that I posed no threat to him or his hopes, there would be then no reason for him to entertain notions of returning that compliment to me!

I was not greatly surprised to perceive no sign of Aunt Ruby for I was fully aware that she moved swiftly, whereas I had walked in quite leisurely fashion owing to the heat of the afternoon and my unwieldy garments. That is until I reached the manor house and, looking down upon its unbelievable transformation, I saw her sitting on something just within its wide open doorway, but the builders were out of sight, and I thought that more than probably they were working at the back of the house. I hurried down the slope and across the garden, anxious to hear Aunt Ruby tell me, although I already knew, that my desire to restore the old ancestral home of the Merricks had been fully justified. For it was beautiful! Snowy white

321

plaster-work, age-blackened timbers, and a red-tiled roof that glowed in the sunlight, as if with pride that it should be privileged to crown a dwelling of such charm.

'What do you think?' Aunt Ruby called as I approached where she sat.

'You know there is no need to ask. What could I think but that my imaginings have become reality. And now, do you not agree it would have been absolutely criminal to demolish it?' I replied.

'We shall see.'

'Where is everybody? I quite thought the workmen would be here,' I said.

'So did I. And the reason for their absence has only just come to me. My dear child, it is Saturday! And as I know the men have been working very long hours to complete this renovation, I presume their master has given permission for them to take their leisure now that it is almost completed and whilst they awaited final instruction. And I can hazard a guess at where they have gone.'

'Indeed?'

'Yes, there is a wrestling contest being held not too far away from here. Somerset men against those of Devon. That is where they will be, no doubt. Tossing back ale and cider and losing their hard-earned money making wagers!'

'In actual fact I am not too despondent regarding their absence, for it means you and I can walk about in peace, without anyone dogging our heels,' I retorted, then asked, 'Have you already been inside?'

'Only so far as where I am sitting now. Yours,

Laura, is the right to be the first person to enter this property as it is, for yours is to be the task of completing the work. I only stepped inside the hall to be out of the sunlight whilst I awaited you!'

'Come then, let us see what there is to be seen,' I said, the first thing to catch my eye being an entirely different staircase, but this was obviously not new, being of mellow, polished oak with an ornately carved handrail and balusters all of a piece with it.

'Look at that!' I exclaimed. 'It certainly suits the rest of the hall perfectly, but surely it was not recently fashioned!'

'I should not think so. From its appearance, I would guess that it came from a building of similar age to this. One which has probably been demolished. I believe that Matthew did stipulate that all work done here must harmonize with the original carpentry. Yes, for it would have looked most odd for timber straight from the sawmill to be set in such a place as that!'

'Indeed it would, and I think that is a beautiful piece of work.'

There were four quite large and two smaller reception rooms on the ground floor, but one of each of these I could see would need to be carpeted, for in these floorboards had been replaced and though the carpenters had done their best to match them to the others, they had not quite succeeded. And as Aunt Ruby had prophesied, the kitchen would have to be completely gutted of everything within it and a fresh start made.

'Antiquity is all very well in its place,' my

companion averred. 'But that place should not be the same one as where food is prepared! I suggest you write to London for catalogues of kitchen equipment and furniture. And what do you intend to do about the plumbing? For the singular absence of anything pertaining to it so far as I can see makes me suspect it is entirely nonexistent!'

'Well, there is a well in the courtyard. I did see that!' I replied, this being received with derisive laughter.

'I thought as much! You have no idea, have you? Laura, you are just like a small girl playing at housekeeping!'

'I can learn,' I answered defensively. 'And I will, too. Just wait and see!'

'Oh, I will, indeed, I will.'

'Let us ascend this new staircase,' I suggested.

'By all means if you go first, for if it is not properly secured your young bones will knit together much more easily than will my old ones!'

And though I smiled at these words, they did inspire me to give the handrail a very sound shaking, only to find it had been well and truly set in place and was as firm as a rock. And then from room to room, we wandered.

'Muslin hangings for the bedchambers during the summer months,' I announced. 'And plush or velvets for the cold ones, each room having a color of its own and being known by it. And downstairs I shall have chintzes and cretonnes, or the same heavier fabrics to combat any possible winter draughts.'

'Possible? My dear Laura, in a house as old as this draughts will be certainties!'

'Then I shall have them seen to.'

'And the inner walls? What is their fate to be?'

'All of the paneled ones to be cleaned and polished, the rest to be replastered and either whitened or given a pastel wash, or hung with suitable paper. I have yet to decide that.'

'Well, er, yes. This place does have possibilities I admit, even though they may be very modest ones,' Aunt Ruby conceded.

'And as I am a very modest person, that will please me quite well,' I said. 'Shall we now go up to the attics?'

'No, not today. Knowing there is a little work still to be done and having seen no sign of anything unfinished as yet makes me think it may well be up there. We can come again on Monday, learn what it is the builders wish to know, and you can set your seal of approval on what they have done already.'

'Oh, before we go, I must see what, if anything, they have done outside. For although they form no part of the main house, I will wish for the outbuildings to be repaired or renewed. This way, Aunt Ruby.'

'Have you ever walked farther than this?' she asked as we stood surveying the same dilapidated scene as I had discovered on my one and only previous tour of inspection.

'Just the length of the old kitchen garden,' I replied.

'So you have not yet seen the quarries nor the site of the hamlet where the workmen and their families used to dwell?'

'No. Is it far?'

'Only a short step away. Come, I will show you. That is if I remember the way, for it is twenty years or more since my feet have touched this soil.'

She led me along a bracken-grown track that emerged amidst the shells of roofless stone cottages, their doors either sagging on broken hinges or mouldering on the ground before them, the empty window frames giving the impression of sightless eyes fixed upon utter desolation.

'That used to be the tommy shop,' Aunt Ruby said, pointing to a building more strongly constructed and larger than its neighbours.

'What are tommys?'

'There is no such thing. That is, or was, just the nickname of the place. Part of the workers' wages was paid to them in metal tokens instead of coin of the realm, and the tokens were then exchanged at the tommy shop for provisions.'

'Could they not be spent anywhere else?'

'No, only there. But even if they could have been, there was nowhere else to take them. This was the one and only shop for miles and could demand what price it wished for anything it sold.'

'Who was the proprietor? For he must have done quite well for himself under those terms!'

'My grandfather, my father, and then my brother owned the shop as well as the quarries, and thus most of the wages paid for work done in the quarries returned to their pockets by way of the shop.'

'What an iniquitous scheme!' I exclaimed indignantly.

'Ah, they were the 'good old days,' as some folk call them.'

'Well for some folk they were,' I replied. 'The Merricks amongst them!'

'Let us go and see what has happened to these quarries. There were two you know, one larger than the other. But I will hazard a guess that you will not recognise them for what they once were.'

'Oh? Why should that be?'

'Just wait and see. We will follow these rails, for there the walking will be easier. A string of ponies used to draw carts containing the stone along these rails, long before our modern railway was ever invented!'

The rails themselves were scarcely discernible, but the grass growing between and at either side of them was shorter than it was elsewhere and when the remains of some further buildings hove into sight I knew we were nearing our destination, even though when we actually reached it I doubted the evidence of my own eyes.

'That cannot once have been a limestone quarry!' I exclaimed.

'Yes, it was, albeit a long time ago.'

'But where was the actual work done?'

'Here. You are looking down on what was once the scene of great activity.'

'But I did not think it would look anything like this!' I had been prepared for a complete eyesore to assault my gaze, but this place was lovely! It was, it was beautiful! Below me lay a lake, and

327

though I knew it must be the result of man's handiwork, its shape was irregular, as if nature had fashioned it. The brilliant blue of the summer sky above us was reflected in its still, clear water, and the steep banks that surrounded it were clothed in a riot of colour: scarlet poppies, the rich azure of cornflowers jostling the white purity of moon daisies, pink spears of foxgloves piercing the golden carpets of buttercups. And just as though petals had detached themselves from their parent flower and taken wing, clouds of butterflies hovered over all in company with industrious bumblebees buzzing their way from bloom to bloom.

'It did not when the quarries were operational. Where you see wildflowers and grasses now was just bare limestone. And of course the water was never allowed to collect as you perceive it today, for pumps were constantly at work draining it away. The seepage from underground springs made it a never-ending task, but now I should think it will be twenty or thirty feet deep. And that building down there was where the overseer could be found when he was not actually engaged lower down in the quarry. It was there too that a tally was kept of each man's labor. Look, down there. Just above the water level.'

'Oh, I see.'

'It is long since I was here last, but I remember the occasion as though it were only yesterday. This quarry and the one just beyond that rise had not been closed for more than a few months then, and during that morning Matthew had had one of his arguments with his father over their reopening. Of course, Matthew had lost, and with the impetuousity of youth — he would have been about sixteen at the time — he had taken his mount from the stables and ridden off in high dudgeon. He did not return for his luncheon, and as the afternoon wore on, I became anxious and set out to find him.'

'And he was here?'

'Yes. I guessed he would be either at the old manor house, which was one of his favorite haunts, or here. And when I found him, I managed to persuade him out of his fit of sulks and persuade him to return home with me.'

'So neither of you have been this way since then?'

'He may have been, but I have not. Ah . . . yes! What a zany I am! It must be here!'

'What? What is here?'

'I must have left it here on that day of which I speak. And I had the house servants search high and low for it, never giving this place a thought!'

'What? What have you lost?'

'A very special riding crop. Of great sentimental value. Oh, I must go to see if it is there!'

'Do you think that would be wise? The place looks derelict, and to get down to it from up here will be far from easy,' I replied doubtfully.

'Heavens above! What kind of young women do they breed nowadays! Have you no spirit, girl? To hear you, anyone would think you were ninety rather than nineteen!'

'I am almost twenty, and I was not aware that great age necessarily endowed a person with what is only common sense!' I retorted with asperity.

'Well, I am going. I shall not be long, and if you are too timid to accompany me, stay where you are until I return.'

There was no mistaking her challenge, and though I had the choice of taking it up or letting it lie, I thought that, if I were not to forfeit any remaining esteem she might hold me in, I had better do the former. I had crossed her will too often of late to do so again now, and though I would much rather have stayed where I was or retraced my steps the way we had come, for what I could see of Aunt Ruby's goal, which was almost completely screened by some very tall rosebay willow herbs, did not look in the least inviting or even interesting, and the slope we must descend to reach it, although pretty enough to view from above, was extremely steep! But this being so and as she had already set off, willy-nilly I felt constrained to follow. For if I did not and she got into difficulties or slipped, there was absolutely nothing to prevent her from plunging headlong into the lake below! So silently fuming, I trod in her wake, to find the going extremely hazardous for the grass was dry and, as my leather-shod feet flattened it, became very slippery indeed! But Aunt Ruby's footwear must have been made from different stuff, for she trotted on ahead of me with all the confidence and surefootedness of a mountain goat! I was too engrossed in watching where I placed my feet to now admire the scenery, but when we stood immediately before the dilapidated building,

I had leisure to inspect it more closely, and I did not like what I saw!

'You are never going in there? It looks a positive deathtrap! Come away, please do!'

As it was erected on a very steep incline, the part of the structure that fronted the lake was supported by stilts made of timber. And though they must have been strong enough in days of yore, as my fingers touched the nearest one, a small portion of it disintegrated into finest powder. And there was a flight of wooden steps leading up to a doorway on the first floor, upon which Aunt Ruby's gaze was resting.

'Nonsense! It is perfectly safe!' she replied.

'I have an idea that somebody may already be up there,' I declared. 'Perhaps some undesirable character whom it would be better to avoid!'

'What an absurd thing to say! This place is deserted and has been for years!'

'Then who or what could have caused those? For we did not make yonder tracks. Ours are over there!' Yes, clear to see was the path we had taken down the slope, for our progress had quite flattened the grasses and wildflowers, but another, slightly less apparent trail led from where we stood back up to the top of the slope but at a different angle.

'Now who would come here? Really, Laura, I cannot understand what is the matter with you today. Oh I see what you mean, but surely the explanation for that is obvious? Some animal has been down here to drink. I did say this was pure spring water, did I not?'

331

'You may be right, but even so that building you wish to enter does look most unsafe.'

'If you think that, then stay down here, but I am going up those steps to seek my riding crop. I shall not be more than a moment or two.'

With the lightness of a cat, she ran up them and though they did creak a little beneath her weight, they stood firm, sufficiently to tempt me to ascend them too, until the thought came to me that I was a little heavier than she, and so I elected to stay where I was. And so I stood there in the hot sunshine, my patience wearing thinner by the minute. What on earth was she doing? Then faintly I heard her call, 'Laura. Are you there? Laura?'

'Yes, I am here. What is it?'

'I have done a very foolish thing. I have wrenched my ankle.'

'Oh dear, I am sorry. Do you want me to go for help?'

'No, no! I only want a little assistance, that is all. Just to get out of here, and then I will rest and should be able to walk home if I am careful.'

'Is it safe for me to come up there?'

'Of course, I would not ask you to if it were not! What a prudent young woman you are! Certainly not one to risk all for the sake of others!'

'I would be a little happier if you described me as being sensible,' I retorted, stung by the truth of this remark. 'For what would it benefit us if we both became injured and trapped in this wormeaten building?'

'Yes, my dear, you are. Extremely! Sensible, I mean. The other was just an unfortunate choice of word. And so if you will be so very kind as to give me your aid, I should really like to get out of this place. I am in a little pain, you know!'

Despite her reassurance I went up those steps with a deal more caution than she had employed, but I reached the top of them without mishap and peered down the length of a long gloomy chamber with only a very small window set high to admit any daylight at all.

'Where are you?'

'Just through here. Mind how you tread for there are one or two empty crates lying about in that outer room, and we do not want you to trip as well!'

Yes, I could dimly discern the outlines of these, and so gingerly I placed one foot before the other, testing each step before I took it.

'How did it happen?' I called as I made my careful way towards her.

'In the most irritating way possible. I did not wish to keep you waiting, and so I made too much haste and caught my toe in the remains of an old rug, twisting my ankle as I fell.'

I could see the doorway through which I must pass to reach her, then stood on its threshold, stepped across it, to be totally blinded, enveloped in a smothering something that was thrown over my head and brought down my body to below my waist, and I heard Aunt Ruby cry sharply, 'Quickly, get her arms up inside it, whilst I secure it around her middle!'

Frantically I tried to disengage myself from within what, by its smell and texture, I guessed was a filthy, old sack. But so taken by utter surprise had I been, so totally unprepared for anything like this to happen that my arms were thrust inside my cloak, and they, together with my head and the upper part of my body, were firmly encased within the nauseating, choking bag. Something extremely strong had been taken several times around my body, thus holding the bag tightly and binding it firmly to my waist! It was similar to being confined in a straitjacket, only worse, much worse, for those constraining garments did leave their unfortunate wearer free to see, to breathe, but as I tried to fill my lungs, I inhaled as well as air, particles of whatever it was the sack had once contained and the irritation that I suffered caused me to splutter and cough until I thought I would surely choke!

But I could still hear, sufficiently well to listen to Aunt Ruby's command of, 'Sit her down, Tansy, lest she do herself a mischief that might look suspicious when the time arrives for her to be found. And the time is not yet ripe for that.'

Yes, somehow I had managed to stay erect, but this was swiftly changed by the simple method of my legs being kicked from underneath me by a sturdily-shod foot.

'You can go, now. Make your way back to the mansion, but be very careful that you are not seen. I shall be finished here and follow in a few minutes. Get on with you, girl!'

I heard the sound of departing footfalls, then silence, and thinking I was alone I began once more to try and free myself, but the sack though old was exceedingly strong, and as I made no headway at all, panic assailed me, and I attempted to scream. But one cannot scream successfully without first filling one's lungs, and as soon as I did a fit of coughing drove all thought of screaming from my mind, for I was too occupied with fighting for my breath to do aught else. By some means I rose to my knees, but this availed me nothing apart from a lusty clout on the side of my head and the sound of Aunt Ruby's voice saying, 'Yes, it seems to be serving its purpose very well, and it will leave no rope marks. And if you cease to struggle, sit down, and take shallow breaths, you will be a deal more comfortable.'

As the blow delivered by some hard object had already knocked me into sitting position once again, I found it easier to profit from this advice than to ignore it.

'What are you doing? Why are you treating me so?' The words I spoke sounded quite clear to me, but her reply made me realise they were not so audible to my tormentor.

'You will have to speak up, my dear. But I can guess what you are asking, and I will tell you this at once. What I am doing brings me no real pleasure. It does not trouble me, but I derive no pleasure from it. And it is entirely your own fault for being so disobliging! First you would not, and then you came to me and said that you would. And that surprising decision of yours brought you a reprieve then, for at that time, I had already started making plans for you to have a very short future! Yes, you bought yourself a further nine months of life at least, for you will understand that I could not

335

have let you live for too long afterward. Not with your unpredictable conscience, for you might have blabbed at any time, and anyway you would have served your purpose. And then after all the planning and preparation, you calmly decide that you will not perform that small service for me. Your utter selfishness and sheer effrontery amaze me, especially when I think of everything I have done for you!'

She relapsed into what I presumed was a silent contemplation of the favors she thought she had granted me, and I sat as still and quiet as a mouse for I had become aware that she was totally deranged, and this knowledge filled me with dread, for I was completely in her power! And her type of dementia did not go hand-in-hand with stupidity. No, cunning was its helpmeet!

'And whoever do you think you are, to dare to cross my will? You, a nobody, an ignoramus only one step removed from the gutter, to dare to say no to me, a Merrick? Well, I have raised you high, and I can just as easily cast you down, even further than you were when first we met. But not yet! It is too soon. You have yet to acquire the haggard and pitiful appearance you must show to the world when you are at last found floating on the lake below. And a few days spent here, as you are now, without food or water, should accomplish much in that direction!' She chuckled, softly, and my blood ran cold.

'And yet in this instance you have been more than helpful. All unknowingly, of course, but helpful just the same. For keeping to your chambers as you have done these last days, you have already prepared the way for what is to come. Yes, your 'miscarriage' will take place this evening, back at Merrick's Mount. Obviously you will not even be there, but nobody will be any the wiser for you will be far too ill to be disturbed, and only Tansy and I will have access to your suite. And such devoted nurses we shall be, she and I! So completely devoted that it will be quite understood when in, yes, I think three days time, you will wander from your apartment whilst one of us is dozing in a chair there. Tansy will be the culprit for that, or at least she will take the blame. It will be presumed you were in a state of delirium when, in your nightrail, you left your bed, quit the house, and wandered here, and either fell or, in the grip of deepest depression, decided to end it all! I believe that depression is quite commonly found to be the aftermath of a miscarriage. And in the meantime, I advise you not to roll about too much, for this place is not so safe as I at first declared. Indeed, I am running the risk of injury to myself by staying here and chatting to you!'

'Please! No! Do not leave me! I will do anything. Anything you say!' for what had I to lose by making such promises?

'No, my dear, it is too late. You cozened me once, but I am not the woman to be bested twice! And I already have fresh plans forming in my mind. Simpler ones! It is proving to be so easy to dispose of you that I regret I did not think along these lines before, so far as David is concerned. And by the time I have got rid of Tansy too, I should be quite adept. She thinks she is soon going to America with a nice fat pension in her pocket. Stupid woman! Her own common sense ought to tell her I could never take that risk! Yes, and then, with David gone and Matthew already doomed, I shall take my rightful place at last! As owner and true mistress of Merrick! And I deserve to. I have run it and cherished it first for one and then another, but in the near future I shall rule there in my own right. Really, to rid myself of you and also to dismiss the idea of putting a bastard in the family cradle has worked out quite well. For me, at least. And so if you remain very still for the next three days and nights, you should be able to recognise Tansy and me when we return to dress you up prettily for your dramatic final appearance and to take our leave of you.'

She moved quietly but swiftly toward the door, thus giving me some idea of in which direction I was facing, but she was not finished even then, for I heard the sound of a key turning in a lock and then naught but silence.

Well, one thing was very certain, I could not, would not, remain as I was for seventy-two hours or more, and then fulfill my destiny by being discovered drowned and floating on the lake! Aunt Ruby had said she was not a woman to be bested. Well, neither was I! And first I had to free myself from this odoriferous, filthy sack. I thought its weakest point might be where it was bound to my body, and so I proceeded to tug at it when I had disengaged my arms from inside my cloak. My aim was to ease it up from underneath its confining rope, but it did not budge even a fraction for it was tied to me so tightly that I could feel its irksome pressure even through the layers of padding within my corset! Oh yes, she had been clever, for as she had not wished for rope marks to be found upon my corpse, so this single one would be well-cushioned from my skin by the layers of padding that lay between it and me. So far I had broken only three of my fingernails, but soon the others were in a like parlous state as I began to try and tear apart the stout fabric of the bag that enveloped me. But it must have been originally made to do a very heavy duty, for it was strong, much too strong for me to rend asunder with my bare hands.

So if brawn would not serve, brain must. Mama had always said that for every problem there was a solution if one applied sufficient thought to it. Aye, and I had found a goodly one for my penurious predicament by coming to Merrick's Mount, had I not? Oh yes, answers might well be discovered, but would they be the right ones? But I had nothing other to do than sit and think, for as I had been told, if I did not inhale too deeply, I was well able to breathe, so that did prove the sack was not air-tight. And now that my eyes had become accustomed to the gloom within it, I realized that a little light did penetrate its fabric. Though not enough to enable me to see where I was or even what surrounded me. No, there was just enough to allow me to perceive the day was still some time distant from sunset, and that knowledge I found strangely comforting, for how I should contrive when darkness fell I shuddered to think!

And so I thought of other things, principally of my own stupid credulity. For just like a gannet, I had swallowed every dishful of lies she had presented to me, and no wonder she had offered such a generous inducement to lure me here in the first place. The fabulous allowance to be paid to me for the rest of my days would not make too great a hole in the Merrick fortune, for those days had never been intended to be many! Just enough of them to enable her to coax me into the conspiracy to rob David of his inheritance, for me to pretend to bear the baby for the requisite time, and once its appearance had been made, for her to silence me forever, probably during the period of my false accouchement. Clearly now I could realise I should never have risen from my bed, for the act of childbirth took its dread toll of so many women that it was quite commonplace. An occurrence most unlikely to be questioned, or even remarked upon! And from being frightened, my mood changed to anger, directed against her for her cynical, callous intentions toward me, a young, innocent, and trusting girl, and then against myself, for being so ridiculously trusting and easily duped. And I had thought I was so clever, that I knew better than did anyone else! Brushing aside Mama's misgivings, attributing the forebodings of Aunt Isobel to her own unfortunate experience, so confident that I could easily cope with any little setback that might come my way. Although truly, this situation in which I now found myself could hardly be described as a 'little setback'! And then

I thought of Matthew. Was he, could he, be aware of what his aunt intended? Had his part in the plot been to speak to me kindly, make me feel wanted, needed, thus to lull me into a false sense of security? To make me agree to be a party to Aunt Ruby's plans in an endeavor to please him? To amuse him? And had my sudden banishment from the dower house been subtly devised to make me think of him so often? For I did, indeed, I did! And what of Aunt Ruby's so casual announcement that he loved me? Lies of hers, lies of his, lies at all? Or was it the truth? He really did? And I did so want it to be the truth! I became conscious of the steady throbbing within my head which by now had increased its intensity tenfold, and as the use of my hands as well as that of my eyes was denied me, I could not even feel my way toward a wall to lean against, so I did the only thing possible. Just as I was, I laid me down and curled up on the floor, and despite my fearful predicament, an overpowering drowsiness took possession of my senses, and I slept.

Hours must have passed before I woke, though at first I thought I was still in the grip of nightmare, as indeed I was, for this was a waking nightmare, just as terrifying as anything the mind might encounter whilst the body slept. Again I struggled vainly to free myself, and during this time, I became aware that no light at all was penetrating between the close woven threads that confined me from the waist upward, and though the absence of it made no real difference to me, the added knowledge that it was now nighttime somehow made my position more fearful than ever! I sat very still, listening. Would there be rats here? Or crawling things? Or wriggling things? Or things that silently crept? What was causing that rustling sound? And surely that little noise came from the scamper of tiny feet? I realized that my petticoats were in disarray, as too was the skirt of my gown, and so I somehow contrived to stagger to my feet so that my clothes might fall back into place. In doing this, I stumbled into something about the height of a desk and thus found myself a seat that was clear of the floor.

Once more my head had begun to ache, and I raised my hands to explore the extent of the injury inflicted by Aunt Ruby. And then for the first time it dawned on me that, ridiculous as this may sound, I was still wearing my once-elegant, now misshapen leghorn hat! The reason for this was because it was firmly secured to my high-coiled hair with a very serviceable hatpin. Sharp and strong and just the tool for laboriously unpicking stitches so soon as I found a seam within the sack.

When at last I released myself, the dawn was about to break, for even though the place was still very gloomy, I instantly perceived a window made up of several small panes of glass, and through the dirt of decades that had settled on these, I could see a lightening in the sky over the far side of the lake. This must be the window through which the overseer of long ago kept his eye on those who hewed and shaped the stone in the quarry below, but for the moment I was content to rejoice in this first stage of my freedom, to stretch out my arms and gulp in great lungfuls of pure, sweet air! And then to divest myself of the hateful, padded corset together with my cumbersome crinoline petticoat. They had no place here, and when I at last managed to effect my escape from here and everything pertaining to the name of Merrick and hie me back to London with all speed, I must be able to move unhindered. I must be agile and swift, alert to any possibility that would aid me to flee from the clutches of Aunt Ruby and that of any other person who sought to do me harm. And so I sat quietly waiting for the true dawn, for then I would be able to see properly and find my way to freedom.

There was nothing on the floor but dirt, certainly no rug nor even the remains of one on which Aunt Ruby could trip. But, of course, that had been just a ruse to lure me up here. There was the desk, a wooden armchair with a broken cane seat, and an ancient three-legged stool. That was the sum total of the room's contents, and so walking very carefully, I crossed to the door. This was of oak, thick and strong, and it looked to be as solid as it had been on the day it was set into place. Its hinges were on the other side for I could see no sign of them, but I could see a lock which told me at first glance that it would defy utterly any puny strength I could bring to bear on it. The window had never been designed to open and was made up of glass panes approximately six by eight inches. There must lie my way I thought, so after wrapping the sack around my right hand and arm, I broke two of them and then essayed to wrench away the verticle bar that had held them in position, only to discover

343

after a great deal of wasted effort that it was made of metal and just as impervious to destruction as would be the iron bars of a prison cell. Then I must try the floor! If it were as unsound as Aunt Ruby had at last declared it to be, my way could be through there. And so on hands and knees, I examined it diligently, hatpin at the ready, poised to prise up any floorboard that looked as though it might yield to such treatment. But every one was neatly dove-tailed to its neighbor and held in place with wooden pegs, so there was not even the head of a nail to work on, and the result of all of my labors was nothing but clouds of disturbed dust.

By now the sun was beginning to climb toward noon, and as I sat on my heels reviewing my situation, I became aware of the void within me that told me my body would like a little sustenance, but more than that, much much more than that, it needed liquid! My throat was so dry it hurt me to cough, which I did often in the dust-laden atmosphere, my lips were starting to crack, and I was completely covered with the grime of years. It was in my hair, my ears, up my nostrils, caked upon my face and sticking to my body, but of far greater concern to me than this acute discomfort was my raging thirst! And there just below me, limpid and cool, clear and sweet, lay a whole lakeful of pure spring water! And I could only gaze at it, thinking of how it would be to swallow great draughts of it, bathe my face in it, even immerse my entire form in it. And whilst I watched, others drank their fill: a vixen and her cubs came down, she with ears a-prick for danger but the little ones came confidently, secure in the knowledge that their mother would shield them from all harm; and further away I could discern three little animals. What they were, I did not know, though they had not only come to quench their thirst but to play as well, for they took turns in sliding down a particularly steep approach to the lake, falling into it, and cavorting merrily in the water, then swimming to the bank, scampering up the slope again and repeating this charming exercise. Seagulls and many other birds arrived, drank and departed, whilst I watched with my tongue almost cloven to the roof of my mouth.

Resolutely I turned away, for I was only making matters worse for myself by imagining how that crystal water would feel against my parched throat, for I admitted to myself that it was beyond my reach, and so I had better turn my attention to the fate that awaited me if I did not find some means to avoid it. One thing at least was in my favour: the element of surprise! For when Aunt Ruby and Tansy came to deliver the *coup de grace* they would not have to deal with a trussed and helpless bundle, to be handled as they chose. No, they would find a very determined young woman who would defend her life with every ounce of her strength! Yes, but what would that strength amount to at the end of three days and nights without food and water? My body had become accustomed to three lavish meals every day, with plenty of tidbits in between, and even now, in this the first day of my incarceration, there was a gnawing emptiness within my stomach that could not entirely be ignored. But to be denied anything at all to drink was amounting to sheer torture, and though I knew I was unlikely to actually expire due to starvation or thirst in that time, I had to face the fact that when I was forced to do battle with these two women for my very existence. It was highly probable I should not pose any real threat to my assailants, for I would be as weak as a kitten!

So somehow I must get out of here before I was put to the test. And I must get out now, whilst my mind was still clear, my grip firm, and my stance steady. And there was one route I had not yet investigated, and that was through the roof! Where I should go from there I had no idea, but if I could manage to get up onto it, I would worry about that, then. I looked upward; the roof was supported by a central beam, and it sloped down from either side of that to meet the front and back walls of the building. This I could see clearly, for there was no plaster ceiling, only secondary beams and joists with laths in between, and above all I knew there must be the greyish-green tiles of the roof. But how to reach it? If I put the stool on the desk and clambered up until I stood on the stool, which was somewhat rickety, I might be able to. And if I first dragged the desk until it was against the front outside wall, I should have that as a support as well as being in a better position, for the rafters were not so high at that point. The desk was heavy but as I had already inspected the floorboards and found them to be sound, I pushed at it with a right good will. There, that was soon done, then the stool atop of it, and then myself. Resting the palms of my hands against the wall, I eased myself upwards until I was standing upright on top of the wobbling stool. I had done it! I had done it! and I could reach! I could reach! Only just, and I would need something with which to push at the laths only just above my head. But what? The only other article within my prison was the broken armchair, and if I could wrench one of its legs loose, that would serve my purpose admirably! And with my initial step toward freedom very close, I became so excited that in my haste to make it I threw caution to the winds, and with less than the utmost care, I made to descend from the stool to the top of the desk and felt the former object tremble beneath my shifted weight, commence to rock despite my desperate efforts to steady it, and then to overturn completely so that I hurtled to the floor, catching the upper part of my left arm on the corner of the desk in passing, and then landing full force with it twisted behind my back! I screamed in agony! Never before had I dreamed such pain existed, and even the mercy of swooning was denied me, for every torn sinew and muscle screeched noiseless protests at such ill usage to my overburdened brain, which was already trying to cope with the now added calamity of the bones themselves being more than probably broken! I tasted a saltiness on my lips and realized that my agony had brought tears to my eyes, and then I crouched there on the filthy floor, cradled my injured arm in my sound one, and whimpered like a beaten cur, with excruciating pain, with utter hopelessness, with fear! And then I wept, great heaving sobs from the depths of my being wracked my entire frame, and they added to my wretched plight, rasping upon my burning throat until I thought I should surely choke. In vain I tried to control them. Think of something else, I told myself. Think of anything! But there *was* nothing else. Nothing existed within the universe or out of it, but my pain, my desolation, and the knowledge that I was doomed to die! And when I felt a slight trembling beneath me, a barely noticeable movement of the floor and a shuddering as if the whole building were just about to collapse, so abject was my misery that I did not even care!

11

Ah, but I did care, for when my thoughts once again became coherent, I became very circumspect in my movements. I had not actually fainted and I had not actually slept, for although I was only dimly aware that the heat of the afternoon sun beating down on the roof above me had been intense, somehow the hours had passed, for I could tell by the gloominess around me that the approach of evening was not too far away, and I instantly recalled the tremor of the building some time since. As I tested the wooden floor and found it to be safe enough, the tremor could only have been caused by one other thing; my heavy fall had accelerated the crumbling of the stilts on which the front of the building was supported, and any sudden movement of mine could make them disintegrate completely, to send the whole structure in which I was imprisoned crashing down into the lake below, with me inside it! Yes, and that would suit Aunt Ruby's purpose just as well, for surely her glib tongue would be capable of telling a tale of my delirious flight and suggesting that somehow I must have become accidentally trapped in this place, which would prove to be as good as a coffin.

I remained where I was for a long while, not daring to move but all the time my mind busy with fresh plans. Only little ones admittedly, nothing on so grand a scale as miraculously escaping through the roof, but it would certainly do no harm if somehow I could draw attention to myself and pray that somebody, somewhere, might be in a position to pay it. My hat! My onetime elegant, now much-begrimed and bedraggled leghorn hat, with its extremely off-white silk rose trimming and long streaming ties of finest gauze! Now if I could thrust that through the window I had broken, suspending it from the frame by one of its ties, if anyone should see it, surely it would make them wonder? And come to find out what it was? And find me? The hat was in one corner just as I was in another; and the window in the far wall away from both. And it is an extremely difficult exercise to crawl on two knees and one hand, all the while being hampered by long skirts and petticoats and the awareness that at any moment you may feel yourself being cast into the eternity of a watery grave!

But at last I managed it, despite an ominous creaking of timber, and then decided that my wisest course was to stay where I was, near to the window. Just in case, in case. And I watched the shadows begin to lengthen, the birds and little beasts come for their evening drink before retiring to lair or roost. And I watched the moon rise, to turn the surface of the lake to a sheet of silver, and one by one, the stars appeared, to gleam like diamonds upon a bed of deep blue velvet. Diamonds! Diamond daisies! Aunt Ruby's seemingly so generous gift which she had never intended to be aught but a loan, and that for only a very short duration! In the stillness of the night, an owl hooted, and then I heard the cry of some hapless tiny creature, and I felt the extra sympathy of one who was similarly placed, trapped, doomed, though its end would come more swiftly and mercifully than would mine, for I had many hours yet to endure before came what by then would surely prove to be a blessed release from my torment.

Did I doze? Had my mind briefly detached itself from the grimness of reality, to take refuge in the happier realm of fancy?

'Laura! Laura! Where are you? Laura!'

Not for months had I heard that voice, that dear voice, low, husky, Matthew's voice! And I wondered if what I feared had come to pass, for it could not be he, and so I must be out of my mind and only imagining I heard it.

'Laura! For the love of God, where are you?'

I was on my knees, peering through the broken

window. Nothing moved; nobody was there; it must have been just my fancy. Though if anyone were nearby, at either side or behind me, I would not see them for the window only overlooked the lake and then across to its other side.

'In here! I am in here!' Forcing my cracked lips apart, I tried to make my whereabouts known, but the clear, shrill cry I hoped I would cause to ring through the air remained somewhere in my throat, and all I could manage was a feeble and quite inaudible croak. I tried again, to no avail. And then I did hear, plainly, David's voice say, 'Do not venture any further, Matt. She would never have come here of her own will. She has too much sense!' Had I indeed? 'And it would have taken a deal of doing to force her all this way. She must be somewhere else!'

They were going to leave me! To walk away and leave me!

'Here! Here! I am here!' This was truly a waking nightmare, to have help so near and all power to summon it denied me, for my voice hardly registered even in my own ears. Make a noise! Any noise! With anything! Quickly, before they depart. Ah, the stool! Where was the stool? Its legs smashed through the remaining glass in the window, and again, and once more for good measure!

'Hark! What was that?' David asked sharply.

What could it be you fool but somebody breaking glass?

'It came from that far room,' Matthew replied, and as he spoke, there was an ominous creaking sound. 'The whole place is about to collapse around our ears,' he added.

'That was what probably caused the glass to break,' David said helpfully. 'The pressure on it.' Lord above, how could anyone be so obtuse?

'You go outside and wait, but I intend to see for myself. If there is anything, I will call you. Keep your distance, David, you are too near to me. And give Virtue and Jeremy a shout, lest they should be needed.'

'Then have a care, Matt.'

'Until she is found, I will take the greatest care. After that, it matters not. Go on, David. Get out of here, and let me proceed.'

It had taken me this while to inch my way across the room to where was the door, and I lost no time in tapping urgently upon it.

'Laura, my love? Is that you?'

'Yes, yes!' But as my answer was only a whisper and surely would not be heard through the door's thickness, I tapped vigorously once again.

'Of course, it is. Who else? She must be injured, or gagged. My God, somebody is going to pay for this! Beloved, be patient for just a little while longer. Just until I can release you. Now, where is the confounded lock? Damnation, the key is gone. She must have been locked in, deliberately! Laura? Dear heart, tap twice if you can hear and understand me.'

This I was very prompt to do.

'Listen, my love. I could break down the door with ease, but to do so might well put you in greater peril. Do you comprehend?'

Two more taps.

'The others must find another way to release you. I shall just depart for long enough to tell them so, and then I will return here straightaway and bear you company whilst they contrive some means of freeing you.'

Another two assenting taps and I had hardly time to assimilate the knowledge that I would soon be out of this hateful place when I heard his voice once again.

'There, I have set matters in train and be very sure they will lose no time, even though they will have to be extremely careful. When you hear a sound on the roof, do not be alarmed, for Jeremy will be up there, making a way through which you will be able to win free. He is my servant, very strong, agile, honest, and true, but a little different from other people in that his form has not reached normal stature, and he is mute. But he can hear well enough, and do not be afraid to put your utmost faith in him.'

'No, I will not be,' but I knew he could not hear my reply so again I tapped twice upon the door.

'I never thought to speak to you again, Laura. I knew I must not, for your dearest sake. In the beginning, I was not too concerned for your safety, for I thought you were cast in the same scheming mold as my aunt, that you knew what you were about and if the worst should happen, that you would deserve it. Her brain conceived the notion I should have a wife, and I knew full well what she hoped would follow. That David would be deprived of Merrick! He and I laughed ourselves silly at the idea, for she did not know about the existence of a secret, as we did. And I let her have her way. I agreed she should go up to London and seek her candidate, quite expecting her to return with some frowsy drab whom she had purchased from out of the gutter. And then I saw you, and at first sight began to have misgivings, for you lay there in your bed, young as spring and much more lovely. But I told myself that appearances are ofttimes deceptive, and the next day I went through the form of marriage with you.'

He paused for breath and to assure him of my attention I gave my double rap upon the door.

'And then I got to know you, to discover you were just as innocent and fresh as you looked! That you were thoughtful and kind and a joy to be with, and I grew to love you! To love you and to fall in love with you! To want to cherish and protect you as one does a treasure beyond price, but also to stroke your silken hair, to touch the petal softness of your skin, to lay my lips upon yours, to feel the warm smoothness of your flesh against mine, tender and yielding. Ah yes, I can say these things with this massive door between us! I longed to, dreamed of, yearned to possess you. To make you truly and utterly mine, to bind you to me forever! Oh God, was ever a man so tormented? But for your sweet sake, I had to be strong. I had to deny myself the delight of your company, the music of your laughter, the enchantment of your smile!'

There was a slight noise above me, coming from somewhere on the roof, and despite my peril, I wished whoever was making it would go away. For I wanted to hear only Matthew, to listen undisturbed to his deep, husky voice saying these magical words; for they in themselves were so wonderfully disturbing that everything else mattered not at all!

'And in return for this stoicism, I did reward myself in some slight degree, for I would keep watch, and occasionally I would see you as you went awalking. Once I fear I startled you, for you called out, but I kept very still and remained silent, for I must never be seen, you see. Least of all by you, my darling, for that I could not bear! To watch fear entering your beautiful eyes, to see distaste wrinkle your dear little nose, to behold those tempting lips of yours curl with disgust? No, my beloved, that I truly could not bear!'

I rapped twice. Again I rapped twice for my heart yearned with pity at his words of such despair. Somehow I must make him understand that regardless of how the rest of the world might view him, to me his looks were of no importance. That I could see deeper than the outer casing of skin that covered him, despite any flaws it might have. And I loved him! I did! All former uncertainties fled away, for now I was sure! This man to whom I was wed. He who was and yet was not my husband, had at least taken possession of my heart. I did not care what he looked like, for what did it matter? Beauty or handsomeness may arouse admiration, but it needs more than either or both of those attributes to inspire true love! And this heady, wonderful feeling that coursed through me could be naught but that, for in my newfound awareness that I really loved him, my wretched state, the dire peril of my plight, and everything else faded into absolute insignificance when set against the knowledge that he loved me in return. My lips were cracked and sore, my throat rasping and raw. There was a large bump on my head, and one shoulder and upper arm still sent agonized reminders to my brain when any sudden movement of mine affected them. I was weary and filthy and hungry and athirst, and yet, despite all of these minor trials, my heart was singing! I basked in the glow of complete contentment, my entire being alight with happiness!

'Laura? Darling? Are you there?'

Two little raps.

'Has Jeremy broken through the roof yet? Two for yes, one for no.'

Above my head there had been sounds of steady activity, though these had been very soft, almost mouselike. Of course, any sudden force employed upon the roof or elsewhere in the derelict building could bring about the end of us all. So a single knock was my reply.

'Ah, yes. He is working slowly and steadily as is best. Be patient, my sweet one. And now tell me, so that there can be no doubt, is my aunt responsible for your being locked in here?' Two raps. 'And was her intention to really do away with you?'

Why deny it? Why try to shield this woman who had planned to murder me in cold blood? But what now seemed worse, she was now intruding into our enthralling conversation, even though it were a trifle one-sided! And I did not want to hear

Matthew talking about her. I just wanted to listen to his deep throaty voice speak of himself, of me, and of us, just the two of us! And so, impatient to banish Aunt Ruby from his thoughts, I answered him with two brisk raps.

'Gently, my dearest. Ah, well I think I have hit upon a notion that will render her harmless in the future. Only trust me, Laura, and I shall ensure that never again will you undergo such an ordeal as this.'

Suddenly there came the crack of snapping wood, and I glanced up sharply for the sound was from above. Jeremy was making a way through the laths, and as I watched, a hole appeared through which could be seen the soft blue of the moonlit sky. Our entrancing *téte à téte* must come to an end, but we should speak further, upon that head I was determined. Two double knocks to inform Matthew that something was happening, and then I saw a rope with a noose at the end of it being gently lowered through the aperture, its other end being secured to the main ridgebeam of the roof.

'Has he won through, Laura?' Then, after I had replied, Matthew said, 'Do as he directs, beloved. Although he cannot speak, he can express his wishes quite clearly. And now lose no time, but do be as careful as you can. For my loved one, you are very, very precious to me!'

And as I assented, my rescuer climbed down the rope with the ability of a monkey. Indeed, when he stood before me I could see he did look rather apelike, for the breadth of his shoulders was immense, and his arms were much too long for the rest of his body, which was supported by very short, bowed legs. His face was nondescript, neither comely nor unsightly, but it did wear a very anxious expression as he gestured toward the rope.

'You are Jeremy!' I whispered. 'Thank you so much for your help.'

His face broke into a grin, and he nodded.

'I have hurt my arm, Jeremy.'

He stood in thought for a moment, then indicated that I should bend my head whilst he slipped the noose over it and drew it down my body until I could sit in it as one would in a swing, and when this was settled to his satisfaction, hand over hand he swarmed up the rope, then sat astride the beam and drew me up after him with as little effort as the lifting of a feather would entail. I think he intended to lower me to the ground in a similar, not too uncomfortable means, but even as I raised my face to the heavens, rejoicing that at last I was free, beneath us there was a groaning noise, and the entire building gave a heart-stopping lurch. Taking my hand in his, Jeremy dragged me, in sitting position, down the sloping roof at the back of my prison. And then, before I was even aware of his intention, he launched the two of us into space, and by the time I realized I was leaping for my life, I had already landed quite safely on a deep pile of bracken, newly cut and set there for just such an eventuality.

'Laura! Thank God! Are you all right?' David was bending over me, raising my head.

'Water!' I whispered, nodding at the same time, then, 'Jeremy, thank you. Thank you all, for you

358

have saved my life! Where is Matthew?'

'Just over there. Jeremy, there is a water flask on my saddle. Fetch it for Lady Merrick, if you please.'

Yes, Matthew was standing about twenty paces away, and though the night was warm, I saw he was wearing a cloak and a wide-brimmed hat. Virtue stood halfway between his master and David and me, whilst Jeremy went scampering up the slope towards where I could hear the jingle of bridle and bit.

'How did you discover where I was?'

'By searching. We had no idea where to look, and none of us had any inkling that anything was amiss until dinnertime this evening. But do not try to talk now. I shall tell you all, later. Just rest and be easy while we wait for Jeremy's return. Fool that I am, I should have had some water ready and waiting.'

I actually felt the grime on my face crumble a little as I attempted to smile, though my rest was only of an instant's duration for all intermingled came creaking, cracking, and grinding noises from the old wooden structure out of which I had only just emerged. And then it tilted to one side, lurched forward, toppled on to what had been its front elevation, then slid slowly down into the lake below. Only a part of it became immediately submerged, and I wondered if my so recent peril of possibly drowning within it had not been so dire after all, but as we watched, planks and beams started to break away and the remainder of it gradually sank until the surface of the waters covered it completely.

I glanced up at David's face, which was set and grim, and then toward Matthew who seemed involuntarily to have drawn a little closer to us. He stood erect, giving me the impression he was far from being so sickly as he was reputed. And yes he was tall, for his stature almost matched that of Virtue, who towered above me! And I sat there staring at this man who constantly shrouded himself in mystery, until perhaps feeling my gaze upon him he turned toward me and then away suddenly, and he stood there tensed, for he was the first to be aware that yet another person approached the scene.

She was carrying a parcel, and confidently she came, and I realized that though Aunt Ruby was visible to us, we were partially screened from her sight by the high-growing foliage that surrounded the area where my prison had stood. The horses too were hidden from view for they had been left at the top of the steep incline just behind us, and even I could not see them nor hear any movement from them. Aunt Ruby paused to survey the disturbed ground on which so recently the building had stood, then, as if to make certain that no trace of me remained, she slowly descended further to the water's very edge and began to scrutinize the floating pieces of timber. It was then that Matthew stepped from his place and followed in her wake. No word passed his lips until some slight sound, possibly made by him, made her turn sharply, espy him, and begin to retrace her steps to meet him, calling as she came,

'Ah, Matthew, so you elected to come this way.

Are the others nearby? I see you have found no sign of her yet, but keep a stout heart, for it is more than likely that she is quite safe by now. Someone will surely have seen her wandering and have given her shelter.'

'Think you so, Aunt?' Matthew's voice was toneless, devoid of any expression.

'Of course, I do. Actually, I only came this way because I was so restless. I knew that the old manor house was an obvious place to search, but I suddenly bethought me of this quarry and the derelict site office. I had no idea it was no longer standing, and I did think there was just a slim chance Laura might have found her way here, and that nobody else might be aware of its existence. It was foolish of me, I can see that now!'

'I was aware of its existence.'

'Well, she is not here, so I may as well go back home and wait to see if the other seekers have been rewarded with more success than you and I.'

'You do not have to wait, Aunt Ruby. I can tell you now! Laura is found! Although she is far from well, she is safe. I should think her physical state may return to normal, though what she will have to suffer mentally after enduring such an agony of mind as she has could well be a very different matter!'

'She is safe? And here? Why did you not say at once? Take me to her, Matthew. The poor child has been in partial delirium these three days past and may be completely out of her senses by now!'

'I think not. She is neither raving nor even hazy in her recollections of what has taken place, and your ministrations are the last thing that she needs!'

'What do you mean, Matthew? And how dare you address me in such a fashion?'

'I will tell you what I mean. I mean that your utter perfidy and ruthless plans and actions have to be halted! And there will never be a better time than now to do it. For year after year you have manipulated others! Nothing and nobody must ever stand in the way of your desires and ambitions! It was you who caused most of the dissent between my father and me, dropping a hint here, letting fall a sly word there. He was not the most patient of men, and I was young and headstrong, and you goaded me into various acts you knew would displease him and then played us one against the other! David had nothing to do with my being sent to Maui. That was your vile deed for which I was blamed, and now the result of your handiwork and scheming stands before you, the untouchable travesty of what I once was! And then as though in some sort of recompense, you brought Laura to me, and in your evil black heart, you hoped I would force her to my will, for what did you care for her, for me, for any child of our begetting, just so long as you could continue to be mistress of Merrick!'

'No, no Matthew! I only sought to please you!'

'You sought to please yourself, and no other! But when you learned that this latest piece of villainy was unlikely to succeed, you decided to wipe the slate clean by disposing of Laura! In a dreadful, unspeakable way, you planned to take her life. No matter that you knew I worshipped the very ground she walked upon. No matter that she was young and lovely, innocent and good! Only your wishes must be regarded, and to hell with those of anyone else!'

'Very well. If you know all, there is nothing more to be said. I shall leave Merrick's Mount tomorrow, and then you will find out the full extent of my worth. You can run your own estate, your own business affairs, your own mansion. What will you do? Move into Merrick's Mount? For if you do, let me assure you that everyone else will move out with a speed that would make lightning seem a loiterer!' She laughed with such vindictiveness that I felt chilled to the marrow of my bones.

'No, Aunt Ruby, I have no plans to do that. But I certainly do not intend that you should depart in style tomorrow, live comfortably elsewhere, and at any time in the future be free to work more mischief! You have harmed my darling; you have attempted to end her life; you have already ruined mine; and so in return, I shall ruin yours! Yes, I have other ideas than that you should leave Merrick! You have always expressed such a deep concern for my lonely existence at the dower house, and now you will end that sad state of affairs by coming to live there with me! We shall be company for each other, and I will be able to keep you under my eye! Virtue will be only too pleased to serve and guard you and to ensure that in the future you will share the fate that your plotting has bestowed upon me. So let us seal our new bargain. Come, dear Aunt, let me take your hand!'

He advanced towards her, fumbling with the

fastenings of what I now saw were gloves! Gloves? On such a balmy night as this?

'No! You cannot! Matthew, for pity's sake, no!' Aunt Ruby's voice was high, almost a shriek.

But Matthew ignored these cries, and as if he had not heard, he continued to approach her, whilst as though in mortal terror, she backed away.

'Matthew! Think! You cannot inflict that hideous curse upon me! Remember the good times we have had. Think of all the things I have done for you!'

I too had heard her utter words similar to those.

'No, Matthew! I beg you. Do not touch me! For mercy's sweet sake!'

She was perilously near to the water's edge, and though my brain told me I ought to cry a warning, I just sat there, mute and immobile, as if I were in a trance, despite being able to see and hear everything that was taking place before my fascinated gaze.

'You had no mercy upon Laura! And attempted murder is an offence that merits a very long prison sentence. But we have no need to go to law over this, for you will serve your sentence with me, at the dower house.'

'I would rather go to prison!'

'I am sure you would, but you have no choice in the matter. So come, dear Aunt, let us be on our way!'

Every word was audible, but Matthew stood between Aunt Ruby and me, and so I cannot swear to what happened next, but I did hear a terrified scream, a mighty splash, and I struggled to my feet only to be held firmly by David's restraining hands. Virtue had run to the lip of the lake where Matthew was quickly divesting himself of cloak, hat, and frockcoat, and then he dived into the timber-cluttered waters. It seemed a very long time passed before he surfaced, to dive again, and again, and yet again. On the fourth attempt, he was successful, for he brought Aunt Ruby with him. I was shocked that neither David nor Jeremy, who had by now returned from his errand, made any move to join them, and I tried to free myself from David's grasp.

'Come, we must go to their aid!' I managed to convey through my still bone-dry lips.

'No, Laura, we must not! We cannot come into such close contact with any one of them now. Jeremy, give her ladyship the flask. Drink, Laura, for there is nothing we can do for those poor wretches down there.'

Though not entirely convinced of this fact, I so craved water that I did drink deeply, all the while watching as Matthew brought his aunt to where Virtue was waiting to receive the burden from him. They laid her upon the greensward and spared no effort in their attempts to revive her, but they toiled in vain. Even from where I stood, I could tell there was no hope; her very stillness proclaimed that all life had left her body. The waters of the lake had claimed it, as she had intended they should claim mine! There followed a low murmuring between master and man, then Virtue began the short climb toward us, but halted when he was still several paces away and said,

'Master say Master David, sir, please to walk

away from Ladyship. He wants to speak to her, private. Jeremy is to stay alongside her.'

What now, I wondered, as David and Virtue both hied themselves off in different directions until they were well out of earshot. I stood with Jeremy, waiting for Matthew to come up to me, and as he drew nearer, I became consciously aware of his hatless state and that the wide brim that had shielded his features from my gaze was now gone. But even so I still did not see his face, for it was hidden behind a mask! He was wearing a facial covering fashioned from some silvery, pliable kind of material, and as the light of the moon glinted on it, the effect was most eerie, even a little frightening. Could I have involuntarily taken a backward step away from this advancing figure? I cannot recall, but Matthew came no nearer, remaining at a distance of five or six yards from me, though when he spoke I could hear his low, husky voice quite clearly.

'Laura, my love, I come to take my leave of you. If things had been different, I think we might have found happiness together, you and I. This love I bear for you is so powerful, so strong, that surely in time you would have found it in your heart to love me a little in return? For I would have striven so hard to find favor in your eyes, that one day I am certain you would have looked upon me with kindness.'

'But I do, Matthew. I already do! There is no need to strive! I do return your love! So please, please, let us talk and make plans sensibly. We cannot live our lives like this! It is too frustrating.

Too cruel! There must be a way for us. All we have to do is find it!' I said.

'My darling, there is only one way, and I have already found it. Now, my dearest one, I must bid you goodbye. We shall never meet again upon this wonderful earth, but if the Lord is merciful and He so wills it, one day I shall feast my eyes upon your lovely face once again. And so, beloved, I implore your forgiveness for the heartache and suffering I have unwittingly caused you. When you think of me sometimes, please do so with charity. And if you can bring yourself to, it would comfort me to know that occasionally you will pray for me. Farewell, Laura, and God bless you. Jeremy, I charge you to guard my dearest wife and keep her safe from all harm!'

Matthew bowed low to me, turned on his heel, and began to walk away.

'No! Matthew! Where are you going? What are you about to do?' I tried to follow him, only to find that Jeremy had taken firm hold of my skirts. 'Let me go, Jeremy. I must discover what it is your master intends!' Though of no great height myself, I was taller than he, despite his immense strength and breadth of shoulder. Thus I only saw the top of his head as he shook it stolidly, until he raised it to reveal a face crumpled with grief, tears coursing freely down it to fall fatly upon his leather jerkin.

'Release me, Jeremy. Do as I bid you! At once!' For I wondered if he knew of something I did not, but just then David rejoined us, as Virtue returned to where Matthew was now standing near to the inert form of Aunt Ruby.

367

'Come, Laura, let us make our way home. There is nothing for us to do here.'

'But what will happen now? What are your half brother's intentions?'

'At this moment, he intends to return to the dower house. He and Virtue will take the remains of Aunt Ruby back there with them for the time being.'

'Oh. Can they manage by themselves?'

'Of course, they can! Our horses are just above us. Shall I carry you up the incline?'

'Thank you, but there is no need for that. If you will allow me to take your arm, I shall manage quite well.'

Only two horses stood patiently waiting, and I enquired, 'Where are the mounts of Matthew and Virtue? Or are they afoot?'

'No, the dower house horses are a little way off. My half brother and his valet will have reached them by now.'

I glanced back the way we had come, to perceive that the others had made better time than had we, to leave behind this beautiful though melancholy scene.

'Now, Laura, you perch in my saddle, so. Jeremy, steady her ladyship whilst I swing up behind her. There! Are you not too uncomfortable? Then let us be on our way.'

We traveled at a leisurely pace, which suited me quite well, for there were many sore and tender places upon my person that would have been happier resting upon feathers than on a leather saddle, but to be so transported was the least of three evils, the alternatives being to either walk home or remain where I was. Home? Did I now regard my destination as my home? For only hours ago had it been my chief ambition to flee from Devonshire, from Merrick's Mount, and never to set eyes on any one of its occupants again!

'How was it that you learned of my plight?' I asked David as we ambled along. 'For Aunt Ruby had planned everything so cleverly that I find the fact that I was missed at all truly miraculous.'

'You have my dear inquisitive wife to thank for that,' he replied. 'She became curious when she overheard some servants' tittle-tattle, and she it was who forced her way into your chambers, to find that maid of yours lying on your bed eating sweetmeats, and you nowhere to be seen!'

'So it was Celia who raised the alarm? Thank heaven for her dear, enquiring nature,' I said, almost forgetting the number of times it had grated on my nerves during days past. 'Yes, my maidservant aided Aunt Ruby to shut me up inside that awful place, and then when they judged the time to be ripe, the two of them were going to return and do away with me altogether. When I looked sufficiently haggard and drawn, they were going to murder me! In cold blood! And Aunt Ruby told me she was then going to kill Tansy, to ensure her silence. She told me that when she and I were alone together. And then it was going to be your turn!'

'What an evil woman she has proved herself to be. I always knew her to be calculating, even ruthless, and utterly selfish, but I never thought

369

she would go to such lengths to have her way.'

'I believe she was mad! Not raving, I do not mean that, but nobody whose mind was normal could have acted as she did and further intended to.'

'Mad or bad, her mind was certainly warped. And if she had but known it, it was all so unnecessary.'

'What do you mean?'

We had just passed the old manor house, and as I spoke, a sharp sound rent the air, swiftly followed by another. Only during my childhood when we lived in the country had I heard their like, but I recognized them instantly. Pistol shots! And they came from the direction of the dower house!

'David! What is Matthew doing?' My cry of alarm was lost to the breeze, as David set spurs to our mount, and we broke into a gallop along the cliff tops. He was forced to draw rein as we threaded our way betwixt the pine trees, and even as we approached Matthew's dwelling an odor reached us that filled me with dread.

Virtue stood on the shallow stone steps with the great door behind him set wide, and through the open doorway, clouds of smoke were billowing, and beyond, the old oakpaneled hall was aglow with a reddish light. Fire! The place was afire!

'Merciful God, the house is alight!' I gasped. 'And where is Matthew?'

As though they were fashioned from stone, David and Jeremy just sat upon their horses, making no attempt to approach the conflagration, not until I struggled to escape the clasp of David's arms, and then he tightened them about me and held me still.

'There is Virtue, but why is he just standing there, and where is his master? He must be inside! Matthew must be inside! We must enter and find him and get him out of there, or he will surely perish! He must be trapped. Please! David! For pity's sake, help him!'

My plea was greeted by a short silence, and then slowly he replied, 'He is trapped, but not in the sense that you mean. And yes, he is inside, but he intends to stay there, no matter what. This is his way, Laura, and he must take it!'

'Can he already be dead? The pistol-shots . . . '

'No. There he is. Up there!'

Every window had been flung wide as if to encourage the fire, and I saw him framed by one of them with a backcloth of flickering light.

'Matthew, please! I beg you! Come out!' I shrieked, and he must have heard my anguished entreaty for the silver-masked face turned in our direction. In silence he stood looking toward us, then he raised his right hand as though in a gesture of final salute. Behind him flames were leaping and could also be seen through other windows on the upper floor. I glanced to where Virtue was still standing on the steps, and he repeated his master's action by raising his right hand. Then the valet turned, briefly regarded the by-now raging holocaust within the hall, and calmly walked into the inferno! I had only taken my gaze off Matthew for a few moments, but during that short time he had left the place where he had been, and my eyes ranged from window to window, seeking him. But he had gone! Then, above the roaring and crackling a third pistol shot splintered the air, shortly followed by a fourth! And I remained still, petrified by purest horror, powerless to move, to cry out, to even weep, whilst before my very eyes such soul-searing tragedy was being enacted, involving my husband, the man I had grown to love!

There were men about us, jostling, gaping, murmuring, but nobody made any attempt to douse the flames, for even I could see that such a task would be impossible. The dower house was old, timber-framed, with most of its inner walls paneled in oak, and its floors of the same combustible material. After weeks of hot, arid summer weather, the ancient dwelling was dry as tinder! No, nothing could have halted that blaze. It must burn until everything had been consumed by the tongues of flame that fiercely blazed within, then presently emerged, licking greedily up the outer walls. With a mighty crash, a portion of the roof caved in. Then the rest of it followed suit, and as if in triumph, the flames leapt even higher, casting showers of sparks that started small outbreaks of smoldering amidst the heat-withered grasses that surrounded what had been Matthew's home.

'You men there, get axes, saws, anything with which to fell the nearest trees,' David at last found his voice to issue commands. 'Jeremy, supply them with what you can. Look sharp now, or the whole countryside will be set ablaze! And some of you do what you can to stamp out any small fires that you see. Yes, strip some of the branches from the trees with which to beat them out. Ah, Rumbelow! There you are! I leave you in charge whilst I take Lady Merrick home. I shall return just so soon as I am able.'

I cannot remember the remainder of our ride back to Merrick's Mount, although I suspect that David spared neither horse nor me in his haste to deposit me safely and hurry back to where was the seat of a fire that threatened to consume hundreds of acres if it were permitted to gain a hold. And even if my ill-used body did protest at being jolted, my brain refused to register it, for at some time it had voiced a protest of its own! It could not cope with so much. It declined to execute its normal functions by telling me that I hurt, that I feared, that I grieved. It withdrew its services completely, and so it was that, drained of all emotion, stunned and silent, dry-eyed and uncomprehending, I was eventually given into Celia's charge. And whether my appearance and general demeanor shocked her into holding her tongue for once, or whether she pestered me with questions, I do not know. It was enough for me to know that there was no sign of my personal maid, that I ate and drank, that I was bathed and anointed, and that I was then put to bed! And once there, I was able to retire into the complete oblivion that only a state of utter mental and physical exhaustion can bring.

12

I slept for all of that day, throughout the following night, and until noon of the day after that, when I was awoken to receive the visit of a young doctor who prodded and poked me, only asked questions pertinent to my health, told me there were no bones broken, put my badly bruised and swollen arm in a sling, and prescribed total rest and a liberal use of the unguent he would leave behind him when he went. Whilst all of this was going on, Celia hovered, anxious to be helpful, as indeed she was. I was mildly surprised at the efficient way in which she assumed authority, giving brisk orders to the goggle-eyed maidservants once the doctor had departed. Of course, the task was hers by right, now! Now that Aunt Ruby was no longer here to keep firm hold of the household reins, now that poor dear Matthew had gone!

Again I was fed, washed, had my hair tidied, and was made generally comfortable. And all the while, Celia asked me no questions apart from those concerning my toilette, and when that was completed, whether I felt I could now sleep for a little while longer.

'No, I am fully awake now,' I replied wanly. 'My brain is still a little bemused, but I am not at all sleepy.'

'Would you like to talk?'

'Yes. No. I do not know. I do not know what to say, where to start. And I tremble to think what your opinion of me must be, though it cannot be lower than my own! But you are still speaking to me, with even a note of concern in your voice! And that you should do so is truly remarkable, for I have behaved in the most abominable fashion! Yes, what I have done and also sought to do is quite unforgivable!' Tears of weakness, of shame, of grief rolled down my cheeks. But Celia, as though seemingly unaffected by the perfidy of my past conduct, came to dry them, murmuring soothingly as she did so, 'There, there, Laura. Do not upset yourself. There is much I do not know, but I have no wish to hear it if the telling of it pains you. I love you as would a sister, and I know you do not have it in you to work real harm against anyone!'

'But I have! At least I intended to before I changed my mind. And if I had not, none of this dreadful business would have happened. Well, it would, but in a different way that would have only affected myself, and I should have richly deserved anything that fate had in store for me! And Matthew would still be alive! And Virtue! And even Aunt Ruby! Oh, it is all my fault! All of it is my doing!'

'Hush, now. I think David should be here. Would you object to him entering your bedchamber? Whilst I am here as well, of course?'

I shook my head, for what right had I to deny him the chance to castigate me? Let him come. Let them all come. I knew I must face him, must face everyone now that my base deceitfulness had become known, so rather sooner than later. Let us get it over, and the first moment I felt my legs would support me, I would quit this place with all speed. And of a surety, there could be nobody amongst the people who dwelt here who would be sorry to see me go! Celia rang the bell which was swiftly answered by her own personal maid, 'Oh, Ada, will you find Mr David and ask him if he will be so kind as to come to her ladyship's apartments?'

When she had gone, to somehow fill the ensuing silence, I remarked, 'But you are her ladyship now, Celia. I suppose, if I am anything, I am the dowager Lady Merrick. Just fancy being a dowager at nineteen! And a widow, too! Oh, Matthew! Oh why, why? Why did he do that dreadful thing? There must have been a solution to our troubles if we had had time to seek and find it. Oh, why was he so hasty? For I grew to love him, Celia, I really did! And he gave us no opportunity to lead a normal, happy life together not even for a little while. And there must have been a way in which we could have done so!'

'There was no other way than the one he took, Laura,' David had entered quietly and now stood looking down on me, his face drawn though whether through grief or tiredness, I did not know. 'Matthew would not have lived to see the beginning of another year, even if none of these recent happenings had taken place.'

'I find that extremely difficult to believe,' I replied. 'For he did not give me the impression he was a weakling, hovering near to death!'

'He was, and he was not. His illness was terminal, but he vowed to die by his own hand before it dragged on to its terrible conclusion. And if I had been he, I should have done the same thing!'

'But why? Why? Why did he do it? We could have spent a little while together, even though he was suffering from this malady, whatever it was. I loved him, David, and he denied me the right to take my place by his side as a wife should!'

'Do you think he did not want to? Do you doubt that you were in his thoughts all the while? Whenever I saw him, he asked after you. Where were you, how were you, and what were you doing?'

'You saw him? I thought only Aunt Ruby did that!' And I felt more aggrieved than ever, if that were possible.

'Yes, I did see him, though I never went into the dower house. He would not allow me to do that, and I had no great desire to, but he and I would frequently converse through an open window. Yes, just as when he got to know you, he would not let you enter, either. He cared for you, and he cared for me, but he did not give a damn for Aunt Ruby's well-being, and so she was permitted to cross the dower house threshold. He always wore gloves though, impregnated with some stuff that was supposed to afford protection against possible contagion, and he kept an air purifier burning day and night. And as he never actually touched her, the risk she ran was not too great. She at least did not seem unduly perturbed by it.'

'You make him sound as if he carried the plague

about his person!' I exclaimed.

'He did! He was a leper! His illness was leprosy! Contagious, revolting, and terminal!'

Aghast, I stared at David. Matthew, a leper? I had heard of the disease, but only with biblical connotations, but I had never before heard of anyone with whom I was acquainted actually having it!

'But how? Why? Where did he get it? And when?'

'If Matt had not been the fellow he was, most probably he never would have caught it. You are aware he spent quite some time abroad? On our plantations in the Sandwich Islands?'

Dumbly I nodded.

'Maui, where our lands lie, is just one island in a group of others, some of which are large and some small. And on one of these other islands is situated a leper colony! It would be about a year before our father died and Matthew came home, that one day he was walking with Virtue in attendance along the deserted beach at Maui. And on that fateful day, he glanced out to sea and espied a poor wretch in utmost difficulty and clinging for his life to an overturned bark canoe. Of course, my half brother dived in, swam to the side of the half-drowned man, and brought him back to the safety of the shore. But whilst the rescue had been taking place, Virtue had hung back, which was quite out of character for him, and when Matthew told him to lend a hand in dragging the fellow up the beach, still he hesitated. Matt himself was spent after his exertions and was in no mood to tolerate this strange disobedience from his servant, so he sharply commanded Virtue to do his bidding and only then did his valet obey him.'

'This man from the sea carried the disease, and Virtue suspected this?'

'Exactly. Matt had taken from the ocean one of the sufferers of leprosy from the colony! This was quite some distance away, but not so far that the tide could not carry him to Maui!'

'But why did not Matthew suspect, the same as did Virtue?'

'He told me he did not even stop to think. He just saw a man in dire need of assistance and went to give it! Only when the man was safely beached did Matt question Virtue's lack of enthusiasm. By then the servant was grey with fear, but also resigned. 'This man has the living death, Master,' he replied to Matt's questioning, and true enough, when my half brother looked closely he could see Virtue was right!'

'But surely Matthew could have seen that for himself at a glance?' I whispered.

'No. In its early stages a person suffering from it does not present a horrific appearance, such as one ofttimes reads about. Leprosy usually affects the vocal chords first, and then impairs the vision, before it manifests itself further by possible insanity and finally death!'

'Celia? Did you know of this?' I demanded, but the fact that she looked as if she might swoon at any moment answered the question for her.

'No, Celia did not know. Nobody knew but myself, Aunt Ruby, Virtue, and Jeremy. Oh, and that priest fellow, Garfath,' David replied.

'But why did Matthew return to England? He told me he was very happy where he was, so why did he not stay there?'

'Because when he did come home, he was not certain that the dread malady had laid its hand on him. He knew it might have, but none of the symptoms had then shown themselves, and so he took the chance of returning to Merrick, though he made very certain he should put nobody else at risk if the worst did come to pass. Oh, Aunt Ruby was aware of all this right from the very start, but she urged him to come, and so he did. For he also knew that if his health and future had been truly blighted by that good-Samaritan act of his, he could live in comfort and privacy for as long as he chose at the dower house, whereas if he had remained where he was and the worst did happen, he would have been forced to leave Maui and join the other lepers on the colony at Molokai. And I cannot imagine a fate more horrendous than that!'

'God in His heaven, neither can I! Oh, David, how on earth did he bear it?'

'As best he could. There were days when he was bitter, but as time passed, he became in a sense, resigned. That was until you came, and though it troubles me to say this, your coming brought him so much delight but also a deal of torment!'

'Oh, if only I had known! I could have done something! Surely I could have helped him, somehow!'

'No, Laura, you could not! Nobody could.'

'But you say Aunt Ruby knew all about this even

before he left the islands? And yet she urged him to come here? And she knew of the risk she was taking every time she went to visit him? I find all this very hard to understand, for she was thoroughly selfish, and I would have thought she would have had a greater concern for her own safety!'

'Oh, she was selfish but she was greedy, too. And she wished to own Merrick with an all consuming passion! Ever since my boyhood, I have been aware of her conniving and scheming, her mischief-making and lies, of the way she would work to set one person against another, yet all the while staying well in the background during any argument. It was she who was instrumental in Matt being sent away in the first place.'

'She told me it was you!'

'She would! Matthew was about to leave college then and was becoming very friendly with an extremely eligible young lady who lived not many miles distant from here. It would not have suited Aunt Ruby for that friendship to have blossomed into romance and then marriage, for she would most likely have lost her position of being the chatelaine of this mansion.'

'Why did your mother never assume that role?' I felt emboldened to ask.

'She had no wish to aggravate a delicate situation, and anyway she did not care for such things. Perhaps you will meet her one day, and then you will see she is not the sort of person to be troubled by such trifles. But this being so, a new bride of the heir to the place would most probably have wanted to take command of the household.'

'She told me there had been an argument, and then some nasty business concerning a dog.'

'There were always arguments in this house. She saw to that! And you must refer to the nauseating death of poor old Herbert? Well, Matt was blamed for it, though she inferred I was the culprit though not very convincingly. But as I knew I did not do it, and later when Matt swore to me that he did not, and I believed him, there remained only one person who could have! And she never had cared for the animal, nor for any other to my knowledge. And, of course, though she pretended otherwise, she was not too displeased to hear of my half brother's illness, for it left her in the position she had held for most of her life, and as you yourself discovered, she intended to keep it for the rest of her days.'

'Through the child, you mean? I do not know what to say regarding that subject.'

'The least said, the better. We had guessed what the plan would be all the while, and when the expected birth was announced we had many merry moments discussing it, though Matt did say you would never go through with it!'

'Well, there at least I did not fail him, and that was what precipitated this ghastly affair that culminated in his own death.'

'Have no regrets on that score, Laura, for it only gave him an added reason to do what he did, but it was not the chief one,' David replied.

'I thought you and he did not get on?'

'In my younger days, we did not. Most probably I was an obnoxious little toad, and our aunt never let an opportunity go by where she could hold him up as an example of all that was boyhood perfection, thus fostering my resentful dislike of him and his virtues. But by the time he was sent abroad, I was acquiring a little sense and in the following years, he and I corresponded regularly and eventually became good friends as well as being half brothers.'

'Oh? All of this is quite different from what I was led to believe.'

'Yes, for some while Matt and I knew what she was about. To somehow deprive me of Merrick, and when she hit on the notion that he should be wed, out of devilment, purest boredom, and a desire to thwart her lifelong ambition, he agreed. But both he and I expected her to find somebody very like herself to play the part of blushing bride, and when you put in an appearance, he and I were utterly confounded and did not know what to do apart from letting matters take their course.'

'Well, they did, but now despite everything you are Sir David Merrick, just as Celia is Milady,' I said.

'No, Laura, that is the cream of the macabre jest. We are not! Sir Charles Merrick was indeed my sire, and I am David Merrick, but I am not true born! My mother and father were never legally married, for she was wed to somebody else when they met and fell in love. She was an actress in her younger days, vital and lovely, but certainly not considered to be one of the *bon ton*. Her real marriage had only been of brief duration, for she and her husband had separated some years before my father and she met, whilst she was playing some theatre in London and my father was there on a pleasure jaunt, and the upshot of their romance was that after attempting to trace the missing husband, though I suspect their unavailing efforts were somewhat halfhearted, they returned to Merrick, and my father presented her to the world as his new wife, though in actual fact she was not!'

'And nobody knew? Or even suspected?'

'Why should they? My father told me of this when I was of an age to understand, explaining that it seemed the simplest thing to do. He had to return to Merrick. He would not leave her behind in London, and if he had brought her here and set her up as his mistress, Aunt Ruby would have made her life a misery. Of course, he could have asked his sister to live elsewhere, but that would have only added fuel to the scandal that would surely have ensued, so he acted as he did. And as my mother had neither the desire nor the experience to run such a mansion as this, everything worked out quite well.'

'I believe your mother has since remarried?' I enquired.

'Yes, but she was then free to do so. She received notification of her widowhood during the time she was supposed to be wed to my father, and though they could then have legally become man and wife, they decided against it. For if they had, it would not have benefited me in any way and would only have caused a great deal of gossip. So they remained as they were, living quite happily in sin.'

'So that means you . . .'

'Are a bastard? Yes, that is so.'

I turned my head to see what were Celia's reactions to these revelations, and David's gaze followed mine. But his wife was sitting calmly in her chair, showing no sign of an imminent fit of hysterics.

'Celia knows, has known all the while. Have you not, my love?'

'Yes, I have, and with the same knowledge, I would wed you again tomorrow,' she answered fondly. 'I have no regrets.'

'Who does know of this secret?' I asked.

'Very few people, Celia and her parents, Matthew, of course, knew, and so does the family solicitor in Exeter. And now you, but nobody else so far as I am aware.'

'Celia's parents were informed of it at the time of your marriage to her?'

'Naturally. And they were not exactly overjoyed at the idea of their only daughter wedding such as I, but my dear wife plagued them until they consented.'

'Indeed, I did! Such tantrums and tears as you would never believe!' Celia interposed cheerfully. 'And I won the day, for my sweet Papa is really so softhearted and romantic, though he would never admit to it. Anyway, the irregularity of David's birth did not matter then for he was the younger son, and Matthew was robust and perfectly healthy, and it was he who would inherit everything. We quite thought we should be known as Mr and Mrs Merrick for the rest of our lives, and I am more than content that this should be so.'

'And Aunt Ruby was ignorant of any of this?'

'That is correct. When Matthew succeeded to the inheritance, he was informed, but only he! Our father stipulated this in his will. He also made me an adequate allowance and gave Celia and me the right to reside here for as long as we chose.'

'So this means the whole estate and title now pass to somebody else?'

'There is nobody else! No legal male heir, and this being so, until Matthew married, everything would have fallen to Aunt Ruby, although she did not know it.'

'What about the clergyman who officiated at Matthew's and my wedding? He is a cousin, is he not?'

'A cousin of Matthew's mother, but with no Merrick blood in him at all. No, Aunt Ruby would have achieved her ambition and have become the owner of everything she had coveted for so long, but she was hoist by her own petard! She was so intent on depriving me of what she thought was my rightful due that she conceived the notion that, if she could persuade Matt to marry, somehow she would contrive to do it. But by finding him a wife, she only deprived herself! For before your marriage to my half brother, she was his only legal kin, but although she was not aware of it, the moment the ceremony was registered, you superseded her! As Lady Merrick, Matthew's lawful wife, but now alas his widow, you are his next of kin, and so all that he owned comes to you! Quickly, Celia, I think she is about to faint!'

'No, I am not,' I asserted, although my voice was high, reedy, and sounded faraway. 'And I cannot possibly accept poor Matthew's estate, for you know what kind of marriage he and I had!'

'It was legal and binding, nevertheless, and there is nobody but you with any true right to inherit. Do you not see, that was why Matthew agreed to the marriage? Oh, he told me of Aunt Ruby's secret plans well before Celia and I went on that visit to Exeter during the New Year. He and I almost fell about, laughing. Of course I duly informed Celia, who was well aware of the situation, and then she and I set off to be entertained by her parents, fully expecting, when we returned, to find some jaded doxy from the slums of London had become the new Lady Merrick. Actually, that was what we all rather hoped for, but you were so very different from the type of person we had imagined would succumb to Aunt Ruby's bribery that we had no idea what to do.'

'I must apologize for being the cause of such disappointment,' I said meekly.

'Oh, Laura, no. Well, in that way you were, I am pleased to say, but when we did get to know you, we were all so glad you are who you are, even though it did complicate matters for us,' Celia replied.

'So, I have been everybody's fool since the moment I came here!' I observed bitterly.

'Please, Laura, do not think any of us regarded you as any such thing!' David answered. 'I have become very fond of you; Celia loves you; and poor Matt adored you. We just did not know what to do for the best! Whether to warn you of Aunt Ruby's scheming and calculating nature and tell you she was only making mischief against her own interest, or whether to say nothing. For if you had let that knowledge slip, there could have been trouble involving you, although we never thought for a moment she would go so far as actual murder! But she could have made life very uncomfortable for you should you have confided in her!'

'Celia, it was you who discovered my absence from my rooms, thereby saving my life,' I remarked. 'And I have yet to thank you properly.'

'Well, in that instance my chief besetting sin, curiosity, proved to be a blessing,' she said, with a smile. 'Aunt Ruby and that body servant of yours turned me away every time I came up here to enquire how you were. They said you were too ill, too weary, resting or sleeping on every occasion I came to visit you, and your bedchamber door was kept locked! And then I overheard my own maid Ada telling one of the house wenches that Tansy was planning to sail to America, and I pricked up my ears. There was something wrong, somewhere, so on that fateful evening I excused myself from going down to dinner by pleading a headache, and just so soon as I guessed David and Aunt Ruby would be seated at table, I hurried here to this apartment. Oh so quietly, I turned the handle of the door leading into this bedchamber, but as usual it was locked, so I went along the passageway to your sitting room. And someone had left the door that gave onto that unfastened, as too was the communicating door between the two rooms. I made no sound as I came in here, lest all be well but you should be sleeping, and there was that creature, lying upon your bed and stuffing herself with comfits!'

'What did you do?'

'I had her off it in less time than a blink would take, and such a slap I gave her across the face that my hand hurt me for hours afterwards! 'Where is your mistress? Where is her ladyship?' I demanded, but the bitch broke free from my grasp and fled, and rather than lose time by trying to catch her, I went straight to the dining room and told David,' Celia replied triumphantly.

'Yes, indeed, I owe you my life!' I said quietly.

'You should have seen Aunt Ruby's face when I burst in upon them and interrupted the meal! And for once, she was bereft of speech, which was just as well, for my husband and I took command! I ordered a search of the house, whilst David set the other servants to seek you in the out-buildings. Of Tansy, there was no sign. She had hidden herself well enough, and I have not seen her since, and Aunt Ruby maintained she had left you sleeping peacefully in the maid's charge less than an hour before. Well, of course, you could not be found, and so all of the men we could mount were sent to scour the countryside, and those we could not, went afoot. David rode straight to the dower house to inform Matthew, and the rest you know.'

'Yes, my life was saved, but alas, those of three other people were lost,' I said slowly. 'It hardly seems a fair exchange now, does it?'

'Dear Laura, two of those lives were already doomed and the other was only lost through its owner's iniquitous behavior. Matthew's voice was affected by his illness as at times was his vision, and faint signs of the disease were beginning to show upon his skin. One had to look closely to see them, and anybody who did not know would not have thought them of any account. But my half brother knew, and such was his revulsion at the sight of them that he magnified them out of all proportion in his own mind.'

'Did he really need to wear that mask?'

'Not in my opinion, for I have seen people who have suffered only from smallpox and, though recovered from it, have been left much more badly marked than was Matthew at the time of his death.'

'So even though you say he was resolved to end his life, he would not have done so yet awhile if it were not for me!'

'Perhaps not for a couple of months or so, but he would have left it for no longer than that. You see, Laura, he could not live with himself as he was. 'Within his revolting, unclean carcase,' as he himself called it. And there was also the possible threat of approaching derangement, and if that did come to pass, Matt feared it would render him incapable of escaping further agonies if he left it too late! And Virtue too was bound to travel the same dreadful path, if he had not chosen to follow his master to the grave as he did!'

'What of Jeremy? What will become of him?' I enquired.

'Jeremy was never in actual contact with my half brother and his valet. They lived quite separately. Jeremy had and still has his own small cottage set well apart and his own stable, in which he keeps his own horse. He too never set foot inside the dower house, for his duties were to fetch the supplies from the home farm, to furnish the dower house with fuel and to make himself generally useful outside. Virtue did everything else, even to tending the horses he and his master rode.'

'What will happen to the beasts?' Celia asked. 'Do they carry the disease, or will they be safe to handle?'

'Matthew took care of that,' David replied, then to me. 'Those two shots we heard before we reached the dower house must have been ending the lives of the animals. We found the remains of them with the others, for Virtue led them into the main hall and destroyed them there before going outside to set the stables ablaze, and then taking a lighted torch to the house itself, thus destroying by cleansing fire everything he and his master had touched or with which they had been in contact. Whilst his valet was so employed, Matthew could have been taking Aunt Ruby into the dower house, and then possibly making what peace he could with his Maker!'

I recalled his last words to me, his request that if I could bring myself to, I should pray for him. But what need would a man like Matthew have for the prayers of such a person as myself? For nobody in full possession of their senses would not cringe before the prospect of being called upon to endure such torment as he had, but he had borne his terrible burden with dignity, stoicism, and a constant regard for others more happily placed than he. And surely the All Merciful God whom I worshipped would not seek to heap further suffering upon his valiant soul. With or without my prayers, which I would murmur anyway. Tears blinded me as in my mind's eye I once again beheld him, standing alone, backed by flickering flame, and resolutely facing his imminent journey into the fearful unknown.

David pressed a handkerchief into my hand saying, 'There, there, Laura. Do not weep for him. He would not have wished for that! He loved you so, and his sole concern was for your welfare and happiness. And as he said, there was no other way.'

'Let her weep, David. Tears are best shed and not bottled up inside,' his wife advised.

'No. Later I shall weep, but not now. There are things to be settled between us first, the most important being that as so very few of us know about the secret of David's birth, why cannot you assume the titles that everyone will expect you to? Would it be against the law for you to do so?'

'I have no idea. And in any event, Celia and I have no great yearning to be known as Sir David and Lady Merrick!'

'But just think of the gossip if you are not! I presume we are not intending to entertain the whole county, even the whole country by giving a detailed account of the recent happenings here? I am quite certain you will have already given those who may be concerned a feasible explanation for the accidental fire at the dower house in which your half brother, his aunt, and servant lost their lives? But if you and Celia continue to style yourselves

as Mr and Mrs Merrick, tongues will surely wag!'
I declared.

'Let them.'

'And what of your mother? Will not the gossip
harm her? I believe she is now Lady Rowan? What
of her position? And Celia's parents, too, will
not remain unscathed by hurtful gibes! Financial
matters we may resolve when I feel a little stronger,
and everything else that may be in question, but
you two must establish yourselves now! Or there
will certainly be the most awkward of situations
arising, which I for one could well do without!'

'But we do not have the right!' Celia objected.

'And who is to know? You either assume the
titles or they will become extinct, so who will you
harm? Not a living soul!'

'We shall think about it,' David conceded, and
I guessed I had won him over to my point of view.
'And now my wife and I will leave you to rest.
Before we go I had better tell you that the tale
I told was you had miscarried the expected child,
and naturally you were upset and had gone to the
dower house to seek comfort from your husband.
Aunt Ruby joined the two of you there, somehow
a fire started, and only you were saved from the
conflagration. That is the gist of the story, and
so when your family arrive you will know what
to say to them if you choose to substantiate my
explanation.'

'My family? Who? How? When?'

'Yesterday I sent a cablegram to your mother,
telling her of the tragedy, although I made no
mention of a baby. That is for you to decide,

393

either way, and my powers of invention could not quite grapple with that small detail. This morning I received her reply that she, your sister, and your aunt would travel down today! I have sent one of the carriages to Exeter to meet their train, though they should have reached there by now and most probably have left and begun their drive here! So you have less than two hours in which to rest, compose yourself, and be ready to greet them upon their arrival. Come, Celia.'

* * *

They brought with them so much prosaic sanity and down-to-earth common sense that at times I wondered whether everything that had so recently come to pass had really happened, or if I had dreamed it! But Aunt Ruby was gone, so too were Matthew, Virtue, the dower house where they had dwelt. And I was indeed the new mistress of Merrick's Mount, the estate and its accompanying fortune. Though this knowledge came a little later and remained a secret between just a few people. Alas, it seemed the very name Merrick bred secrets and deception, but this was an unavoidable one inflicting hurt on nobody. Mama was the same as ever, dignified, gracious, and so self-possessed, never remarking on the grand style of living that we enjoyed at Merrick's Mount, nor letting it be known she herself was not accustomed to being waited on by so many servants. But I did see her eyes resting approvingly on gleaming silver and glittering crystal, Persian carpets and delicate porcelain figurines. Aunt Isobel too retained her countenance by the simple process of keeping a still tongue, but Tiffany, dear, dear Tiffany, after losing her initial shyness, was quite awestruck at our palatial splendor and enthusiastically applauded everything she saw.

'Ooh, Laura! Fancy actually living in a place like this! It must have been like taking up residence in a museum! Were you not terrified when first you came here?'

'Well, I was a little nervous,' I admitted. 'But I soon got used to it.'

'I know I never should. I am afraid to even sit down lest I flatten a cushion, and the liveried footmen appear to be so grand that I hesitate to merely address them!'

(Ah, but those days have long gone, have they not, Milady? For now that you are Theophania, Viscountess Farnol, at some time in the future to become the Countess of Rougemont, when the occasion arises you can command your own retinue of servants with a hauteur that is the equal of anyone's!)

David and Celia did adopt the titles by which the rest of the world assumed they now should be known, and Celia veritably blossomed, running the mansion as though she had done so for years, for I left everything of that nature to her. But she and her husband as well as myself were deeply appreciative of Mama's wise counsel pertaining to what should be done regarding the burial and memorial services and of the funeral panoply that would be expected upon the tragic, sudden demise of Matthew and his aunt. It was my mother who sent formal notification to *The Times*, replied to the many letters of sympathy and condolence, consulted Mrs. Sweetbriar and Flint, thus learning of local customs to be observed on sad occasions such as this. Yes, Mrs Lambourne became the staunch support of we last three people to bear the name Merrick, and very thankful we were that she did!

It transpired Mr Peppercorn was not the family solicitor, he only undertaking certain little tasks for Aunt Ruby when she visited London. No, Mr. Westering was the Merricks' man of business and he, David, Celia and myself were close-closeted for a whole afternoon making our arrangements, for since Matthew never troubled to make a will, as David had said, everything now came to me. The entail on the property was now broken, as there was no true male heir, and though Mr. Westering did demur when I made my proposals and David and Celia stoutly disagreed with them until I felt an urgent need to box their ears, in the end I had my way. They were to have Merrick's Mount as their residence, for I intended to set up house at the old manor just so soon as it became habitable.

'No, no, Laura! I will not hear of it! That will not do at all!' Celia cried.

'My dear, I am depriving myself of nothing. I have never liked this place, whereas you do! And I shall be more than happy to dwell cosily in my own little home near where I shall work. Now as to upkeep and finances. I intend, with Captain Quillian's assistance, to reopen the quarries! That was dear Matthew's wish, and I shall see that it is fulfilled. Also it will give both Seth and myself something worthwhile to do. The entire property at Maui, David, is yours, to keep and run, or sell as you choose. I want nothing to do with it. The very name of the island gives me feelings of melancholy and regret. And my desire is we should share the income from the estate here at Merrick, the rents from the tenant farms, and things of that nature. The actual capital and the family jewels we can decide upon at a later date. Those are my wishes Mr Westering, and it will please me if you will have the requisite papers prepared for me to sign.'

'No, Laura, we cannot accept this overwhelming generosity,' David said firmly.

'I am afraid you must. Who has more right to it than you? Certainly not I! I actually give you nothing, for only a legal quibble has tossed this property into my lap in a wholly ridiculous fashion! And I think you will agree I have not left myself entirely penniless! Now I shall retire to my chambers. I feel a headache coming on, and I know any hint of an argument would only aggravate it. Good afternoon, Mr Westering. Whenever you call with the documents that require my signature, I shall be pleased to receive you. If I withdraw now, my headache will most probably be gone by dinnertime, so I will see you, Celia, and you, David, then.' So what could they do, but as I wished?

The last small pieces of the puzzle now fell into place, for Mama remarked upon Aunt Ruby's many little kindnesses toward me, including writing to her supposedly on my behalf almost upon my arrival at Merrick's Mount. This initial letter told of how

397

I had broken my right wrist by slipping on some icy ground. (So clumsy of you, Laura! Whatever must she have thought?) Thereafter the two of them had sustained quite a lively correspondence, Mama writing as she thought to me, and Aunt Ruby penning regular replies to these missives, presumably at my dictation! Yes, even in those early days, she was preparing me like a lamb for the slaughter! Of course, I did not let my mother know there had been no such injury, for how could I have accounted for my 'benefactress's' course of deception without disclosing the whole of her well laid plans and my own stupidity? No, the fewer people who knew the truth of the sorry tale, the better. Though even to this day I have to choose my words with care, for none of my kinfolk are fools!

And the two mysterious horsemen had been Matthew and his valet, out for a moonlight ride in the crisp, newfallen snow. And poor David was quite guiltless of spying on and following me, for my sad, lonely husband had himself told me that he was the silent watcher, just trying to catch a glimpse of me. Oh, if only I had known!

One by one ten years have passed, and it amazes me, when I think about it, that I shall soon be thirty! Approaching middle-age! Though those years have not dragged by but have been busy ones, and that has made my life if not rapturously happy, at least tolerable. What I had planned did come to pass, and this stretch of the Devon coastline has altered out of all recognition from what it was like when first I set eyes on it. For now it bustles. It has come alive again! Seth and I are joint partners in a very thriving venture. We have had built new cottages for the quarry workers and their families, but I have made certain there is no tommy shop and have encouraged small shopkeepers to set up their businesses quite independently, and the hamlet we originally built now looks as though one day it might grow into a village! The new wharfs and quay are hives of activity, and this being so I am pleased I suggested they be constructed a little way further from my home than were the old ones. For, yes, I live at the manor house with just a small staff to run it and the faithful Jeremy to care for my modest stable of horses.

At my suggestion, Celia invited David's mother and her husband to stay at Merrick's Mount, for I was curious about the lady and wished to meet her. Whilst I still resided there, they came, but far from being the slightly vulgar though goodhearted creature of my imaginings, Lady Rowan showed herself to be the very epitome of gentility, never saying a word out of place nor behaving in any way that would give cause for an eyebrow to be raised, at least not until I got to know her very well! For after all, had she not been an actress? And upon my soul, she was a very good one! She was received at Court and now mingled with the highest in the land, and it was during one of her ensuing visits to her son's home at Merrick's Mount that she met my sister, was so taken by Tiffany's loveliness and charm that she offered — nay, insisted — on bringing her out in grand style, presenting her at one of Her Majesty's rare 'drawing rooms,' for though the Queen was still mourning the death of Prince Albert and had retired to Windsor, she had begun to emerge from there on infrequent occasions. I journeyed up to London, where my family still lived, for this great event, taking with me the diamond daisies for Tiffany to wear with her court gown and the nodding plumes that adorned her lovely golden hair. They looked so exquisite on her that I made her keep them. They also set off her bridal gown to perfection, for she was the reigning toast of society, the belle of every ball, and of the many suitors who clamored for her hand in marriage, she chose a young beau who, though not the richest nor the one with the grandest title, was the man whose love she wholeheartedly returned. So at least her dreams of romance and happiness came true, and every summer she and her adoring husband Viscount Farnol bring their brood of a small boy and little twin daughters (and now with yet another one on the way), together with nannies and nursery maids, to stay with Uncle David and Auntie Celia at Merrick! And during the time of the visit, Celia positively radiates joy for she dotes on children in general and the Farnol cherubs in particular. Indeed, it is at her insistence that they stay where they do for, 'You are so busy with the business, Laura, and there is so much more room at the Mount than in your poky little manor house!' Alas, Celia has not yet borne a child of her own, and as time passes, her chances of becoming a mother do not increase. Therefore it has been agreed just between herself, David, and me that if their marriage does remain childless and Tiffany's coming baby should prove to be a second son, one day in years to come, he shall have Merrick!

Yes, the mansion seems to have awoken after spending so many decades drowsing in its stately splendor, and this in itself is strange for the people responsible for the change are none of them true born Merricks, for there remain none such. But carriages arrive and depart from its pillared *porte cochere*, bringing or carrying away Celia's parents, her brothers, their wives and children, David's Mama and stepfather, Tiffany, her husband and infants, though my Mama and Aunt Isobel always stay with me at my cosy manor, where they can enjoy a little peace.

And, of myself, what is there to say? A widow but never actually a wife: a dowager, yet still a maiden! I realized long since that so this would remain for the rest of my days, for though I have grown very fond of Seth in the manner of friendship, and several times he has asked me to marry him, I cannot bring myself to say yes. Folk urge me to become his wife. It would be so suitable, and I should no longer have to live as I do in my lonely state, but I merely smile at this advice and change the subject of conversation. For I cannot reveal the true reason why I do not, will not, consent to end my supposed loneliness by wedding Seth, though I can set it down on paper for none to read but myself. And the truth is, I never am alone! Wherever I go, whatever I do, Matthew is with me! Constantly I feel his presence, for in the most comforting way, he haunts me. And it delights me that he does! He is here beside me as I pen these words, he knows my innermost thoughts, my secret and silent dreams. For my love for my husband has not faded as the years have passed, rather it grows stronger, steadier, as if indeed we were spending our lives together and the first wild passion of our love has deepened into a more mature, less turbulent emotion. Sometimes I wonder how it will be when Matthew and I do come together once again. Will it be as a fond but staid middle-aged couple or will our love bloom afresh? Shall we cling to each other rapturously, or quietly and gently embrace? But I know that whatever comes to pass, will be right for us, will be ordained as was our meeting and our parting, though whilst I am waiting for that moment I can still dream of what might, what will be.

And as I grow older, I become more and more patient, for now that the headstrong impetuousity of youth is far behind me, I know all I have to do is wait. For every hour that passes takes me a tiny step nearer to the man I love. Each fresh, new sunrise brings us just a little closer. Yes, for though he has gone before me, my beloved waits for me on the other side of the veil, a veil that daily becomes a shade lighter, a fraction more transparent, a veil that on one glorious day will disappear completely, so that again we shall stand face to unblemished face, and unhindered, he will take me in his arms and hold me close, there to rest upon his dear heart for all eternity.